ONE
INDIAN
GIRL

Chetan Bhagat is the author of six bestselling novels—*Five Point Someone* (2004), *One Night @ the Call Center* (2005), *The 3 Mistakes of My Life* (2008), *2 States* (2009), *Revolution 2020* (2011) and *Half Girlfriend* (2014)—which have sold over ten million copies and have been translated into over a dozen languages worldwide.

In 2008, *The New York Times* called him 'the biggest-selling author in India's history', a position he has maintained until date. Almost all his books have been adapted into hit Bollywood films. He is also a Filmfare-award-winning screenplay writer.

TIME magazine named him as one of the 100 most influential people in the world and Fast Company, USA, listed him as one of the 100 most creative people in business globally. His columns in *The Times of India* and *Dainik Bhaskar* are amongst the most widely read in the country. He is also one of the country's leading motivational speakers and has hosted several TV shows. Despite all the above, he is only human and can be totally stupid sometimes.

Chetan went to college at IIT Delhi and IIM Ahmedabad, after which he worked in investment banking for a decade before quitting his job to become a full-time writer.

He is married to Anusha and is the father of twin boys, Shyam and Ishaan. He lives in Mumbai.

ONE INDIAN GIRL

CHETAN BHAGAT

RUPA

Published by
Rupa Publications India Pvt. Ltd 2016
7/16, Ansari Road, Daryaganj
New Delhi 110002

Sales centres:
Allahabad Bengaluru Chennai
Hyderabad Jaipur Kathmandu
Kolkata Mumbai

Lyrics on page 106 have been taken from the song 'Let Her Go' by Passenger
(Nettwerk Records); on page 134 from the song 'Sorry' by Justin Bieber
(Def Jam Recordings, Universal Music Group); on page 244 from the song 'Chittiyan
Kalaiyan' from the movie *Roy* (T-Series); and on page 247 from the song 'London
Thumakda' from the movie *Queen* (T-Series).

While every effort has been made to trace copyright holders and obtain permission, this
has not been possible in all cases. Any omissions brought to our attention will be remedied
in future editions.

This book is a work of fiction. Names of persons, organizations, businesses, characters,
incidents, places and events are fictional and a product of the imagination of the
author. Any resemblance to actual events or places or persons, living or dead, is entirely
coincidental. Any references to hotels, places, businesses, locations, and organizations and
businesses, while real, are used in a way that is purely fictional, and have no resemblance
to any existing organization, location etc., and any use thereof is not intended to harm,
disrespect, defame or derogate any third party.

ISBN: 978-81-291-4214-6

Second impression 2016

10 9 8 7 6 5 4 3 2

The moral right of the author has been asserted.

Printed at Replika Press Pvt. Ltd, India

To all Indian girls
especially the ones
who dare to dream
and live life on their own terms.

To all the women in my life,
thank you for being there.[*]

[*]*Despite me being a total pain sometimes.*

Acknowledgements

Hi all,

I can't possibly thank everyone who has contributed to this book. Every woman who ever came into my life has played a part. You all know who you are, so in case I missed you out, like always—sorry.

The ones I would like to thank here are:

God, for giving me so much.

Shinie Antony, my editor, friend, guide. She's been with me from the start and continues to be the first reader of all my books.

My readers, for blessing me with so much love. It is because of you that I get to do what I love—tell stories.

The hundred-odd women I interviewed for this book, including that Serbian DJ, the IndiGo flight attendants, the hotel staff wherever I stayed, the various people I met at my motivational talks, the co-passengers on planes. There was a phase when I discussed this book with every woman I came across. Thank you for opening up and sharing your innermost feelings. It made the book.

Alphabetically—Abha Bakaya, Aditi Prakash, Alisha Arora, Amit Agarwal, Angela Wang, Anubha Bang, Anusha Venkatachalam, Ayesha Raval, Avni Jhunjunwala, Bhakti Bhat, Ira Trivedi, Jessica Rosenberg, Karuna Suggu, Krishen Parmar, Kushaan Parikh, Meghna Rao, Michelle Shetty, Nibha Bhandari, Prateek Dhawan, Rachita Chauhan, Reema Parmar, Shalini Raghavan, Virali Panchamia, Vivita Relan, Zitin Dhawan— for all the inspiration, support and feedback at whatever point during the journey of this book, or even my life.

The editors at Rupa, for their relentless attempts to make the book better.

The salespersons at Rupa, the retailers who carry my books, the online delivery boy or girl who brings my books to my reader's doorstep—thank you.

My critics. For helping me improve and keeping my ego down.

My mother Rekha Bhagat, the first woman in my life. Anusha Bhagat, my wife. Thanks.

My kids. For having a little less dad so there can be a little more author.

My extended family. Brother Ketan. In-laws. My cousins. Everyone who has ever loved me.

With that, it's time for *One Indian Girl*.

Prologue

Some people are good at taking decisions. I am not one of them. Some people fall asleep quickly at night. I am not one of them either. It is 3 in the morning. I have tossed and turned in bed for two hours. I am to get married in fifteen hours. We have over 200 guests in the hotel, here to attend my grand destination wedding in Goa. I brought them here. Everyone is excited. After all, it is the first destination wedding in the Mehta family.

I am the bride. I should get my beauty sleep. I can't. The last thing I care about right now is beauty. The only thing I care about is how to get out of this mess. Because, like it often happens to me, here I am in a situation where I don't know what the fuck is going on.

1

'What do you mean, not enough rooms?' I said to Arijit Banerjee, the lobby manager of the Goa Marriott.

'See, what I am trying to explain is...' Arijit began in his modulated, courteous voice when mom cut him off.

'It's my daughter's wedding. Are you going to shame us?' she said, her volume loud enough to startle the rest of the reception staff.

'No, ma'am. Just a shortage of twenty rooms. You booked a hundred. We had only promised eighty then. We hoped to give more but the chief minister-had a function and...'

'What do we tell our guests who have come all the way from America?' mom said.

'If I may suggest, there is another hotel two kilometres away,' Arijit said.

'We *have* to be together. You are going to ruin my daughter's wedding for some sarkaari function?' my mother said, bosom heaving, breath heavy—classic warning signs of an upcoming storm.

'Mom, go sit with dad, please. I will sort this out,' I said. Mom glared at me. How could I, the bride, do all this in the first place? I should be worried about my facials, not room allocations.

'The boy's side arrives in less than three hours. I can't believe this,' she muttered, walking to the sofa at the centre of the lobby. My father sat there along with Kamla bua, his elder sister. Other uncles and aunts occupied the remaining couches in the lobby—a Mehta takeover of the Marriott. My mother looked at my father, a level-two glare. It signified: 'Will you ever take the initiative?'

My father shifted in his seat. I refocused on the lobby manager.

'What can be done now, Arijit?' I said. 'My entire family is here.'

We had come on the morning flight from Delhi. The Gulatis, the boy's side, would take off from Mumbai at 3 p.m. and land in Goa at 4. Twenty hired Innovas would bring them to the hotel by 5. I checked the time—2.30 p.m.

'See, ma'am, we have set up a special desk for the Mehta–Gulati wedding,' Arijit said. 'We are doing the check-ins for your family now.'

He pointed to a makeshift counter at the far corner of the lobby where three female Marriott employees with permanent smiles sat.

They welcomed everyone with folded hands. Each guest received a shell necklace, a set of key cards for the room, a map of the Marriott Goa property and a 'wedding information booklet'. The booklet contained the entire programme for the week, including the time, venue and other details of the ceremonies.

'My side will take fifty rooms. The Gulatis need fifty too,' I said.

'If you take fifty, ma'am, we will only have thirty left for them,' Arijit said.

'Where is Suraj?' I said. Suraj was the owner of Moonshine Events, the event manager we had appointed for the wedding. 'We will manage last minute' is what he had told me.

'At the airport,' Arijit said.

My father ambled up to the reception desk. 'Everything okay, beta?'

I explained the situation to him.

'Thirty rooms! The Gulatis have 120 guests,' my father said.

'Exactly.' I threw up my hands.

Mom and Kamla bua came to the reception as well. 'I told Sudarshan also, why all this Goa business? Delhi has so many nice banquet halls and farmhouses. Seems like you have money to waste,' Kamla bua said.

I wanted to retort but my mother gave me the Mother Look.

They are our guests, I reminded myself. I let out a huge breath.

'How many from our side?' my mother said.

'Mehta family has 117 guests, ma'am,' Arijit said, counting from his reservation sheets.

'If we only have eighty, that is forty rooms for each side,' I said. 'Let's reallocate. Stop the check-ins for the Mehtas right now.'

Arijit signalled the smiling ladies at the counter. They stopped the smiles and the check-ins and put the shell necklaces back in the drawer.

'How can we reduce the rooms for the boy's side?' my mother said in a shocked voice.

'What else to do?' I said.

'How many rooms are they expecting?' she said.

'Fifty,' I said. 'Call them now. They will readjust their allocations on the way here.'

'How can you ask the boy's side to adjust?' Kamla bua said. 'Aparna, are you serious?'

My mother looked at Kamla bua and me.

'But how can we manage in only thirty rooms?' I said and turned to my father. 'Dad, call them.'

'Sudarshan, don't insult them before they even arrive,' Kamla bua said. 'We will manage in thirty rooms. It's okay. Some of us will sleep on the floor.'

'Nobody needs to sleep on the floor, bua,' I said. 'I am sorry this screw-up happened. But if we have forty rooms each, it is three to a room. With so many kids anyway, it should be fine.'

'We can manage in thirty,' my mother said.

'Mom? That's four to a room. While the Gulatis will have so much space. Let's tell them.'

'No,' my mother said. 'We can't do that.'

'Why?'

'They are the boy's side. Little bit also you don't understand?'

I didn't want to lose it at my own wedding, definitely not in the first hour of arrival. I turned to my father. 'Dad, it's no big deal. His family will understand. We are here for six nights. It will get too tight for us,' I said.

Dad, of course, would not listen. These two women, his wife and sister, controlled his remote. For once, both of them were on the same page as well.

'Beta, these are norms. You don't understand. We have to keep them comfortable. Girl's side is expected to adjust,' he said.

I argued for five more minutes. It didn't work. I had to relent. And do what the girl's side needs to do—adjust.

'You and Aditi take a room,' my mother said, referring to my sister.

'Let her be with her husband. What will jiju think?' I said.

'Anil will adjust with the other gents,' Kamla bua said.

Over the next twenty minutes the two women sorted the extended Mehta family comprising 117 people into thirty rooms. They used a complex algorithm with criteria like the people sharing the room should not hate each other (warring relatives were kept in different rooms) or be potentially attracted to each other (mixed gender rooms were avoided, even if it involved people aged eighty-plus). Kids were packed five to a room, often with a grandparent. Kamla bua, herself a widow, dramatically offered to sleep on the floor in my parents' room, causing my father to offer his own bed and sleep on the floor instead. Of course, Arijit kept saying that they would put extra beds in the room. But how can you compare sleeping on an extra Marriott bed with the Punjabi bua's eternal sacrifice of sleeping on the floor?

'I am happy with roti and achaar,' Kamla bua said.

'It's the Marriott. There is enough food, bua,' I said.

'I am just saying.'

'Can you please focus on the reallocations? We all need to be checked in before the Gulatis arrive,' I said.

In the middle of this chaos, I forgot what I had come here for. I had come to change my life forever. To do something I'd never believed in my whole life. To do something I never thought I would. I had come to have an arranged marriage.

Here I was, lost in logistics, guest arrangements and bua tantrums. I took a moment to reflect.

I will be married in a week. To a guy I hardly know. This guy and I are to share a bed, home and life for the rest of my life.

Why isn't it sinking in? Why am I fighting with Suraj on chat instead?

Me: Major screw-up on rooms, Suraj. Not cool.

Suraj: Sorry. Really sorry. Political reasons. Tried. Really.

Me: What else is going to get screwed up?

Suraj: Nothing. IndiGo from Mumbai just landed. We are ready to receive guests. See you soon.

I went to the Mehta–Gulati check-in desk. All my family guests had checked in. Some did grumble about sharing a room with three others but most seemed fine. Mom said that the grumblers were the jealous types, the relatives who couldn't stand the fact that we had reached a level where we could do a destination wedding in Goa. The supportive ones, according to mom, were those who understood what it was like to be the girl's side.

'Do not use this "girl's side" and "boy's side" logic with me again. I don't like it,' I said. Mom and I were sitting in the lobby, ensuring that the staff readied the special check-in desk for the Gulatis.

'Can you stop waving your feminism flag for a week? This is a wedding, not an NGO activist venue,' my mother said.

'But...'

'I know you are paying for it. Still, beta, protocol is protocol.'

'It is a sexist protocol.'

'Did you figure out your parlour appointments? Aditi also wants hair and make-up all six days.'

I love how my mother can throw another topic into the conversation if she doesn't want to answer me.

'Of course she does,' I said.

'Now go change,' mom said.

'What?'

'You are going to meet the boy's side in jeans and T-shirt? And look at your neck!'

'Again you said "boy's side". And what's wrong with my neck?'

'There is no jewellery. Go change into a salwar-kameez and wear a chain from my jewellery box.'

'I have just arrived. I am working to settle the guests in. Why am I expected to doll up? Is the boy expected to dress up right after he gets off a flight?'

My mother folded her hands. When logic fails, she does this, brings both her hands together dramatically. Strangely, it works.

I relented and stood up. She handed me the key cards to her and my room. I went to her room first. I took out a gold necklace, the thinnest and least hideous of them all. *Why am I agreeing to this?* I wondered even as I wore it. *Maybe because I failed when I did things my way. All the women's empowerment and feminism bullshit didn't really take me anywhere, right? Maybe Kamla bua and mom's way was the right way.*

I went to my room. Four huge suitcases were crammed into the walking space in the corridor. Two giant bags belonged to my sister, who had essentially packed a retail store's worth of dresses for herself.

I opened one of my suitcases, took out a yellow silk salwar-kameez with a slim zari border. My mother had told me, no cottons this week. I undressed. I looked at myself in the mirror. My wavy hair had grown, and now reached my shoulders. I looked slim—the two-month diet before the wedding had helped. The black La Perla lingerie I had purchased in Hong Kong also gave a little lift here and a little tuck there. *Expensive underwear can make any woman look sexy*, a little voice in my head said. Some men in the past had called me sexy, but they could have been biased. *Why am I always so hard on myself? Why couldn't they have genuinely found me sexy?* Well, it didn't matter now. I would be undressing in front of a new man soon. The thought made me shudder.

I walked closer to the mirror. I saw my face up-close. 'It's all happening,

Radhika,' I said out loud.

Hi, I am Radhika Mehta and I am getting married this week. I am twenty-seven years old. I grew up in Delhi. I now work in London, at Goldman Sachs, an investment bank. I am a vice president in the Distressed Debt Group. Thank you for reading my story. However, let me warn you. You may not like me too much. One, I make a lot of money. Two, I have an opinion on everything. Three, I've had sex. Now if I was a guy you would be okay with all of this. But since I am a girl these three things don't really make me too likeable, do they?

I am also a bit of a nerd. My sister, Aditi, and I went to school together in Delhi at Springdales, Pusa Road. She is just a year older than me. My parents wanted a son for their firstborn. When Aditi came, they had to undo the damage as soon as possible. Hence, my father, SBI Naraina Vihar Branch Manager Sudarshan Mehta, decided to have another child with his homemaker wife, Aparna Mehta. Sadly for them, the second was also a girl, which was me. It is rumoured that they tried again twice; both times my mother had an abortion because it was a girl. I confronted her on this topic years ago, but she brushed it off.

'I don't remember, actually,' she said, 'but I am happy with my two daughters.'

'You don't remember two abortions?'

'You will judge me, so no point telling you. You don't know what it is like to be without a son.'

I had stopped asking her after that.

In school, Aditi didi was a hundred times more popular than me. She was the girl boys had crushes on. I was the girl who started to wear spectacles in class six. Aditi didi is fair-complexioned. I am what they call wheatish in matrimonial ads (why don't they call white-skinned people rice-ish?). We look like the before–after pictures in a fairness cream ad; I'm the before picture, of course. Aditi didi started dieting from age twelve, and waxed her legs from age thirteen. I topped my class at age twelve, and won the Maths Olympiad at age thirteen. Clearly, she was the cooler one. In school, people either didn't notice me or made fun of me. I preferred the former. Hence, I stayed in the background, with my books. Once, in class ten, a boy asked me out in front of the whole class. He gave me a red rose along with an Archies greeting card. Overwhelmed, I cried tears of joy. Turned out it was a prank. The entire class laughed as he squeezed the rose and ink sprayed across my face. My spectacles protected my eyes, thankfully.

That day I realized I had only one thing going for me—academics. In class twelve I was the school topper. I ranked among the top five in Delhi, which, come to think of it, was a major loser-like thing to do. Unlike me, Aditi didi had barely passed class twelve a year ago. However, she did win the unofficial title of Miss Hotness at her farewell. In some ways, oh well, in every way, that was a bigger achievement than topping CBSE.

Have you heard about the insane cut-offs at Delhi University? I am the kind of student that causes them. I scored a 98 per cent aggregate in class twelve. Then I joined Shri Ram College of Commerce, or SRCC. People say it is one of the best colleges for nerds. At SRCC, I realized that I was nerdier than even the regular nerds. I topped there too. I never bunked a class. I hardly spoke to any boys, I made few friends. With bad school memories, I wanted to survive college with as little human contact as possible.

I finished college and took the CAT for MBA entrance. As you can guess, nerdy me hit a 99.7 percentile. I made it to IIM Ahmedabad. In contrast, Aditi didi had finished her graduation from Amity University the year before and wanted to get married. She had two criteria for her groom. One, the boy had to be rich. Second, well, there was no second criterion really. She said something like she wanted to be a housewife and look after her husband. Fortunately, rich Punjabi men in Delhi who can't woo women on their own are only too happy to oblige girls like her. Aditi didi married Anil, owner of three sanitaryware shops in Paharganj and two Honda CR-Vs. They had their wedding the same year I joined IIMA.

'You should also get married soon,' didi had told me. 'There's a right time for a girl to marry. Don't delay it.'

'I am twenty-one,' I said. 'I haven't even done my master's yet.'

'The younger the better. Especially for someone like you,' she said.

'What do you mean *especially* for someone like me?'

She never explained. I guess she meant for someone as nerdy as me or as wheatish as me or someone whose breasts weren't the size of footballs, as Punjabi men prefer.

I joined IIMA. I finally found nerd heaven. Everyone studied, and just when you thought you had studied enough, the institute gave you more assignments. My mother called on a regular basis, primarily to discuss her favourite topic. 'Start looking at boys at least. Anil's circle has many good, rich guys.'

'I am not going to marry a man from the circle of sanitaryware shop owners, mom.'

'Why?' my mother said, genuinely confused.

'You know what, I am not getting married for several years anyway. Forget it. I have class now. Bye.'

I finished with IIMA. Overachiever me had a job offer on Day Zero, the prime slot for recruiters. I got an offer to be an associate at Goldman Sachs, New York. The job paid an annual compensation of 120,000 dollars.

'Forty-eight lakh rupees a year, four lakhs a month, mom,' I told her on the phone.

I heard nothing in response. Most likely she had fainted. My father had never crossed a third of this amount in his twenty-five-year career with the State Bank of India.

'Are you there, mom?'

'How will I ever find a boy for you?' she said.

That was her prime concern. Her twenty-three-year-old daughter, who grew up in middle-class West Delhi, had cracked a job at one of the biggest investment banks in the world and all she cared about was its impact on her groom-hunt.

'Stop it, mom. What boy?'

'Who wants to marry a girl who earns so much? If the boy earns less, he won't consider you. If he earns more, why would he marry a working girl?'

'I have no idea what you are talking about. But I am moving to America. I have a great job. Can you save your melodrama for another time?'

'Your father wants to speak to you,' she said and passed him the phone.

'Goldman Sachs? American, no?' he said.

♦

My room phone rang, startling me back to reality. *I am in Goa, not IIMA*, I reminded myself.

'Where are you? The Gulatis are ten minutes away,' my mother said.

'Huh? I am here, mom. In my room.'

'Are you dressed?'

I looked in the mirror.

'Yeah, almost.'

'Come down fast. What are you wearing?'

'The yellow salwar-kameez. Zari border.'

'Silk?'

'Yes.'

'You wore a chain?'

'Yes.'

'Come then.'

◆

'Hey, remember me?' I heard a voice behind me. I turned around.

'Brijesh,' I said to my husband-to-be. 'Hi.'

I didn't know what to do next. *Should I look shy? Should I giggle? Should I give him a hug?* Like an idiot, I shook hands with him while he adjusted his black-rimmed spectacles with his left hand. Unlike how he'd looked in the Skype calls of the past few weeks, he was thinner, his white kurta and blue jeans hanging a bit on him. His neatly combed side-parted hair made him look like those schoolboys whom teachers first ask to become prefects. I smelled strong aftershave.

I was in the lobby. The boy's side had arrived. They crowded around the special check-in desk. The hotel staff brought in trays filled with glasses of coconut water.

'I made them get the coconut water. It wasn't part of the package,' Suraj told me. He was trying hard to compensate for the rooms' disaster. He gave me a printout of the week's plan. I glanced at it.

Radhika weds Brijesh: Itinerary for the week

Day 1: Arrival, check-ins, briefing, relax in resort

Day 2: Goa Darshan Tour for elders and children (11 a.m.-6 p.m.)
Bachelor Party for Mr Brijesh Gulati at Club Cubana (8 p.m.)
Bachelorette Party for Ms Radhika Mehta at LPK (8 p.m.)

'You have organized buses for the bachelor parties?' I said.

'Yes, ma'am. The buses will be there at 7.30 at the front entrance.'
I read further.

Day 3: Bhajan and Puja in function room (4 p.m.)

Day 4: Mehndi—counters for all ladies in function room
      (12-6 p.m.)
Day 5: Sangeet in function room (8 p.m.)

'The choreographer is here for the sangeet practice?' I said.

'No, ma'am. He will arrive in two days. He said that's enough time for practice.'

I looked at the itinerary again.

Day 6: Wedding at the Grand Ballroom and the Main Lawns (8 p.m.)
Day 7: Checkouts and departures (12 noon)

Suraj handed over the other sheets with details about each function and venue.

'Sorry about the rooms' goof-up, madam. Everything is under control now,' he said.

Suraj had just left when Brijesh came up behind me.

'This place is beautiful. Great idea to have a wedding in Goa,' he said. His accent was 90 per cent Indian and 10 per cent American. From a distance I saw my parents at the Marriott entrance, greeting Brijesh's parents and their relatives with folded hands. I focused back on Brijesh. 'Thank you. I always wanted a destination wedding,' I said.

Awkward silence for ten long, slow seconds. *What are we supposed to say to each other? Should I break the ice? Should I say, hey, we can officially start having sex in a week? Shut up, Radhika. Shut the fuck up.*

'You look,' Brijesh paused, searching for an apt word, 'beautiful.'

Could you do no better, Mr Groom? Stop it, Radhika, I scolded myself. *Yeah, stop it, Radhika!* I have to tell you about this bad habit of mine. I have this little person, this inner mini-me who keeps chattering about every situation or person around me. Sometimes, this mini-me overwhelms me so much I have to think hard to remember what just happened.

'Thank you,' I said. 'Thank you, Brijesh.'

And what sort of a name is Brijesh? Can it be more unfashionable? Radhika, you are going to marry a guy called Brijesh. You will be Mrs Brijesh Gulati. That's terrible. Okay, stop it. Stop it, Radhika. He's come a long way. He's a nice guy. That's what matters, right?

'Yellow looks nice on you,' Brijesh continued.

Actually, yellow sucks on me, what with my famous wheatish complexion. I wore this because mom wanted a sunflower in the lobby when the Gulatis arrived.

Okay, he is trying.

'Thanks,' I said. *Say more, you stupid girl.* 'Your kurta is also nice,' I said. *Duh, could you be more stupid?*

'Hello, beta.' A man in his early fifties along with his wife came up to me. They seemed too enthusiastic to be complete strangers. It took me a second to place them. All right, they were my in-laws. Mr Aadarsh Gulati and Mrs Sulochana Gulati. *Radhika, behave. Don't say anything stupid. Be like mom. Be like Aditi. What would Aditi didi do? She would touch their feet. C'mon, dive, then.*

I bent down. I touched the feet of people I had only Skyped twice in my life but who now deserved my total respect. My parents had met them several times, of course. Dad told me they were nice people. *Nice people? How does anyone figure out nice people? Are there any nice people in this world?* See, my mind won't stop chattering. Ever.

'How was your flight, uncle?' I said.

'Just one hour from Mumbai. Not like Brijesh, who has come from halfway across the world,' Aadarsh uncle said.

'For you, of course,' Sulochana aunty said and cupped my cheeks. She planted a big kiss on my forehead. I guess, considering this is a country where in-laws burn brides, they did seem like nice people.

More of Brijesh's relatives swarmed around us.

'Come, come, see the dulhan,' one of the aunts said. The monkey was out of the cage and there was a free sighting in the lobby. A crowd gathered around me. I tried to remember as many names as possible.

'My mother's sisters, Rohini masi and Gunjan masi,' Brijesh said, 'and that's dad's brothers, Purohit chacha and Amit chacha.'

Bob-bob went my head as I wished them all. If I saw anyone with even a hint of white or dyed or henna-tinted hair, I went for their feet. Exactly as my mother would expect me to. Amid the introductions and obsequious respect going on, Brijesh pulled me aside.

'Hey, is this too much for you?'

I shrugged.

'Is there somewhere we could take a walk?' he said.

There, he was being sweet. I had told him earlier I wanted to get to know him better, and he was making an effort.

'Sure. Let's go to the poolside,' I said.

2

Palm trees along the Marriott pool swayed green in the breeze. The 5 p.m. December sun lit up the hotel's cottages, casting gentle shadows everywhere. We went down the walking path, with the hotel to our left and the Arabian Sea to our right. I felt overdressed in my sunflower outfit as other hotel guests roamed around in shorts and vests.

'So you just arrived yesterday from San Francisco?' I said.

'Yeah, landed last night,' he said. 'I wanted to maximize my leave. One week for the wedding. A couple of days after that at home in Mumbai. Then Bali for our honeymoon. Used it all up, actually.'

The word honeymoon caused a jolt in me. Mini-me woke up again.

Honeymoon! After a dozen-odd Skype calls and meeting once over a day trip? A week in Bali with this man I am walking next to. Will we be naked? Stop it, Radhika. Focus on the moment.

'Must be tiring, flying so much,' I said.

'I saw you. Not tired anymore.'

I smiled. *The man is trying. Maybe I should too.*

Brijesh smiled back. He had innocent teacher's-pet eyes. 'How's Facebook?' I said.

'I had a busy month. Just finished an enterprise project. So much work, front-end interfaces, back-end systems, underlying APIs.'

'APIs?'

'Application programme interface. Set of routines, protocols and tools for building software applications. How software components interact, basically.'

I nodded, having understood not a word.

'You have no idea what I am talking about, right?'

I laughed.

'I know. Not the most exciting job in the world,' he said, his voice flat.

'Come on, you work at Facebook. It's quite cool.'

'People think it is Facebook so there's nothing to do. We post pictures all day or something.'

'I am sure it is pretty high-tech behind the scenes.'

Should I talk about more personal stuff? He will happily discuss computer code for two hours if I let him. Radhika, take control.

'You like your job?' I said.

Brijesh shrugged. 'It's nice. A lot of smart people. Always stuff happening. Pays well. Stock options. Flexi time…'

'What about that start-up idea?' I said. He had mentioned setting up his own software company when we'd met earlier.

'That's there. I still want to do it,' Brijesh said.

'So then?'

'Facebook is hard to leave. The salary, stock options and benefits. Plus, I would need funding. Arranging all that, leaving that level of security takes a lot. Just simpler this way.'

I nodded. We had to talk beyond work. Fortunately, he switched topics.

'I love Goa,' he said. 'I am here after a decade. We came here from our engineering college. Of course, not to such fancy resorts. We stayed in a simple place. Ate at the shacks.'

'I love the shacks.'

'You will love San Francisco too,' he said.

'I have lived in New York. Never on the West Coast.'

'California is different from New York. More laid-back.'

'Even our group at Goldman is supposed to be more chilled out in San Francisco.'

'How's that coming along? Your transfer done?'

My phone buzzed twice.

'Sorry, phone. Maybe mom needs something,' I said.

'Sure,' Brijesh said.

I had two messages from an unknown number. The number started with '+1'. Someone in the USA, I figured.

'Hey, heard you are getting married. True?' said the first message.

'This is Debu, by the way. Hope you remember me,' said the second. Debu? Debashish Sen! After what, like, three years? Debu was messaging me?

'Hi,' I typed back. He replied immediately.

'Hi, Radhika. How are you? Took me a while to hunt for your number. Been wanting to talk to you.'

'Everything okay?' Brijesh said, noticing how preoccupied I was with my phone.

'Huh? Yeah, all good,' I said, my voice nervous. I lowered the phone and clenched it in my hand.

'So, all done?' Brijesh said.

'What?'

'Your transfer. We were just talking about it.'

'Huh? Yes, yes. It's done, mostly. I will have to shuttle between London and San Francisco a few times, for my existing investments. But it is done.'

My phone buzzed three more times, vibrating in my hand. I should have ignored it. However, there is something about buzzing phones—my obsessive compulsive disorder makes me look at them. After all, it could be mom or Aditi didi. It wasn't.

'Hey baby. I just want to say I am sorry,' Debu's message said. He continued:

'I found out you are getting married.'

'I couldn't believe it.'

I had to reply to this.

'Why? You didn't think anyone would?' I typed back.

Having reached the end of the garden, Brijesh and I turned around to stroll back.

'We have to find a place to stay. Facebook is in Menlo Park, Goldman Sachs is downtown, right?' Brijesh said.

'Huh? What is downtown?' I said, my mind still on Debu's message.

'Goldman Sachs. San Francisco office,' Brijesh said, each word slow and deliberate. After all, he was speaking to a distracted idiot like me.

'Yeah, Goldman is on California Street, downtown.'

My phone buzzed a few more times. I swore to myself not to check it. I focused on Brijesh.

'So we have to decide whether we'll stay downtown or near Menlo Park, which is in Palo Alto,' Brijesh said.

'Yeah, sure.'

'Sure what?'

'You are right.' I had no idea what he just said.

'I said you have to choose. Downtown or Palo Alto?'

'Why do I have to choose?'

'Radhika, are you okay? I said, we have to choose where we'll stay.' I finally figured out the conversation.

'Uh-oh. Well, I am easy, actually. You are already staying in Menlo Park, right?'

'Yeah, but my lease expires in two months.'

Just one little peek, I told myself. I will have a quick look at the phone and then pay full attention to Brijesh.

I lifted the phone. Among the many messages from Debu, one read: 'I love you.'

Fuck. Fortunately, I did not blurt the word out. I immediately shut the phone. I placed my hand on my face.

'I was keen to move out anyway,' Brijesh said. 'Radhika, are you okay? Everything under control?'

'Actually, I need to go back. Mom needs something. Jewellery issues,' I said.

'Ah. Indian weddings,' Brijesh said.

Yeah, I had lied to my husband-to-be, within one hour of his arrival. What a wonderful bride I am going to make, isn't it? See, I told you, you won't like me very much.

'So I will see you again soon?' I said.

'Of course,' Brijesh said, with a twinkle in his eye. 'I am going to be your husband, you are going to see me all the time. Come, let's walk back.'

I gripped my phone tight as if otherwise the messages would leak out and fall on the floor. Brijesh left me at the lift lobby, where he met one of his cousins who wanted to talk to him. The lift door shut. I pressed the button to the fourth floor, and took a deep breath. I checked my phone. It had tons of messages from Debu.

'For the past few months I have been thinking of you constantly.'

'Only had the courage to text you now.'

'I made the biggest mistake. I didn't value you.'

'I love you.'

What the hell is he talking about?

Ting! The lift reached my floor. I walked up to my room and rang the bell. Aditi didi opened the door.

'Where were you?' She gave me a mischievous look. 'With Brijesh?'

I smiled, as if caught red-handed. *I am the coy bride. I have to smile whenever my would-be-husband is mentioned.*

Didi had opened one of her suitcases. It was the kind of giant bag murderers use to hide bodies. She had six dresses spread out on the bed.

'What is Brijesh like?' she said, as she unfolded a red dress.

'Decent. Getting to know him,' I said, plonking myself on the sofa.

I took out my phone again. *Why? Why am I taking out my phone again?*

Aditi didi continued to talk. 'I didn't know Anil at all before marriage. You just get to know each other better after the wedding. The honeymoon helps.' She winked at me.

I nodded, even as I wondered what to reply to Debu.

'I really do,' Debu texted again. The guy who earlier took ten days to reply to a text was now sending ten texts a minute.

'Are you high?' I replied. Debu and I ended up having a chat.

'No. It is 5 in the morning here. I am having my coffee. This is not a drunk text.'

'Good. Then you need to know I am getting married in five days.'

'What? So soon?'

'Yes. Guests are already here.'

'Whom are you getting married to?'

'Someone not as insecure as you…' I typed and deleted.

'Brijesh Gulati…' I typed and deleted again.

I decided to not reply. Didi held up two dresses, one blue and one red.

'Which one should I wear for tomorrow's bachelorette? Honest opinion,' she said.

'Both are good. Which is your favourite?' I said.

'I like the red. But it's really short. Is it screaming for attention too much?' she said.

Of course, it is. But that's what you have always wanted, sister. Why stop yourself now?

'It's fine. Wear whatever you like,' I said.

'I'll wear the blue. It's till the knees. More elder-sister-of-the-bride types.'

'You are only a year older.'

'Yeah, that is also true. And tomorrow is the only day I get to wear a Western dress. I only wear Indian after that. I am one of the few girls here who can actually carry off a dress like this.'

She lifted her red dress. Yes, Aditi didi with her super-slim soup-and-salad-diet figure could carry it off.

'Red, didi. End of debate,' I said.

My phone buzzed.

'Babes, who are you getting married to?' Debu said.

I replied, 'It doesn't matter. You are not in my life anymore, Debashish.'

'Can you call me Debu at least?'

'I am busy, Debashish. I don't have time for this.'

'Where's the wedding?'

I didn't respond.

'You didn't invite me?' he said, needling me again.

Asshole, you didn't even return my calls, I wanted to say but didn't.

My phone rang. Debu was trying to call me. I cut the call. I typed back a message.

'Don't call me. I told you I am busy. There are people around.'

'So just reply to me. Where is the wedding?'

'Why?'

'Just curious.'

'Whatever,' I typed back.

'I can call friends around and find out. So why don't you just tell me?'

'Goa.'

'Wow! Destination wedding and all.'

I didn't respond. To distract myself I asked Aditi didi a deep existential question: 'What shoes are you wearing with this?'

'Oh see, now that's an issue too. I have these four-inch-heel red stilettos, but that's definitely attention-seeking.'

'Yeah, plus we are going dancing. Would be difficult in high heels. I am wearing flats.'

My sister feels her deepest bond with me when I discuss clothes and shoes with her. She came up to me and pulled my cheeks. 'You can't wear flats for your bachelorette. How cute you are. You don't know anything.'

Yes, I may be a distressed debt specialist. I may have rescued bankrupt companies and structured complex takeovers. I may be a vice president at Goldman Sachs. But if I prefer flats because they are comfortable, I know nothing. I had kept a black dress for tomorrow's party. Didi had a look at it. 'Too simple,' she said. She went on to accessorize it for me. As she opened her jewellery box, I checked my phone again.

'Where in Goa?' Debu had sent me a message.

'Why?' I said.

'Can I call, please?' he said.

'No.'

'It's at a resort?' he said.

'Debu, you are in New York. Focus on your work there. Didn't you have a girlfriend?'

'Who?'

'Never mind.'

'I am sorry, Rad.'

'It's okay. Life goes on. It has gone on.'

'Yeah, true. But I made the biggest mistake. And you are getting married now. Like now!'

I sent a smiley back.

'Where will you live after your marriage? Hong Kong?'

'No. I moved to London from Hong Kong a year ago.'

'Oh. So London?'

'San Francisco.'

'Ah. IT guy?'

'I have to go, Debashish.'

'Still mad at me?'

'No. I really have to. I have to get ready for dinner with the guests.'

'Okay. I am just asking casually. Where is the wedding?'

'Marriott,' I said.

'Nice! Must be beautiful.'

'Stop chatting on your phone. Who are you talking to anyway? Everyone we know is here in Goa for the wedding,' Aditi didi said.

'Huh? Nobody. Just....work,' I said, keeping my phone aside. After the bridegroom, the bride had lied to her sister.

'Take this, my body necklace. Your dull dress will liven up,' she said.

'My dull dress is Prada, didi,' I said.

'I don't care. It needs to have a get-up, no? It is too sober. You are too sober.'

I didn't think I was going to remain sober. Not after Debu's next message.

'I am coming,' he said.

'What?' I typed back, mouth open.

'I am coming to India. Let me check flights.'

'Are you nuts?'

'No, really, I want to talk to you.'

'Debu, calm down, okay? This is not funny.'

'At least you called me Debu again.'

'Whatever. I have to go. Please don't message.'

'See you soon. Bye.'

'Go to work. Bye.'

'Again you are lost in your phone. What is wrong with you?' Aditi didi said.

I looked up as I re-entered the real world.

'Everyone's meeting for dinner soon. Get ready.'

'Can't I go like this? I just wore this.'

'No. You are the bride.'

'So? I have to change every two hours?'

'Just go shower, okay? And don't take your phone inside.'

3

'Didi, let's go, the bus is waiting,' I said. Aditi didi had spent the last two hours changing in and out of a dozen dresses. Finally, she wore the red one she'd always wanted to wear.

'Is it showing too much cleavage?' she said.

Isn't that what you want? I am the bride, goddammit. It is my bachelorette party. Can't you make me the priority at least for this week?

The room phone rang. I picked it up.

'Hey,' Brijesh said. I had started to recognize his voice. That's a good sign, isn't it?

'Hi, Brijesh. All set?'

'Yeah, my gang is in the bus. I am calling from the reception.'

'Oh, you boys go ahead. The driver knows Club Cubana, right?' I said.

'Yeah, he does, it is in Arpora. Your bus for LPK is here too. Coming?'

'Soon.'

'I wish we were going to the same place,' Brijesh said.

I laughed. 'That's sweet, Brijesh, but that's the point of a bachelor party. Your last night out without the annoying spouse. Boys and girls go separately tonight.'

'You are not annoying,' he said.

'Clearly you don't know me yet.'

'I wanted to see you before we left. My gang wanted to see all the dressed-up Mehta girls.'

'Your gang is not laying an eye on my innocent cousins.'

I ended the call and turned to Aditi didi, who continued to adjust her dress in front of the mirror. 'Didi, you do realize it is *my* bachelorette?'

◆

'There it is,' said Jyoti, my second cousin, pointing at a huge flaming-yellow lit-up sign for Love Passion Karma or LPK. The club, half an hour from the hotel, was located at the waterfront of Nerul River and decorated in an over-the-top Paleolithic era theme, with stone caves and giant stone statues of the early man in the lawn. We were a group of fifteen girls. Suraj had also arranged two bouncers for us. We had a table in a semi-private area, with balloons and champagne bottles.

Nice job, Suraj, I thought.

'Some of the girls seem too young, madam,' the club owner told Aditi didi.

'Everyone is above eighteen,' didi said firmly.

'Some people in your group do look underage, ma'am,' he said.

'It's okay. Give them soft drinks. But get my sister drunk tonight.'

'No, didi,' I said in vain as the owner brought a round of tequila shots. I had to take two. Jyoti asked for another round. Rajni, our neighbour's daughter, wanted the music louder. Shruti, my childhood friend from school, wanted Honey Singh songs. Saloni, Aditi didi's best friend, felt we should play drinking games until someone puked. There is nothing as crazy as fifteen Punjabi girls determined to go out of control. I took out my phone. I had a message from Brijesh.

'Club Cubana is nice. Thanks.'

'You are welcome. How is it going?' I said.

'Three drinks down. And you?'

'Was made to consume tequila shots.'

'Wow. Wait, the boys are teasing me for chatting with you.'

'Ha ha, go have fun.' I kept my phone aside.

Aditi didi wanted to raise a toast. Two waiters arrived and poured champagne for everyone.

'For my only darling sweetest sister. Someone who only studied and worked hard. She did nothing naughty in life. Nothing bad ever.'

Yeah right, I thought but simply smiled as Aditi didi continued, 'Oh yes, she's the good girl. If I barely passed, she topped. If I became a housewife, she became a hi-fi banker. If I had the boobs, she had the brains.'

All the girls laughed. The muscular bouncers blushed. My phone buzzed. *Must be Brijesh,* I thought. *He's sweet. He's trying to make a connection.*

'Hey, am at JFK airport. Figuring out last-minute tickets,' Debu had messaged instead.

'What?' I typed back.

'Fifteen hours to Mumbai. Then a quick connection to Goa.'

'Debu, are you serious? Stop it, will you?'

Aditi didi caught me staring at my phone.

'Look at my baby, chatting with her husband-to-be. At least leave him on your girls' night out,' she said. Everyone laughed. Aditi didi took a big gulp of the champagne. I gulped at what I saw next.

Debu had sent me a picture of the Air India counter at JFK. He followed it up with a smiley.

'Take another shot,' one of my cousins egged me.

Yeah, just shoot me instead.

'Miss you,' said another message.

'Will you shut the fuck up and go home?' I typed in response. Damn, I almost pressed send before I realized the last 'miss you' message had come from Brijesh.

I deleted what I had written and retyped, 'Aww, sweet,' adding a few smileys. I couldn't think of anything more imaginative. With care I switched chats from Brijesh to Debu.

'Please don't bother me. Go home,' I said.

'Girls,' my sister made an announcement, 'what say we take away the bride's phone for the evening?'

'Huh? No, didi, no,' I said in vain as Aditi didi snatched my phone from my hands and placed it in her handbag.

'It's your last night out as a bachelorette. You better do crazy things and not waste it on the phone,' Aditi didi said.

I wanted to tell her I had enough craziness happening on the phone.

'Okay,' Aditi didi announced. 'Let's play "challenge the bride". Everyone will give the bride a dare. And Radhika has to do it.'

I looked around. Our table was in one corner of the restaurant. In the middle, several people sat on bar stools. Half the customers were Indians who had come to Goa for the Christmas holidays. Others were mostly European and American tourists.

Jyoti gave me the first task.

'See that bald white guy over there.' She pointed at a forty-something man sitting at the bar. 'Find out his name and the country he comes from.'

'That's too easy,' didi said.

'Get his name, country and slap, no wait, kiss his forehead,' said Shruti. Everyone laughed and cheered at the suggestion.

'No way,' I said.

'Yes way. Here take this. Bottoms up.' Saloni gave me a half-filled champagne glass. I gulped it in one go. My head felt light.

'Go!' Aditi didi clapped her hands.

I walked up to the bar.

'Hi there,' I said to the man. He wore a white vest and jeans. He had two rings on his right hand and a dragon tattoo on his right shoulder.

'Hi there, young lady,' he said. His accent sounded Australian. I had to confirm it.

'Are you an Australian cricketer?'

He laughed. 'No, mate, I am Australian but I am no cricket player. Like watching it, though.'

'Aren't you Philip Lee?' I made up a name on the spot.

'Is he even a player?' he said and sipped his beer.

'You aren't Philip?'

'No,' he said. 'Can I buy you a drink, young lady?'

'Well, who are you then?'

'I'm Mark. What drink would you like?'

'A tequila shot.'

Mark ordered a pair of shots. I had accomplished two out of the three tasks.

'Cheers,' he said as we took the shot.

I kept the glass on the table.

'You here on holiday?' Mark said.

'Actually, I am here to get married.'

'Really?'

'Yeah. I have to go. Bye, Mark.'

Before he could react I kissed his head.

'Thanks for the drink,' I said and scooted out of there.

The girls gave me a standing ovation. Everyone had a shot as a mark of respect for my courage.

'Okay, no more,' I said as Mark winked at me from the bar.

The girls were hysterical. We finished four champagne bottles. We ordered four more. I don't really know when we started to dance. The DJ played tracks like 'Subah hone na de' and 'Baby doll'. Some men in the club tried to flirt with my little cousins. Aditi didi shooed most of them off. We had selfie binges as the fifteen of us took photos in every possible permutation and combination. An hour later, another group of boys arrived at the club. It took us girls a minute to realize the situation.

'Oh my God. It's Brijesh jiju and his gang!' Saloni said.

Brijesh came up to me on the dance floor.

'Not allowed, not allowed,' Jyoti said.

'You were at Club Cubana. What happened?' Shruti said to Akhil,

Brijesh's maternal cousin.

'Nothing. We had a few drinks. Then we thought, when we have the most beautiful girls in Goa partying alone, what are we doing here?' Akhil said.

Shruti blushed. Even though the girls protested at the boys coming here, they secretly liked it. This is how we girls are. At times we want to be wanted, even when we deny it. My bachelorette wasn't really a singles' party now. However, I was too drunk to care.

'You look too beautiful,' Brijesh said. The DJ switched to Honey Singh's Blue eyes, a slow couples-only type song, possibly to get drunk single men off the floor.

'Obviously you have had too much to drink,' I said. Nobody could find me 'too beautiful' otherwise.

'Well, I have had a few. But I always find you really beautiful,' Brijesh said.

Sweet, I thought. The tequila in me gave him a hug.

'I messaged you,' Brijesh said, 'several times.'

'You did? Oh, where's my phone? I don't even know where my phone is.'

'I wanted to check if you would be okay if we come. I tried to stop the boys.'

'It's okay. The idea is to have fun. All this segregation is not to be taken seriously,' I said.

'Nice music,' he said.

'You want to dance?' I said.

'I am not much of a dancer,' Brijesh said.

'Neither am I,' I said.

I held his shoulders as we swayed gently to Blue eyes. The girls went into an 'aww' and 'how sweet' overdrive.

See, I can be a 'good' girl. *Am I not trying to be a good girl?* I told mini-me, my personal chatterbox and eternal critic. Mini-me, however, had slept off. Alcohol does this to her. I guess that is why most people drink anyway. To shut up their inner critic. So they can do whatever the hell they want.

'Ouch, Brijesh, you are stepping on my toes,' I said.

4

It was 4 in the afternoon. Everyone who'd partied last night had a hangover. We had come back to the hotel at 6 in the morning and gone straight for breakfast. I remembered sitting with my mother and ordering pancakes. I couldn't eat much, as I kept dozing off.

'Wake up. This is so wrong, what you did. Brijesh's parents will think what an uncultured and irresponsible girl they are getting. Who drinks like this?' my mother had said, shaking me non-stop.

'Even their son did. In fact, he puked and passed out at the club,' I'd said.

'He's a boy.'

Even in my exhausted, hungover and sleepy state, my feminist antennae were up. I stared at my mother.

'So what if he is a boy?' I said. Clearly, the alcohol-induced confidence had not left me.

'Eat quickly. Get some rest. There are bhajans today. Please wear something decent. Why do you youngsters have to do such parties the night before bhajans?'

'Why do you oldies have to do bhajans the day after our party?'

'Just because you have started to make money you will say anything?'

I had kept quiet. I didn't mention that this uncultured and irresponsible daughter of theirs was paying for her own wedding. One crore rupees, or 150,000 dollars, wired from my salary account as the wedding budget. Did she even care?

I had had to gulp down a glass of orange juice to calm myself. *You have screwed up your life enough, can you please behave for a few days?* the voice inside told me. *Ah, good morning, mini-me. When did you wake up?*

I remembered being escorted to my room. Aditi didi slept diagonally across the bed, still in her red dress. I changed into my T-shirt and pajamas, slid didi's legs aside and lay down. My head hurt like someone had hammered it a few times. I closed my eyes.

Didi woke me up at 2.30 in the afternoon.

'Get up, we have bhajans.'

'They are at 4. Why are you waking me up now?' I said. Didi drew open the curtains. My eyes hurt from the daylight.

'You need time to get ready. Here, you have to wear this orange saree.'
'No,' I said and pulled a pillow on top of my head.

I woke up eventually. I grumbled about the entire process of dressing up, which only women have to endure. The hotel sent a hair-and-make-up lady to our room. She blow-dried my tangled hair. The noise from the hair-dryer hurt my head even more.

We reached the function room downstairs. It had been converted to look like the inside of a temple. Marigold flowers in parabolic shapes adorned the walls. At the centre was a huge picture of Sai Baba. My parents believed in him more than any God. Statues of other Hindu gods—Krishna, Ganesha, Lakshmi and Vaishno Devi—were also kept. The bhajan singers set up their mikes.

The younger lot sat at the back of the room. Most of them were holding their heads. Brijesh's friends and cousins wore crisp silk kurta-pajamas. They had taken a shower in order to look fresh. They passed around strips of Combiflam and bottles of water to nurse their hangovers.

My girls did no better. Most of them leaned back against the wall and snoozed in their elaborate lehengas and salwar-kameezes. The way Indian girls transform themselves from party chicks in short dresses to fully clad, chaste, virginal bhajan attendees is almost a visual effects' miracle.

The bhajans began. The singers had a wonderful voice. However, when you are hungover even the best melody sounds like an electric drill. Brijesh looked at me and smiled. I gestured that I wanted to sleep. He passed me a Combiflam strip. I popped a pill.

'You are not well?' Kamla bua said.
'Just tired,' I said.
'I have an Ayurvedic medicine. It works better,' Kamla bua said. Nothing in the world works better than Combiflam, I wanted to tell her.
'Nice bhajans, bua,' I said instead.

The angels of Marriott brought us cups of black coffee. I had two. I swore not to drink again, ever. Okay, at least not this week. The coffee helped me wake up somewhat.

'Come and pray in front, beta,' one of my aunts told me.

Brijesh and I went ahead and bowed before the gods. The singers sang a special song for us. I looked at Brijesh. He had his eyes shut and hands folded. He was actually praying. I felt guilty for not praying with as much sincerity. *Because you are a fraud*, mini-me told me. *Will you ever shut up?* I said to mini-me.

I went back and sat with the girls. Brijesh joined the boys. The crowd participated in the next bhajan, one of the more popular ones. Despite the loud music, I found it hard to keep my eyes open. However, I woke up with a jolt when a bearded man in his late twenties entered the room. He had curly hair and wore a white kurta-pajama.

'Oh God. Debu?' I blurted out.

'What?' Rajni, who sat next to me, said.

'Nothing,' I said.

He went up to the Sai Baba picture with confidence. He knelt down, bowed and touched his forehead to the ground. Done with his prayers, he went to the men's section and sat down. He clapped his hands as the singers sang the next bhajan.

What the fuck is he doing here? Did I just say, or think, the F-word in the puja room? Who cares? Am I imagining this? No I am not. What the fuck is Debu doing here?

He looked at me and smiled. Brijesh smiled at me at the same time as well. I fake-smiled at both of them. I had to talk to Debu. *How? Where is my phone? Damn, where is my phone?*

'Where is my phone? Haven't seen it today. Did I leave it in the club?' I whispered to Rajni.

'Aditi didi kept it last night, right?'

I tapped Aditi didi's shoulder. She sat in front of me, wearing a magenta salwar-kameez with the dupatta covering her head. She sang with full fervour. Nobody could have guessed how well she had matched every step of Sunny Leone's Baby doll at LPK last night.

'What?' she said. I gestured that she return my phone. She rummaged through her handbag.

'Here,' she said and handed it to me.

I had only 5 per cent battery left. I checked my messages. Brijesh had sent me some about leaving Club Cubana and coming to LPK. Debu had sent messages about taking off, and then one about him having landed in Goa.

'What on earth are you doing here?' I messaged Debu.

He didn't see his phone. He seemed to be in bliss, lost in the bhajans. *Fuck, what is wrong with him?* It took me a minute to get his attention. I gestured to him to look at his phone.

He saw the message. He replied with a few wink smileys from across the room.

'Really, what are you doing?' I typed back.

'Nice surprise, no?' he messaged.

'Cut the nonsense, Debu. My entire family is here.'

'Yeah, I saw. His too. I saw the groom. Golden silk kurta, lots of red threads around his wrist, right?'

'What do you want, Debu?' I sent a message.

'To talk face-to-face.'

'I can't.'

'I have come all the way. Please.'

'My phone is dying.'

'Meet me.'

'How?' I said.

'You say. Anytime. Anywhere.'

I thought hard.

'After the bhajans. At the hotel gym.'

Nobody would go to the gym after bhajans. He replied with a thumbs up.

◆

Debu sat on the bench press. He held a dumbbell in one hand and did bicep curls. I stood in front of him.

'Are you crazy?' I said. I looked around to see if anyone I knew had come to the gym. Apart from one old white man on the treadmill and a gym trainer, there was no one.

'Thank you for coming,' he said. 'By the way, you look gorgeous in this orange saree. Wow. Just wow!'

'Whatever. And can you keep that dumbbell down?'

'Just trying to make it look natural,' he said.

'You are in a kurta. I am in a sari. We don't look natural here. Debu, what is wrong with you? You literally took a flight and came down?'

'Yeah. I am quite jetlagged actually. I feel like having breakfast. Want to grab some?'

'Will you stop it? You have no idea how I have come here. Everyone will be looking for me at dinner.'

'We can go there. I can eat.'

'Debu, this is not a joke. My family is here. Their reputation is important. How could you just walk into the bhajans' place?'

'I wanted to pray. For my mission to be successful.'

'What mission?'

'To win you back. The most important thing in the world for me right now.'

I must say, for a second I had no answer. I looked at him. He still had his trademark two-week beard and curly hair. He had gained a bit of weight, but also become more fit. Or maybe it just felt like that in the gym.

'How are you, baby?' he said.

'Don't "baby" me,' I said, loud enough for the American man on the treadmill to turn his head towards us for a second. I continued, 'You have any idea what you made me go through? And you just cut me off.'

'I was an idiot. An insecure twenty-four-year-old.'

'And what are you now? A stupid twenty-eight-year-old?'

'Maybe. But I am old enough to realize you are the best thing to have ever happened to me.'

'What?' I said, then keeping my composure, 'It's over, Debu. It's been over since long back. You didn't even return my calls.'

'I am sorry.'

'It doesn't matter. Now I have to ask you to leave. Go visit your parents in Kolkata. You are in India anyway.'

'New York, baby.'

'What about New York?'

'Don't you remember the days in New York? We had issues, yes, but how can you forget all the happy memories?'

He looked into my eyes. He seemed to be in pain. For the first time in my life, someone had crossed half a planet to come for the usually unlovable me. And it is hard to keep yelling at someone who has done that for you.

'You forgot, baby?' he said again.

'No, Debu, I have forgotten nothing,' I said, my voice soft.

New York

Four Years Ago

5

'Bay-gulls. That's how you pronounce them, spelt b-a-g-e-l-s,' Avinash said at the breakfast counter on 85 Broad Street, worldwide headquarters of Goldman Sachs.

Avinash, a batchmate of mine from IIMA, had also made it to Goldman Sachs. He had worked abroad before his MBA. He knew a lot more than me about the way things worked in America. He picked up the doughnut-shaped bread, slit it horizontally with a black plastic knife and smeared it with cheese.

'Bagel and cream cheese, classic combo,' he said.

'Thanks, Avinash,' I said, fumbling with my plate, my handbag, my umbrella and my senses. I had worn a Western-style office suit for the first time in my life. Even for my Goldman Sachs interview at IIMA campus I had worn a sari.

Is the skirt too tight? Is my ass looking too big? Is my hair in place? Mini-me was in overdrive, the perfect day for her to knock me out.

Two hundred other fresh recruits had arrived from all over the world. For our ten-week associate training, we had to report at 7.30 in the morning. Classes began after a quick breakfast, and ended at 6.30 in the evening.

Partners and senior employees from various departments, such as Corporate Finance, Equities and Distressed Debt, took sessions on what actually happened in their group. The partners, no more than 200 in the entire firm of 20,000 people, held the senior-most positions in the firm. They held equity in the bank and made the most money. Their annual compensation could reach tens of millions of dollars every year.

'Open the Goldman Sachs business principles,' said Gary Colbert, a senior partner who looked like a rich grandfather in his gold spectacles. Goldman took great pride in its fourteen business principles.

'Long-term greed,' Gary said. 'Read that line in the principles. That's what we aim for here.'

Greed and investment banking went together. Goldman was honest enough to admit it. They just didn't mind delaying their greed, for it made the pay-off even better. Gary recounted his journey from joining Goldman as an operations assistant thirty-five years ago.

'Everyone works hard at Goldman, no exception. If you want an easy life, look elsewhere,' Gary said. Well, it was too late for me to look elsewhere. I was already in New York. Trainees circulated horror stories about new associates spending nights in the office and sleeping on office couches.

Two weeks into our training Avinash came up to me.

'I have a group of Indian friends in New York. We are meeting up for drinks tonight. You want to come?'

'I have to finish the merger model spreadsheet,' I said.

'You are still a muggu,' Avinash said, referring to me as someone who mugs up, or studies, all the time. My IIMA reputation would not leave me so easily.

I had lied to Avinash. I had a haircut appointment. After moving to New York, I had decided to leave my nerdy, unfashionable days far behind. An associate trainee in my class had gorgeous shoulder-length hair with waves, exactly how I wanted mine. She had made a booking for me at a salon on 32nd Street.

Of course, I couldn't tell Avinash this. Muggu Radhika doing her hair? He would laugh in my face. The news would spread like wildfire in the IIMA alumni groups.

'You are in New York, will you live a little?' Avinash said.

'Where are the drinks?' I said.

'At Whiskey Blue. It's a bar at the W Hotel. Right opposite the Benjamin Hotel, where you are staying.'

Some problems in the world seem to exist solely for women. Like not having anything to wear. I realized I had nothing nice for tonight.

'I am not sure, let me see,' I said.

'What let me see? Just come, Muggu,' he said.

◆

For the rare breed of girls like me that hates shopping and has serious retardation in the areas of the brain that help you pick a dress, Banana Republic is the answer.

'Hi, miss. God, you have a gorgeous colour,' one of the African-American female sales assistants said. *Say that to my mother. She stays up at night wondering who will marry me with this skin colour.*

'I have to go for drinks, with some friends,' I said, 'and I suck at shopping. Can you help?'

When you have no clue, best to surrender. The only shopping I ever did in my life was for textbooks.

'I'll take care of you, girl,' the shop assistant said.

She picked a navy blue lace dress for me. It fit well, but ended mid-thigh.

'Too short?' I said.

'Not at all. It's summer. You look lovely,' she said. Even though she was paid to say it, it felt good. 'I would wax those legs, though,' she added.

Ouch! That hurt.

'Unless you like it natural,' the salesperson corrected herself, switching back to classic American political correctness.

◆

I entered Whiskey Blue at 9. The plush bar and lounge had decadent leather sofas and dim lighting. Avinash noticed me first.

'Hey, you are late,' he said, 'and wow.'

'What?'

'Your dress. I almost didn't recognize you.'

Was that an 'oh my God, you look good' wow? Or was it a 'what the fuck are you wearing' wow? Before I could ask he introduced me to the others.

'That's Ruchi, Ashish, Nidhi, Rohan and our dreamer-philosopher, Debu,' Avinash said, 'and this is Radhika, guys, my batchmate from IIMA, top mugger and now at Goldman Sachs, like me.'

Fuck you, Avinash.

'She doesn't look like a mugger,' Debu said. He shifted to make space for me.

We occupied two sofas. Ruchi, Ashish and Nidhi sat on one. Rohan, Avinash, Debu and I sat on the opposite side. The waiter asked for my order.

'I don't really drink a lot,' I said.

'Don't worry, they only give you one glass at a time,' Debu said. I smiled.

He looked into my eyes. He did have a philosopher look about him, with his beard and uncombed hair.

'Wine?' he said. 'It's light.'

'Sure,' I said.

'A glass of Shiraz for the lady,' Debu said to the waiter. Nobody had ever ordered Shiraz for me, which I later learnt is a type of grape. Nobody had ever referred to me as a lady either.

'Cheers,' Debu said once our drinks arrived.

Everyone lifted his or her glasses. Debu continued, 'To the fresh-off-the-boat people, Avinash, Rohan and Radhika. Welcome to the USA, welcome to New York.'

I learnt more about the others. Rohan had come from IIMC. He had a job at Morgan Stanley. Nidhi and Ashish were dating each other. They had worked at Merrill Lynch for two years.

At one point, when the others were lost in conversation, Debu turned to me.

'Goldman Sachs, eh? That's a big deal. What is it like?' Debu said.

'It's okay,' I said. 'I am still in training. Most of it is going over my head. How about you? Are you in a bank too?'

Debu laughed. 'Far from it. I am not a numbers guy at all. I work in BBDO. An advertising agency on Madison Avenue.'

'That is so cool,' I said.

'The only somewhat creative career I could find.'

'Where are you from?' I said.

'I grew up in Kolkata. Then went to SRCC in Delhi, then did my master's here...'

I cut him mid-sentence.

'SRCC? You went to SRCC? Which batch?'

'I graduated three years ago,' he said.

'What? You are one batch senior to me.'

We realized that despite attending the same college we had never seen or met each other.

'Sorry, I can't recall seeing you,' I said.

'I was under the influence. Justifying the use of grass to stimulate my creativity. So I don't blame you.'

'I studied most of the time. I don't blame you,' I said. Both of us laughed. A little bit of wine from my glass spilt on my leg. He offered me a tissue. Even in the darkness, I noticed him look at my legs.

Oh, so this is how guys check out girls? Thank God it is dark. I need to book a waxing appointment soon.

'Where are you staying?' Debu said.

'Right across, at the Benjamin Hotel. Only for training, though. Will look for an apartment soon.'

He lit up a cigarette. He offered me one. I declined.

'Can I say something?' he said.

'Sure,' I said.

'That is a nice dress you are wearing,' he said.

'Oh, thanks,' I said. The mix of compliments and wine made me giddy.

'But if you want me to cut the price tag, I can. Sixty-nine ninety-five. Good buy,' he said. He pointed to the tag, still attached to the back of my dress.

My face colour changed to match that of the red wine. I had never been so embarrassed in my life.

'Or I can let it be if you want to return the dress. The return policy is great in the USA,' Debu said.

I fumbled to find the price label on my back. He laughed, picked up a cutlery knife from the table and cut the tag.

'What's up, guys?' Avinash asked as he noticed Debu bent over my back.

'Nothing. I liked the dress. Just wanted to check the brand,' Debu said.

'You advertising types, always curious,' Avinash said.

Post-drinks the group decided to go to Ray's, a famous place for pizzas.

'What's your favourite cuisine?' Debu asked me as he ate his pizza slice.

I had no favourite cuisine. I couldn't say Indian. It sounded too unfashionable.

'Chinese,' I blurted out.

'I know a great Chinese place. Would you like to go sometime?'

Did he just ask me out? Nobody has ever asked me out. Thank you, Banana Republic. Oh, maybe he is just being helpful. He is saying he will tell me of a Chinese place I can go to sometime, alone. Is that what he means?

He looked at me, waiting for an answer. *Say something, Radhika.*

'Huh? Yeah, why not? You can tell me the address, or if they deliver...'

'I meant with me.'

'Oh,' I said and became quiet. *Say something else, you stupid girl.*

'Yeah. Just you and me,' Debu said.

My heart began to beat fast. *Is this what people call a date? Can I ask him to clarify?*

'Okay,' I said, letting out a huge breath, 'we can.'

'Next Friday?' he said. Thoughts darted across my head. *Isn't he too forward? Wait, he is just fixing a time. Else how will it ever happen? Will it look too cheap and desperate if I say yes? Will he think I am a slut? Why is there no user manual for how girls should live on this planet?*

'Friday?' I said and shut up, like a bimbette. He must be wondering how Goldman ever hired me.

'Yeah. Weekend. No office next day,' he said, his voice uncomfortable. He didn't know if I was trying to blow him off or just being the usual idiot that I am.

'Okay,' I said. The effort it took me to say that okay felt like lifting seven heavy suitcases.

'Cool. I will message you the time and address.'

'Sure,' I said.

'Only if I have your number,' he said.

'Oh, of course. I'll give it to you,' I said.

6

'Distressed Debt: Special Situations Group,' the slide on the projection system read. The associate training class became radio silent. Distressed Debt was the hardest group to crack and join in Goldman Sachs. In any year only one or two associates were offered a role in the group. Those who made it earned the fastest promotions and the best bonuses.

Everyone had waited for this presentation.

'Good morning, everyone,' said the speaker on stage in a British accent. 'I am Neel Gupta, partner at the Special Situations Group in the Hong Kong office.'

I looked up from my desk. He was six feet tall, lean and had a muscular frame. He had high cheekbones and a light brown complexion. He had salt-and-pepper hair, more pepper than salt, actually. He wore a crisp white shirt, a pinstriped navy-blue suit and a matching tie.

'I will be giving you an overview of the Distressed Debt Group, in my view the most exciting place to be in Goldman Sachs.'

I sat next to four American girls: Maggie, Angela, Jessica and Carolyn. They looked at each other and made he-is-so-hot gestures.

If he wasn't a partner he could be a model in one of those ads that show distinguished men buying expensive watches.

'He is gorgeous,' a girl behind me whispered.

Focus, Radhika, I told myself as he switched to the next slide.

The slide showed various stages in the life of a business. It started with the inception and start-up stage. It went on to growth, maturity, decline and demise.

'Angel funds, venture capital and private equity. These guys help companies that are just born or are growing up. In clinical terms you can call them the maternity ward.'

He turned his back to us to see the slide. All the girls in the class exchanged glances with each other. The girls from the Hong Kong office felt extra lucky to have such a hunk in their office.

Neel continued, 'We, on the other hand, belong to the death ward. We come in when the company has failed, when the time has come to either try something drastic or...'

He dramatically paused at the 'or' for a few seconds before he spoke again. 'Or the time has come to pull out the life support, or liquidate and close the company. How easy do you think that is?'

He moved around the classroom and stopped right next to me. He had great perfume on, the kind that makes you want to go closer and smell it some more.

'You, young lady. You think it is easy to shut down factories and fire people?'

I was gobsmacked. I didn't expect to be asked a question in the GS training class, which had people from around the world. *What if I said something stupid? What if everyone laughed at my Delhi accent?*

I got up, nervous.

'Sit down, young lady,' Neel said. 'Answer from your seat. Where are you from?'

'India, sir.'

'Ah, I grew up there. Moved to the UK when I was ten. Anyway, so when would you recommend closing a business?'

'When all other alternatives have failed. When keeping it alive means throwing good money after bad. When hope dies, I guess.'

'When hope dies. Nice way to put it. But isn't it heartbreaking when that happens?' Neel said.

I remained silent. He moved to the front of the class.

'Can you blame the undertaker for burying dead people? If people are dead, they need to be buried,' Neel said.

His macabre analogies made his point clear. It also added notoriety, a level of excitement to distressed debt. What Neel said next helped further.

'I became a partner in twelve years. Other parts of the firm, it takes twenty or more. Our associates make what VPs make in other groups. I am not allowed to reveal numbers, but if you stick around in distressed debt you will end up a very wealthy man or woman.'

Goldman Sachs never liked to discuss wealth in public. This, despite the fact that everyone at the firm was essentially there because of the money. Trainees whispered they had found out Neel's equity in the firm on the Internet. He had thirty million dollars' worth of Goldman Sachs shares. His hotness level spiked even more.

His session ended with thundering applause. He made a final announcement before he left.

'We only have a few places in the group. Those interested, apply with the training coordinator. We will shortlist and get back to you,' he said and looked in my direction. 'Do try. It'll be worth it.'

Did he just signal me to apply? Did he like my answer? My phone buzzed. Debu had sent a message.

'Tao restaurant. 58th Street and Park Avenue. 8 p.m. Okay?'

Damn, I almost forgot. I had a date, or at least a 'let's meet for Chinese food' tonight. Before that I had something even more important. I had a waxing appointment.

◆

'Ohohoh... Slower, that hurts,' I said to the waxing lady.

'You haven't done this before?' said my fifty-year-old waxing lady Catherine politely, while ripping the waxing strips off me most brutally.

I was lying down in my underwear. I had come to Completely Bare, a funky 'high-tech meets comfy chic' waxing studio on 68th Street and Madison.

'I have. Twice in my life. In India. Years ago,' I said.

'Really? Did it hurt then?'

Hell yeah, it did. Aditi didi had made me do it for a wedding in the family. I almost broke family ties with her after that. If only Debu knew what I was going through to have a plate of noodles with him. Catherine dipped a spatula in a bowl of molten wax.

'Cold wax hurts more, but the results last longer,' she said. She applied the wax on my upper thigh, then put a white strip of cloth, six inches long and two inches wide, on that. Hair clung to it. I felt the Armageddon coming.

'Can't you give local anesthesia or...oww...oww...oww...'

'Relax, honey,' Catherine said.

I clenched my teeth and closed my eyes. I imagined myself in the Middle East. They punish women with lashes if they do something awful like driving a car, offering men their opinions or something totally immoral like exposing their elbows in public.

'Fifty lashes for Radhika.' I imagined a fatwa on me as Catherine went to work. She finished my legs from the front and flipped me around. I felt like a fish being scaled before dinner.

'You don't want a Brazilian?' Catherine asked me. 'It is only fifteen dollars more.'

'What's that?' I said. Catherine rolled her eyes.

'It's everything gone, honey. Down there too.'

It took me a second to figure out what she meant. Then I realized the embarrassment and pain involved.

'Do girls do it?' I said.

'Everyone, honey. The boys don't like them bushes anymore.'

Okay, I thought. *It's only fifteen dollars more. I am Indian after all, and Indians like bargains, even if they involve pain.*

'You want it?' Catherine said.

Maybe I can do this. This is not for Debu or tonight. This is for me. Enough of being a frumpy nerd, Radhika. Do it.

'Sure, I'll take the Brazilian,' I said.

I don't want to go into the details of what happened next. It started with Catherine examining bits of me nobody else ever had, while she shook her head in disapproval. After that she applied molten wax on body parts that were clearly never meant to ever come in contact with molten wax. *Why do we women put ourselves through this? Why can't boys… oww…oww…oww.*

I think I would prefer the lashes in Saudi Arabia.

'There we go,' Catherine said after her ten-minute sadism experiment ended.

'I might faint,' I said.

'You will get used to it,' Catherine said. 'Trust me, he will love it.'

There is no he, I wanted to tell her. I am only going to have wonton soup with him. Not wanton sex.

Catherine came back with a strip of crystal dots.

'And as a special promotion, we are giving all customers who got a Brazilian a free Swarovski service. Allow me. This won't hurt at all.'

I couldn't believe what happened next. Catherine made a pattern with thirty crystals down there.

Once done, she told me to stand up and look into the mirror.

'I look like a stripper,' I said.

'You look sexy.'

'I can't walk out with crystals on my…you know.'

'Don't worry. They wash off in a couple of days. Faster if you rub with soap.'

Debu called.

'Hey, done with training? You will be on time, right? Or should we make it 8.30?' Debu said.

'I am done. Was just taking care of some…internal issues. See you soon,' I said.

◆

'You look,' he paused, 'wonderful.'

'Thank you,' I said.

'Your dress is lovely too.'

'Look, no tag today,' I said and turned around. Both of us laughed. I was wearing a military green lace dress I had picked up from Gap. It ended well above the knees, exposing enough leg. However, I still don't think Debu noticed the hundred dollars I spent fixing my limbs. The dim lighting and the restaurant table covering my legs did no justice to the hour I had spent in the torture chamber.

Debu ordered a set dinner for us.

We sat down in the upper level of Tao, a large-sized restaurant by New York standards. Downstairs, we could see a giant Buddha and the Zen koi pond.

'Nice place,' I said.

'Did you know they shot the *Sex and the City* movie here?' Debu said. I didn't. 'So how was your day?'

'Good. We are pitching for this new sportswear brand called Under Armor. If we get the campaign it will be awesome. How's Goldman?'

'Still in training. Busy. It will get even more hectic after work begins.'

I told him about Neel's distressed debt presentation. I recounted how I was questioned in front of the entire class.

'So I am thinking, I won't apply to distressed debt. It's quite difficult to get anyway. Plus, the job seems too difficult,' I said.

'How can you not apply?' Debu said. 'You are from IIMA. You will crack it.'

'People in my class are from top colleges around the world. Harvard, Stanford, you name it.'

'So what? You answered the question the partner asked you in the presentation, right?'

I looked at Debu. He had listened to me with full attention. His deep black eyes flickered in the candlelight. I leaned back on my seat and crossed my legs. They felt unusually smooth. I remembered why and smiled.

'Why are you smiling?' he said.

'Nothing.' I shook my head.

'Listen,' he said and placed his hand on mine. 'You have to apply. Too many Indians come to this city and get overwhelmed. Don't be underconfident. You can do it. You will.'

'Thanks. And you will win Under Armor,' I said.

'Cheers to that,' he said and we lifted our water glasses. The waiter arrived with our food—chicken noodle soup and vegetable fried rice. The soup seemed a little too bland for my taste. I stuck to the fried rice.

'You aren't having the soup. You don't like chicken?'

'I eat meat, but I prefer vegetarian,' I said.

'I am vegetarian too,' he said.

'Really?'

'I am a Bengali. For us, fish and chicken are vegetables.'

Both of us laughed.

We chatted through dinner. He told me about his parents in Kolkata. His father owned a printing press. It didn't really make much money now. His mother stayed at home. Debu grew up dreaming about being a painter. He settled for commercial art as the practical choice. His parents had saved enough to send him to do a course in design and arts in the US. He secured the current job through campus placement.

'Advertising sounds cool,' I said, 'that too Madison Avenue. Best place to do it in the world.'

'It's not as cool on the inside. There's constant politics. The money isn't great. I have been lucky to work on good campaigns. However, juniors don't usually get much creative work.'

'I am sure it is not just luck. You must be really good.'

He looked at me and smiled. He ate with chopsticks. I tried but failed. Mini-me told me to not make an ass of myself and use a fork and spoon. I complied.

'Thanks for the compliment,' he said. 'Dessert?'

I saw the menu. It had choices like sweet red bean pudding and tofu ice cream.

'Red bean pudding?' I said. 'What is that?'

'Rajma,' Debu said. 'Rajma kheer of sorts.'

'Yuck,' I said.

'Chinese desserts are not famous. There's a reason—they suck,' he said.

'Bengali desserts are the best,' I said.

Debu's chest swelled with pride.

'Bengali men aren't too bad either,' he said.

Did he just flirt with me? Is this flirting? Am I supposed to respond with something clever?

'As sweet as their desserts?' I said, one eyebrow up.

See, I can flirt back. Nerds can flirt.

He never expected a comeback. He took a second to take in my response.

'Why don't you try and find out?' he said.

That's enough, Radhika, this is going into dangerous territory, I told myself. *Deflect, change the topic, fast. You don't want to be judged as a slut on the first date.* See, this is what I do. When I am with a man, I behave like I am sitting for a test. Answer the question properly. Act naïve as if I don't understand his double meaning. Don't just be. Perform.

'Don't know about the men. I'd love to have a rasgulla though,' I said, my voice as innocent and dumb as possible. 'Alas, this is Manhattan.'

'Fear not. We Bengalis have left imprints everywhere. Would you like to go to a rasgulla place?'

'Here? Now? In Manhattan?'

He nodded and smiled. The bill arrived.

'Should we split?' I said and took out two twenty-dollar bills.

He thought about it for a second.

'Actually, no. Can I treat you this time?' he said.

Isn't that what dates are? I said to myself. *But then, what about gender equality?*

'Why?' I said. 'We can split.'

'No,' he said as he took the money out of his wallet. 'It's not that much. You can buy the rasgullas.'

❖

Debu and I took a yellow cab to 28th Street and Lexington Avenue, in an area called Murray Hill.

'It's also called Curry Hill,' Debu said as we stepped out of the taxi. I could see why. Indian, Bangladeshi and Pakistani restaurants dotted both sides of the road. Some resembled roadside dhabas back in India, complete with bright tubelights and plastic chairs.

'Is this even New York?' I laughed.

'It's Midtown Manhattan,' Debu said. 'You like it?'

'I love it. In fact, you could have just brought me here first.'

'Darn, wasted money at Tao. Didn't realize you could be a cheap date.'

Date. He used the word date. I am on a date. I felt thrilled at the prospect of being on a date. Even if at a ramshackle parantha shop called Lahori Kebab.

'Can we have a parantha?' I said.

'Huh? Didn't we just eat?'

'I am Punjabi. Rice isn't dinner.'

We walked into the shabby but brightly lit restaurant. Debu ordered two tandoori paranthas with gobi stuffing inside.

'Green chillies on the side, please,' I said, my mouth salivating at the prospect. I noticed four seedy-looking Indian guys in the restaurant. They wore neon construction-worker jackets. I caught them staring at my legs.

Yes, finally I have an audience for all that effort, I said to myself.

'Let's sit down,' Debu said as he noticed the workers.

Nobody has ever checked out my legs, I wanted to tell him. Let me enjoy the moment. *Oh well, better be the good girl, you exhibitionist,* mini-me said.

The restaurant had Indian desserts Post paranthas, we had two rasgullas each.

You better skip lunch tomorrow, mini-me said, *there is no point in waxing fat legs. Elephants don't wax, do they?*

'I love how you eat. You are enjoying this,' Debu said to me.

'Sorry. I haven't had Indian food in weeks,' I said.

He wiped my lips with a tissue. I smiled at him.

'There are a couple of Indian restaurants in Brooklyn too, where I live,' Debu said. He was referring to another borough of New York, south of Manhattan.

'You live in Brooklyn?' I said. Most of my Goldman class planned to take apartments in Manhattan. They considered Brooklyn too far.

'Yeah. Told you. Advertising is glamorous only on paper. They don't pay. That's the only place we can afford a decent apartment.'

'We as in?'

'I share it. Two other guys from work.'

'Oh okay. I need to find an apartment soon too,' I said.

The bill arrived. I paid this time, a total of eight dollars. We stood up to leave.

'You want to see a movie next week? Shah Rukh's *Don 2* is releasing,' Debu said.

'They have Indian movie theatres here?' I said in excitement.

'Just a couple. But they do,' he said. 'Next Friday?'

I nodded. The food in my mouth prevented me from talking.

Date two, baby, I said to myself and mentally high-fived.

7

One month later

On the last day of associate training, I received an email from my training manager, Jane Rosenberg. She had called me to her office.

I wondered if I had done anything wrong. I had skipped class to meet Debu a few times. Had they found out?

Debu and I had watched two movies, one Yankees baseball game and one Broadway musical called *The Lion King*. We visited quaint restaurants all over Manhattan and ate Italian, Middle Eastern and Indian food.

I had fallen in love with New York. I had also started liking Debu, even though things weren't romantic yet. *Why wasn't he making a move? When would I have my own boyfriend? Would I ever have my own boyfriend?* Perhaps it was because of these insecurities inside me, but I wanted things to change soon.

Our next date was tomorrow. I had picked a short wine-coloured dress, my boldest so far.

'Jane asked you to come to her office as well?' Mark, an American associate about my age, came up to me.

'Huh?' I said, as I came back from my thoughts about what shoes to pair with my wine dress. 'Yeah. How do you know?'

'You are copied on my email. It's you, me and another associate, Carl Wong.'

◆

I reached Jane's office on the sixteenth floor of 85 Broad Street. Jane, in her forties, sat at her desk, lost in her computer.

'Welcome. You must be the new associates,' Jane said as we sat down.

I looked at Mark and Carl. They seemed relaxed in contrast to a jittery me.

'I have called you here because I have fresh offers for you. The three of you have been selected for the Distressed Debt Group.'

'Yes!' Mark said and fist-pumped. Carl and Mark high-fived each other.

'Really?' I said. Has there been a mistake? I wanted to ask. Sure, I had applied. I had also met a few people as asked. However, I didn't really think I had a chance.

'It's a tough challenge but a great opportunity,' Jane was saying. 'Are you going to accept this or do you want to be in another department?'

'Yes, of course, I accept,' Mark said. 'Am going to kill it.'

'Totally accept,' Carl said; his voice had an American accent even though he was ethnically Chinese.

'You, Raa–dee–kaa?'

'Yeah. Well, I am thinking.'

What was I thinking? *Has there been a mistake? Can I do this? Is this too difficult?* This is what girls like me do. The boys in front of me jumped up in confidence. I, on the other hand, triple-guessed and quadruple-guessed myself.

Mini-me, will you be supportive and be quiet for once? I took a deep breath.

'Yeah, I accept,' I said.

I signed the offer letter and felt a surge of excitement. I wanted to share this with someone. I decided to call home later when India woke up. However, mom and dad would have little idea about my achievement.

'Debu,' I said as I called him after I left Jane's office, 'I got distressed debt.'

'Didn't I say you could do it?'

'Yeah, you did. We will see if I can last. What are you doing?'

'You will do amazing. I'm at work. Busy with a presentation. We are meeting tomorrow, right?'

'Yeah. Can it be my treat? Training ended, I did make it to the best group. I think we should celebrate.'

'Sure. I can't wait,' Debu said.

I made another important call.

'Completely Bare? I want to book a waxing appointment.'

◆

'Champagne, madam, just as you ordered,' the waiter said. He poured two glasses and kept the bottle in an ice bucket.

We had come to Aquagrill at Soho. The restaurant specialized in seafood. Debu had told me he used to have fish with every meal back home in Kolkata. We chose the set dinner.

The waiter arrived with an appetizer made of salmon and asparagus.
'This is amazing,' Debu sighed.

'You like seafood, that's why I chose this place,' I said. He nodded and grinned, his mouth full of food. I found his curly hair, beard and smile more adorable every time I met him.

My dress ended high on my thighs. I had not eaten any lunch to avoid love handles. I wondered if he noticed.

'We have seen each other every week since the first time we met, right?' he said. I gazed at his lips.

Yes, we have, but why haven't we kissed yet? Is it wrong for a girl to think that? Should he be asking me that instead? Where are the rules?

'What are you thinking?' Debu said. He snapped his fingers, as I didn't respond.

'Huh? Oh, nothing. Just nervous about my new assignment, I guess.'

How can a girl admit she is thinking about kissing? Isn't that what super-sluts do?

'Relax. You can crack anything. You are really smart. One of the smartest people I've met.' I looked at him.

Wow, a man who acknowledges a woman's smartness. Now I want to kiss him even more. Are you going to make a move, Debu? Or will you keep eating that shrimp cocktail in the martini glass?

I brought my legs close and enjoyed their smoothness against each other. *Debu, make the right moves, and you could be a really happy man tonight.*

'Distressed debt. Sounds scary, though,' Debu said.

How do I change the topic from distressed debt to my amazingly waxed legs? I couldn't. I drained my champagne glass.

'It is,' I said. 'You have to negotiate with hard-nosed business owners. They sometimes refuse to pay the bank. You have to seize properties. Squeeze out value.'

'Wow,' Debu said. 'Doesn't sound like a regular banker on a desk job.'

'Yeah,' I said. 'Also, there are hardly any women in the team. It's a man's job.'

'What nonsense,' Debu said. 'Why can't a woman do it? They are better negotiators.'

I like this man. A lot. Go on, Debu.

He continued, 'It's all this bullshit men spread. To scare women out of a role or position. Fact is, men are shit-scared of talented women like you.'

'Thanks, Debu.'

Okay, I had a challenge bigger than distressed debt tonight. I had to ensure Debu made a move, so some naughtiness could happen. Of course, because I am a woman, I somehow also had to pretend to be innocent, as if I had no role to play in making anything happen. I had to steer him without him realizing he had been steered.

The waiter brought us our final course of codfish served with miso sauce.

'Wow,' Debu said as he took a bite, 'best fish I have ever tasted. In fact, maybe the best thing I have ever tasted.'

'Yeah. Well, there's still dessert, save the best for the last,' I said.

Was that double meaning? Fuck, don't slutify yourself.

He laughed. *Did he get the reference?*

'You know Bongs and mishti,' he said. *No, he didn't. Be careful. Always give out a chaste good-Indian-girl vibe.*

'How's work?' I said.

'It's great. Under Armor account is almost in,' he said and crossed his fingers.

'I am sure it will come in,' I said.

'It will be my first big win. My boss said if I get it I get promoted to senior creative associate.'

'That sounds a lot cooler than distressed debt associate.'

He laughed.

'You get the bucks. That's cool enough,' he said.

Somehow I never wanted to discuss the money I made with Debu. I had to shift the topic back to him.

'Under Armor is a cutting-edge brand. I saw their store yesterday. Great stuff,' I said.

'I can't wait to work on their campaign.'

We had a dark chocolate mousse cake with orange sauce as our last dish.

'Great choice of restaurant, Radhika,' Debu said. 'At first I thought this place too fancy, but look at the food. Wow.'

We finished our meal and the bill arrived. The waiter handed it to Debu, but I plucked it from his hands. I had told Debu it would be my treat. I had a quick look. The bill came to 200 dollars. I placed the cash in the bill folder and handed it to the waiter.

'Is it a lot?' Debu said. 'It is, isn't it? Why did you spend so much?'

'Look, I wanted to celebrate with you. My only true friend in New York. So thank you for being there.'

I held my champagne glass high. He did the same and made a toast.

'Congratulations. To my talented friend Radhika, who will kick ass at distressed debt and show the men how it is done,' he said.

◆

We decided to walk from Aquagrill to the Benjamin Hotel, a half-an-hour stroll. From there Debu could get a direct '4' train to Brooklyn. I had thirty minutes to get this man to make a move. A part of me wanted to scream, Oh Debu, just kiss me already.

Of course, a lifetime of brainwashing to be a 'good Indian girl' would never allow me to do that.

He didn't make any move. However, he did say amazing things on our walk.

'It's really important that women do well. It sets an example for other younger women. It inspires them,' he said.

'Who am I inspiring?' I said, my mind filled with alternate thoughts. *Did he notice my legs yet? Did dinner make my stomach less flat? Are my boobs in place? Can this guy walk slower so I can keep up in my heels?*

'Of course you are an inspiration. To your younger cousins, for example. I am sure they will see their Radhika didi and want to be like her.'

I laughed.

'What?' he said.

'I don't know. My sister Aditi has more fans. She barely graduated. She knows make-up and clothes way better than me, though.'

That is when Debu said something, something even better than the amazing things he had said about my work and intelligence.

'You have great taste in clothes,' he said.

Oh, I love this man. He must be partially blind but I love this man.

'Really?' I said. I found it hard to take a compliment that didn't involve grades or job interviews.

'Yeah. You have this subtle, understated style. This red dress, pardon me, but...'

'But what?' I said. *Is it ripped somewhere?* I thought in horror.

'Pardon me, but it makes you look so hot,' he said.

Oh Debu! Bless him, gods. Give him any advertising account he wants. For the first time in my life, apart from when I had fever, I had been associated with the word hot. Someone in this world found me hot. Hot. *Fuck, Radhika, someone called you hot.* My soul break-danced inside me.

'Really?' I said, my tone as casual as possible, even as I fished for more.

'Yeah. You don't mind me saying that, I hope.'

Do I mind? Bring it on, dude. We have ten more minutes to reach the hotel. Please keep praising me. The shallower the better. Make it only about clothes, looks and legs. Those are the compliments I miss. Of course, I have to say it in a way that he doesn't think I am too keen.

'No, I don't mind. Usually we talk about more intellectual and work-related stuff. It is strange but no, it's okay. Curious to see how you men think,' I said and giggled like an idiot.

'I think you have a nice figure,' he said.

Which part, which part? I wanted to scream in excitement. *Do you like my waist? Boobs? Ass? Be articulate, Debu.*

'Really?' I said, dragging out the word, as if I never expected this. I punched his shoulder—subtle encouragement and fake shyness all rolled into one.

'Yeah. Your legs, I mean…you have nice legs.'

'Oh, so that is all you like about me?'

Desperate, lame, stupid. What was that, Radhika? I told myself as I fished. Oh I didn't just fish. I sent a fishing team with a trailer to catch a shipload.

'No, no. I like your face too. Your hair. Your eyes. Your whole personality, actually.'

'Yeah, yeah. Now you will say all this. It's about the legs, right?'

It better be about the legs. I paid 100 dollars to Completely Bare.

'No, no. Sorry… I mean…'

'Relax, Debu. I am kidding,' I said and squeezed his warm hand. I didn't want to let go of it. However, I didn't want it to count as a move either. *Why do we girls have to follow so many rules? If he likes my whole personality, why can't I be fully me?*

I released his hand. We walked past a Barnes and Noble bookstore and had to cross a traffic signal. He used it as an excuse to hold my hand. We crossed the road together. He didn't release my hand afterwards.

I gave him a sideways glance. He smiled at me.

'My sister is considered the prettier one, actually,' I said.

'I find that quite hard to believe. Unless she is Miss Universe or something.'

I smiled at his indirect compliment. I felt like running my fingers through his curly hair.

He continued, 'Actually, even if she is Miss Universe. I find you really pretty.'

Sweet lies, they do have a place in life. I sighed.

'Thanks, Debu,' I said.

We reached the Benjamin Hotel. We had made some progress. We had held hands, but only that. *Did I intimidate him? Did he totally lie but actually not find me attractive? Is he scared?*

'So this is where I live. Train stop is right there.' I pointed at the subway sign.

'Sure,' he said. 'I had a great time. Thanks for the treat.'

'You are welcome,' I said. 'Bye.'

My heart sank a bit. I didn't want him to go.

'Hey, just one thing. Doesn't have to be today,' he said.

'Yeah?' I said.

'You have your sister's photo in your room? Wanted to check. I am sure the claim that she is prettier is false,' he said.

Was that a move? He mentioned my room. Did he want to come upstairs? Or he could technically want me to go up and bring down some pictures. Heck, I had Aditi didi's photos on my phone. So is this a move? Will someone tell me, please?

I smiled at him.

'No, really,' Debu said,

'That's sweet. So are you.'

'Pretty?'

I laughed. 'No. Handsome. Smart. Creative too.'

'Thanks,' he said.

'Okay, I think I have some photos on my laptop upstairs. You want to come up?' I said.

8

'No way,' Debu said. 'She is not prettier than you.'

'Oh, come on,' I said. 'Aditi didi is so nice-looking.'

'Listen, sure she is, but not more than you. No way. You have better features.'

'That's not what my mother led me to believe,' I said.

'Must be the Punjabi thing. The whiter the skin, the prettier the person. Nonsense,' he said, somewhat agitated.

We sat on the edge of the hotel bed, my laptop in the middle. I had a two-year-old family album open on the screen.

'All my life I have been this nerdy, studious girl. Aditi didi is considered the looker.'

'Sorry, she's your sister, but she dresses like she is going to a party even for random family pictures at home.'

'She is like that,' I said.

'You did wear horrible glasses though,' Debu said.

I laughed.

'I switched to contacts a year ago,' I said, and pointed to a picture of my family in our living room. 'That is dad. Simple, quiet man. Just doesn't want people in society to say anything critical of him. This is my mother. Dominates dad totally.'

Debu examined the pictures as I spoke again.

'I miss home,' I said. 'Seeing these pictures I miss India. I want to watch TV serials with my mother and do nothing.'

'Says the new hotshot distressed debt banker. Too late, girl.' Debu laughed.

I made a mock-sad face.

I need a hug. Move things forward, Debu. Do I have to give you an instruction manual?

'It's a sweet family,' Debu said.

'It is,' I said. I wanted to stall the conversation with short, boring replies. Awkward silences lead to many interesting things.

Unfortunately, certain intellectual Bengali men don't often get the hint.

'Have you read *The Beauty Myth* by Naomi Wolf?' Debu said.

'No, what's that?'

'A landmark feminist book. It talks about how women are culturally bullied into feeling conscious about their looks all the time,' he said.

'Really? Well, to a certain extent it's true,' I said.

'Yeah. Do men compare their physicality with their siblings so much?'

'I guess not.' At another time or place, like at one of our Friday dinners, I would have liked to engage in this intellectually stimulating conversation. Not now. I had other things on my mind.

'Exactly,' he said, 'she says it is a way for men to control women and...'

'My feet are killing me,' I interrupted him. I removed my shoes. I brought my feet up on the bed. My short dress inched up a little further on my thighs. Debu forgot his chain of thought. I guess there are ways for women to control men too.

'Sorry, what were you saying?' I said. I squeezed and released my toes.

'Huh?' he said. 'Nothing. I will give you the book.'

'Not used to walking long distances in heels,' I said.

'Do you want me to give you a foot massage?' he said.

And the Republic Day bravery award finally goes to Debashish Sen, I wanted to announce.

'Really?' I said. 'You know how to?'

It was one of those stupid things girls sometimes say. We know it is stupid but we say it anyway to act naïve or whatever.

I loved his hands on my feet.

'Wow, that's nice,' I said. He pressed my feet timidly, as if I would get up and slap him any second.

He massaged my shins. His hands slowly moved up to my knees. I didn't stop him.

'Do you have lotion?' he said. I pointed to the bedside table. He took a bottle of moisturizer and splashed it on my feet. I jerked as the cold lotion touched my skin. He put his warm hands on my legs. He moved them in a sliding motion from shin to knee.

I closed my eyes. I could feel his hands reach above my knees. Nobody had ever touched me there before, unless you count the waxing torture-chamber lady. Tingles of pleasure ran up my thighs.

He became bolder every minute, going higher. We didn't exchange a word. He reached the seam of my dress. His fingers danced tantalizingly upon my thighs.

Is this all moving too fast? a voice within me said. Heck, I didn't care.

'Is this okay?' Debu said.

I nodded. I opened my eyes. I signalled him to bring his face closer to mine. He leaned forward. Our lips met. I kissed for the first time in my life.

I could feel he had bottled up his desire too. His lips refused to leave mine. Our tongues touched. I lost track of time, space and orientation. I had seen kisses in the movies. I had imagined what my first one would be like. But this was better. Better than anything I had seen or imagined.

'You are so beautiful,' he whispered into my ear as he nibbled my earlobe.

He placed his hand on my breast, over my dress. He wanted to slide his hand in but couldn't. I would have had to remove the entire fitted dress to give him access.

I pushed back his chest.

'Is this going too fast?' I said. Like any guy would actually say, 'Yes, it is.'

'No. Of course not. It feels right,' Debu said, one hand on my thigh.

He moved his other hand to my back, trying to find the zipper for my dress.

'There's too much light,' I said. Sure, he had praised my body. However, I had never taken off my clothes in front of a man. I couldn't with so much light.

He switched off all the lights in the room. The window curtains remained open. The dim light from the Manhattan skyline was just about enough for us to see each other.

I had worn a new matching pair of red lingerie from Triumph, in anticipation.

Debu pulled my dress off. He unhooked my bra from behind. He removed his shirt as well.

'What are you making me do, Debu?' I whispered as I held my unhooked bra in place with my hands. I felt I had to make it seem like he made me do this. Never mind the pre-planned lingerie.

'Just go with the flow,' Debu said, standard boy-speak for 'let me please have sex without interruption'.

He pulled the red bra out of my hands. He grabbed my breasts.

'Not so hard, please,' I said.

'Sorry,' Debu said.

'You have done this before?' I said.

He took a few seconds to answer.

'If I say yes, will you ask me to stop?' Debu said.

I laughed.

'No, silly. Just that this is my first time,' I said.

'I had one girlfriend before. Two years back.'

'Can we not talk about that now?' I said.

He kissed my nipples. He moved up and kissed my collarbone. He kissed my chin and then my lips for several minutes. He tugged at my panties. My heart beat fast. Was I really going to get fully naked in front of a man?

I guess it was too late. He pulled down my panties. He removed his trousers and underwear. I had not seen a naked man so up-close. I wanted to get a good look, more as an anatomy lesson. However, he held me tight and continued to kiss me. His hands reached higher on my thighs.

'Your legs are so soft,' he said. I decided to take a life membership at Completely Bare.

He touched me between my legs. The Brazilian had made everything smooth.

'Wow, you are wet,' he said.

I wasn't just wet. I was soaked. The good girl in me wondered if he would judge me for it.

He bent and brought his face closer between my legs.

'What are you doing?' I said.

'Huh? Going down.'

'Down where?' I said.

'Down. There.'

'Really? Your mouth? There?'

'Yeah. Just relax.'

I can't really describe the next ten minutes. His tongue felt the exact opposite of the brutal waxing strips. Every flick transported me to a state of extreme pleasure. *Why don't people do this all the time? Wow, why didn't anyone tell me sex feels so damn good?*

He put a finger inside me. I winced once.

'Careful,' I said.

'Does it feel good?' he said.

I nodded, my eyes closed.

He continued to work with his tongue. I became more aroused. I soon reached a point where the intensity became too much.

'Stop,' I said.

'What?' he said.

'Come here,' I said.

He came up close. I kissed him, which was a little strange considering where his mouth had been just now.

He climbed over me.

'May I?' he said.

Was I going to have sex? Had I finally grown up? But wait, should I?

'I have protection,' he said.

Damn, did the guy anticipate this? Was I too easy?

'I happened to have it in my wallet,' Debu said, as if reading my mind. I didn't want to think anymore. I gave him the slightest nod.

He entered me gently. It hurt a bit. Frankly, his tongue had felt better. *However, this is what people call sex*, I thought, *so I guess this is what we have to do.*

Radhika Mehta, you are finally having sex, I said to myself and mentally high-fived myself. It felt like a major milestone in life, on par with getting into IIMA or scoring Goldman Sachs. Or distressed debt. *Will that job be tough? Okay, why am I thinking about distressed debt when there is a man in me?*

'You feel so amazing,' he said.

I was glad he felt that way. As for me, I couldn't see what the big fuss was about sex.

How do I ask him to do that 'going down' stuff again? Is it too late? What is the protocol in bed?

His strokes became faster. He gripped me tight on my shoulders and groaned. I guess he had had an orgasm. He gasped for a few seconds as he went lax on me.

'Wow,' Debu said. 'Amazing, isn't it?'

So, how did I feel after having sex the first time? Well, you know how you sometimes wait for a big Salman or Shah Rukh movie for months and then it finally arrives? You go for the first day first show, and then the movie is not bad, but not so great either.

'Yeah, was amazing,' I said. I guess it's just polite to agree with people in bed.

He slid off me and lay on the side. He stared at the ceiling. We held hands.

'You are wonderful. Thank you,' he said.

'Thank you'? What on earth was that? Is the show over? Why is he plopped like a phone without charge now?

'Was it good?' I said.

'I repeat, amazing. I am so spent and finished.'

'Finished?'

'Satisfied, I mean,' he said.

'Debu.'

'Yeah.'

'Can you make me spent and finished too? Please?'

'Huh?' Debu said. He turned to me, surprised.

'That going down thing you did. Can you do it a bit more?' I said.

'Sure, baby.'

Good. I guess that didn't make me the shy and coy girl all Indian girls should be. Maybe it even made me seem like a slut. However, I would rather be a spent and finished slut than a good but frustrated Indian girl.

Five minutes later, I moaned out loud too. Wow. I pressed his head hard between my legs. My legs shook, and then my whole body. *Okay, so this is what an orgasm feels like.*

'How are you?' he said.

I hid my face in embarrassment.

'What? I said, "How are you".' He laughed.

'Spent. And finished.'

9

Two months later

'We are stuck in this MegaBowl deal,' said Jonathan Husky, vice president and my boss in the Distressed Debt Group.

My phone buzzed in my pocket. I checked the time. It was 7 in the evening. I had to meet Debu in an hour. It seemed undoable.

We sat in the meeting room of the Goldman Sachs Distressed Debt Group. From the Goldman side, there was Jonathan, Clark Smith, who was another associate in the group, and I. We also had a representative from each of the seven banks that had lent to MegaBowl, a Boston-based builder of bowling alleys. While people who played in their bowling alleys had fun, their creditors had a different story. MegaBowl had defaulted on fifty million dollars' worth of loans.

'There are no assets,' Jonathan continued. 'The company has nothing apart from lots of bowling pins and bowling balls.'

Recovering fifty million dollars would require a lot of bowling balls, I thought. The bankers looked at each other in silence, sympathizing with each other for their collective stupidity in lending so much money to MegaBowl.

'Tell us what to do,' one of the bankers said. 'We just want out. I can't deal with their stupid CEO.'

My hand went into my handbag and grabbed my phone.

'Radhika.' Jonathan saying my name startled me. 'Please share the plan.'

Damn, I needed a minute to tell Debu I couldn't make it tonight. I released my phone and brought my hand out of my bag.

'Eh, sure, Jonathan,' I said. I shared the special booklets I had prepared for the meeting.

'Our basic premise,' I said, opening the first page, 'is to keep MegaBowl as a going concern. There is little value in liquidation, just about six cents on the dollar. However, it is fifty cents if we allow the CEO to continue.'

'Fire him,' Dirk Grigly, a fat and bald banker from Bank of America, said. 'He has caused all the mess.'

'He has, yes,' I said, 'but we need him to stabilize operations for now. We also have to retrench people and cut salaries. Let's use him to do the dirty work.'

I walked them through the plan. It would enable the company to reduce its size and reduce costs.

The bankers pored over the booklets. I thought of an excuse I could use to take out my phone. I didn't want Debu to leave for the restaurant.

The bankers cared little about my boyfriend.

'What's the guarantee it is going to work?' one of the lenders said.

'There isn't,' I said, 'but now that we have finally valued the business, twenty-five million is maximum recovery. Or fifty cents on the dollar.'

'We can offer thirty cents,' Jonathan said, 'and you can be out of this.'

That's how we worked. Bid at thirty cents, hoped to recover fifty.

'Thirty cents?' Dirk said. 'That's nothing.'

'Goldman is taking all the risk here of reviving it,' Jonathan said.

The creditors huddled together.

'Should we leave you alone for ten minutes?' Jonathan said and stood up.

Yes, this was my chance to make my call. Jonathan, Clark and I left the room.

I rushed back to my cubicle.

I called Debu.

'Hey baby, where are you? I was just about to leave. Did you see my messages?' Debu said.

'No, I just stepped out of a never-ending creditor meeting.'

'What?'

'We are about to close a deal. My first, actually.'

'It's 7.30. We have an 8 o'clock reservation. Comedy Cellar doesn't allow you late entry.'

'I am so sorry. Can you cancel it, please?'

'We've already paid. Fifteen bucks each.'

'I know. I am so sorry.'

'What? Really?' he said, his voice low.

'Can I make it up to you? Tonight? Come over to my place.'

'When?'

'Have your dinner and come over. I will join you soon.'

I hung up and waited at my desk. I had rented a one-bedroom unit in Tribeca, one of the closest residential neighbourhoods from Wall Street. Debu had an extra set of keys, as he came over on a regular basis.

I had gone to his place in Brooklyn only a few times. A typical bachelor pad, it had more beer than groceries in the fridge. He shared the apartment with two other guys, offering us little privacy. They kept their house keys under a potted plant outside the house. When I asked Debu why, he said, 'Just simpler baby, we lost six duplicate keys in the last three months.'

My desk phone rang. Jonathan had called from the meeting room.

'Can you and Clark come over?' he said.

Clark and I reached the meeting room.

'Clark, Radhika, I am happy to say the lender group here has agreed. We have a deal. Your first, right?'

'Yes. That is great news,' I said.

'Radhika, we need a quick term sheet. The remaining documentation can be done later.'

My heart sank. A term sheet would take a couple of hours. Jonathan and Clark took the lenders downstairs for a drink to Harry's Café & Steak, two blocks from the Goldman building. I worked at my desk, drafting the term sheet with all the deal conditions.

Jonathan came up to my desk late at night. He looked at his watch.

'Ten minutes to midnight. Oh no. Sorry about this. You should go home, Radhika,' he said.

'Just mailed you the final term sheet.' I logged out of my computer.

'Well done. You were fantastic in this deal. You are a real asset to the group,' Jonathan said.

I felt a warm glow of happiness inside me as I left the Goldman building. Jonathan's words stayed in my head. I couldn't wait to share them with Debu.

◆

'I am sleeping, baby,' Debu complained as I switched on the bedroom ceiling light.

'Sorry,' I said as I switched the light off. I turned on the bedside lamp instead.

'What time is it?' he said in a sleepy voice.

'12.30,' I said.

'What?' he said, and opened his eyes wide. 'You were in office until now?'

'Yeah. What to do? My first big deal. You know what Jonathan told me?'

'What?'

'Radhika, you are a real asset to the group.'

'Why not? They seem to be dumping all their work on you.'

'Nothing like that. They stayed late too. Many little things one has to be careful about in the documentation. It took me a while.'

'Did you eat dinner?'

'No, baby,' I said.

'What?' Debu sat up in bed.

'I didn't get the time.'

'This is terrible. Wait.'

He got off the bed, walked up to the open kitchen in the living room and took out a tray of eggs from the fridge.

'I'll make you some bhurji,' he said, 'have it with bread.'

'Go to sleep. I will have some cereal.'

'Have something hot.'

'I will have my hot boyfriend then. Come here.'

I pulled him by his T-shirt and kissed him.

'Sorry I was late. Let me make it up to you,' I said.

He pushed me away.

'Wait, eggs first.'

He got busy whipping the eggs. He cut onions and tomatoes and placed a saucepan on the stove. Ten minutes later he served me my dinner.

'Try,' he said.

I took a bite.

'How is it?' he said.

'Yum. Thank you.'

'Welcome.'

'Debu, listen.'

'What?'

'I love you.'

'I love you too. Just don't get to see you much.'

'Sorry, baby.'

'Let's move in together. That way I will see you at least.'

I became silent.

'I will share the rent. Don't worry.'

'Not that, silly. But that's a live-in. That means we are in a serious relationship.'

'Aren't we?' Debu said.

I smiled at him.

'Keep the place clean, okay?' I said.

10

One year later

'I will think about marriage later, mom. I am still new at my job. Let me focus on that. Please,' I said.

I ran down the subway steps to the Wall Street station platform. The Friday evening rush hour made it difficult for me to hear her.

'What?' I said, as the sound of an arriving train drowned her words.

'Job is not that important,' she said. I could hear sounds of her making tea in her kitchen. It was 8.30 in the evening for me, 6 in the morning for her. Jonathan had made me do a presentation twice, giving me a dirty look when he noticed some inadvertent typos.

'It is important. I am in the most challenging group in the firm. Everyone here thinks I am one of the best,' I said.

'What about everyone here thinking why isn't Mr Mehta's second daughter getting married? Is something wrong with her?'

'Really, mom? You think something is wrong with me?'

I stepped into the number 3 train. The doors shut. I had just three stops to Chambers Street in Tribeca, a five-minute subway ride. Somehow, speaking to mom made it seem much longer.

'It's been a year since you have been abroad. Your sister married two years ago. Let us at least start looking. It takes a while, you know.'

'Aditi didi wanted to get married. I don't.'

'You don't?'

'Not yet. Look at my life. I just finished work. It's 8.30 at night here.'

'What kind of a job is this? Making girls stay so late.'

'Can you stop criticizing every aspect of my life? I am not ready to get married or even look at any options.'

Well, I didn't need more options. My option had messaged me thrice as he waited for me for dinner.

'So what do you want?' mom said.

'Many other things. I want to do well at work. I want to be promoted this year, get a good bonus. I want to travel. Enjoy New York. Come home and visit all of you.'

'Is there a boy?' she said.

My heart skipped a beat. My mother's sixth sense had sprung up.

'No. Not really,' I said. I guess telling her about my live-in status with a guy for the past one year would be too much to share at one go.

'Meaning?'

'I have friends. Like this guy, Debashish. He is also from SRCC.'

'Debashish who?' she said, her voice curious.

'Debashish Sen. Senior in college. Didn't know him then. Works in Manhattan at an ad agency.'

'Bengali?' she said, a tinge of disgust in her tone.

'Yeah. Why?'

'Nothing. They are smelly, no? They eat a lot of fish.'

'What nonsense!'

'Anyway. I hope he is just a friend.'

I had an urge to tell her that we had contraceptives on our grocery list.

'Yes. I hardly get time. But I have met him.'

'Met him?'

'In groups, nothing more,' I said hurriedly.

Why am I not telling her? I should tell her. However, this Debu has to get his act together and tell me first.

'You are not the boyfriend and love types. Aditi was like that.'

'What is that supposed to mean?' I said, my voice loud enough to startle two skinny girls sitting next to me.

'Nothing. You are the studious types. What boyfriend and all you will make? We will have to find someone for you.'

'Really, mom? You would do that for me? Thank you. How can I ever repay you?'

'It's okay. We are parents. It is our duty.'

She doesn't get sarcasm at all. I wanted to lash out more. I wanted to say, Sure, thanks, mom, do hook me up with someone. For who else would take your unlovable daughter?

I chose not to aggravate the situation. I took a deep breath instead.

'My station has arrived. You made tea?'

'Yeah, I did. I can talk some more. Your father is still in the bathroom.'

I stepped out of the train. I climbed up the stairs and came out to Chambers Street. My house was a six-minute walk from here.

'How's dad?' I said.

'Waiting for his tea. He still has to figure out what to do with his retired life.'

'Did you get the money?'

'It was too much, beta.'

'Just tell dad to change his car, please. At least get a Honda City. That Maruti belongs in a museum.'

'I will tell him. We feel bad taking money from our daughter.'

'Why? If I were your son it would be okay?'

'Yes. But you are not, no?'

'So what? I am your child. Why can't I help improve your lifestyle?'

'With sons it is different. It's like your right.'

'Mom, you know all this stuff irritates me a lot. I have had a long day. I was in office for thirteen hours. Can you please say something nice?'

'We miss you.'

'I miss you guys too.'

'We feel bad. Our daughter is working thirteen hours a day and sending money home. We may have limited means after dad's retirement, but things are not so bad.'

'Again, mom,' I said, my voice upset, 'you have to stop. Let me do things for my family.'

'Don't shout at me. It's early morning here.'

'Well, you have to stop irritating me.'

'I am not irritating you. You keep saying "family". If you don't get married how will you have a family?'

'Bye, mom. I don't want to lose it. Please go have tea with dad.'

'Did I say anything wrong now? It's a fact, no?'

'I have reached home. I have to take the lift. I will talk to you later.'

'As you wish. All you kids behave in this hi-fi manner now. Call whenever. End whenever. Shout whenever. I am just your mother.'

I took three deep breaths.

'I am sorry for shouting at you,' I said.

'You are becoming too aggressive. If you stay like this who will...'

Before she could say that my aggression would hamper my chances of getting married, I had to end the call.

'Sorry,' I said, 'I am sorry.'

'Go rest. Don't work so hard.'

◆

I entered the apartment. Debu sat in the living room watching football on TV. He wore a loose grey T-shirt and a pair of black shorts. He held a can of beer in his hand.

'Hey,' he said, his eyes not moving an inch from the screen.

'Hi,' I said, my voice curt. *Is it too much for him to get up from the sofa and give me a hug?*

I removed my jacket and placed it on the dining table. I saw takeaway bowls from Mr Chow, a Chinese restaurant in Tribeca.

'You ordered in?' I said.

'Yeah. Felt too lazy to make anything. Plus, there was this game.'

'This food is too greasy for me. You could have ordered something healthier.'

'Mr Chow is cheap. Have you seen the portion sizes? It will last us two days.'

I dumped my handbag on the dining chair. Sometimes, I wished Debu wasn't so obsessed about saving a few bucks.

'I fought with my mother. I called her to have a chat and ended up yelling at her.'

'Uh huh,' he said, eyes on TV. 'That's not nice.'

'Debu, can you please shut the TV off for a minute?' I said. Screamed, in fact.

Debu looked mildly surprised. He didn't switch off the TV, but muted it. He turned to me.

'What happened, baby?'

'I've come home after a long day. Can you just pretend to be happy to see me?'

'Of course I am happy, baby.'

'Give me a hug. Don't just say "hey" when I enter the house.'

He sprang up from his seat. He came up to me and hugged me.

I pushed him away. 'Not when I have to ask. And be interested. My mom and I had a huge argument.'

'What about?'

'Guess.'

'Your marriage? Her whole "who will marry my poor daughter" routine?'

'Yes, Debu,' I said, glaring at him. 'You are so clever to figure it out. But seriously, who will marry her poor daughter?'

My mother and I had at least one blowout per week about my marriage. Debu knew about it. I hoped he would get into action and propose a plan. Of course, a stupid minor league American football game was more important. I continued to glare at him.

'What?' Debu said. 'Stop letting her affect you so much. She's regressive and old-fashioned.'

He took a paper plate and scooped some noodles on it. He handed it to me, a cheap portion of chowmein to compensate for my uncertain future.

'Debu, really? Is that what you think I am upset about?'

'It's not?' he said, his face blank.

Why don't guys ever get it? It's never just one thing with women. It's a long day at work, dirty looks from my boss, seeing women thinner than me in the train, arguing with my mother, coming home to a disinterested boyfriend and then eating greasy food for dinner that would make me even fatter than the skinny girls on the train. Oh, and add boyfriend never having the guts to discuss our future.

'No,' I said, in as patient a voice as possible, 'it isn't only that.'

'Oh,' he said, genuinely astonished.

'Debu, what the fuck!'

'What? What did I do?'

'What did you not do?'

'The hug? I am sorry about the hug, baby.'

'It's not the hug. It's us. Are you so thick or are you pretending to be so?'

'Be clear, baby.'

'Don't baby me.'

I pushed my plate away. I didn't want to eat this cardiac arrest on a plate. I didn't want to listen to the 'baby, baby' crap.

'What's the matter?'

'Debu, where are we going?'

'Meaning?'

I picked up the remote and switched off the TV.

'Us. Where is this relationship going? My mother wants me to get married. Are you listening?'

'But you don't want to, right? Not right now, right?' he said, puzzled.

'But where do you see us in the future, Debu?'

'I love you, baby. I mean, Radhika. And you love me. We love each other so much. Who else do we have, really?'

'Love is fine. Yes, I do love you. Frankly, sometimes I feel I am too involved with you. I can't even think of another guy. Maybe that is why I flare up with mom.'

'So that's good, no?'

'But do we have a future? Or are we just sharing rent and having sex?'

'Don't talk like that.'

I walked across the room and sat on the sofa. I switched on the TV again.

He came and switched it off.

'Why did you switch on the TV?' he said.

'You won't talk,' I said, 'and you tell me not to talk. So what to do? Let's pretend there is no problem.'

'Okay, I will talk,' Debu said.

'Sure. I am listening.'

'It's my job. I am waiting for this promotion.'

'It's supposed to come through next month.'

'Yeah, but you never know. It's crazy. Two of my peers told my boss I don't deserve the promotion. Advertising is dog-eat-dog. I am so stressed.'

'Well, that's terrible. But how is this relevant when it comes to us?'

'I want to be a senior creative director. Get a raise. A few more accounts. I want to be a little more solid at work before thinking about marriage. I want to focus on my career, not get distracted.'

'I am not asking you to marry me next week.'

'I just… Okay, fine, I want to get past this promotion. Win a couple more accounts. I will be ready to take the next step then.'

'What do I tell mom?'

'Tell her about me. Tell her you have a boyfriend.'

'She's not like that. She will flip out. I will tell her once, and at the right time. When it is time to take things ahead.'

'Your wish,' he said. 'Come here.'

I didn't move from my seat. He came to me and held me.

'I love you,' he said.

'Me too. Sorry I snapped at you.'

◆

We lay down in bed. He ran his fingers up and down my arm.

'Not tonight, Debu,' I said. 'Just not in the mood.'

'You will feel better.'

'No,' I said.

He placed a hand on my breast. I pushed it away.

'Focus on your career, Debu, don't get distracted. Goodnight.'

11

'Foreclose on the company properties first. Scare him so he plays ball,' I said to Jonathan. We stood by the coffee machine in the office pantry. We were talking about MedTron, a semiconductor company gone bust.

'That's true. Smart suggestion,' Jonathan said.

I made two espressos and passed him a cup.

My phone rang. Debu. I looked at it and kept it aside.

'Go ahead, take it,' Jonathan said.

'It's a personal call. I can call back,' I said.

'No, go ahead. I'll see you back at your desk.'

Jonathan left the pantry. I picked up the phone.

'Hi,' I said. 'A middle-of-the-day call. Nice!'

'Well, you are speaking to a senior creative director of BBDO,' he said.

'Oh my God! It happened! Congrats, Debu. This is headline news.'

'Thank you. You are the first person I called.'

'Of course. We totally need to celebrate this.'

'It's okay. They promoted two others too.'

'It's huge. You know it is. Anyway, I got to go. Need to make some calls. What time will you be home today?'

'7.30. Why?'

'Nothing. I might get a little late. Okay, Mr Senior Creative Director, bye!'

I hammered out a quick plan. I messaged Avinash, Ashish and Nidhi.

'Kind of big news. Debu got promoted. My boyfriend is a senior creative director! Surprise celebration drinks. Our place. 7 p.m. sharp. 55B, 50 Franklin Street, Tribeca.'

Within minutes everyone confirmed. I messaged a few others. Some wanted to bring their friends along. In half an hour, I had a mini-party organized with about a dozen confirmed guests. Finally, I dashed Debu a message.

'Busy day. May get late. Have dinner and sleep.'

◆

'Surprise!' everyone shouted in unison as a clueless Debu opened the door. His shocked and dazed expression had everyone bursting into laughter and made my hours of frantic preparation worthwhile. I had ordered pizzas from Ray's. The salads, nuts and bar snacks came from Whole Foods. Champagne was chilling in the freezer. It was the first time Debu and I had so many guests in our little apartment. Chatter and laughter filled the living room. It made my world seem complete. My house felt like a home. I dimmed the lights and turned up the music.

'What a great party!' Nidhi said.

'Template for you. You never do such surprises for me,' Ashish, now her husband, said.

'We are married. They are boyfriend and girlfriend. There's a difference.'

'Whatever,' Ashish said. Nidhi laughed.

I felt a tap on my shoulder. I turned around. It was Debu. He looked deep into my eyes.

'I love you,' he said.

'I love you too,' I said.

Debu pecked me on the lips. Avinash whistled. Everyone looked at us. I covered my face in embarrassment. The house felt warm and fuzzy. I had never been happier in my whole life.

'I just told you this afternoon. How did you do all this so fast?' Debu said.

'I took the rest of the day off.'

'Thank you for making me feel so special, superwoman.'

'You are welcome. But you are still helping me clean up after the party, okay?' I said.

◆

Three months later

'Superb job on MegaBowl. We will recover thirty million, not twenty-five. Well done, Radhika!' I read Jonathan's old email on my laptop. He had copied Jon Cruz, a partner in the Distressed Debt Group. Jon had sent a 'well done' email as well.

'Baby, shut your laptop. Come, lie down,' Debu said, in a drowsy voice. I was sitting next to him on the bed. I had switched off the room lights. However, the glare of the laptop screen bothered him.

'It's still too bright. What time is it?' Debu said.

'11.30,' I said. 'Only a few more minutes, I promise.'

He exhaled noisily.

'What are you working on?' he said, putting his arm around my waist. I nudged the laptop higher to accommodate him.

'My own performance review. I have to turn it in tomorrow.'

'You are amazing,' he said and nuzzled my shoulder.

'Unfortunately, no such option here. I have to write details on all the deals I worked on in the past year.'

'They know you are good. Come, sleep. Let me hold you.' He pulled me closer.

'You sleep. I know the laptop is bothering you. I will sit in the living room,' I said.

'It's cold.'

'I'll turn on the heat in the hall,' I said. I kissed Debu on the forehead, climbed off the bed and shut the door.

I went into our living room, adjusted the thermostat and sat on the couch. I opened my laptop again and read the performance review form.

List instances where you added significant value in a deal.

I had worked on three deals this last year; MegaBowl was the deal I had contributed to the most. I entered the details. Last year, when I joined the firm fresh out of college, we had had a fixed bonus. My performance review would decide my bonus this year.

I reached the last question.

What is your overall assessment of your performance on a scale of 1–5, based on the classification below:

1: Significantly below expectations

2: Below expectations

3: Meets expectations

4: Better than expectations

5: Significantly better than expectations

I pondered on my overall rating for a few minutes. Choosing a '5' felt pompous. I settled for a '3' and pressed 'submit'.

'Done?' I heard Debu's voice from the bedroom.

'Yeah, coming,' I said.

◆

I tiptoed across to Partner Jon Cruz's cabin; his secretary asked me to wait as Jon ended a call. Bonus day in Goldman altered the air in the office. Inside, people felt huge anxiety and excitement. Outside, they had to pretend to be cool, like it was any other day. Of course, it was anything but that. Bonus is what bankers work for, and the 'number' defines whether you are good or not. A zero bonus or a ridiculously low number could even mean a signal to leave the firm.

Jon Cruz would communicate the bonus to everyone in the New York distressed debt team. I had a base salary of 120,000 dollars a year. I felt a 30,000 number would be good, translating to three months' salary. Anything higher, say a thirty-five or forty, would make it a rainbow in my sky.

'How you doing?' Jon said, staring at his screen. He always tried to relax the person before he shared the number. He had the magic spreadsheet with all the bonus data open on his computer.

'I am good. How are you feeling?' I said.

'A bit like Santa Claus today.'

I smiled. But only a little. In a partner's office one always had to be poised.

'Your first real bonus, right?' he said.

I nodded.

'How you do think you have done?' he said.

'I guess I will find out,' I said.

He laughed. 'Well, people like you around here. The worst rating in all your reviews came from you. You gave yourself a three; almost everyone else gave you a five.'

I was speechless. Joy hopped through me like a rabbit as I realized people had noticed my twelve months of slog.

'So your bonus for the year is 150,000 dollars.'

'What?' I blurted out. I shouldn't have but I did. What did he just say?

'What do you mean what? Like it?' Jon said.

'Sorry, how much did you say again?'

'150,000 dollars. So your total compensation is 120,000 base plus 150,000 bonus. You made 270,000 dollars for the year.'

I felt dizzy. I pressed my feet hard on the floor to keep my balance. Two hundred and seventy thousand dollars, I repeated the number in my head to absorb it. It converted to 1 crore and 50 lakh in rupees. *Stay calm, stay calm, stay calm,* I kept repeating to myself.

'You also get a base increment. It is now 140,000 a year. Keep it up.'

'Well, yeah. Thanks, Jon. I will do my best,' I said, my vocal chords not too cooperative.

'You sound funny.'

'Sorry. It is a big number for me,' I said.

Jon laughed. 'You deserve it. By the way, it is one of the highest bonuses at the associate level this year.'

'Thanks.'

'But I must add that bonus numbers are confidential. Please do not share them with anyone in the firm.'

'I understand,' I said.

'Good. Back to work now.'

I felt lightheaded as I returned to my seat. I looked at Craig in the adjacent cubicle. I wanted to high-five him. I couldn't. I simply smiled. I opened a financial model spreadsheet on my computer. However, my mind couldn't focus. I had to share my bonus news with someone. India would be asleep, I couldn't call home. I called Debu.

He didn't pick up.

Probably in a work meeting, I thought. I called Debu again after half an hour. He still didn't pick up. I heard Jonathan and Craig make lunch plans with their significant others.

Where is Debu when I need him?

Finally, Debu called back after an hour.

'What's up?'

'Want to meet for lunch?'

'When? Now?'

'Yeah.'

'I am at work. Can't step out. Too much politics happening on an account.'

'I got my bonus number,' I whispered to him.

'Oh. Cool. Tell me.'

'I want to share it face-to-face.'

'You will tell me at home tonight?'

'Let's go out,' I said.

'Really?'

'Yeah. I will pick a place near your office. Come straight from work. 6.30?'

12

I booked Nerai, a highly rated Greek restaurant a ten-minute walk from the BBDO office. I sent Debu a message after making the reservation.

'Nerai, 55 East 54th St., 6.30.'

I left work at 5.30 p.m. I had to walk to the South Ferry station and take the '1' train to reach the restaurant. I decided to take a taxi instead. Heck, I deserved a twenty-dollar cab ride today. The yellow New York taxi took the FDR drive, a highway along the east side of Manhattan. The cab whisked me to 49th Street without a traffic signal. From there the taxi drove westwards towards Nerai's location.

I reached early and surveyed the restaurant at leisure; Greek paintings on white exposed-brick walls. I scanned the wine list and ordered a bottle of Greek red wine.

I received a message from Debu.

'Sorry, stuck at work. Running ten minutes late.'

'No issues,' I replied.

'Order something. Very hungry,' he responded.

I ordered a watermelon and feta cheese salad along with a trio of dips. The food arrived. Debu didn't. I kept waiting.

He entered the restaurant at 7 p.m.

'I am so, so sorry,' Debu said.

'It's fine,' I said. I stood up and we hugged.

He removed his long black overcoat and hung it at the back of his seat.

'Too much work?' I said as we sat down.

'Just politics. On who gets credit for a campaign. Ever since my promotion I spend more time managing politics than doing anything creative.'

'You are senior, after all. That's what managers do.'

'Yeah, I guess. Oh, food is here. How is it? I am starving.'

'I have not tried. Was waiting for you.'

Debu picked up pita bread and had it with the hummus dip. I ate some salad. His hunger satiated after a few bites, Debu spoke again.

'Anyway, how are you? Big day?' he said.

I smiled. He continued, 'Not telling me on the phone. Dinner out on a weekday. You do like your suspense.'

'Nothing like that. I wanted to share it in person.'

He rubbed his hands together. 'So, what is it?'

'Jon called me this morning to his room. I told you about Jon, right? The partner.'

'Yes.'

'So he told me I had received good reviews from other people.'

'See, I told you. You are a star.'

'Well, it's nice when a partner praises you.'

'What's the number, babe?'

'I will tell you…'

'I can't wait anymore.'

'My bonus for the year is…don't tell anyone, okay?'

'Whom will I tell?'

'A hundred and fifty.'

'A hundred and fifty what?' he said, sounding confused.

'150,000 dollars.'

'150,000 dollars?' he repeated my words.

'Yeah.'

'You mean total compensation? You get 120 already, so thirty more bonus?'

'No. One-fifty is the bonus. Total comp is 270.'

Debu's mouth fell open. It stayed like that for a few seconds before he spoke again, one deliberate word at a time.

'You made 270,000 dollars last year?' he said. His big eyes seemed even bigger.

'Yeah.'

'Oh,' he said in a low voice. 'Holy fuck! These banks.'

'Well, not everyone had this number. They told me it is one of the highest for associates of my level. I had a five rating.'

'Nice,' he said in a muted voice.

The waiter arrived to take Debu's order. He opened the menu and took five minutes selecting his dish; probably figuring out which item offered the best value.

'One lamb kebab and one falafel, please.'

The waiter left.

'You okay with the order, baby? Wanted anything else?' Debu said to me.

'No. Though you seem more interested in the menu than listening to me.'

'No, no. Anyway. You were saying?'

I smiled. 'That I had the highest bonus among the associates.'

'That's nice, babe. I mean, I can't even imagine that kind of money. You know, I barely reached an 80,000 compensation even after the promotion.'

Why does he have to tell me his salary now? I already know it.

'You are doing very well too,' I said. I regretted saying it the next instant.

Why did I have to add a reassuring and patronizing, 'You are doing very well too'? As if telling a kid who is second in a race, 'You ran well too.'

Thankfully, I don't think he noticed. I continued, 'There's no doubt you are awesome at BBDO. You are one of their best.'

'People are stupid in my company. You won't believe what happened in this campaign.'

Okay, what just happened here? Why has it become about him? Isn't this, like, my big moment?

The waiter arrived with a bottle of red wine. Debu looked at him, surprised.

'I ordered Greek wine to celebrate my big bonus. A whole bottle!' I signalled the waiter to pour us two glasses.

'Cool,' he said. 'Nice.'

Cool. Nice. Will this guy ever move on from these words to say something more substantial?

The food arrived. His face lit up.

'This lamb smells so good. Baby, you pick the best places. Really, nobody picks restaurants in New York like you do. This is so close to my office too. Will come here with my team.'

Mr Debashish Sen, I do other things besides pick restaurants. Like make a ton of money for a girl my age. Heck, I make a lot of money for anyone any age. I also got a top rating in my reviews. Can you at least praise me a little for it?

'This is yum. Try the lamb. It's so soft. Outstanding,' Debu said, ten times more enthusiasm in his voice than the 'nice' he'd uttered for my bonus.

I served myself. I wondered why I didn't feel ecstatic about my bonus anymore.

Why am I so keen for his praise? I have earned that bonus. Jon, one of the most senior partners at Goldman Sachs, has recognized my work. Still, I want Debu to also acknowledge it. Why? Why do we girls have this defect? Why do we need our men to praise and validate us in order for us to feel accomplished?

'How is it? Lamb is so tender, no?' he said.

'It's nice,' I said. 'Fuck you' is what I wanted to say.

So even if it is a defect, even if I do need him to praise me, why can't he? When he got a promotion I'd jumped up and down and thrown a surprise party for him. He can't get past the tenderness of his lamb?

I kept silent and did not meet his eye. He had known me long enough—a year and a half, to be precise—to figure out I was upset.

'I am proud of you, baby. So proud of you. You worked hard for it. I know it,' he said.

'That does feel nice to hear. Thanks,' I said and squeezed his hand on the table.

'I am sorry. I still can't get over the number. It's insane. You have less than two years of work experience.'

'Distressed pays well. My deals made a lot of money. So a bit of luck too. But yeah, even I was shocked when I heard it.'

'You make, like, three times as much as me? Mindblowing.'

Why did he have to say it like that? Why compare? I wanted to tell him about my base increment too. I don't know why but I decided against it.

'Well, between two people someone will end up earning more. Some industries pay more, as simple as that,' I said.

'Hmmm…' He stabbed a piece of lamb with his fork.

'Let's go on a nice vacation. Anywhere. Europe? Hawaii?' I said.

He laughed. 'Feeling rich?'

'I *am* rich. *We* are rich. Let's go shopping this weekend. You will come?'

'Maybe. You told your parents?'

'I will. I will call mom when she wakes up.'

'They will be so happy.'

'I hope so. I wanted them to buy a Honda City. I think I will ask them to get an even better car.'

'You are a great daughter. They will be so proud of you.'

'Thanks. Debu, I have one question.'

'Yeah?'

'Are you proud of me? For real?'

'Yeah, I am.'

We looked into each other's eyes. Together, we had made a place for ourselves in this new city. We had not only survived, but also thrived. He had been promoted. I had done well. We were good for each other. I held on to his hand. He cleared his throat to speak. I wondered if he would say something romantic.

'Sorry, but are you going to eat that last piece of lamb?' he said.

◆

'A hundred and fifty thousand dollars. So one-and-a-half lakh dollars,' I said on the phone to my mother.

'Tell me in rupees,' she said.

'It is forty-five to the dollar now. So, around 70 lakhs.'

'That's your bonus?' I heard a vessel drop.

'I am sending some money to your account. Please go shopping,' I said.

'You had a 70-lakh-rupees bonus?' my mother repeated.

'Yes.'

'In addition to your salary?'

'Yes.'

'What kind of work do you do anyway?'

'What is that supposed to mean?'

'I have never heard anyone earn that much.'

'I told you, I am in distressed debt. So we work with companies in trouble.'

'How can you make money if those companies are in trouble?'

I laughed, 'We do. Is dad around?'

'Yeah,' she said and shouted out for him. 'Listen. Come here. Your daughter made 70 lakhs!'

Her voice could probably be heard across the whole colony they lived in. So much for Goldman's confidentiality clauses.

I narrated the entire bonus story and calculation to dad. After a minute of stunned silence, he spoke in an emotional voice. 'Even the SBI chairperson doesn't make that much. You are twenty-four years old. My little girl has become such a big shot.'

I found it difficult to hold back tears.

'I am still your little daughter, dad. The one who held your finger on the way to the school bus stop.'

'You are my sweetest little one,' he said.

'Remember you used to tell me to stand on my own feet? To not worry about anything else, to just do the best I can? That's all I did, dad.'

I heard him sob. My father cries more than all the women in the house.

'I am so proud of you,' he said.

'I love you. I miss you,' I said.

'Come home soon,' he said.

'I will. I will take a vacation at Christmas time. What do you want? Can I get you anything?'

'Get my little girl to me soonest.'

I hung up the phone. I realized I had cried after a long time. Who knew 270,000 dollars could make you so emotional?

13

'Cheers!' Jonathan raised a toast. 'To my amazing associates, Craig and Radhika.'

We lifted our glasses. As per distressed debt tradition, the entire group went out for drinks on the Friday night of the bonus announcement week. We had come to Harry's Café & Steak, a five-minute walk from the Goldman building. Harry's was a Wall Street institution, where senior bankers and CEOs lunched and closed some of the biggest mergers and financial deals. Around twenty of us from the Distressed Debt Group congregated in the bar area. Jon Cruz came only for a few minutes; he chatted with senior MDs and vice presidents before leaving for the weekend at his Hamptons beach house.

'See you, guys. And enjoy yourself. It's on me,' Jon said as he left the bar, leaving his credit card behind.

People had invited their significant others, which meant wives, husbands, girlfriends and boyfriends. Even I had invited Debu. I had finally gathered the courage to make him public to my team. Until now my group considered me a geek, in a relationship with her financial models. Tonight they would see my man.

White-gloved waiters passed around champagne glasses on silver trays.

'Happy with your number?' Craig said to me. Confidentiality clauses apart, bonus gossip was just too hard to resist.

'It's my first real one. Of course I am happy,' I said, trying not to reveal too much.

'I am sure they paid you really well. They love you here,' Craig said. I wondered if he had a hint of snark in his voice. I couldn't tell.

'Hey, is that Jonathan's wife who just arrived?' I said, deflecting the topic. I pointed to the Harry's entrance. I recognized her from the pictures on Jonathan's desk.

'Yeah, that's Clara,' Craig said.

Clara, a tall American blonde who worked in the Metropolitan Museum of Art, was wearing a long purple dress.

'You have someone coming too?' I said.

'Amanda is coming in a few minutes,' Craig said. I remembered him mentioning his girlfriend to me once. She was an aspiring actress, working on an off–Broadway theatre production.

'How about you?' Craig said.

'I have a friend coming,' I said.

'Friend?'

I laughed. 'Okay, boyfriend. Sorry, I just haven't told anyone in the firm.'

'I didn't know you have a boyfriend.'

Craig raised his glass and touched it to mine. I took another sip of my champagne.

'I never mentioned him,' I said.

'Well, today we'll get to see him,' Craig said, 'the boyfriend of our superstar associate.'

'I am still a lowly minion,' I said.

'You are good. I hate to admit it, but you are better than me. They will make you VP in six months. You wait and see.'

'I don't know…'

'Amanda is here,' Craig said in a higher pitch.

A gorgeous blonde with grey eyes entered the bar. Everyone in the group, men and women, paused their conversations to look at her. She had curly golden hair, and her make-up was impeccable, oxblood lipstick and smoky eyes.

She came and hugged Craig. For a few seconds, despite being an associate, Craig became a superstar in the room.

I checked my phone.

'Still stuck at work. Sorry,' Debu had messaged.

'Come soon. Everyone is here,' I replied.

Craig introduced me to Amanda. The waiter gave us another champagne glass each.

'I have heard so much about you,' Amanda said.

'You have?' I said.

'Craig mentions his deals, and how you are a tough negotiator. And that you are really good,' she said.

I laughed.

'I am not. I get lucky sometimes,' I said. Well, that is how I take compliments. I don't say thank you. I just deny the compliment.

'I love the colour of your skin,' Amanda said.

'Really? I wish I had yours,' I said. She laughed. All the men around us noticed her laugh.

'So I hear you are an actor?' I said.

'Yeah. Doing a small theatre part right now. Auditioning for television and movies. It's hard, though. So I also work as a part-time piano teacher.'

'You are so pretty. I am sure it will work out,' I said.

'Too many pretty women in New York,' Amanda said.

'But you are the prettiest,' Craig said and kissed her on top of her head. She giggled. Craig introduced her to Jonathan and a couple of other VPs. All the men listened to every word Amanda had to say.

I wanted to be Amanda. I don't know why. I scolded myself for thinking that way. Amanda didn't have a real job. Amanda didn't know how to make financial models. Amanda couldn't close a financial deal. Amanda didn't make 270,000 dollars a year. *But Amanda is so hot. Amanda also has men hovering around her, hoping to get her a drink. Where is my one and only man?*

'Debu, where are you?' I sent a message again.

He didn't reply for an hour. Meanwhile, I met the better halves of everyone in the distressed debt team. I finished three glasses of champagne. The wooziness in my head told me I needed to slow down a bit.

Debu called me at 9.30.

'Where are you, Debu? Everyone is leaving. Did you get my message?' I said.

'Yeah. Shit happening at work. I will tell you about it later.'

I could hear crowd noises around him.

'Where are you now?' I said.

'I came downstairs for a drink with my team.'

'Debu? You were supposed to come to my office party for drinks tonight. I wanted to introduce you to everyone!'

'Stupid politics happening. I have to talk to people. I will come.'

'When?'

'In an hour?'

'It'll be over. Really Debu? You had to do your office stuff on the one day I call you?'

'I got stuck. I can't tell you the backstabbing that happened here.'

'Debu,' I said, my voice confident after the champagne, 'I don't care about your office right now. You said you would come.'

'I thought I might. Listen, it's just bankers, right? It's anyway not my scene.'

'Really? I am a banker too.'

'You are different. But they talk about money and deals and...'

'Debu, they are people too. Today, everyone has come with their significant others. I told Craig you are coming. What do I tell him?'

'That I am stuck at work. What else?'

'So they'll think I made up my boyfriend.'

'What?'

'Nothing. Bye.'

'So should I come in an hour or not?'

'Don't. Drink with your backstabbing colleagues. It's okay. Bye.'

I hung up. I picked up a glass of champagne and knocked it down bottoms up. Jonathan noticed me.

'Someone doesn't like to go slow and savour their French bubbly,' he said.

'Hey, Jonathan,' I said.

'Craig told me your boyfriend is coming. Is he here? Would love to say hi.'

'He's stuck at work, sadly.'

'Oh, that's unfortunate. What does he do?'

I don't know what the fuck he does, I wanted to say in reflex. His not showing up, the four glasses of champagne and my realization I wasn't as pretty as Amanda had all added to my frustration. I took a deep breath to compose myself.

'He works in advertising. On Madison Avenue,' I managed to say.

'Oh, nice. The creative type.'

'I guess.'

'The banker and the creative. Interesting combination.'

'Yeah...where's your wife?'

He introduced me to Clara, who told me she couldn't believe how hard we all worked.

Forty-five minutes later the crowd frittered away from Harry's. In smaller groups, people left for their own respective dinner plans. I had none. I walked out into the freezing cold and tried to find a cab. I couldn't, given it was Friday night. I walked into the subway and looked at my phone. Debu had not called or messaged. Dizzy with alcohol, I realized I had not eaten anything for a long time. I came out of the train station. On the walk home, I picked up a pizza slice for myself from a small takeaway deli. Even in my incoherent state, I wondered if that idiot Debu had eaten dinner. I packed another slice for him, just in case.

I reached home. Debu was sitting on the sofa, hypnotized by ESPN.

'What the…you are here?' I said. He stood up and came forward to help take away the pizza boxes and my handbag. I removed my winter coat and placed it on the hanger.

'I just arrived. Ten minutes ago. Honest,' he said.

'You ate dinner?' I said.

'No, not really. Just some bar snacks.'

'Come, let's eat. I got pizza,' I said.

'Thanks, baby.'

'Don't "baby" me. Just eat.'

'What? You upset? Everything okay?'

Is he a moron to ask?

I didn't respond. We sat facing each other at our small white dining table in the living room. I took out the pizza slices from the boxes and put them on plates. Strings of molten cheese hung from slices.

'Looks yummy,' he said.

I looked at the cheesy pizza slice and thought of Amanda. *I bet she doesn't eat this stuff. No wonder she looks like she does.* My anger multiplied at the thought of eating this calorie bomb dinner. I pushed my plate away.

'What, baby?' Debu said, mouth stuffed with food.

'I am not hungry.'

'Why?'

'I can't eat this. Too fattening.'

'You only bought it, baby.'

'Yeah, because I am stupid. Okay? And stop calling me "baby".'

Debu put his pizza slice down.

'Listen, I know you are upset. I didn't come for your party. But I had a really rough day.'

'So it is about you now?' I said.

'They took me and two of my juniors off the Under Armor account.'

'What? How?' I said. 'That was your account!'

'I told you. Politics. They called it reshuffle. However, they stole it from me.'

'It all happened today?'

'They announced it today. But they had plotted against me for months. All planned.'

'Sorry to hear that. You still have other good accounts, right?'

'I am fucked.'

I didn't know what to say. He had told me about the politics in his group for months. The initial excitement Debu had had about working in advertising had disappeared. Many in his team often excluded him from client meetings, a worrying sign.

'What were you doing outside the office then?' I said.

'I was with my people. Trying to figure out what happened.'

'Did you?'

'They fucked me. What is there to figure out?'

'So you could have come for my office party instead of a drink with the boys after work.'

'Radhika, is your office party all you care about?'

'No. But I am wondering if you care about me at all.'

'What do you mean? So I didn't come to a stupid banker thing. Big deal.'

I stood up and slammed my fist on the table.

'It was not a stupid banker thing. It was *my* thing. I got a huge bonus this week. This was the celebration. I wanted you to meet my team. I wanted them to meet you. Don't you get it?'

'Sit down. Can we eat dinner?' he said.

'I don't want to eat,' I screamed.

'Don't throw a tantrum. Are you drunk?'

'No,' I said.

'A bit high?'

'It doesn't matter. I can still think more clearly than you.'

'What?'

'You need to change your job. Every day you bicker about the politics. What are you going to do about it?'

'I don't know.'

'Of course you do. Are you happy at your job?'

'Not exactly.'

'However, you are stuck there. So you need to go out there and apply again.'

'BBDO is prestigious. How to leave it?'

'Screw prestigious. If your group is not good, change. There is stuff happening in digital advertising. You tell me about it so much. Find a job in that.'

'I can't. It's not easy. And they are start-ups and uncertain...'

'Whatever, Debu! So stay here, fine. But quit complaining so much.'

'I can't even share and vent with you?'

'You can. But at some point, do something about it. You don't, Debu. You don't do anything about us. You don't do anything about the job you don't like.'

'What do you mean I don't do anything about us?'

'My mother calls me every week. She wants me to start looking at boys. I tell you every time she says that. Do you ever take the hint?'

He kept quiet. I had brought out all the touchy topics at one go.

'You have seen how my career is going at the moment. If only it was okay, I would have thought about it.'

'So do something about the career, Debu,' I said.

I left the room. I took a shower and went to bed. I switched off all the lights.

Debu changed and slid into bed next to me. He placed his arm around me. I brushed it aside.

'Come here, baby,' he said.

'Go to sleep,' I said.

14

'We made a ten-million-dollar investment. We will now recover thirty-six million dollars,' I said.

I made my final comments on the last presentation slide. We had invested in City Properties, a Manhattan real-estate firm gone bust. Fortunately, the property market had improved after our investment and we tripled our money.

'Fantastic. We should sell. Now that is what I call a home run,' Jon said. 'What a deal! Well done, Radhika.'

'Jonathan and Craig guided me through it all,' I said.

I came back to my seat. I called Debu. I wanted to tell him about Jon's praise.

'Hey,' he said.

'What's up?'

'Just working on a pitch. I don't think we will get it, though. How about you?' Debu said.

'I am at work. Another deal closed.'

'You called for a reason?'

'Yeah,' I said. However, at that moment I didn't want to tell him my success story. Perhaps it was better not to share it than to do so and not get an enthusiastic response.

'What is it?'

'Well,' I said and wondered what to say next. Why was I hiding my success from him?

'I just had a good day at work,' I said.

'What? Managed to make more money?' He laughed.

He was being funny. Still, I didn't like what he said, or maybe it was just his tone. I ignored his barb.

'No just... I don't know. I just felt good. Grateful for what we have. We should be grateful, no, Debu? We have so much. We have independence, jobs, health, family, a great city we live in and love. We have love. It's a lot to be grateful for, isn't it?'

'Yeah, baby. We do.' He sounded like he was about to yawn. 'That's sweet. Anyway, I better go back to my pitch.'

'Sure. Sorry I disturbed you.'

'Bye, baby,' he said and hung up.

I went back to my screen.

'Killed it.' Craig came to my desk and high-fived me.

'Don't we always?' I winked at him.

◆

'Hi, this is Radhika Mehta from the New York office,' I said. I had dialled into a conference call with our Asian office in Hong Kong. Owing to the time difference the call had been scheduled late, at 10 in the night. I took the call from home, sitting on the living room sofa. Debu read a book in the bedroom, waiting for me to finish.

'Hi, Radhika. This is Peter Wu from the Hong Kong office,' a voice on the phone said.

'Josh Ang from Hong Kong,' came another one.

'Jonathan from the New York office,' Jonathan said.

I placed the phone on speaker mode so I could have my hands free. I had made myself a cup of mint tea, and cupped it in both hands.

Jonathan introduced the deal.

'We are dealing with a company called Luxvision, a spectacles and sunglasses manufacturer. Radhika has already sent out the info memo. Currently in trouble, has no cash. The only assets are some factories in China.'

Goldman Sachs excelled in working together across offices. While the deal came from New York, we would engage the Hong Kong office to help us out. Josh and Peter would visit the company plants in China to see if the factories actually existed, and if they had any value.

'Client is saying the factory is in Shenzhen, just across the border from Hong Kong,' I said.

'Easy then. We could do a day trip,' Peter said.

'That would be good,' I said. 'They are saying the factory is in the heart of town, and if we close it down we could rezone into residential use and sell apartments.'

As I finished my sentence, Debu tiptoed into the living room. I placed a finger on my lips to signal him to be quiet. He nodded and pointed at the fridge. He walked up to the fridge and took out a cup of strawberry yoghurt. He offered me some. I declined and sipped my tea. I smiled at how domesticated we had become. He could be in the kitchen doing his thing. I could sip my tea and work. I sent him a flying kiss. He smiled back.

I tuned back into the call.

'Shenzhen is growing fast. Depends on the location and local permissions. What about the workers?' asked Josh, a VP in the Hong Kong Distressed Debt Group.

Debu sat at the dining table and ate his snack. The call continued on the speakerphone.

'Two hundred workers. If we continue the manufacturing they stay,' I said.

'Though if we keep the business running it is only worth forty million. If we sell the land for apartments, it is seventy million,' Jonathan said.

'Wow,' Peter said, 'huge difference in value.'

'Yeah, so obviously we want the workers out and to explore the land sale option,' I said.

'Okay, give us a few days, we will make a visit and revert,' Jon said.

'Hope we get good news,' I said.

The call ended. I hung up and shut my laptop. I noticed Debu.

'Hey, you are still here,' I said.

He scraped out the last of his yoghurt.

'Yeah. I was listening to bits of your call.'

'Boring banker stuff, right?'

'Kind of. However, I think I sort of understood what is happening.'

I stretched my arms above my head.

'It's a new deal. Company gone bust, factories in China,' I said.

'Yeah, and you guys are trying to close it down, sell the land for apartments.'

'True. The factory is old but in a great location. China is growing fast, so this is the heart of town now. Ready for bed? It's late.'

'No, wait, what about the workers?' He came to sit on the sofa next to me.

'They will have to be let go of. We will give them some compensation,' I said.

'And their families? What about getting new jobs?'

'Debu, they will figure it out. We will give them a few months' salary as compensation. They will find another job meanwhile.'

'It's not that easy. What kind of blatant capitalism is this?'

I looked at Debu in shock.

'What?' I said. 'Seriously? Blatant capitalism?'

'You are trying to make the most money.'

'Well, yeah, that is my job. We invest money, so we want good returns on it.'

'But why do you have to fire people?'

I rolled my eyes.

'Is this a Bengali communist thing? Bengalis love communism, right?'

'I don't know. It just feels wrong, what you are doing to make money.'

'I am not doing anything wrong. We are doing what is legally possible and trying to generate maximum value.'

'To make some rich Goldman Sachs partners even richer? What about the workers at this factory?'

'Debu! Goldman Sachs has not created trouble for the workers. The company management screwed up, borrowed too much money, ran their business badly and went bankrupt. Hence the workers suffered. We are simply there to clean up the mess.'

'Like vultures. They could say they have come to clean up when they are actually feeding themselves.'

'That's not such a nice analogy, but yes. You could say that. Yes, even in the financial system, you need the mortuary.'

'You make money doing this.'

'So? We also take huge risks. Nobody wants to touch these companies otherwise.'

I finished my tea. I went to the kitchen sink and washed the cup.

Debu came up behind me.

'You like your job?'

I turned to him.

'Yeah, Debu. I love it. I am good at it. It's exciting. I am learning so much. It's a great firm. I am paid well. It kills me at times with work but I love it.'

'I don't know. Just doesn't feel right. I hope the job doesn't harden you.'

'Harden me?' I said. 'What are you talking about?'

'You were this sweet, innocent girl when I met you. You had a soft side.'

'I still do. I am the same person. This is a job. I am more than that.

I do it and come home to cuddle with you. Don't I?'

'Yeah,' he said, sounding unconvinced.

'You applied to digital ad agencies?'

'I will. Soon.'

'I thought you said you would.'

'I will, Radhika. Don't keep pushing me so much. See, this is what I mean. You have become hard.'

'I am just concerned,' I said and threw my hands up in the air. 'I want you to be happy in your job too. I want you to settle down so we can take the next step.'

'What step?'

I'd had enough of him faking ignorance. He knew exactly what I was talking about. With great effort, I kept calm and spoke again.

'About marriage. How many times do I have to bring it up?' I said. 'I feel like I have to beg you.'

'You don't have to beg me.'

'So how long do I fend off my mother?'

'I have told you. I am not ready.'

My breathing became fast. I couldn't take this anymore.

'We won't get married tomorrow, Debu. But we have to make some plans. I have to tell my parents I have someone in my life, so they don't knock on every door in West Delhi to find a boy for me. I want to tell them soon.'

'What do you want from me?'

'Tell me what is your plan for us. You want to get married in one year? Two years? Three years? Something at least.'

'I think it is too soon to think about all this.'

'We have dated, sorry, lived-in for about two years. I think it is absolutely the time to at least think about this.'

'I think it is not,' Debu said.

'I think it is,' I said. We locked eyes.

'And so you must be right. After all, you get the higher bonus, so what do I know, yeah?' Debu said.

I gasped. I raised my hand and pointed a finger at him.

'What the fuck! What did you say?'

'Nothing,' he said, probably regretting his statement.

'Did you just bring my bonus into our marriage discussion?'

'No, I didn't.'

'You did. I don't even think about it anymore. Is it on your mind?'

'No, I don't care.'

'You sure? If I were the sweet and innocent girl you met, whatever that means, you were also the sweet boy who talked about feminism while we walked in Manhattan. Remember? *You will inspire other girls? Women need to show men they are no less?*'

'I don't care about your bonus. Okay? That is not what this is about.'

'So then what? Explain to me. Why is it wrong for us to discuss the future if we have lived with each other for almost two years?'

'I am not sure,' he said.

'About what?'

'I don't know. Suppose we marry each other. We will start a family, have kids, right?'

'Yeah, of course,' I said.

'So I am thinking. I don't know. I had this idea of what the mother of my kids would be like.'

'Huh? Mother of your kids?' I said. Sometimes, Debu talks such whacko stuff, I wonder what they smoke in their ad agency offices.

'Yeah. It's important, right? What kind of mother I want for my kids,' Debu said.

'Sure. I want a good father for my kids too. Can you come to the point?'

'So are you going to keep working like this or leave work once you have kids?'

'I don't know. I haven't decided yet. I'd like to work if possible.'

'You think you can?'

'Let's see. Will have to work it out. If I make as much money as I do I can afford full-time help, take a house close to work, have our parents come…'

He interrupted me.

'See, this is what I am not sure about.'

'What?'

'When you talk in such practical terms.'

'What do you mean?'

'Like, if you are like this, in this hard job, "fire the workers" kind of role, would you even be affectionate towards our kids?'

'What the fuck, Debu!' I shouted.

'See, now you are losing it. Then you say you want to discuss things!'

'This is not a discussion. You are talking bullshit. Making sweeping judgements.'

'I am not. Okay, I like you. I love you. But I want my kids' mother to be at home for them.'

'Maybe I will be. If needed.'

'See, you are not sure. You have this hi-fi mega-paying job.'

'My job will have nothing to do with my commitment as a mother. Do you get it?'

We stared at each other in silence for about thirty seconds. He finally spoke again. 'I don't think I can do this. Really, I can't.'

My heart stopped for a second. Did he just propose a break-up? Oh my God, had the only man who ever loved the unlovable me threatened to leave me?

I turned my volume down and spoke in a calm voice. 'Debu. What's the matter with you? Why are you being like this?'

He shrugged.

'Work stress?'

'No.'

'Is it the call? Listen, this is the distressed debt business. Don't get so affected. It's business.'

'Not only that.'

I checked the time. It was midnight. I had to wake up at 6.30 to prepare for an early morning meeting.

'Debu, calm down. Sorry I snapped at you. I will try to be understanding, okay?'

I went up behind him and hugged him.

'This is not the time to talk about such things. It's my mistake,' I said.

'It's fine,' he said, disentangling my arms.

'Shall we go to bed?' I said.

He nodded.

We slipped under the sheets. I took off my nightsuit and drew him closer.

'I'm tired. Goodnight, baby,' he said and turned away from me.

Within a few minutes he had slept. I, on the other hand, kept awake all night, wondering what I would do if the one man who loved me decided to leave me.

◆

Since I hadn't slept I got out of bed at 5 a.m. I spent the next hour making breakfast. I made pancakes, Debu's favourite. I also cut fruit, boiled some eggs and made toast. I wondered why I was doing this. Was it because I couldn't sleep? Or did I want to calm Debu down? Or to show I could be domestic enough to be a good mother? Or did I want to prove that I could be sweet and innocent, which probably translates into docile and submissive?

I wanted Debu to wake up and be happy. I wanted it more than the China deal or a bonus or anything else. I scolded myself for feeling that way, but I couldn't help it. His words about me not being potential mother material had shaken me up.

Wake up, Debu, eat the pancakes and please tell me I am lovable.

He entered the living room at 6.45. I had already laid out the plates and placed a jug filled with orange juice on the table. I switched on the electric hobs and put a saucepan on it.

'Wow,' he said, rubbing his eyes.

'Good morning,' I said in my most cheerful voice.

'What are you doing?'

'Making pancakes. You love them, remember? You want them with maple syrup or honey?'

'Maple syrup. Is it the weekend?' he said in a puzzled voice as he dragged a dining chair out to sit.

'No, Wednesday. I just thought I would cook us something special.'

On typical weekdays we would gobble down cereal and milk and rush out of the house.

I kept a plate of blueberries, raspberries and blackberries in front of Debu.

'Fancy,' he said.

'Berries are good for you. Start with this while the pancakes get cooked.'

He waved his hands.

'Don't you have to go to work?' he said.

'I do.'

'You had an important meeting in the morning, right?'

'Yeah. I will have breakfast with you and then get ready.'

The smell of buttery dough filled the living room. The pancakes turned golden-brown. I arranged two of them on a plate, drizzled maple syrup on them. I cut a banana into thin slices and arranged them around the pancakes.

'How about you?' Debu said as I gave him his plate.

'I am making more,' I said.

Does he think I am less hardened now? I wondered. He ate in silence, perhaps wondering if this was a dream. I made my pancakes and sat in front of him.

'They are delicious,' he said.

'Thank you.'

'I should say thank you. You put in so much effort. What time did you wake up to make all this?'

'Five. Just an hour earlier,' I lied. I hadn't slept at all.

'You do look tired.'

'It's okay. I will be fine.' I cut a piece of pancake.

'Radhika, I want to say something,' Debu said.

I know you will say sorry. It is okay, I said to myself. He must feel guilty now after he saw how much I care for him.

'What?'

'This is really sweet.'

'Thanks. So are you. A sweet gesture for my sweet boyfriend.'

'Thank you, Radhika. This is really sweet but…'

'But what?'

'Today you are making breakfast like this. This is awesome. But I am not happy.'

'Not happy about what, baby?'

'Us.'

'Why? Is this about last night? We were both angry,' I said. I found it difficult to swallow the slice of banana in my mouth.

'It's not just about yesterday or about being angry. I have been thinking about it for many days. Weeks, actually.'

'Really? And you didn't discuss it with me?' I said. I felt a little stupid about cooking all morning.

'There is nothing to discuss. I know I am not happy.'

'You are bored of me?'

'Don't be stupid.'

'So?'

'I am being calm, okay? But I have an image of the wife I want. The mother of the kids I want. I am not judging you, but I think I want a housewife.'

'What?' I said. My fork almost fell out of my hands.

'It's what I have seen growing up. I go to work, make the money. Wife takes care of the home. Simple needs, happy family.'

'What are you talking about, Debu? Didn't you say women could achieve anything today? Didn't you encourage me when I had to apply for distressed debt?'

'I did. I still admire you. I respect all women who achieve big things. I think it is great...'

'But you can't be with them?'

'I don't know. Maybe not. Maybe I could. But you made me think about marriage and I did. I visualized a future home. I would like my wife to be there for me and my kids.'

'And I can't be that?'

'Will you leave your job?'

'Why, Debu? Why do I have to leave it? I like it. It's rewarding and fulfilling to me.'

'What about the home?'

'What about the home? You are going to work too, right? Why can't I?'

'Oh, so you want to work and I stay at home?'

'I didn't say that, but why do I have to choose one of the two?'

'I get it.'

'What, Debu?'

'You make more money. I should quit my job, right, not the high-flying you?'

'Will you stop it? Stop calling me high-flying or whatever. When you do well I am happy for you. Am I not? Why can't you be?'

He looked at me once and then sideways. I let out a deep breath and spoke again, as calm as possible.

'Nobody needs to quit if they don't want to. We can still have a good happy family,' I said.

Debu kept quiet. I could tell my words did not convince him.

'Say something,' I said, putting my cutlery down.

He remained quiet, continued to eat in silence. Tears welled up in my eyes. I wiped them with a tissue.

He placed his hand on mine.

'Don't cry,' he said.

'Don't make me cry and then say "don't cry",' I said, my voice breaking.

'Leave all this banking and morning meetings. You are stressing yourself out.'

'I am fine,' I said as I continued to cry. 'I am fine.'

'You are this simple Indian girl. You need to love and be loved.'

'Yeah, I am,' I said, sniffling as I composed myself.

'I will take care of us. Don't you just want to be there for me and our future kids?'

I checked the time.

'It's 7.20. I really need to rush.'

I walked towards the bathroom. Debu spoke behind me.

'See. This is what you do. I am discussing something with you,' he said.

I turned to him at the bathroom door.

'I have a morning meeting. I am presenting a deal. I told you.'

'But I am discussing something important. Leave the meeting today.'

'I can't. I have to present the China deal.'

I went into the bathroom, took a quick shower and changed from my nightclothes to a white shirt and black trousers. When I came out Debu was still sitting at the dining table.

'This is what I fear. Even as a mother this is what you will do. Then what?' he said.

I didn't respond. I stared at him for five seconds. He cowered a little, nervous at what I would do next. I reached the entrance door and opened it. I stepped out of the house. I glared at him one more time and slammed the door shut.

15

'Whoa, big party night yesterday?' Jonathan said. We sat in the meeting room waiting for others to arrive.

'No, I was at home. We had the China deal call, right?' I said.

'But your eyes. They are red.'

'I didn't sleep well, actually.'

'Deal stress?'

'Life stress.'

Jonathan smiled.

'I know the feeling,' he said.

Craig, Jon and a few other VPs and associates from the Distressed Debt Group arrived in the next few minutes. I presented the Luxvision deal to get everyone's views.

'I would get a local Chinese property developer involved soon,' Jon said.

He was right. China had too many regulations; you needed a strong local partner to navigate the system.

'Sure,' I said. 'Hong Kong office is visiting the factory. Will ask them to talk to a few developers too.'

I finished my presentation and sat down. Another team presented their deal. My head hurt from lack of sleep. I was trying my best to pay attention to the speaker when my phone buzzed in my trouser pocket. I ignored it at first. It buzzed a few more times. The meeting room was dark as the speaker made a slide presentation. I slid out my phone and held it in my hand beneath the table. I had several messages, all from Debu.

'Radhika, I can't do this anymore.'

'Think whatever of me but this is not what I want.'

'Trust me. You are not an easy person to be with.'

'I want a simple life. I just want a simple Indian girl.'

'I want to break up. I will move out.'

'Will leave the rent for this month on top of the fridge. Bye.'

My face froze as I stared at the screen. I couldn't react in front of the team. I clenched my teeth so my eyes wouldn't stream.

'Excuse me,' I whispered to Jonathan next to me and stood up.

'I need to step out,' I whispered and tiptoed out of the meeting room to confront the darkness I faced in my life.

I went to the ladies' room and re-read the messages.

I called Debu. He cut my call. I called twice again.

'Can you call me?' I sent him a message.

He didn't respond. I came back to my cubicle, sat in my seat and covered my face with my hands. Tricia, a sixty-year-old American secretary in our group, glanced at me.

'You okay?'

I nodded, my lips a flat line.

'Just tired,' I said with effort.

'Are you going to call me?' I sent a message again.

'There is nothing to talk about,' he replied.

I called him. He cut my call again.

'Am busy,' his message said.

'What could be more important than this?' I responded.

'Can you leave me alone, please?' came his answer.

My eyes welled up. I didn't want to cry in office. I sucked in my breath.

'We have lived together for two years. Is it that simple to end it?' I sent him a message.

'I should have ended it earlier,' he said.

I called him. He picked up.

'I have told you I can't talk. Stop calling me, please.'

'Can we talk later?' I pleaded as my voice began to quiver.

'I really have to go. Bye,' he said.

That was that. My face red, I knew I had to leave the office before I disintegrated.

'I am just going out for a walk,' I called out to Tricia. 'Feeling a bit uneasy.'

'Fresh air will do you good,' Tricia said.

'Tell Jonathan to call on my cell if he needs me.'

I stepped out of 85 Broad Street. The sun shone bright, taking away a bit of the chill. It was a beautiful day weather-wise, but it felt like my worst day in New York so far. I felt like calling him again, but resisted the temptation. I kept staring at my phone, hoping he would call me back. He didn't.

I roamed up and down Wall Street a dozen times. I didn't have anyone like Debu in New York. Sure, I had some friends at work and outside. However, I couldn't imagine this city without Debu. *Maybe he is just upset*, I told myself. But he had seemed so cold and firm when he spoke to me.

I went back to work after an hour. I somehow finished the day. I didn't eat any lunch. I left office at 5 in the evening and took the subway back and reached home.

I switched on the lights of the living room. I went to the bathroom. I saw the counter didn't have Debu's perfume or his beard trimmer. The clothes-hook in the bathroom did not have any of his clothes. I went to the bedroom, opened the closet—nothing.

I felt like someone had kicked me in the stomach, hard.

No, this is just a nightmare. I didn't sleep all night so I am imagining all this.

I sat on the bed and stared at the empty closet. Then I cried. And cried. Till my eyes were as empty as Debu's cupboard.

◆

'Please, Debu. The house is so empty without you,' I said.

I held on to the pole in the subway compartment. Debu had left home five days ago. I had called him every day, trying to convince him to come back.

'It is your house. You stayed there alone before me, right?' Debu said.

'Yeah, but now it is our home.'

'It's not. It's rented. Too much rent, if you ask me.'

The train shook as it shifted tracks. I found it tough to balance myself.

'You know what I mean,' I said.

'It's okay. You will get used to it,' he said.

'I can't. Please, Debu. Don't you miss me?' I said. A part of me felt horrible for grovelling before him like this. I teared up in front of everyone in the subway.

'I am just a habit. Trust me,' Debu said.

'My stop has come. I will call you from home,' I said and hung up. It gave me an excuse to call him again after a while. Maybe he would be convinced this time?

How desperate are you? mini-me said. *Yes, so I am a little desperate, but only for love. There's nothing wrong in being desperate for love, right?*

At home I sat on the bed and called him again. He took my call. I heard noises in the background.

'I've come out for drinks. With office people. Can we talk later?'

'Talk to me for two minutes, please,' I said. The house felt lonely as hell. I needed him near me, if not in person, then at least on the phone.

'Come on chat. But only two minutes,' he said. Of course, like an obedient slave, I agreed to whatever scraps he offered me.

'Wassup,' he sent me a message.

'How was your day?' I replied.

'Was fine. Is that what you wanted to say?'

'I can't sleep at night.'

'You should.'

'I beg you, come back.'

'Not that again, Radhika. Please. Have told you my decision.'

'What is my fault? Just tell me. I will change myself.'

'It's fine.'

'You want me to not work? Leave my job? Just say it.'

'Do whatever. Your life.'

'Debu, please!'

'Listen, office people here. Got to go. Bye.'

He didn't respond after that. I opened the fridge, found a bottle of white wine, poured myself a big glass. Then another and another.

I sent him a message in my drunken state.

'I love you, Debu.'

He didn't respond.

'I will do anything for you. Nothing else matters,' I sent another one.

'Love you, Debu. More than anyone else,' I continued my message barrage, as the wine inside me meant I had no limits anymore. From desperate I had now moved to full-on pathetic. I saw the 'typing...' notification on WhatsApp. He was going to respond! Joy filled me in anticipation of his response.

'How do you say "stop bothering me" nicely?' came his reply.

I poured myself a fourth glass. I needed to pass out and, well, not bother him anymore.

16

A month after Debu left we closed the Luxvision deal. The China factory site did have real-estate potential. With the right local partners, we could see a good profit on the deal in two years. We had closed a complicated deal. Jonathan wanted to celebrate.

'I am buying a round of drinks. Harry's at 7,' he said to Craig and me in the afternoon.

Craig did thumbs up from his cubicle.

'Radhika, you on?' Jonathan said. I gave him a blank stare. In the last month I had worked on autopilot. I showed up at the Goldman office in the morning, sat in my seat, worked on my computer and left post 8 in the evening. I wanted to reach home as late and as tired as possible. If I had spare time or the energy to think, I would message and call Debu. He had stopped taking my calls or responding to messages sometime back. But it didn't deter me.

I didn't socialize with anyone. I ate cereal with milk from tetrapacks for breakfast and dinner. I skipped lunch. I spoke very little to mom. And when I did I asked her meaningless questions like what she had made for dinner or what the temperature was in Delhi.

I slept no more than two to three hours a night. The rest of the time I stared at the bedroom ceiling or watched American TV infomercials about slimming products promising eternal fitness and happiness.

Hence, when Jonathan asked me a simple question, it didn't register with me.

'You don't have plans this evening, do you?' Jonathan said.

I shook my head. I didn't have plans. *I will never have plans.*

'Come for drinks at Harry's then. Luxvision deal-closing drinks.'

'Sure,' I managed to say.

Of course, heartbreak, alcohol and I are an explosive combination. Everyone celebrated the end of all the hard work on the China deal with champagne and martinis. I drank my glass of wine to kill the pain that just would not go away. I couldn't believe I loved this guy so much. I tried to find reasons to hate him. How he used to sit watching TV doing nothing. How he would not shower on weekends until the evening. How he would scan the menu to order the cheapest dishes. Yeah, he isn't worth it, Radhika, I tried to tell myself. It didn't work. In fact, the things that annoyed me about him made me miss him more. I slipped to one corner of the bar with my second glass of wine. I watched my colleagues chat and laugh from a distance.

I listened to the song playing in the bar. It was Passenger's Let her go.

You only need the light when it is burning low
Only miss the sun when it starts to snow.

How did Passenger know what I was going through? God, I missed Debu. I wanted him to hold me like he did every night. It meant more to me than any stupid job or stupid deal.

'What's up, Radhika?' Jonathan came up to me. 'Come join us.'

'In a bit. Taking it easy. Plus, I like this song.'

Staring at the ceiling in the dark
Same old empty feeling in your heart
Cause love comes slow and it goes so fast.

Jonathan raised his glass. I raised mine as well and touched it to his. *I could quit this job. Sure, that's what Debu wanted.*

'Enjoying yourself in the distressed group?' Jonathan said.

I shrugged. I couldn't pretend to be cheerful anymore.

'What?' Jonathan was puzzled.

'I don't know. I can't really say.'

Even though Jonathan was a colleague, my boss and I totally should not have done this, I burst into tears. *Fuck, why do I cry so much these days?* I swallowed hard to curb my tears. *I am not going to make a fool of myself in front of my coworkers.*

'Anything we can help with?' Jonathan said, surprised.

I shook my head, keeping my gaze down.

If there is one thing Americans understand, it is not to invade someone's personal space. Jonathan figured something was amiss.

'I am going to let you be. Join us if you want to. Okay?'

I nodded.

'Thanks,' I mumbled.

I decided to quit my job. No deal or company or job was worth it.

I only enjoyed all this when I had Debu. I needed love. Unfortunately, Goldman doesn't hand out love at bonus time. I debated whether I should tell Jonathan now. However, he seemed to be having a fun conversation with Craig. I didn't want to spoil anyone's mood.

I did bottoms-up on my third or fourth or fifth glass of wine. I tried to call Debu to tell him about my decision to quit work. He didn't pick up. I decided to tell him face-to-face. I gestured to Jonathan that I needed to go. He gave me an understanding nod.

I came out of Harry's. The wine made me feel weightless, airborne. At a florist kiosk on Wall Street I bought a dozen dark red roses. I checked the time—7.30 p.m.—and hailed a yellow cab.

'Tiffany on Fifth Avenue, please,' I said.

I reached the Tiffany store just a few minutes before its closing time. 'Rings, for men,' I said.

The polite salesperson took out several gold and platinum rings. I chose a classic men's platinum band.

'Excellent choice. That would be 2,000 dollars,' the salesperson said.

I took out my credit card.

'Thank you. Would you like it gift-wrapped?' he said.

'Yes, please,' I said.

I rushed out of the store and hailed another cab.

'Brooklyn Heights, please.'

The taxi took the FDR, crossed Brooklyn Bridge and entered Brooklyn. It took me forty minutes to reach Debu's building. He had moved back to his apartment with his old roommates. The elevator of his building had shut down for temporary repairs so I climbed up the five floors to reach his apartment. I was about to ring the bell but paused. I wanted to give him a complete surprise. I had come with news of a resignation, a bouquet of roses and a ring. I wanted him. I was ready to be his girl, just the way he wanted me to be. I lifted the potted plant outside his house. I found the bunch of house keys under it.

I opened the door. It was dark in the living room. I switched on the lights. I wondered if anyone was home. Two bedrooms had their doors ajar. These belonged to Debu's roommates.

I walked up to the third bedroom—his. I could hear music. Yep, Debu was inside. I knocked twice. I don't think he heard it. Had he slept off while listening to music? I checked the house keys. I tried them one by one on the bedroom door with my right hand since I held the bouquet and the blue Tiffany box in my left. One of the keys worked. I gently opened the door. I just wanted to slip into bed with him. A tiny bedside lamp was switched on. It took me a second to process what I saw: Debu and a white girl lay there naked, intertwined with one another. I couldn't breathe. In hindsight I realize I should have shut the door and dashed out. Instead, I froze.

'What the fuck…' Debu said as he saw me.

'I…I…sorry…sorry…'

'Oh fuck,' the American girl said as she saw me. She had a large tattoo of a bird on her left upper breast. She also had a pierced upper lip. I don't know why I stood there and noticed all this and did not just run out.

'Radhika?' Debu said.

I started to shiver.

'You know her?' the girl said.

'Huh?' Debu said as he visibly wondered what to tell her. 'Used to. What are you doing here, Radhika?'

'Nothing,' I said. My face was on fire with embarrassment. *What the hell was I doing here anyway? With a bouquet and Tiffany box in my hand?*

Then, in a second, I was gone. I turned around and ran out of his house. I don't know if he came after me. I don't think he did. Not that I looked back. I simply ran and ran, down the stairs and on the empty streets. I wanted to disappear into thin air. In the middle of the road I prayed for a cab, but none came.

'Don't cry, don't cry, don't cry, Radhika,' I mumbled, rocking myself. I had to keep it together until I reached home. Or at least until I found a taxi. My hands trembled, my knees wobbled.

'Don't, Radhika,' I said out loud even as I let go. My legs felt weak. I kneeled down on the road and cried. I didn't just cry, I howled. A couple of people from the ground-floor apartments peeped out from their windows to look at me. I didn't care. *Where did I go wrong?* I looked at the sky. *I am sorry, God, but what wrong did I do?*

The image of Debu with the tattooed white girl wouldn't vacate my head.

An NYPD police car came up on the road and stopped near me.

'You all right, lady?' a cop spoke to me from inside the car.

I looked up at him and nodded.

'You live here?'

'No. Tribeca.'

'You want to go home?'

I nodded.

'Come, we can drop you to the subway station.'

I sat in a police car for the first time in my life. Five minutes later, he dropped me at the Clark Street subway stop. I swiped my Metrocard and took the number 2 train to Chambers Street. Like a corpse I reached home. Once inside, I sat on the sofa and looked at my hands; I still had the bouquet and ring. I threw them on the floor and called home.

'I miss you, mom,' I said.

My mother sensed my sad, tired and devastated state.

'What happened, beta?'

'Nothing.'

'Say what happened.'

'Nothing. Just homesick.'

'We miss you too.'

'I love you, mom!'

'Love you too, beta. It's late, sleep now.'

'Goodnight, mom.'

I lay down on the sofa and passed out.

◆

'Hey, what's up, dealmaker? Come on right in,' Jon said as I knocked at his office door.

I came in and sat down in front of him.

'So, Jonathan told me,' Jon said.

'Yeah, I figured,' I said.

'Personal reasons?' Jon said.

I nodded. I had sent in my resignation.

I had really tried to get back to normal. But New York wouldn't let me. Every street, every nook, every inch of Manhattan made me think of him. Hell, I was such a wreck that every advertisement hoarding (because Debu worked in advertising, you see) made my heart sink. Every restaurant menu took me back to dinners with him. Even in my own house the kitchen, the couch, the bed, everything screamed his absence. I had no plan for the future. I only knew I couldn't bear to be a minute more in this city, where I had loved and lost the only man who loved me. I looked out of Jon's window. I saw the Hudson River, and the buildings of Brooklyn past it. Brooklyn—the word itself made my eyes well up.

I swallowed hard. I hate girls who cry in office. Let alone in front of a Goldman Sachs partner. *Don't be a crybaby*, I scolded myself.

'Can I have some water?' I said instead.

'Sure,' Jon said.

I poured myself a glass of water, took a slow sip but the tears slipped out anyway. I lifted the glass higher to cover more of my face. It didn't help. My body shook as I started to cry. Some of the water spilled on his table.

'I am sorry,' I said.

'It's okay,' Jon said. He passed me a box of tissues. If this were an Indian office, the boss would have asked five times what happened, and would require all the gory details. In strait-laced America, no matter what, they let you be, unless you want to share.

'I hope you feel better,' Jon said as I wiped my face.

I nodded.

'Listen, I am not going to tell you what to do. However, you do know how much we value you,' Jon said.

'Yeah,' I said, staring at the glass before me to avoid eye contact.

'So if there is anything we can do to keep you… If you need a long break or time off, anything…'

I shook my head.

'What next?' Jon said.

'I have no idea. Leave New York. Maybe go home.'

'You want to tell me what the issue is?' Jon said.

I kept silent.

'Sorry, it's not my place to ask. You don't have to tell me. Just wanted to help if I could.'

'I can't be in New York,' I said.

'Okay. Do you need to be someplace specific?'

'No. Just not New York. Too much baggage.'

Jon nodded, leaning back on his ergonomic Herman Miller chair.

'A relationship ended. I didn't realize I was this attached. Or it would hurt so much.'

'Hmm…'

Jon was probably wondering how his favourite associate could be so foolish as to leave a job and a city over a guy.

'Now every corner of Manhattan reminds me of him,' I said.

'You could always move to Brooklyn,' he said and smiled, pointing to the window.

He looked at me. Of course his joke had not worked.

'He lives in Brooklyn now,' I said in a plain voice.

'Sorry, sorry. I was just being funny. Didn't work, obviously,' Jon said.

'You probably think I am insane. To throw away a career for a guy. That too a guy who is not with me anymore.'

'I don't judge people. And I know you are not insane.'

'Thanks, Jon. Anyway, I want to thank you. I have had a wonderful experience…' I said as he interrupted me.

'Wait. How about we keep you? But we transfer you?'

'Transfer?'

'To another office within the group.'

'Where?'

'Wherever we have offices. Your last deal was that China one, right?'

'Yeah. Luxvision.'

'So that deal needs to be monitored until we exit. You could do it from Hong Kong. That will get you started. Plus, find new deals there. Asia is growing.'

'Hong Kong?' I said.

'That's as far as it gets from New York by the way, on this planet,' he said and smiled.

'You are saying I could transfer to distressed debt in Hong Kong?' I said.

'I could make some calls,' Jon said. 'See if they can accommodate.'

Jon was being modest; a partner of his stature calling the Hong Kong office meant they would oblige him in a second.

'I know nothing about Hong Kong.'

'Lots of Chinese people,' Jon said. 'Seems like a fun place from what I have seen during my travels.'

'I already submitted my resignation. I sent you an email.'

'I have already deleted it,' Jon said, clicking a button on his computer mouse.

Both of us smiled.

'Thank you, Jon. Thank you so much.'

'I will call Neel. He is the partner there. You know him?' Jon said.

'Not much. He did a session during associate training, right?'

'Smart guy. I will talk to him. How soon can you move?'

'When is the next flight?'

17

'JFK, please,' I said to the cab driver.

I sat in a yellow cab to the airport. It was almost 5 in the evening. Finally, the movers had left and I had surrendered the keys to my Tribeca apartment.

My new job offer had come through, with only one brief call with Neel as an interview. Given Jon's recommendation, Neel said this was a formality and more a 'welcome to Hong Kong' call. Human Resources sent me a new offer. Given the high rents in Hong Kong, they added a housing allowance of 60,000 dollars a year to my base salary.

I had decided to quit and go back to West Delhi with a zero salary. Maybe I would have yielded to my mother's badgering about getting married. I should have been serving tea and mithai in trays to prospective grooms. Instead, I had a welcome brochure from the Goldman Sachs Asia-Pacific Relocation Group in my hand. I might not have love in my life, but I did have Uncle Goldman Sachs taking care of me. The brochure said I would be staying at the Shangri-La Hotel in Hong Kong until I found a new apartment.

The cab passed the Tweed Courthouse near the Manhattan side entrance to the Brooklyn Bridge. From a distance, I could see the skyscrapers of the Financial District. Even though I had wanted to get out of New York at the earliest, I felt a tinge of regret. I had become attached to the city of my firsts—first job, first boyfriend, first independent home and, well, first break-up.

'Could you stop here for a second, please?' I said as the cab reached the bridge.

The driver slowed down the cab.

'Can I walk across the bridge? You can meet me on the other side.'

'The entire bridge? That will take you half an hour.'

'I have time. Can I have your number?'

He gave me a business card with his name and number.

'I am gonna have to keep the meter on,' he said, chewing gum.

'Sure, I will call you when I reach the other side.'

I stepped out of the taxi and climbed the steps up to the pedestrian walkway of the bridge. The Brooklyn Bridge is an old cable-stayed-cum-suspension bridge in New York City. Completed in 1883, it connects the boroughs of Manhattan and Brooklyn by spanning the East River. Around a mile long, it has a pedestrian walkway in the middle, above the automobile lanes.

If you have seen movies set in New York, you would have probably seen scenic shots of the Brooklyn Bridge. I began my walk. The orange-coloured sky at sunset and Manhattan's skyline on my left seemed like a perfect last memory of the city. The peak hour traffic passed below me. I noticed that the bridge with its trusses resembled the Howrah Bridge in Kolkata.

Pain singed my heart; Kolkata reminded me of Debu. I had told myself to not think of him. That's what sucks about love. It takes away your control over your thoughts. Any trigger, anything that somehow could be connected back to Debu, would spark a fire of memories inside me. I just wanted my last walk in the city to be peaceful. Alas, no such luck. I approached Brooklyn. I wondered if Debu would be home already. Or if the tattooed white girl would be waiting for him. One of his roommates had told Avinash, who then told me, that the girl was a waitress at Chipotle, a Mexican fast-food chain. I didn't ask further. I wondered if he loved her so much that he never thought of me. Or did he miss me?

Focus on the walk, breathe, I told myself. *Why doesn't the brain listen once in a while? Why can't it just take in the beautiful view? Isn't it the brain's job to figure out a way to avoid pain? So why is it only generating thoughts that kill me?*

I reached the midpoint of the bridge. Tourists took pictures of the panoramic scenery. I took out my phone to take a last snapshot of New York as well. After I clicked the picture, I opened my WhatsApp. I don't know why I did it, but I checked Debu's profile. He had the same picture as always, of him posing next to The Lake, at Central Park. He was online. I took a deep breath, typed 'Hi' and pressed send.

He read my message but didn't respond. I didn't want him to think I was chasing him again. I typed another message.

'I am leaving New York.'

You know the most annoying thing in the world? When it says 'typing…' on WhatsApp but then the 'typing…' vanishes. I have a cab waiting. *Debu, say what you have to say fast, please,* I said in my head.

'Good' came his response. *Could he be any meaner?* So okay, I had barged into his apartment. I had even entered his bedroom. Sure, he was mad at me. But did he realize that the person he'd lived with for two years was leaving the city, the country or even the continent?

'I meant I am leaving now. On my way to the airport.'

He then did another mean thing you can do on WhatsApp. He sent me a thumbs-up smiley. Who made that stupid smiley? What the fuck is that thumbs-up supposed to mean?

Like an idiot I continued to send message after message. All in the hope of a scrap of emotion or validation. This man had the ability to make me feel wretched in seconds.

'I am moving to Hong Kong.'

'Great. More money for you, I hope.'

Really? He had to say that? I decided to ignore his snide comment.

'So I am leaving New York forever,' I said. I meant, *I love you so much, this is what I have to do to get over you. And I am so lonely and scared, can you please say something nice before I go to a strange country, I beg you.*

He did not respond for a minute. I checked the time. I had to reach the other end soon. I sent him another message to prompt him to respond.

'Just wanted to let you know. No chance of me bothering you now, I guess,' I said. *I am grovelling now. At least say something nice.*

'Thank you for that. This way you can achieve your goals. And I can find someone caring,' he said.

That hurt. I gripped my phone tight, to prevent my fingers from typing again. I like to humiliate myself, but I guess I had to set limits on how much.

No more, I said to myself. I took a deep breath. On an impulse, I tossed my phone into the East River. Tourists around me gasped in disbelief as I tossed a working iPhone into the water. The next minute I felt stupid. However, it ensured I didn't have a phone on me for the next few hours, particularly at the airport. Of course, I could have simply deleted his contact. However, that wouldn't stop me from expecting him to respond or from checking my phone every two minutes. No, I had to toss that humiliation device into the river. People with little emotional self-control must take drastic steps. I resumed my walk towards Brooklyn. As I stared at the wooden pathway, a question crossed my mind.

Damn, how will I reach the cab driver without my phone?

◆

I did manage to find the taxi—by borrowing a tourist's phone and using the card the driver gave me. In twenty minutes we reached JFK airport.

'Terminal 7 please, Cathay Pacific,' I said to the driver as we approached the airport driveway.

I checked in and waited to board in the Cathay Pacific lounge. A part of me felt glad I had lost my phone. If I didn't I would be calling Debu right now. I thought about his curt responses. Couldn't he have said, 'All the best, baby. I am sorry it ended this way'? He could have even sent a 'Let's be in touch. I still care about you'. Was I so horrible? Was he so relieved to be rid of me?

Lost in these thoughts, I boarded the Cathay Pacific plane with its dark green interiors. I sat in the plush business-class seat, courtesy my bank, the only one in the world that seemed to care about me.

A pretty Chinese girl in a fitted red cheongsam dress came up to me. She offered me a glass of champagne. I declined. I had no reason to celebrate. I looked out the window as the plane started to taxi for its long sixteen-hour flight. My eyes filled with tears. I felt lost in my luxurious surroundings. Too sad to stay. Too sad to leave. *Perhaps this is how it will be from now,* I thought. *I will remain sad forever.* The plane took off. I continued to cry as New York became smaller and smaller in my window.

The flight attendant noticed my tears. After the seatbelt signs went off, she came up to me with a hot towel and tissues. I used the hot towel to wipe my face. The heat felt nice on my skin.

'Thank you,' I said.

'Would you like to eat something, ma'am?' she said.

I shook my head.

'Maybe just the starter? We also have a lovely carrot-and-ginger soup.'

I nodded. She pulled out my tray table and placed a white cloth on it. She took another cloth napkin and placed it on my lap. She brought me a tray of food. It contained fresh salad, soup and brown bread. I had not eaten all day. I finished everything on my tray.

Later, she offered a raspberry pudding for dessert. After I ate it all up she brought me hot peppermint tea. I enjoyed her full attention.

Is this the kind of wife men want?

'Ready for bed?' she said.

I nodded. She adjusted my seat and converted it into a flat bed. She placed a white sheet and pillow on it. As I lay down, she draped a quilt over me. I realized something. Debu wasn't the only one. I also wanted someone like this lady to take care of me. Why can't women get a wife?

18

I wiped a tear from the corner of my right eye. A bit of kajal came away on my finger. I sat down on the leg raise machine. Debu continued to look at me with an apologetic expression.

'I have not forgotten anything, Debu. But I don't need to be reminded of it either.'

'I am sorry, baby,' he said and touched my elbow. I pushed his hand away. I stood up to leave.

'I need to go. And you have to stop calling me baby.'

I tried to walk past him. He blocked me.

'What?' I said.

'Please. Stay. Listen to me. Please.'

'What's the point? I have literally a hundred people waiting upstairs.' My phone rang.

'See, it is my sister,' I said.

'Tell her you need ten more minutes.'

'What for?' I placed a finger on my lips to signal Debu to be quiet and answered the call.

'Yeah, didi. I went to the washroom…no, not in the room…I am coming. Give me five minutes…no need to come fetch me…I will come on my own.'

I hung up. I saw Debu. His eyes, his dreamy puppy-dog eyes, continued to look at me.

'What?' I said.

'I made the biggest mistake of my life,' Debu said.

'It doesn't matter,' I said. Even though I said it didn't matter, I did feel good inside. At least he finally felt some regret.

'You were the best thing that happened to me. Seriously,' Debu said.

'Why? That white chick didn't work out?'

'Who?'

'That girl. Who was with you when I…'

'No. We tried. There was no intellectual match.'

'Oh, you care about a girl's intellect too now?'

'Of course I do. I always did. That is why I liked you.'

'That is also why you dumped me.'

'I told you. I made a mistake. A big mistake. Monumental mistake.'

'You said my job would harden me. What else did you say? You had a vision for the mother of your kids. You wanted me to quit working.'

'I am sorry. I became a little insecure.'

'Oh, really? Now you realize it! You weren't a little insecure. You were monumentally insecure.'

I realized my volume had increased. A body-builder-type white guy stared at us through his bicep curls.

'Do you have any idea how much I loved you?' I said.

He kept quiet, his head down. I noticed the thick curls on his head. I continued, 'I was ready to quit my job. Just to make you happy. I came to Brooklyn to tell you I would resign. I wanted to propose to you that night. You wanted a simple family. I was game. I even bought a ring.'

'You did?' he said, looking up, his eyes wide.

I shook my head.

'All pointless, Debu. My family is upstairs. Can I go now? And I suggest you leave Goa soon too.'

He grabbed my hand. I extracted it, almost in reflex.

'What are you doing, Debu? My would-be in-laws are in this hotel.'

'I know. I just...' And then he did something I have never seen him do. He started to cry. Puzzled gym trainers must have been wondering why a grown-up man was crying in their gym even before he had begun to exercise.

'Don't make a scene, Debu,' I said. I tried to remain unaffected, but to see him cry like this choked me. He knelt on the floor.

'Please, baby. Please, I beg you,' Debu said. 'I have come all the way from New York.'

I looked around. The last thing I wanted was anyone noticing us.

I held Debu by the shoulders.

'Get up, please.' I pulled him up.

I handed him one of the hand towels kept in the gym. He used it to wipe his face and compose himself.

'Stop being the victim here, Debu. Remember how you treated me? You would not take my calls. You were rude on messages.'

He nodded his head vigorously.

'You were, you were...' I searched for the right word.

'An asshole. Yes,' he said.

'Good. So now, you are doing these tears and trips. But how did you treat me earlier? Even on my last day. I still remember. You sent me a thumbs-up smiley. That's it.'

'I said "I will miss you" ten minutes later. You didn't reply.'

'You did?'

'Yeah. Why didn't you reply?'

'I tossed my phone in the river.'

'What?' I shook my head and threw my hands up.

'No point digging up the past.'

'Why not? After you, I tried to be with several people. I dated other girls. Nobody connected with me like you did. Nobody had the complete package of qualities like you. You are smart, caring and humble. You are easy to live with. You kept our little apartment so well. I still remember how you gave me that surprise party when I got a promotion. Which girl does that?'

Anger filled me. I wanted to slap him. My arm tightened.

'What? You want to slap me, right? Do it.'

I looked around. Everybody seemed busy with their own exercises. I lifted my hand and slapped him hard across his cheek.

'Ow!' he howled. 'You actually slapped me?'

I flexed my fingers; my hand hurt.

'Now you tell me all that? You couldn't say it earlier? I gave you surprise parties, yes. But how did you react when I got my first bonus?'

'Like a dick.'

'Exactly. Where did your feminism go?'

'My feminism didn't go anywhere. My masculinity did. I told you, I felt insecure. How can my girl make three times as much as I do?'

'So what? I work in a bank. It pays better. You chose your passion, advertising. Why did you have to compare? Wasn't it all our money?'

My phone rang again. This was my mother.

'Bye, Debu.'

'Two minutes. Please.'

I cut the call.

'What?' I said.

'I didn't value you. I am sorry. I had to lose you to realize how amazing you were. Like that Passenger song. Let her go.'

I knew that song. I had cried to it. I wanted to tell him but I didn't.

I took deep breaths to not lose it again. I had to remain serene for dinner, like a good Indian bride should be after bhajans.

'Well, too bad. Anything else? Have a safe trip back otherwise,' I said.

'I have a plan,' he said.

'Plan?'

'Yeah. Swap the groom.'

'What?' I said, my hands on my hips.

'I understand you have your entire family here. You can't stop the wedding. But I am ready. I want to marry you right here in Goa. I will call my parents from Kolkata, maybe some close relatives and...'

I cut him short.

'Hold on there. What did you say? We get married? Right here?'

'Ask yourself, Radhika. I am your first love. Sure, I made a mistake. But I want to amend it. I want you more than anything else in the world. So I can get married now. Your parents will freak, but at least they'll know it is not a cancelled wedding. The boy's side, yes, they will be upset too. But I will handle it.'

'You have really thought it all out.'

'I had time on the long flight here. I realized I couldn't lose you at any cost.'

'And what makes you think I want to marry you?'

'Because I know. Deep down, you still have feelings for me. I will keep you happy, Radhika. Do whatever you want. Just be with me.'

I sat back on the leg press machine again. I covered my face with my palms; this wasn't happening. No, I couldn't be facing this. *This is a horrible dream*, I told myself. *When I remove my hands from my face, Debu will be gone*.

However, he stood there, looking at me like he did years ago when we first fell in love.

'Just agree and I will handle everything else.'

'This is not a joke, Debu. My entire family, Brijesh's entire family, is here.'

'Brijesh is the person you are getting married to?'

'Yes,' I said.

Did I just show that I was considering Debu's idea? Was it just about how to manage the family embarrassment now?

'I am here for you. We can go back to how we were. Remember our tiny apartment?'

'Of course,' I said, my voice softening.

My phone rang again.

'They will send search parties for me!'

'I will wait for you. Will you think about this and let me know?' Debu said.

'I don't know. My mind is not working. I better go.'

'I am in the resort across the road. They didn't have rooms here at the Marriott.'

'I know,' I said. *Thank God for small mercies.*

◆

Day four

'How are you?' Brijesh smiled at me. We were on the sandy beach for an early morning stroll. When he'd asked me out on a morning walk the previous night, he said he wanted to catch up before the relatives woke up.

'Sleepy,' I said and yawned. I checked the time: 6.30.

'I am sorry. I shouldn't have kept it so early,' he said.

'No, it's fine. Once people wake up, chaos begins,' I said

I had worn pink lycra leggings and a white top. He wore a grey tracksuit. We were both barefoot. Occasionally, the waves would splash high and run through our toes.

'Didn't sleep enough?' he said.

'Four hours. It is okay,' I said. Sleep deprivation delayed my reactions to recent events. Debu had flooded me with messages all night, right from reminding me of our first date to asking me how long before I took a decision.

'The bhajans were wonderful. Such a great idea,' Brijesh said.

'My mother's idea, actually,' I said.

'Yeah, it just makes the whole event more pure,' Brijesh said.

Sure, especially pure if the bride goes to the hotel gym to make escape plans with her ex-boyfriend.

'Mehndi today then?' Brijesh said.

'Yeah,' I said. 'Not much for you to do.'

'Oh, they have plans for me too. They will apply turmeric paste all over me.'

'Marinating the groom before the roast?'

Both of us laughed.

He held my hand; I didn't protest. How could I? We were getting married. He clasped it tighter, and although it felt a bit weird, I held his hand too, not merely leaving my hand in his. I wanted support, perhaps, to decide what I needed to do.

'You happy?' Brijesh said.

I looked at him. His smile was childlike. He was visibly thrilled to hold my hand.

'Yes, I am happy, Brijesh,' I said. To make others feel better, women lie about their feelings all the time. It's amazing how easily it comes to us.

'So I told you about Menlo Park, right? I thought we could take a place there or near the Goldman office. That way, at least one of us can be home quickly if necessary.'

'Sounds good,' I said absently.

'Although, if my start-up happens, I don't have to be in Menlo. We could be near your office in that case. If I ever take that step, though.'

'I am sure you will,' I said.

He shrugged his shoulders. The morning sun was on our faces. I had worked hard to remain on a plan of regular diet and exercise before the wedding. I hoped I didn't look fat in my tight workout clothes.

'You are beautiful,' Brijesh said, as if reading my mind.

I don't know why, but I laughed. I suck at receiving compliments anyway, and laughing in the compliment-giver's face is another way of deflecting them.

'Did I say something wrong?' Brijesh said.

'No,' I said and smiled. 'Thank you.'

'I have never said this to a girl. Ever,' he said.

I looked at him. He looked like an earnest schoolboy, even though he could work the world's most complicated computers.

'Well, I should be flattered then,' I said.

We walked in silence. After a few minutes I checked my phone. It had a message from Debu.

'Good morning, beautiful.'

'Who is it?' Brijesh said.

'Huh? Nothing. Didi woke up and is looking for me.'

'Really?'

'Yeah, let's go back,' I said.

'I thought we could have breakfast outside. At a beach shack. Just us,' Brijesh said.

My phone buzzed again.

'I love you,' Debu had sent another message.

I released Brijesh's hand. I couldn't hold my groom-to-be with one hand and use the other to check love messages from my ex.

'We better get back,' I said.

'Anything happened?'

I nodded. Brijesh didn't say anything after that. We walked back to the hotel. I kept a little distance from him, so he couldn't hold my hand again. I held my phone tight and ignored any incoming messages.

We reached the hotel elevator for my wing. I turned to him before I stepped into the lift.

'Sorry, Brijesh. I know you're making an effort so we get to know each other better. I am trying too. But somehow I just can't right now. Too much on my mind.'

He smiled.

'We will have plenty of time after marriage.'

'You are very sweet,' I said

He blushed as he hid his smile. Oh, it would kill me if I had to stab him in the back and run away with someone else. Why couldn't Brijesh be an evil groom? Like the ones in the movies, the ones who shoot innocent pigeons for fun?

I waved him goodbye.

'See you at mehndi,' he said.

'No boys allowed there, mister,' I said.

He smiled. I gave him an extra-wide, almost fake smile in return. Thankfully, the elevator door shut. I heaved a huge sigh of relief as Brijesh disappeared from sight.

'God help me,' I said as the lift started to climb up the floors.

19

'Put your phone aside, Radhika didi. How will he apply the mehndi?' Sweety, my eighteen-year-old cousin, said.

Four mehndiwallahs had set up stalls in the function room. Suraj had also arranged for a bangle stall. The function room turned into a stock exchange of hotly traded gossip as women of all ages assembled to apply mehndi and choose bangles. Waiters served hot masala tea along with snacks like mini samosas and jalebis. As women waited their turn, they discussed topics ranging from the latest lehenga trends to the creepiest uncles to who slept with whom in Bollywood.

I had a dedicated mehndiwallah called Puran Singh. He claimed to be an artist who only specialized in bridal mehndi.

'You would not have seen any dulhan with such beautiful mehndi,' Puran said as he went to work at a slow pace. The other mehndiwallahs worked at triple the speed with my cousins.

'I can use the phone with one hand, see,' I said to Sweety.

I used my right hand as he applied mehndi on my left.

'Who are you messaging? Brijesh bhaiya?' Jyoti, my second cousin, said. Everyone burst into laughter.

'Are you excited about the first night? What will you do?' Sweety said. Everyone giggled again.

'My sister is innocent. Please don't corrupt her,' Aditi didi said. According to her, I was clueless about men. It was partly my fault. I hadn't told them about my relationships. I couldn't. Neither Aditi didi nor my mom would get it. For them relationships meant one thing—to get married as fast as possible.

Saloni, Aditi didi's best friend, held my chin.

'You know what will happen on the first night? Do you have any experience?'

Well, does having regular sex for several years count?

I shook my head. I could at least try to be the demure bride.

'Come, I will tell you,' Saloni didi said. She brought her mouth close to my ear.

'Just drive him crazy. Tear off all his clothes and drive him crazy,' she whispered.

It was supposed to be an outrageous statement. I was supposed to get embarrassed. I played the part and blushed, so my cousins and friends could enjoy the show. I hid my face in Saloni didi's shoulders. I don't know why I did that. *Just to entertain the crowd? Or to make them believe I was actually 'innocent'? Why do I have to be this fake?*

The girls finally left me alone as their turn came with the other mehndiwallahs. I checked my phone.

'Baby, I am waiting,' Debu had sent me on WhatsApp.

'I know,' I replied.

'It's not that difficult. Just tell them you have another guy.'

'Whom do I tell?'

'Anyone. Your mother. Your sister.'

'Is this a good idea, Debu? I am really confused.'

'It's love, baby. It's meant to be confusing. Even I was about you. But now I am sure. I want you to be Mrs Radhika Sen.'

The name Mrs Radhika Sen made me squirm a little.

'Madam, don't move so much,' the mehndi guy said as I furiously typed with my right hand.

'Not sure if I will change my surname.'

'Don't,' he said.

I didn't respond. He typed after a minute.

'Is that a yes, though?'

'I don't know, Debu. I am at my mehndi. Hard to use the phone too.'

'Baby, please, just say yes.'

I kept the phone aside.

'I have been doing this for twenty years. You have the most beautiful hands of them all,' Puran said.

'You say this to every bride?' I said.

He looked at me and smiled, showing his paan-stained teeth.

'Actually, yes.'

I smiled back, shaking my head. My phone buzzed again.

'Your left hand is almost done. Will need the other one soon,' Puran said.

I nodded and checked my phone. The message had not come from Debu. It came from an unknown international number. It began with '+852', the code for Hong Kong.

'Hi. It's Neel,' the message said.

'Madam, can I have your other hand? And don't move your left hand now. It has fresh mehndi,' Puran said.

'Give me one minute,' I said to the mehndiwallah.

'Hi, Neel,' I replied.

'I heard you are getting married. In Goa.'

'Yeah.'

'Cool. Office people told me.'

'Yes. What's up?'

'I am in Sri Lanka. Due diligence on a deal.'

'Okay.'

'Can I call you?'

'Radhika, focus on your mehndi or I will kidnap your phone again,' Aditi didi said.

'Ten seconds,' I implored Aditi didi.

'Too caught up right now,' I typed back.

I pressed send. I kept the phone aside on the cushion next to me. Puran held my right hand and started to apply mehndi. He had spent two hours to make an intricate floral pattern on my left hand. He needed the same time on my right.

My phone screen lit up on the beautiful cushion. I had another message.

'It's urgent,' Neel said.

I couldn't respond. I did not have any hand free.

He called. I used my pinkie finger to disconnect the call.

He sent another message, 'Listen, please talk to me for two minutes.'

I couldn't. How do I tell him? He continued to send me messages, one after the other.

'Don't move, Radhikaji,' Puran said.

Neel continued with his messages.

'I have a lot to tell you.'

'Been meaning to reach you sooner.'

'Are you going to reply at least?'

I can't, I screamed in my head as Puran Singh drew an intricate circle on my right palm with henna paste. The messages kept popping up.

'You know what. This can't be done on chat.'

'Or even on a call.'

'Some things are just better discussed face-to-face.'

'So maybe I should do that.'

'Yeah.'

'Okay then. You are reading my messages but not responding.'

'So yeah. Face-to-face.'

I sat there, exasperated and helpless.

'Bhaiya, can you hurry up?' I said to Puran.

'It is shaadi ki mehndi. How can you hurry it up? You saw your left hand? I have to make this equally beautiful.'

I saw my phone flicker every few seconds.

'Damn,' I mumbled to myself. I had to respond before he did anything crazy. I had enough on my plate already.

'There you go,' Puran said after two hours.

'Thank you. Thank you so much. Can I go now?'

'Yes. But you won't give me any special gift?'

I gestured to my sister. She gave the mehndi guy a 2,000-rupee tip. He smiled and folded his hands to say thanks.

'Don't wash your hands for four hours. Will make the colour last beyond the honeymoon,' Puran said.

'Did you say four hours?' I said.

◆

I told my cousins I needed to use the restroom. I ran up to my room. Aditi didi followed me there.

'How will you use the restroom with your hands like this? Come here,' she said.

Aditi didi unfastened my salwar drawstrings.

'I will come in with you?' she said, pointing to the bathroom.

'Fuck it. I am washing my hands,' I said.

'No, wait...'

I ran into the bathroom. I placed my hands under the running water at the washbasin tap. The mehndi stains were dark orange rather than the deep dark brown I could have achieved had I shown more patience. However, I needed my fingers. I had to respond to Neel and prevent another layer of chaos in my life.

'Hey. Sorry. Couldn't respond earlier,' I hurriedly typed a reply.

'It's okay,' Neel replied in an instant.

'What's up?' I said.

He called me. I picked up the call in the bathroom.

'Hi,' I said.

'It's been so long since I heard your voice.'

'What's the matter, Neel?'

'How are you?'

'Can you hurry up, please? What is it?'

'I have something important to tell you.'

'What?'

'Like I told you, it is better in person.'

'Not pōssible. Just tell me.'

'You are in Goa, right? Which resort?'

'Neel, I am with 200 people here. Can this wait?'

'Which resort? Or should I call your office to find out?'

'Just tell me what you have to. I am at my wedding. You are on due diligence.'

'Yeah, at some remote copper mine in the south of Sri Lanka. Don't ask. No flights from here. Wait, let me check my computer.'

Aditi didi knocked on the bathroom door.

'Seriously, Neel, I have to go. Bye.'

'Okay, bye. Congratulations,' he said.

'Oh well. Whatever. Bye now.'

I came out of the bathroom.

'What? You washed away the mehndi?' Aditi didi said.

'It's still a strong colour,' I said. I began to change into my workout clothes.

'It's your wedding mehndi. You couldn't be patient for a few hours?'

'Sorry, didi. I am not as nice a girl as you. Okay?' I said, irritated.

'Arey? Why are you snapping at me? And why are you changing into these clothes?'

'Sorry for being rude, didi. I just need to get some air. I am going for a walk on the beach.'

'With whom?'

'Alone.'

'Why? I will come with you.'

'No, didi,' I said, my voice firm. 'I want to be alone. No Brijesh. No you. No mom and dad. Can I get an hour? I need to clear my head.'

Aditi didi came and patted my cheek.

'What happened?'

'Nothing. All this wedding stuff is just too much. I need an hour.'

She gave me a hug.

'Go. I will cover for you.'

◆

I walked on the beach outside Marriott. I continued further north until I had left the hotel behind. I saw that Brijesh had messaged me. I decided not to open it. I couldn't deal with anyone. I focused on the orange sun, which sank deeper into the water every minute. My mind was filled with thoughts. *How did Neel find out? Oh well, it isn't difficult if you work in the same firm, even if in different offices. What's he doing in Sri Lanka? Making even more money, I guess. Why did he call me? Why didn't he tell me what he wanted to? What's with all the suspense?*

'Radhika,' a voice from behind startled me.

'Debu?' I turned around. He wore a white printed T-shirt and Bermuda shorts. He came running to me, huffing and puffing as he caught his breath.

'Are you following me?' I said.

'No. I stay in that property,' he said and pointed to a hotel building at a distance.

'Don't stalk me.'

'I am not...'

'Oh really?'

'I am just waiting for your reply. I hung out at the beach all day. Honestly, I saw you alone so I couldn't resist. Sorry.'

I looked around.

'I don't want anyone to see us,' I said.

'There's a shack on the other side, nobody will find us. Can we talk?' he said.

'No, Debu.'

'Please,' he said.

I checked the time on my phone.

'Ten minutes,' I said.

We went to King's Shack on Miramar beach. We sat on sea-facing cane chairs. The evening sea breeze cooled our skin. He ordered a beer.

I had a glass of water.

'How was your day?' he said.

I showed him the mehndi on my hands.

'That's pretty.'

'Thanks. What did you do?'

He lifted the left sleeve of his T-shirt. He had a two-inch tattoo on his upper arm. It said 'Radhika'.

'What the hell, Debu?' I said.

'I had nothing to do all day. I decided to get one. I should have done it a long time ago.'

'You are getting tattoos with my name while I get married to another man? Have you gone mad?'

'I love you, Radhika. Call it madness if you want.'

It is not just what Debu says. It's how he says it. It can make even the most hardened bitch of a heart melt. He placed one hand on his chest and looked at me with his drooping eyes. He brought forward his hand to hold mine. I shook my head. He withdrew.

'Please, baby,' Debu said, 'one more chance.'

'I have to go back,' I said. I signalled the waiter to give us the bill.

'I have made the plan. You break the news to the family just one day before your wedding. I will have my parents, aunts, uncles and cousins come down. My parents will do the talking with yours. Don't worry. You just handle the boy's side.'

'Me?'

'Yeah. Don't give them too much time to react. Just say you can't do this and they can leave. You don't have to tell them about me until our wedding is over.'

My heart started to beat at turbo speed.

'Debu,' I said.

'It sounds crazy, baby, but this is the only way. Your relatives will murmur a bit, but at least they won't say that the wedding was cancelled. As for the boy's side, who cares? We will be in New York in no time.'

'What?'

'You can get a transfer back to New York, right? Or if you want to remain in London, I can come there. Will do whatever you say. I am sure you are in an important role now.'

'Debu, what are you talking about? All this…okay, now I need to go,' I said.

I stood up and walked out of the restaurant. He followed me. He came up close behind me and whispered, 'Have faith in me, baby.'

My phone rang. Brijesh. I stepped aside to take the call.

'Hey,' I said.

'I sent you a message.'

'Sorry, I didn't see.'

'Where are you now?'

'I'm,' I said and wondered what to say, 'around. Just around only.'

'Another sunset walk? Like yesterday?'

Debu went back to pay the bill and smiled at me from a distance. I spoke to Brijesh. 'No, I don't want to go for a walk.'

'Oh okay,' Brijesh said, disappointed.

'But I need a drink,' I said.

'There's that open air lounge in the Marriott…' he said as I interrupted him.

'No, away from the Marriott. Somewhere else. I need to get away,' I said.

'Should I ask for a car?'

'I want some fresh air. Also, I don't want to go with a driver. Can you arrange a bike?'

'You mean one of those rental Activas?'

'Yeah. Can you ride one of those?'

'Well, yes. I did in college.'

'Good. See me outside the Marriott in fifteen minutes.'

I hung up.

'All good, baby?' Debu said, coming out of the shack.

'I am going out with Brijesh,' I said.

'Oh,' he said, sounding disheartened.

'I am not doing this to hurt you.'

'You can hurt me. I hurt you as well. But please think. This is about our future. You can't be with a guy you don't love.'

'All this is messing me up, Debu. I need to breathe.'

'Sure, baby. Take your time.'

'Thanks. Now don't come near me. Stay put for five minutes while I walk away.'

He nodded. He opened his arms wide, asking for a hug. I looked around. Nobody could see us. I hugged him. He wouldn't release me.

'It feels so nice to hold you, baby,' he whispered.

'It's enough, leave me now. Please,' I said in a soft voice.

20

'Careful,' I said. The Activa wobbled on the bumpy road as we came out of the Marriott driveway.

'I haven't ridden one of these in five years,' Brijesh said. I wondered if I should hold him from behind. I could, considering I would be his wife in three days. However, I didn't want him to think I was too easy either. I kept my hands on his shoulders instead.

We passed through a narrow road between rice fields. He went fast. The breeze made my hair fly all over my face.

'This is fun,' I said.

'Great idea, Radhika,' Brijesh said. 'Dump the relatives. Do our own thing.'

'Where are we going?' I said.

'Anjuna. That's where we hung out when we came on a college trip.'

Thirty minutes later, we reached the rocky Anjuna beach and parked the bike. We walked for five minutes and reached a shack called Curlies. We sat on adjacent easy chairs, both of us facing the Arabian Sea. I removed my sneakers to rest my feet on the sandy floor of Curlies.

'Beer?' Brijesh said.

'Sure,' I said. He asked a waiter to bring us two Kingfishers. Two tables away, I saw another Indian couple. The girl wore red and white bangles on both hands, a wedding chudaa; they had just gotten married. Must be their honeymoon. They held hands, but it seemed a little awkward. Arranged marriage, maybe. I looked at Brijesh. We would be a married couple too by this weekend. Brijesh smiled as he handed me a half-pint Kingfisher bottle.

'What did you tell your folks?' Brijesh said.

'I told Aditi didi that I am going for a walk with you.'

'They don't know you are at Anjuna?'

'No,' I said, 'mom will freak out.'

I sipped my beer.

We watched the sun go down. A young singer at Curlies sang and played the guitar. The Goan sunset became even more poignant with the music. The singer sang Justin Bieber's song, Sorry.

Is it too late now to say sorry?
Yeah, I know that I let you down
Is it too late to say I'm sorry now?

The song made me think of Debu. He had come all the way from New York. Sure, he had been a jerk. But don't people make mistakes? Wouldn't most men react the same way if their girlfriend earned triple their salary? *All he wants now is to marry me. Doesn't he deserve a chance?*

'You seem lost,' Brijesh said. 'Am I so boring?'

I shook my head. I scolded myself for letting my mind go back to Debu again and again. *And why am I rationalizing his behaviour so much? Is it again my female manufacturing defect, saying things like 'But isn't that what most men would do'?*

Focus on the man you are with right now, mini-me screamed at me.

'No, you are not boring. It's a lovely place. Thanks, Brijesh,' I said.

I still didn't like his name. Hated it, in fact. Why did it have to be so unfashionable? 'Meet my husband, Debashish Sen' versus 'Meet my husband, Brijesh Gulati'. Eww.

Girl, stop daydreaming.

'We came to Goa on a mechanical engineering college field trip.'

'Engineering field trip to Goa?' I said.

'Well, we convinced the college authorities there's enough industry in Goa.'

'Like draught-beer-brewing machines?' I said.

He laughed. 'I admit it was a bit of a fraud. But we did visit the Goa Shipyard and Vedanta's iron ore facility.'

'For ten minutes?'

'Fifteen minutes. Rest on the beaches. But hey, we submitted a report and everything.'

I took another sip of beer.

'This is what happens at NIT? Goa trips in the name of industry visits?' I tut-tutted.

'Some of our classmates did go to the Bhilai Steel Plant. They hate us till today.'

We laughed together. *Okay, I can do this,* I told myself. He may not be the most interesting guy around, but the engineering college stories did make him more human.

'You seem to have had fun in college.'

'I'm not as boring as you think.'

'I didn't say you are.'

'Actually, I am. Particularly when it comes to talking to women. But with the boys, I did have fun.'

'Yeah? You like boys?' I said and winked at him.

'No...no I meant...' he said and blushed.

I laughed. 'I am teasing you.'

'I know. Sorry. You got me.'

'You think women are different?' I said.

He shrugged.

'They are, right? Women are not like men,' he said.

'Well, in some ways not. But in many ways, yes.'

'Of course, we are all people. People are the same,' he said.

I tried not to stare at him too much. I wondered if he ever thought about things like gender equality.

'Brijesh, do you know what is a feminist?'

'Sort of. But what exactly is it?' he said and blinked his eyes. He genuinely didn't seem to know.

'You haven't heard the word "feminist"?'

'Of course I have. I sort of know what it is. Equal rights for women, right? Is that the definition?'

'Feminism is a movement that seeks to define, establish and achieve equal political, economic, cultural, personal and social rights for women. A feminist is someone who believes in this movement.'

'Wow,' he said.

'What wow?'

'The way you said the definition. It's cool.'

'Thanks. But are you one?'

'Never really thought about it. Never faced a situation where I had to be one. But I guess, yes.'

'You are?' I said.

'I think all human beings should have equal rights. It's not men versus women, it's human versus human. Feminist is a wrong term. It should be humanist. The right question is "Are you a humanist?" Well, everyone should be,' he said.

'True,' I said.

'Are you a feminist, Radhika?'

'What do you mean? I am a woman.'

'Not all women are feminists.'

'Really?'

'Mothers who treat sons better than daughters. Are they feminists?'

'No,' I said.

'Women who judge other working women as not being good enough mothers. Are they feminists?'

'No. I see your point. Yes, I consider myself a feminist,' I said.

'Can I say something?'

'Sure.'

'I don't think anyone has to specifically call himself or herself a feminist. If you are a fair person and want equal opportunities for all, that's a start.'

I looked at him and smiled.

The waiter brought us another round of beer. The sun had vanished, leaving behind a dark grey sky. We watched the waves splash on the beachfront.

'What else did you do in Goa on your field trip?' I said.

'Stuff. Stuff you don't want to know.'

I got interested. 'Oh, really. Like what?'

'Nothing.'

'Try me.'

'Okay, checking out all the firang women on all the beaches.'

'You mean leching at them?'

'Of course not. I would call it more a studied observation,' he said.

I laughed.

'Engineers are sick,' I said.

'They are. Deprivation does that to us.'

'What else?'

'We smoked up.'

'What? Weed?'

He nodded.

'You had weed in Goa?' I said.

'Yeah. You can get it at Anjuna. There are some shops behind the shack. I don't know if they still operate. But we scored from there.'

'Mr Brijesh Gulati, you do have a past.'

He laughed. 'Most of it is around studying to top the class and get a scholarship to the USA. But yes, we did some fun stuff.'

'Should we try some?'

'You want to smoke weed? Now?' he said, startled.

'Yeah. Or is it too much for a good Indian bride to smoke a joint a couple of days before the wedding?'

'No, no, nothing like that.'

'Too feminist?'

'No, Radhika. Nothing like that. How can we smoke up? We have all our relatives here.'

'Not at Anjuna. See if you can get some.'

He looked at me. I gave him a wicked grin. He stood up.

'Give me fifteen minutes,' he said.

◆

'Come behind the rocks. Nobody will see us,' Brijesh said as I took a drag

We had left Curlies and come up to a remote corner on Anjuna beach. Brijesh rolled three joints. We started with our first one.

'You have done this before?' he said.

'No, but I always wanted to try,' I said.

'Go slow,' he said.

With each drag my mind became more calm, my senses more numb. The stress of Debu hovering around the Marriott went up in smoke. Brijesh also didn't feel as unfamiliar.

'Wow, this reminds me of my college days,' he said.

'Bet your parents never thought this is the kind of bahu they are getting,' I said.

He shrugged.

'What kind of bahu?'

'This kind. Smoking up on the beach before her wedding. It's not what good Indian bahus do.'

'If their son can do this, why can't the bahu?' he said.

'Now that is feminism,' I said and high-fived him.

'Everything doesn't need hi-fi labels like feminism. Just logic. If I can do it, you can do it.'

'You are sweet.'

'Isn't sweet the word women use when they aren't attracted to a guy but don't want to hurt him either?'

'Smart you are, Mr Facebook. Not too duh about girls.'

'Well, in this aspect I am good. Been Mr Sweet all my life.'

'Sweet is good,' I said and took the last puff of the joint.

He smiled.

'Shall we head back? It will get late,' he said.

'Yeah. Save those two joints for the Marriott. We will need them.'

We rode back on the Activa. This time I held him around the waist. Maybe it was the beer and the joint, but it didn't feel odd. We passed through the same rice fields, now invisible in the darkness. The headlight of the Activa showed us the road. We stopped at a crossroads to confirm the way.

'We take a right from here, yes?' I said, placing my chin on his shoulder.

'Yeah,' he said.

As we turned, we passed two cops at a checkpoint. They stopped us.

'Licence,' one of the cops said.

Brijesh stood up from the Activa and sifted through his pockets. He took out his wallet and checked inside. He couldn't find it.

'Oh, I think I kept it in the hotel safe,' he said.

'What?' the cop said.

'I have a California licence. From the USA. I left it at the hotel, sorry.'

The cops looked at each other.

'We have to fine you,' one cop said. He took out a challan booklet.

The other cop turned to me.

'Madam, this is not right. You should not drive without a licence.'

'We are tourists. Sorry.'

We had to pay a fine of 400 rupees. Brijesh took out a 1,000-rupee note from his wallet. The cops gave him the change. As Brijesh put the wallet back in his pocket, a small paper bundle fell out.

'You dropped something,' the cop said and picked it up. He held it in his hand and brought it closer to his face. He sniffed at it once, and gave it to his colleague.

Damn.

'Can both of you step aside, please? Give us the Activa keys.'

'What's the matter?' I said.

He lifted up the paper packet.

'This is marijuana. It is illegal. We need to take you to the police station.'

21

'Anjuna police station, mom. Opposite Children's Park. The driver will know. Please come quietly with dad. Don't tell any of the relatives.'

'What are you doing in the police station?' my mother said, her voice hysterical.

'Stop shouting, mom. I am here with Brijesh.'

'Brijesh? Brijesh and you are at the police station? Why?'

'If you come here I can tell you. Bring dad, okay?'

'What about Brijesh's parents?' mom said.

'He has called them separately. They are coming too.'

'Oh God. What is going on? Are you safe?'

'Yes. Mom, Brijesh didn't have a licence.'

'Licence? Why?'

'We went for a ride on an Activa.'

'Activa? There are so many cars we have hired.'

'Mom, just come.'

I hung up the phone. Brijesh sat next to me. Sub-inspector Samuel D'Souza sat in front of us.

'Where did you buy it?'

'It's common in the lanes of Anjuna beach. I am sure you know,' Brijesh said.

'Are you suggesting we know and do nothing about it?'

'No sir,' I said. 'Sorry.'

I elbowed Brijesh to be quiet.

'When is the wedding?' the sub-inspector said.

'Friday,' I said.

'In two days. And this is how you start your married life. Doing drugs?'

'It's not a drug, sir. It's mild herbal stuff. In fact, in California it is legal,' Brijesh said.

The sub-inspector gave us a stern look.

'Is this California?' he said.

'No, sir,' Brijesh said, head down.

'What is this place?'

'Goa, sir.'

'What do people come here to do?' the sub-inspector said.

'To party, sir?' Brijesh said, in a soft voice.

'No,' the sub-inspector shouted. 'People come here to have a good, clean, peaceful holiday. Not to do this nonsense.'

'Yes, sir,' Brijesh said, his tone apologetic.

I pressed my teeth tight to prevent a smile. A snigger slipped out. The inspector turned to me.

'Are you finding this funny?' Sub-inspector D'Souza said.

'No, sir,' I said, keeping a straight face.

Brijesh's and my parents entered the police station. They saw us, sitting across from the sub-inspector.

'What happened, inspector?' my father said.

'Are you the parents? Come see what your children are up to,' Sub-inspector D'Souza said.

◆

'You are too much, Radhika,' my mother said. I sat in a car with my parents. Brijesh sat in a separate car with his own folks. The naughty kids had to be separated, I guess, as we made our way back to the hotel.

'I am sorry, mom,' I said for the seventh time, 'and thank you, dad.'

My father had finally made the cops thaw. Dad figured out a contact in State Bank of India in Goa, who in turn knew the police commissioner of the state. A few calls, tons of apologies and a wedding invitation to the entire police station was what it took to finally make the sub-inspector melt.

'Both of you are going to start a life together. Have kids together. Is this how mature adults are expected to behave?' the sub-inspector said before we left. My father kept quiet as he sat in the front seat of the car. My mother continued to talk. 'I have never heard of any girl drinking and smoking drugs before her wedding. Never.'

I kept quiet. She continued, 'If our relatives find out, what will they think? Out-of-control girl.'

I wanted to react. However, I clenched my fists tight to restrain myself. She didn't stop.

'What will the Gulatis think?' she said. 'They must be questioning their decision tonight.'

'Okay, mom, that is enough,' I said.

'What enough? Drinking beer. Having charas-ganja. Is this even a girl?'

'Their son did the same.'

'So?'

'What do you mean, so? Why aren't you saying they must be ashamed of their son too?'

'He is a boy. He will do his mischief. Why do you have to do the same? Is this your so-called equality?'

'Mom. It's done. Can we please be quiet until we get to the hotel?'

She faced me with folded hands.

'I can be quiet. But you also have to behave. I beg you. Can you please control yourself until your wedding?'

'And what after that?' I said. 'I am no longer your headache?'

She glared at me. I looked away.

'Will you behave?' she said finally.

'Okay fine,' I said.

'Good.'

We reached the hotel. All of us got out of the car.

'Sorry, dad,' I said to him.

'I trust you to make the right choices, beta. Don't embarrass us.'

◆

I sat on the bed, well past midnight. Aditi didi lay down next to me.

'Weed? Grass? You did grass with Brijesh?'

'One shared joint. Still we got into so much trouble.'

'How did you even get the stuff?'

'Brijesh scored it from the lanes in Anjuna.'

She turned to me, surprised.

'I thought both of you are the studious types.'

'We are not that dull, didi,' I said.

'Proud of you, little sister,' Aditi didi said.

I heard two knocks on the door. Didi and I looked at each other.

'Wait,' Aditi didi whispered as she stepped off the bed. She went to the door and looked through the keyhole.

'Who is it?' she said out loud.

'Oh, sorry. Excuse me, wrong room,' I heard a faint voice.

Didi came back to bed.

'Who?' I said.

'I don't know. Some man in a suit. Anyway, tell me more about the police station drama. It's too funny.'

◆

'One-two-three-four. Come on, start,' Mickey, the choreographer, shouted as he switched on the music. The song London thumakda filled the room. Five of my aunts, including Richa mami and Kamla bua, were practising on stage with the choreographer.

'Follow my moves,' he said.

Mickey had a lean body. In black tights and a black T-shirt he looked like an insect compared to my well-fed, substantial Punjabi aunts. The aunts moved. The makeshift stage groaned under the pressure.

'Don't bang your feet so hard. Grace, grace,' Mickey called out. Placing his right hand on his head he twirled.

I practised in another corner of the function room, along with my cousins. Mickey's assistant Vikram was to teach us our moves.

'Faster, faster, match the beat of the song,' Mickey said and clapped on the stage. The aunts moved their bottoms left and right twice, before circling around. Kamla bua made a face. She hated so much action this early in the morning.

'Ladies,' Vikram said to my group, 'I will show you once and then you follow.'

Vikram played DJ wale babu. The rap song required us to be jerky to match the erratic beat.

Bam! I heard a loud noise from the stage. Hotel staff rushed to the scene. My aunts and the choreographer huddled around Richa mami, who had fallen down. A hundred and ten kilos of Punjabi mass lay on the floor, wrapped in an oversized white salwar-kameez.

'Who hired this idiot choreographer? Such difficult steps for us,' she shrieked, holding her ankle.

'Sorry, madam, sorry,' Mickey said.

'What sorry?' Kamla bua said. 'You should see who can do what step.'

'Yes, madam.'

The hotel staff brought a first-aid kit and sprayed a pain reliever on her leg. Two waiters helped Richa mami stand up.

'Can we take a break?' Kamla bua said.

'But madam, the sangeet is tonight,' Mickey said.

'We haven't even had breakfast. Won't we get weakness if we do dance without breakfast?' Richa mami said.

She was right. Punjabis need calories, by the hour, every hour.

◆

My cousins and I took a table by the window at our family's dedicated breakfast buffet area. Some of them were rehearsing their steps even now. I went to the breakfast counter and picked up a plate.

'Can I have whole-wheat toast, please?' I said to a waiter.

'Would you like that with peanut butter and honey?' said a voice behind me.

I turned around. My eyes almost popped out of my face.

'Neel?' I said out loud.

'Hi,' he said. He looked the same, handsome as hell. He had gelled hair, a salt-and-pepper stubble and a lithe frame. He wore a black suit and a white shirt, both crisp.

'Neel?' I whispered his name again, more aware of my surroundings. 'What are you doing here?'

'I told you. I have to talk to you face-to-face. I came to your room last night. Another lady answered. So I left.'

'My sister,' I informed faintly, looking around rapidly. 'Keep your voice low. How did you even get here so fast? Weren't you in some copper mine in Sri Lanka?'

'I just...' he said and paused. 'I took a chartered flight. Doesn't matter. Can we talk?'

'You chartered a plane to come here?' I said. Neel did not meet my eyes.

The waiter brought me whole-wheat toast.

'I have to go,' I said.

'I know,' he said.

'You can't come here. This is our private family dining area.'

'I know.'

'Neel, look at me.'

He looked at me finally then, and I remembered those eyes. Those eyes and a lot more.

Hong Kong

Two Years Ago

22

'This is your desk,' said Bianca, a secretary in the Distressed Debt Group. 'Look outside, you even have a Hong Kong harbour view.'

It took me a while to adjust to my new surroundings. Goldman Sachs in Hong Kong is located at the Cheung Kong Centre skyscraper in Central, occupying the sixtieth to the sixty-eighth floors. The distressed debt team is located on the sixty-seventh floor. From the floor to the ceiling windows of the glass-and-steel building, one can see the Hong Kong skyline and harbour towards the north. In the southern direction, one has views of the Peak, the top of the green hill on Hong Kong Island.

Hong Kong is an ex-British colony, now under Chinese control. The British exited in 1997, but left behind one of the most modern, developed and efficient cities in the world. Consisting of the Hong Kong Island, the Kowloon peninsula and New Territories, this city of seven million inhabitants is one of the busiest global financial centres. Compact, brightly lit and buzzing, Hong Kong overwhelms you upon arrival with its insomnia and beehive activity.

'A company broker will call you. To help with the house-hunting,' Bianca continued. 'And here are some other helpful contacts.'

She gave me a file of all the people who would help me in my relocation.

'Neel will meet you in his office at 9,' Bianca said and left.

I logged into my computer, arranged the stationery on my desk. I put up a few family pictures on my cubicle walls. At 9, I walked up to Neel's corner office.

'Ah, Radhika. Come on right in,' Neel said.

He wore a white shirt, silver cufflinks and a blue Hermes skinny tie. I had not seen him since associate training two years ago. His office had panoramic vistas of Hong Kong. The sunshine pouring into the room made his skin glow.

He gave me a firm handshake.

'Thank you for having me in your group,' I said.

'It's our pleasure. We don't normally get high performers from New York here. How are you settling in?'

'I am good. Just arrived over the weekend.'

'Where are you staying?'

'Shangri-La.'

'Nice. Hey, did you have any breakfast? Want to step over to the breakout area for a coffee?'

'Sure,' I said.

We took the elevator down to the sixty-first floor. The Goldman breakout area is a café of sorts, where the staff often take a break for meals.

Neel and I went up to the counter person. Neel turned to me. 'What would you like?'

'Whole-wheat toast. With peanut butter and honey,' I said.

'Toast? And what?' the counter person said.

'Peanut butter and honey,' I said.

'Huh?' she said.

'*Faa sang zoeng mat mgoi*,' Neel said. The woman smiled and nodded.

'Thanks,' I said.

'No issues. I don't really speak Cantonese. But learning a few words is never a bad idea,' Neel said. He ordered a black coffee and bagel for himself.

We took our food and sat at a window-facing table. He briefed me about the group.

'We are ten professionals here. It isn't as large as New York. However, we are growing faster than any other Goldman office.'

I nodded and listened with full attention.

'You will work with Josh Ang and Peter Wu. They look after China and Korea respectively. There may be special deals from time to time you might get pulled into.'

'Looking forward to it,' I said.

'Good. We have a morning team meeting every day at 8. That is when everyone talks about their deals.'

'Okay.'

'I want you to speak up. I encourage people to raise questions so we challenge each other,' Neel said.

'Of course.'

'Feel free to come into my office. Josh is your immediate boss, but we don't really believe in formal roles here. There's some peanut butter on your lip.'

'Oh, really?' I said and wiped my lip with a tissue. 'I am sorry.'

'The other side.'

I shifted the tissue and felt my face turn red. Neel smiled. He looked even more gorgeous when he smiled.

'Welcome to Hong Kong,' he said.

◆

'We have a Bank of East Asia distressed debt auction coming up. There are fifty loans, sold as a portfolio. Bids due in two weeks,' Josh said at the morning meeting.

'Two weeks? That's tight,' Peter said.

All banks accumulate bad loans over time. Sometimes the bank feels it is easier to sell off those loans at a discount rather than chase the borrowers. To speed up things, they sell those loans as a portfolio, or in a bunch. In a sense, it clears their entire dirty plate in one shot. However, for bidders like us it means a crazy amount of work, evaluating what is on the plate.

'We can pass. People are busy with other deals, right?' Neel said.

'Actually, I could look at it,' I said. All eyes turned to me.

'I can. I don't have too much going on,' I said.

'It is fifty companies. You'll have to go through them all. You sure?' Josh said, in his mixed American and Chinese accent.

'We have two weeks. I can work weekends too,' I said.

'I could spare two days too,' Peter said.

'So can I,' said Simon, another Taiwanese analyst in the group.

Neel tapped his fingers on the conference room table.

'Let's do it,' he said finally, and stood up to signal end of the meeting.

For the next two weeks, I camped in my cubicle. Boxes of documents to be reviewed for the bid surrounded me. I only went back to the hotel to sleep, shower and change. One Friday night I didn't even do that. I worked straight through the night and watched the Saturday morning sunrise from the office window.

'Radhika, what are you doing here?' Neel's voice startled me.

I turned around. In workout clothes, he looked different from his usual formal self. He was wearing a black Under Armor T-shirt, a brand that reminded me of Debu. The portfolio work had kept him off my thoughts over the last few days. But now I felt pain flood my heart. *When will I get over that man*? I wondered.

'Good morning, Neel,' I said. 'Just wrapping up the bid. Will have it ready Monday morning.'

'You have dark circles under your eyes. Did you even go back last night?'

I smiled and shook my head.

'This is too much, Radhika. You have to maintain a balance.'

He placed his hand on the edge of my cubicle door. I could see his bicep flex through his sleeve.

'Going to the gym?' I said.

'I'm going on a mountain hike. I prefer working out outdoors.'

'That sounds like fun.'

'Yes. More than half of Hong Kong is country parks. Beautiful hikes.'

'I have heard.'

'Hope you see a bit of this city and not just this office.'

'I will. Just want this portfolio out of the way,' I said and then covered my mouth as I yawned.

'Radhika, you need to go home.'

'I will. Soon. What brings you to office?'

'Left my mobile phone behind yesterday. Just picking it up for the hike.'

He went into his office and came out after a few minutes. He saw me staring at my spreadsheet.

'Still here? Go rest.'

I smiled.

'Twenty more minutes. Tops,' I said.

'I'm leaving. Good work, Radhika.'

'Thanks. Bye, Neel, have a nice hike,' I said, eyes on my monitor.

He walked away from me and paused. He turned around and came back.

'Radhika, there's something I want to tell you.'

'Okay,' I said and shifted my gaze to him.

'There's a confidential deal. Some distressed companies don't like the world to know they are in distress. It can affect their business.'

'Sure, I understand,' I said.

'This one is in the Philippines. Only the Goldman Sachs Asia head and I know about it. I can't even discuss it in the morning meeting.'

'Oh, okay,' I said.

'I need an associate on the deal. Would you like to be on it?'

The prospect of more work in my current exhausted state made me feel even more tired. However, to be in a confidential deal and work with a partner meant a lot.

'Sure,' I said, 'what's the timing?'

'You finish the bid. Then I will brief you. We'll also need to meet the company people.'

'Sure. What sector is it?'

'I'll tell you. Real soon. Bye now. And get out of here fast,' he said.

◆

What the hell, I said to myself. Debu had unfriended me on Facebook. For the first time in Hong Kong I had finished work early and come back to my hotel at 5 p.m. The team had liked my final presentation on the portfolio. We had submitted a bid for fourteen cents on the dollar for the loans. Exhausted, I had been looking forward to a calm evening in the hotel and a good long sleep. However, I made the mistake of opening my laptop and logging on to Facebook. Like an idiot, I searched for Debashish Sen's profile. I couldn't find him on my friends' list.

Damn. I typed his name for the third time. Yes, he had unfriended me. I could understand why. Actually, I could not understand why. I wasn't some stalking witch who would cast an evil eye on his posts and pictures. Sure, we had broken up. People break up. They don't have to vanish like this.

I didn't have his phone number anymore. I had deleted all his previous emails. I felt like calling Avinash to ask for Debu's contacts again. I stopped myself and turned on the TV instead. Most of the channels were in Chinese. One channel showed a soap opera. I couldn't understand one word. However, I saw a girl on the screen cry, probably for her lost love. I don't know what it triggered in me, but I joined her. I clutched my pillow tight and cried. I had resisted this so perfectly for weeks. Ever since I came to Hong Kong I had buried myself in work. I thought I had made great progress with my break-up. Now I was back to square one.

Why did he unfriend me? I cried even more. I switched off the hotel room lights, opened the minibar and found little whisky and vodka bottles. I drank four of them, bottoms up, and lay down in bed. My head hurt as it sifted through images of Debu. *Will I ever get over him?*

I closed my eyes. I slept, or passed out, as weeks of sleep deprivation caught up with me.

I woke up as my phone rang. I had a bad headache. I opened one eye and saw the caller. It was Neel.

Damn. Damn. Damn. I switched on the light, ran into the bathroom and splashed water on my face. Only then did I pick up the call.

'Hello?' I said, my voice unclear.

'Sorry, were you sleeping? Is it too late?' Neel said.

I checked the time. It was only 8.30 p.m.

'No, no. Just took a nap. I am sorry. I left office early today.'

'You deserve the rest. Sorry to wake you up.'

'It's fine. I needed to anyway.'

Focus, Radhika. It's a partner on the line.

'I just called to ask if you could come to the office tomorrow at 7.30 a.m.?' Neel said.

'Huh? Yes, sure.'

'I can brief you on the Philippines deal. Better we talk about it before everyone arrives.'

'Of course,' I said.

◆

'El Casa Seaplane and Resorts,' I read the tasteful aquamarine-coloured cover of a brochure Neel handed to me.

He took a sip of his black coffee and kept the cup aside. He played with one of his blue sapphire cufflinks as he spoke to me. 'You know much about the Philippines?'

'One of the Southeast Asian countries, right?'

'Yeah. Seven thousand-plus islands. Couple of main ones though. Manila is the capital.'

'Okay,' I said. I took notes in my notebook.

'The company is El Casa Seaplane and Resorts. They borrowed too much. Business nosedived due to a cyclone. Trouble. Hence at our desk.'

I scribbled down whatever I could. Neel continued to speak.

'Palawan is in the south of the Philippines. Often voted as one of the most beautiful islands in the world.'

'Sure,' I said, jotting down at a frantic pace.

'Around Palawan there are tiny, super-exclusive, privately owned islands. El Casa operates ten resorts, each on one of these private mini-islands.'

I flipped through the brochure. It had stunning aerial pictures of the boutique tropical island resorts. The brochure said that none of El Casa's resorts had more than ten rooms.

'It says rooms are 1,000 dollars a night,' I said, surprised.

Neel smiled.

'Yes, so it is mostly super-rich foreign tourists. Locals can't afford it.'

'How does one even get there?' I said.

'You fly from Manila to Palawan, and then take one of the company seaplanes to the resorts.'

'Expensive operation,' I said.

'Yes. So when business takes a nosedive it gets really tough,' Neel said.

Neel told me that Typhoon Haiyan, one of the deadliest tropical cyclones, had hit the Philippines last year. It had left thousands dead. The country had still not recovered from it. High-end tourists still avoided the Philippines, making El Casa suffer. I took notes as Neel continued to talk.

'Owner is Marcos Sereno. Fifty years old, first generation, liquor baron. Tough businessman, respected in the community. El Casa is a passion project for him. So he is touchy about the world finding out it failed.'

'You have the financials?' I said.

Neel slid a five-inch-thick set of documents towards me.

'This contains everything. The existing lending banks want to get out. Marcos wants to cooperate, as long as his reputation stays intact.'

'Understood,' I said. 'I will go through all this.'

'Good. And let's go to Palawan next week and meet Marcos.'

23

'Orange juice or champagne?' a Cathay Pacific flight attendant said. She offered Neel drinks on a tray.

'Orange juice, please. Too early for champagne,' Neel said.

I took the same. We sat next to each other in the business-class cabin of the morning flight to Manila. I was on my first real business trip, travelling to a different country. I looked outside the window as the plane took off, making Hong Kong's skyscrapers look like Lego toys down below.

'So what did you think of El Casa?' Neel said.

'Oh, wait,' I said and opened my laptop bag. I took out the printout of my financial model.

'Keep this aside for now. Tell me your gut feeling on the business,' Neel said.

'My gut feeling?' I said, surprised. I was just an associate. Why would a partner care about my gut feeling? Wasn't it my job to just make the financial model and rattle out the numbers?

'Yeah, I'd like to know. Do you even like the business?'

I took a few seconds to collect my thoughts before I spoke again. 'In some ways El Casa is a rare asset, so quite valuable. In other ways it is a pain, as there are limited buyers for this thing. Also, I can't imagine Philippines law being the most investor-friendly,' I said.

'Good. I like how you think, in several directions at the same time,' Neel said.

'Thanks,' I said, embarrassed by his praise. I fumbled through my sheets.

'So what do we do here?' Neel said.

'We get a buyer,' I said.

'Meaning?'

'We talk to big hotel chains. This business needs a high-end global brand. Otherwise people are not going to come,' I said.

'Hmmm…' Neel said.

'I am thinking Aman Resorts, Four Seasons. Something in that category,' I said.

Neel looked at me. I saw pride in his eyes.

'You are smart,' he said.

'Not really,' I said, like a stupid fool.

'What do you mean?'

'Nothing. Thank you, I meant. Would you like me to show you the financial model?'

'Sure,' he said.

Over the next hour I went over the numbers. The company had fifty million dollars worth of loans. It could probably repay only half. Neel listened with full attention, cross-questioning me several times.

'That's good. I think we have a sense of what is going on here,' he said when I finished.

The flight attendant served us breakfast: fruit, cereal, milk and omelettes.

'I could also build another scenario…' I said as Neel interrupted me.

'Enough. Do you only think about work?'

'No, I just…'

'Let us enjoy our meal. No more talking shop.'

'Sure.' I ate a strawberry with my fork.

'How do you find Hong Kong?' Neel said.

'Efficient. Everything is close by.'

'You found an apartment?'

'Yes. On Old Peak Road. I am moving in next week.'

'It is a good area,' Neel said.

Old Peak Road passed through the Midlevels, an area midway to the Peak. A one-and-a-half bedroom apartment in this expat area cost me 6,000 US dollars a month in rent.

'Where do you stay?' I said.

'Repulse Bay. On the South side. You should visit. I do team dinners at my place sometimes.'

'Sure,' I said.

He applied jam on his toast. I noticed his slender fingers. I continued to gaze at them until he spoke again, startling me.

'Kusum would love to meet you,' he said.

'Kusum?' I said.

'My wife. We have two kids. Siya and Aryan. Seven and three.'

Of course, a man so amazing had to be married.

'Oh, how nice,' I said.

'Yeah. How about you?'

'Well, I am not married,' I said and smiled.

'Of course. But where's your family?'

'Delhi. Mom and dad. I have an elder sister.'

'Great. You close to your parents?'

I paused for a few seconds to think before I answered.

'In some ways I am close. Dad is really quiet. I am close to my mom. But we fight a lot,' I said.

Neel laughed.

'Really? Over what?' he said.

'The stupidest things. Mostly it is about her obsession to get me married.'

'Oh, you are young. Why marry so soon?'

'Exactly. If only she would get that.'

'Typical Indian parents, right?' Neel said.

I nodded.

'When did you leave India?' I said

'When I was twelve. I grew up in London after that. Undergrad at Oxford. Harvard for my MBA later. Met Kusum there, actually.'

'Oh, college sweethearts,' I said. I realized I should have shown more restraint. I was speaking to a partner, my boss's boss.

'You could say that,' he said and laughed.

The captain's announcement about the flight landing interrupted our conversation. When the plane hovered above Manila, Neel spoke again.

'Why did you leave New York?' Neel said.

'Personal reasons,' I repeated my rehearsed answer.

'Oh, I am sorry. I didn't mean to...' Neel said as I interrupted him.

'I had a break-up. A bad break-up.'

Neel looked at me. He raised his long eyebrows.

'Really?' he said.

'Yeah, why?' I said.

'You moved all this way for a guy?'

'Worse. Not for a guy. But for a guy who didn't want me.'

Again I felt I had crossed the line of acceptable conversation with a partner. Neel fumbled with his seatbelt as he searched for a suitable response.

'Well, anyway. Welcome to the Philippines,' he said.

The flight landed with a gentle thud.

◆

'I spent years to build El Casa. No logic why I did it. Just wanted to show the world how beautiful my country is,' Marcos said.

We sat in the El Casa office in Palawan across from the owner and CEO, Marcos Sereno, who had a portly frame and wore a Hawaiian shirt.

We had taken another short flight from Manila to Palawan and come for the meeting straight from Palawan airport. On the way, I saw a sleepy city full of palm trees and long, powdery beaches.

'Your country *is* stunning. It was evident even in the short journey from the airport to here,' Neel said to Marcos.

'You have to see the resorts. This is nothing,' Marcos said dismissively.

'Yeah?' Neel said.

'You are staying at one tonight, right?' Marcos said.

'We had actually booked a hotel in Manila on our way back. Our Hong Kong flight is tomorrow,' Neel said.

Marcos waved a no with his hands.

'Forget Manila. Crowded and polluted. You stay at my resort.'

'But…' Neel said before Marcos interrupted him.

'I insist. My seaplane will take you there.'

'Sure,' Neel said. Apart from being gracious to our client, we wanted to see the quality of the resorts anyway. Marcos told his secretary to arrange two rooms at the El Casa Pengalusian Island.

'Now let us talk business,' Marcos said after he delegated our travel arrangements.

'My colleague Radhika here has prepared some numbers,' Neel said.

I passed out copies of the financial model.

'I have tried to value each resort,' I said. Over the next ten minutes I walked him through my assumptions and projections. After I finished, Marcos took a deep breath.

'What now?' Marcos said.

I looked at Neel. It was time for him to speak.

'We need a new buyer. However, nobody will buy a company with a fifty-million-dollar loan on it. We have to settle the banks at a discount first.'

'They will settle,' Marcos said.

'But we want them to settle at a low price. We have to paint a terrible scenario for the banks. Say the business is worth almost nothing. You will have to play along,' I said.

'Really?' Marcos said.

'Yes. So they will sell the loans to us cheap. We will then find a new buyer. From our profit, we can give you 20 per cent,' I said.

Marcos's eyes widened. He looked at Neel.

'She's good,' Marcos said.

'Only my best people for you. Any other issues, Marcos?' Neel said. Marcos turned to me again.

'Will the new buyer fire people?' Marcos said.

'Depends on the new owner,' I said.

'I don't want that. No firing people. They are my people,' Marcos said.

I looked at Neel. We had a deadlock. The value of the company would drop if the new buyer had a no-layoffs clause.

'No firing anyone for five years. Okay?' Neel said.

Marcos looked at me. I pursed my lips.

'Fine. We can build that in. But if we do, do we have a deal?' I said.

'This girl is a quick one,' Marcos said to Neel and grinned.

'In my group, we like to close deals,' Neel said.

Marcos extended his hand.

'Let's do it,' Marcos said

We shook hands. We had an in-principle agreement.

'I'll send in the term sheet tomorrow,' I said.

'Is she always so obsessed with work?' Marcos said. 'No urgency. Send it in a few days. This is the Philippines. There's more to life than work here.'

There's nothing else but work in my life, I thought. I smiled at Marcos.

'Try my beer. Number one in the Philippines,' Marcos said as he opened the fridge behind his desk.

◆

'Okay, this is a little scary,' I said as I tied the flimsy seatbelt around me. Neel and I sat next to each other in the compact four-seater El Casa seaplane. The seats were tiny, our heads inches from the roof. The pilot gave us a thumbs-up sign, indicating take-off.

'What plane is this?' Neel asked the pilot.

'Amphibious Cessna 208 Caravan, sir,' the pilot said. The plane could take off and land on water as well as land. We took off from the local airport at Palawan. The turboprop noise made it difficult to talk. Neel saw my petrified face.

'You okay?' he screamed so I could hear him.

I nodded and blinked my eyelids. He grinned.

'Breathe,' he said.

I exhaled and inhaled a few times. The plane took off. I looked outside the window. The crystal-blue sea, white beaches and the green cover of trees below me made me forget our precarious position.

'Wow,' I blurted out as I saw some of the most breathtaking scenery I had ever seen in my life.

'It really is spectacular,' Neel said.

Fifteen minutes later, the plane hovered over the Pengalusian Island. Less than half a kilometre long and only two hundred metres wide, the rice-grain-shaped island seemed tiny from the top. The beach ran all across the perimeter of the island. On the southern tip, a few huts became visible.

'That's the resort,' the pilot said. 'The rest of the island is just left untouched. All natural.'

I closed my eyes as the plane landed on its water skis. When I opened them, Neel and the pilot were looking at me. Both of them had a grin on their faces.

'I am sorry. It's beautiful, but scary,' I said.

We stepped out of the plane into the sand. Two porters took our bags. The resort manager greeted us.

'You must be Mr Marcos Sereno's special guests,' he said. 'Welcome to El Casa Pengalusian. I am Carlos, the resort manager.'

He showed us our respective rooms. Each room was a little cottage on stilts, built above a clear blue water lagoon.

'If you sit in the balcony,' Carlos said, 'you can see fish in the water below you.'

I kept my belongings in the luxurious room, which had wooden floors and a thatched roof. I felt tired. I went up to the reception area where I found Neel in conversation with Carlos.

'Pretty stunning place you have here,' Neel said.

'Thank you, sir,' Carlos said.

I joined the two of them.

'Carlos, can I talk to you later?' I said. 'A few business-related questions about the resort?'

'Sure. Mr Sereno informed me,' Carlos said.

Neel smiled at my attempt to do due diligence at every opportunity. Carlos excused himself and left us in the lobby area. The sun shone bright, though there was only one hour to sunset.

'Beats working on a bank portfolio, doesn't it?' Neel said.

'Totally,' I said and laughed. 'This is the best deal ever. How beautiful is this place?'

'Yeah, glad we came. I had no idea this is so amazing.'

'We will find a buyer, right?' I said.

'Gosh. You are unbelievable. Just look at the view. Worry about the buyer later,' Neel said.

'Sorry,' I said.

We walked out of the lobby to face the sea in front of us. Rock formations in the middle of the ocean made the view even more dramatic.

'What's your plan for the rest of the evening?' Neel said.

'I have to make the term sheet,' I said.

'Come on. Do it back in office. Want to take a walk around the island before dinner?'

'Sure,' I said.

'Let's change into workout clothes. See you here in thirty minutes,' he said.

◆

Neel and I walked on the two-kilometre trail that circled the island. Every nook and corner had spectacular scenery. Warm seawater touched our shoes as we walked on the sand near the water. If God hired an architect to design heaven, this was how it would be done.

'Let's keep it brisk,' Neel said and increased his stride. He now walked in front of me, looking even better in his workout clothes: knee-length black shorts and a neon-green Nike T-shirt.

I wore a white T-shirt and grey trackpants.

'You are really into fitness,' I said.

'I try,' Neel said.

'The hike that day. Walk today.'

'Well, when you get to my age, your metabolism drops. Not easy to remain fit.'

'You look so fit,' I said. I wondered if I should have said it. I had just noticed a partner's physical appearance. Well, who in the office hadn't?

'Thank you. I am old now. Forty-five.'

'That's not so old,' I said. *Okay, why did I have to say that?*

He laughed. 'Really? How old are you? Sorry. I shouldn't be asking a lady that.'

'I am twenty-five. Well, twenty-six soon.'

'That's incredibly young. Look at you, already on big deals.'

'I am lucky.'

'Don't say that. You are good. You work hard. That's when luck creeps up on you.'

I turned to him and smiled.

'Thanks,' I said.

'But you are twenty years younger. I feel even older now,' Neel said.

'You are a partner at Goldman Sachs at forty-five. It's pretty young. Plus, you look good.'

Now why the fuck did I have to say that? 'You look good'? You are with the head of distressed debt for Asia. Radhika, control your tongue.

'Thank you. Don't get to hear that so much these days,' he said.

We circled the entire island and returned to the resort.

'Dinner in an hour? I will take a shower and see you at the restaurant,' he said.

'Sure,' I said.

'I might run a few more rounds of the island before that,' he said.

'I feel like a slob,' I said.

'Relax. You must be tired. See you soon.'

24

'Champagne, sir, courtesy Mr Marcos Sereno,' Carlos said as he kept a bottle of Dom Perignon in a chiller next to us. We sat in the open-air restaurant in the resort, located in an alcove. The sun had set. The clear sea reflected the palette of the sky. The restaurant had only six tables, each with several lit candles on it.

Ours was the only occupied table.

'Would you like some?' Neel said as he lifted the bottle.

'Yes, please,' I said.

Like a gentleman, Neel stood up and poured the champagne for me.

'Thank you,' I said.

'You are welcome,' Neel said. We raised our glasses in a toast.

'To many more deals,' he said.

'Especially ones involving private island assets,' I said. Both of us laughed.

Waiters brought us various kinds of seafood, all caught fresh from the sea. Everything tasted delicious.

One of the waiters brought us a heart-shaped red velvet cake.

'For the lovely couple,' he said in a Filipino accent.

The waiter's words left me stumped. I struggled to speak.

'Oh, actually, we...' I said. Neel intervened.

'Thank you for the cake. Didn't have to be heart-shaped, as we are not a couple.'

The waiter looked at both of us, surprised.

'We are here on a business trip,' I said. The waiter became even more confused. Who comes to Pengalusian Island on work?

Neel smiled.

'Thanks for the cake,' he repeated. The waiter left us. We burst out laughing. Neel poured us both another glass of champagne.

'Okay, that was a little weird,' I said.

'Totally. Did not expect that.'

I could feel my head swim after two drinks.

'Though I must say I was flattered,' Neel said.

'Really? Why?' I said, pretending to be ignorant even as I fished for more compliments.

'Well, even at my age he thought I could be with you. That's a compliment.'

'Well. True that,' I said. 'All that running is surely helping.'

We clinked our glasses. I don't know if it was the champagne, the beautiful setting or that Neel made me feel comfortable, but I found it easy to talk to him.

'You should come here with your wife,' I said.

'Huh?' he said, slightly surprised. 'Yeah, Kusum would love this place. Who wouldn't?'

'So you guys met in college? Love at first sight?' I said. I don't know if I had overstepped the line. After three glasses of champagne, all so-called lines seem pretty blurred anyway.

'Yeah, you could say that, yeah,' Neel said, after deliberating for a second.

'Sorry, didn't mean to pry.'

'No, it's fine. Kusum and I were in the same class. She was born and brought up in the USA. I mostly lived in the UK. Both of us were desis, yet Westernized. I guess we connected.'

'How wonderful,' I said.

'Yeah. Absolutely,' he said. He became quiet. He took a big sip from his glass and spoke again. 'How about you? In love pretty hard? Moving countries.'

'Never again. This love business is not for me,' I said. I took a knife and cut across the heart-shaped cake.

'That's symbolic,' he said. 'A knife through your bleeding red velvet heart.'

I laughed.

'Pretty much what happened. Discarded like used tissue. Switched like a TV channel,' I said.

'Ouch, I am sorry,' Neel said. 'Though, excuse me, I am a bit surprised.'

'Surprised?'

'Like who were you dating? Brad Pitt?'

I laughed. 'Not really. Just a regular guy. Job on Madison Avenue. Why?'

'How on earth could any guy leave you?' Neel said.

His words felt like cold menthol balm on my bruised, wounded heart. I could have cried, but girls who cry in front of their bosses are losers, and those who do in front of the boss's boss are the biggest losers.

'I am not...that...great,' I fumbled for words. What I wanted to say was 'Tell me more about why I am great.'

'Are you kidding me?' Neel said and counted on his fingers. 'You are smart, successful, fun to talk to, young, hard-working, funny and, well, I shouldn't be saying this as your senior, but you know...' He paused mid-sentence.

'You know—what?' I said.

'I don't want to talk out of turn.'

'It's okay.'

'Well, you know, you look pretty good. Very good, in fact.'

Wow, did Neel Gupta just try a line on me? But wait, did Neel Gupta actually find me good-looking? And did he mean all those other wonderful things he just said?

I felt loads of self-esteem shots being injected into my bloodstream.

'You are just saying all this to make me feel good,' I said. It meant, *say more.*

'No. Why would I? I mean it. You are, professionally and personally, one of the most amazing people I have ever met,' Neel said.

I swear I felt the sand shift beneath me. Neel stared me right in the eyes. We had a moment of silence as I heard the splashing waves. I absorbed his compliment. Someone as cool as Neel found me attractive. It was all too much. Something had to short-circuit in me as I gave the most idiotic response.

'It's okay if I send Marcos the term sheet by tomorrow evening, right?' I said.

◆

One month later

'Whole-wheat toast. *Faa sang zoeng mat,*' I said. I had finally learnt to order breakfast at the Goldman café. Neel and I were the early arrivals, at 7.30 a.m.

Neel took his black coffee and a bowl of oats. A month since our Philippines' visit, we had the term sheet signed. We had also reached settlement with the banks.

'I can't tell you the details. But I have good news,' Neel said.

'We have a buyer?' I said, excited.

'Shh!' Neel said and placed a finger on his lips. 'Yes. We could be going to meet Marcos soon and finish the deal.'

'Cool,' I said. 'Take over the loans on one side and sell the company on the other.'

'What we call back-to-back deals. No risk on books. Best deal ever,' Neel said. We gave each other a thumbs-up. He reviewed the deal-closing documents.

'Looks good. Fingers crossed. Buyer on board soon,' Neel said.

I kept the documents back in my laptop bag. These last few minutes of our daily café meeting had become my favourite part of the day. It was when Neel and I discussed things apart from work.

'How is your new apartment?' Neel said.

'I love it. Thirtieth floor, great view. Still doing it up,' I said.

'Check out IKEA, they have good home stuff. Neat designs, good price,' Neel said.

'Sure. Will go there. Need to join a gym too.'

'Have you tried yoga?'

I shook my head. 'Maybe at school in India,' I said, 'when it was compulsory.'

Neel laughed.

'Check out Pure Yoga. They have a great studio. I go sometimes,' Neel said.

'Okay. My birthday is coming up next week. Maybe I will treat myself to a membership.'

'Oh, great. Happy birthday in advance.'

'Thanks. So you do yoga too. How do you do it all?' I said.

'If you love yourself, you will take care of yourself, right?'

◆

I counted the twenty-six pink roses. The bouquet on my desk had a maroon ribbon wrapped around it. It came from Armani Fiori, located in Central. Part of the Armani brand of Italian designer Giorgio Armani, the bouquets in the shop would be no less than 200 dollars at least. I removed a small white envelope tied to one of the roses. A card inside said, 'Happy Birthday—From the team.'

I sat back in my seat, surprised. The hard-nosed and tough Distressed Debt Group isn't known for affection and flowers. Bianca passed my cubicle.

'Happy birthday, Radhika,' she said.

'Thank you,' I said, 'and thanks for the flowers. The most beautiful bouquet I have ever seen.'

'You are welcome. We don't normally do it. But you are new. Maybe that's why Neel wanted it.'

'Neel?'

'Yes, he told me to order it. He even selected the arrangement.'

I thanked everyone for the birthday wishes in the team meeting.

'The flowers are an exception. Don't get high hopes,' Josh said.

'Mostly we gift each other bad loan documents,' Simon said. The team burst into laughter. I looked at Neel. He smiled at me.

'A team from the Metropolitan Bank of Tokyo is in town. They want to meet for potential co-investments,' he said, making it clear that the bouquet and my birthday didn't warrant any more discussion.

◆

'That's Tanaka-san, Shin-san and I am Sugimula,' said Arai Sugimura, head of the Distressed Debt Group at Metropolitan Bank of Tokyo, as he introduced his team. In Japan, the tag 'san' is applied out of respect, sort of like 'shri' in Hindi. We exchanged business cards, held in both hands, as is the norm in Asia.

'La-dhi-ka-san,' Arai said. 'Do I say youl name light?'

'It's fine,' I said and smiled. The Japanese bankers bowed to us as they sat down. Bianca asked us if we needed anything. Everyone agreed to have Chinese tea.

'It's an honour you came to visit us,' Neel said, turning on his client-charm button. 'How can we do business together?'

'Gupta-san, it is plivilege for us too,' Arai said. 'Goldman Sachs is ples-ti-gious bank. Youl gloup has good leputation in malket.'

Bianca came back with teacups and a kettle of tea. She placed them on the table and left.

'Thank you. It's all due to my great team,' Neel said, waving his hand at us.

Neel poured tea for himself. As did Josh and Peter.

'La-dhika-san,' Arai said.

'Yes?' I said.

'Would you mind?' he said and pointed to the kettle. I realized he wanted me to pour tea for his team. I looked at Neel and Josh. They seemed confused, but gestured that I do it anyway. I poured tea for the Japanese team and a cup for myself.

Arai explained his desire to co-invest with our group. Nobody else from Arai's team spoke a word. In Japan, when the boss talks, you remain silent.

'So what kind of deals al you looking at?' Arai said. 'Any polt-folios?'

Arai had the typical Japanese problem of being unable to speak the R sound, which he substituted with L.

'Radhika bid for one recently, maybe she can talk about it,' Josh said.

'La-dhika-san?' Arai said.

'Yeah, I can tell you about this local Bank of East Asia auction...' I began to speak but Arai interrupted me with his laughter.

'Excuse me?' I said, wondering if I had said anything wrong.

'Solly. I thought La-dhika-san youl secle-taly. How can lady do dist-lessed debt?' Arai continued to laugh. His minions also grinned, taking their boss's cue.

Neel pursed his lips. He looked at me once and turned to Arai.

'The young lady here is one of our best distressed debt analysts,' Neel said.

'Yes, yes, of coulse. By the way, I lemember a joke when you said lady,' Arai said.

None of us responded. He continued, 'You know what they say about lady?' He turned to Josh. Josh didn't answer.

Arai continued anyway, 'When a lady say no, she means maybe. When she says maybe, she means yes. When she says yes, well, she is not a lady.'

His colleagues found the joke extra funny and laughed out loud. Peter, Josh, Neel and I looked at each other.

'Arai-san, I understand this is amusing to you. But frankly, this makes us quite uncomfortable,' Neel said.

'Solly. You may continue,' Arai said.

I took a deep breath to regain my composure. I spoke again.

'Yes, so I was saying,' I said.

Neel stood up.

'Actually, no,' Neel said and paused before he spoke again. 'No. This won't work out.'

'What?' Arai said, his face serious.

'We look for fit in a partner. Sorry, Arai-san, we won't be able to do business with you,' Neel said.

'We have billion dollars to invest. Lot of fee for Goldman Sachs on that.' Arai looked stupefied.

'I understand,' Neel said, 'but...'

'Actually, it's okay, Neel,' I said. 'Arai-san, if I can tell you about the portfolio...'

Neel shook his head.

'Arai-san, Tanaka-san, Shin-san, thank you for coming. I am sure you will find a great partner. We will pass. We anyway have a lot on our plate,' Neel said. Josh and Peter stood up, somewhat surprised. The Japanese bankers looked at each other.

'Josh will see you out,' Neel said and left the room.

◆

'Hey, Radhika, come on in,' Neel said.

I went into his office and sat down in front of him. He wore a pink shirt and a red Hermes tie. His face reflected a bit of pink from his shirt.

'By the way, happy birthday,' he said.

'Thank you for the flowers.'

'They are from the team,' Neel said.

'Bianca told me you chose them.'

'Oh, she did? She doesn't understand confidentiality.' Neel grinned.

He played with his cuffs. He would do that when he was nervous. Or excited.

'Neel, about the meeting with the Japanese bankers...'

'Yeah. What douchebags.'

'You cancelled the deal?'

'Well, we can't work with sexist people like that. They made you so uncomfortable.'

'I was taken aback a bit, yes. But an odd comment here or there doesn't bother me.'

'It's not okay, Radhika,' Neel said, raising his voice loud enough for even Bianca to notice.

'There was business there,' I said.

'So?' Neel said.

I looked at him. We exchanged a glance. I don't know if I imagined it, but it lasted a heartbeat longer than it should have between a partner and an associate.

'Listen, Radhika. I am not going to allow anyone to treat you like this,' he said and immediately corrected himself. 'I mean, not going to allow anyone in my team to be treated like that.'

'All right. But I was fine,' I said.

'No. Don't be fine. No business is worth that. We can let it go, okay?'

I looked at Neel.

'Thanks,' I said in a subdued voice.

'You are welcome,' he said. 'Now, what are your birthday plans?'

'I have a few calls with prospective El Casa buyers tonight.'

'Gosh, you are incorrigible,' Neel said.

'It's not so bad. Simon has organized drinks. A couple of Goldman associates are coming.'

'Nice. Have fun,' he said.

I wondered if I should invite him. He read my mind.

'I would have come, but it will be awkward for the rest if a partner shows up.'

'I understand. No issues,' I said.

'Happy birthday again, Radhika,' he said.

I came back to my desk. I touched the petals of one of the twenty-six roses. My phone rang. I had a call from India. I picked up the phone.

'Hey, sister,' Aditi didi said. 'Happy birthday. I came home today. We miss you.'

25

One month later

'Here you go, whole-wheat toast with peanut butter and honey,' Neel said and passed me my breakfast. I gestured him a thanks with a thumbs-up. I was on a conference call. I was now vice president; my expected promotion had become official two weeks ago. We sat in the Goldman café at 7 a.m. We had a potential buyer for El Casa called Greenwood Hospitality, a US-based company that owned fifty boutique hotels worldwide. On the call were Maddox Dean, MD in the mergers' department in New York; Philippe Greenwood, owner of Greenwood; Neel and I.

'Philippe, the docs are watertight here. I think we should close this soon,' Neel said.

'I don't mind,' Philippe said, 'just that your price of fifty million is too high. How about forty?'

Neel looked at me. I shook my head.

'Too low,' Neel said.

'Let's lock at forty-five,' Greenwood said.

Neel looked at me.

I nodded.

'Done,' Neel said. 'Can we close the docs soon, please?'

'This is fantastic,' Maddox said. 'We have a deal.'

'Super. We'll go down to the Philippines and close it with El Casa next week,' Neel said.

The call ended.

'Congratulations,' I said.

'How much is the final profit?' Neel said.

'Twenty million, net, to us,' I said.

Neel and I high-fived each other.

◆

'How did you guys do it?' Marcos said, as he flipped through the documents. Even though he tried to hide it, the smile wouldn't leave his face. He had a bankrupt business that faced foreclosure and mass lay-offs. Now he would get five million dollars next week in his account as a settlement fee for his cooperation. Not to mention a global buyer who would keep his resorts alive.

'That's what we do. We close deals, Marcos,' Neel said.

'Wonderful. You are staying for several days this time, I hope,' Marcos said as he signed the documents. 'Stay on a different island each night.'

'I wish,' Neel said. 'But there's a lot of work back in Hong Kong. We will leave tomorrow.'

'Same place then? Pengalusian?'

'Yes,' Neel said.

'You saved my people their jobs. Thank you so much,' he said.

I collected all the documents Marcos had signed. Neel shook hands with Marcos.

'Pleasure doing business with you,' Neel said.

◆

I stood in front of the mirror at the Pengalusian Island Resort and turned from side to side. I wondered if my black shorts and the white gunjee over my pink sports bra revealed too much. Neel had suggested a run before our deal-closing celebration dinner. 'Let's burn calories before we consume them,' he had said.

'It's fine. Be cool about it,' I said to myself and checked myself out one last time. Okay, so the shorts were a little too short. The gunjee was, well, a little too short too.

I met Neel at the reception area. He wore a blue workout T-shirt and black cycling shorts. He also had blue mirror-tinted Raybans on.

'Wow, you've transformed,' he said. The sunglasses covered his eyes. I couldn't tell if he was staring at me. I thought he did. Maybe I wished he did.

'I haven't run in the longest time,' I said.

'We'll just jog. Three rounds of the island?'

'Two, please.'

He laughed.

'Okay, let's go,' he said.

We jogged around the periphery of the tiny island. We had walked this route on our previous trip. However, today the island felt even more dreamlike. Despite the bright sun, a cool breeze kept the temperature just right. We jogged on the beach away from the water, which slapped lazily against the shore. Neel ran slower to match my pace. This way he remained only a few steps ahead of me. I noticed his muscular legs. He had perfect, sculpted calves. He ran in flawless, graceful form. I, meanwhile, gasped, kicked and panted through the two-kilometre route. I wanted to quit after the first round. However, Neel wouldn't let me.

'Enough,' I said, holding my stomach.

'Come on, you are doing great,' he said.

For the second round he remained behind me. I looked back from the corner of my eye. I don't know if he noticed my legs. It would have been hard to miss them, considering my shorts bunched up even more when I ran.

'I am done,' I said, gasping for breath as I finished the second round.

'Mind if I run a bit more?' he said.

'Sure,' I said and exhaled noisily.

'See you in an hour for dinner,' he said and ran ahead. Soon, he disappeared into the sand and green foliage of the island.

I came back to my room and showered. I opened my suitcase and took out a white flowing dress with a floral print. It seemed perfect for an island resort dinner. The dress had a deep neckline; I wore a bead necklace to cover it. I applied make-up, and created a smoky effect around my eyes. I realized I had not dressed up to look good since my New York days with Debu. Also, I noticed the name 'Debu' didn't sting as much anymore. I applied perfume and translucent strawberry lip gloss. I looked at myself in the mirror one final time. If I made an effort I could look nice.

Will he like how I look? The question floated in my head. Mini-me scolded me, *He may be friendly, but he's still a partner, and married. Get it?*

26

I reached the restaurant before Neel. I sipped a glass of champagne as I watched the sunset. He arrived twenty minutes later.

'Sorry I am late. I ran extra rounds,' Neel said.

He wore a white T-shirt and beige shorts.

'It's okay,' I said. He pulled out a chair and sat in front of me.

'Wow,' he said, his gaze on me.

'What?' I said.

'You look…well, different,' he said.

'Good different or bad different?' I said.

'You look stunning, actually. This dress really suits you.'

He had given me his first direct compliment about my looks. While working on El Casa we had become freer in terms of talking to each other. However, we still maintained propriety. We didn't discuss feelings, for instance. We didn't make personal comments. In fact, we never even called each other a friend.

And yet, today his compliment didn't feel out of place.

'Thank you, Neel. That's sweet of you,' I said. There, I had become so much better at taking a compliment.

He removed his Birkenstock sandals so his feet could touch the sand. I kicked off my heels too.

'Where's my drink?' Neel said and signalled the waiter. The waiter poured champagne for him.

'So how do you feel after the run?' Neel said.

'Good,' I said, 'but I need to build my stamina. People older than me are whipping me and doing extra rounds.'

Neel grinned. The waiter brought us the set menu choices. I chose the vegetarian option. It consisted of an avocado and rocket leaf salad, followed by mushroom truffle pasta. Neel chose a seafood chowder soup and pan-seared salmon cooked in a mango salsa.

'To El Casa, your first big deal in Asia,' Neel said and raised his glass.

'To Greenwood, their new buyer.' I touched his glass with mine.

'What a resort, isn't it?' Neel said. He pointed to the scenery ahead of us. Only half of the sun remained in the horizon. The deep orange-coloured sky had turned a silky texture.

'The most beautiful place I have ever been to,' I said.

'Same for me. With one of the most beautiful minds I know,' Neel said.

'Yeah, sure. It's only my mind that's beautiful,' I said. *I am a fisherwoman. I fish, fish, fish.*

'Of course not. But it isn't appropriate for me to comment on the rest of you. Protocol,' he said.

'We need to get something straight,' I said and sat upright.

'What?' Neel said.

'Are we friends or are we colleagues or are you my super-senior boss?' I said.

'That's a tough one,' Neel said.

'Is it?'

'Well, yes. Fact remains I am the head of the group. You are the VP. Cheers.'

We touched glasses again. I took a big gulp.

'So that's who we are. Colleagues?' I said.

'Well, no. I feel like after all those breakfast meetings I know you somewhat. You know me too. In fact...' he said and paused.

'In fact what?'

'In fact, I am going to miss our breakfast chats the most after this deal,' he said and stared into the horizon. 'Our oatmeal and peanut-butter-toast conversations.'

'Don't forget the honey,' I said.

He laughed.

'I will miss our breakfasts too,' I said.

'Well, life goes on. Another day, another deal,' Neel said.

'Wait. So we are not friends?'

'Can we be?'

'Why not?' I said.

'Many reasons to not be. I am your senior. Twenty years older. Married. Two kids. You, on the other hand, young and single. Smart and attractive.'

'Attractive?' I said and smiled.

'Yeah, of course. You are really attractive, Radhika. I am just being factual.'

Ah, the sweet, soothing feeling of receiving a compliment from a worthy man.

My life, at this moment, felt perfect.

'Thank you,' I said. 'You are pretty cool too.'

'What is this? An overworked bankers' self-praise society?' Neel said.

We laughed. The waiter refilled our champagne glasses.

'We are friends,' Neel said. 'I don't see you as a junior now.'

'Do note I get too casual with friends. Tell me if I overstep the line. After all, you are my senior,' I said.

'I am not the typical senior. You can be honest with me. Speak your mind.'

'Really?'

'Yeah. Try me,' Neel said.

'Okay. What do you truly think of me?' I said. 'As a person.'

He wiped the water droplets on his glass with this thumb.

'Go on, hit me. Be frank,' I said.

He smiled.

'You are smart, of course. But you are also simple and a little lost. You are one of the most attractive women I have met. Yet, you need external validation, a lot of it. This could be because you have self-esteem issues. You are sensitive, but have closed yourself. After what has happened in New York perhaps.'

'Wow,' was all I could say, impressed and speechless at his observations.

'A bit too frank?' he said.

'Yeah, ouch,' I said and laughed. 'But not bad. You do observe more about me than the financial models I create.'

'Oh, but your work is stellar. You could be partner one day. Radhika Mehta, Partner, Goldman Sachs. Here's to that,' Neel said and raised a toast. He finished his glass in one shot. I followed him. The cloudless sky looked even more beautiful as little stars became visible at dusk. A slow French song began to play in the background. I couldn't understand the lyrics, but could feel the pain of the singer.

'Partner Radhika. With a lot of deals under her belt. But lonely, without love,' I said.

'What nonsense. Radhika with a lot of love,' Neel said.

'Whatever. I don't think so. Which song is this? It's beautiful.'

'La vie en rose. Life through rose-tinted glasses. Famous French song. But seriously, that's what you think? You won't find love?'

'Yeah. My biggest fear, perhaps.'

Neel gave me a look of disbelief.

'You want to talk about New York?' he said.

The waiter brought us another champagne bottle. Over the course of dinner and a few more glasses of bubbly, I told him my entire New York story. He listened with full attention, nodding at every significant moment.

'And so, that's it. I dropped the phone in the East River. Came to Hong Kong,' I said.

I wiped a slow tear rolling down my cheek. I didn't think of Debu much now. However, repeating the story was not a breeze.

'You could have just dropped the SIM card, you know. And wiped the phone to factory settings,' Neel said.

I looked at Neel. He kept a poker face. I don't know why, but we burst out laughing.

'It's okay, crap happens in life. Mostly it's for the good,' Neel said.

'More champagne, sir?' the waiter said as he picked up our second empty bottle.

'Actually, no I am pretty...' Neel said as I interrupted him.

'Actually, yes. We'd like another one,' I said.

'Really?' Neel said, looking at me as the waiter left.

'Well, I have told you a lot about me. We still have to cover you. We need a drink for that.'

Neel shrugged and smiled.

'Okay, bring it on,' he said. 'What's your read on me, as a person?'

'Well,' I said, resting my left palm on my glass. 'You are a bit of an enigma.'

'Enigma?'

'Yeah, mysterious. You are smart, clearly an overachiever. Fit, good-looking, charming.'

'I could get used to this. Go on,' Neel said.

'But...' I said.

'But what?'

'I don't know if you are truly happy. You should be, right? You have everything the world aspires for, right? But you don't seem truly happy.'

'I am happy. Look at me. Being paid to be on an island.'

'Yeah, you get paid. A lot. But that's not all it takes to be happy.'

He didn't respond. He looked searchingly at me.

'What makes you think I am not happy?' he said slowly.

'I feel you put on a mask. This perfect mask. Hard-working family man, controls his diet, exercises regularly. It's almost too perfect. Like your perfectly ironed shirts, there isn't an out-of-place crease. You know what they say in due diligence, right?'

'What?'

'If it is too good to be true, it probably is too good to be true,' I said.

He looked at me, his eyes wide in surprise. He put his glass down.

'Did I cross the line?' I said, a little anxious.

He shook his head.

'No, no. It's okay. What else makes you feel this way?'

'You never talk about your family.'

'I do. I told you. Kusum. My two kids.'

'Factual stuff.'

'Meaning?'

'It's like data. No feelings.'

'Okay,' Neel said. 'Wow. You learn something every day. So that's what you think about me.'

'I am sorry if I said something inappropriate.'

'No, it's cool,' he said and smiled.

The waiter cleared our dinner plates. He brought us mango with sticky rice as dessert. I cut a piece of mango with my knife and ate it with a fork.

'Your wife is happy for all your success?' I said.

'Yeah,' Neel said, after some deliberation. 'She is. We have been together twenty years. She has seen my entire journey.'

'Twenty years? Wow, so you guys met when I was five,' I said.

'Ouch!' Neel grinned. 'Now you make me feel really old.'

'What is it like being married for so long?' I said.

'It's nice. You build a life together, a lot of memories together. You bring kids into this world.'

'Yeah, does sound beautiful.'

'And yet, because you have been with a person so long, it doesn't stay the same. Issues crop up. Many issues. Many, many issues.'

I sensed Neel had stuff bottled up.

'Okay. Well, you can talk about it if you want,' I said.

'I am not going to bore you. I don't have an exciting story with iPhones being thrown off the Brooklyn Bridge. Just stupid domestic stuff.'

'Hey, I had an old iPhone. I would have upgraded to a new model anyway.'

Both of us laughed.

'You are funny,' he said.

We finished our meal.

'I ate too much,' I said.

'Me too. Let's take a walk?'

'Another walk? You are Mr Hyperactive, aren't you?' I said.

He grinned. He picked up a flashlight—there was one on every table. I lifted two glasses and the unfinished third bottle of champagne.

'What?' Neel said.

'We will take this along,' I said.

'Kind of defeats...' Neel said and I nudged him.

'Come,' I said. We walked barefoot on the same route as our jog a couple of hours ago. However, the island took on a new form in the darkness. The trees appeared pitch black, as did the sea. I could see white streaks where the waves broke, due to the phosphorescence and the moonlight. We walked close to the shore this time. The water lapped at our feet, warm on our ankles. Neel's flashlight showed us the way. We walked in silence, with no sound apart from the splashing waves. The lack of conversation didn't seem awkward. In fact, it seemed perfect. I spoke after a while.

'You must be tired,' I said. 'You ran five rounds.'

'A little bit,' Neel said but walked on.

We reached the northern tip of the island, which had a C-shaped alcove. The waves became gentle here and made no sound. Rock formations on the beach jutted out of the sand. At a distance we could see fishing boats as nearby islanders went out for a night's catch.

'Can we sit for a bit?' I said.

'Sure,' he said.

We sat down on the cold sand in absolute silence. He switched off the flashlight. The moonlight was just about enough for us to see each other's faces. I poured myself a glass of champagne. He looked at me, shook his head in disbelief and grinned. I poured him a glass as well. He took a sip. I turned my head back to look up at the sky.

The night sky had so many stars, it felt like someone had sprayed it with silver paint.

'Wow, look at the gazillion stars above,' I said.

He turned his gaze up to the sky as well.

'Unlike Hong Kong there is no pollution here, and no backlight from the city.'

'Yeah, I have never seen stars in Hong Kong,' I said.

'Do you recognize constellations?' Neel said.

I shook my head. He pointed at the sky with his index finger.

'See, that's Ursa Major, or the Great Bear,' he said, outlining the group of seven stars.

I kept looking at his finger. He kept talking.

'That's Ursa Minor, Little Bear. That's the North Star,' Neel said.

'How do you know all this?' I said.

'Used to have a telescope once. Can you imagine, these stars are all navigators had when they sailed centuries ago. No GPS.'

'Unbelievable,' I said.

My neck hurt from keeping my head tilted for so long. I lay down on the sand instead. This way my eyes could face the sky above me and I could be comfortable.

'Easier to see this way,' I said. Neel looked at me once and lay down as well. Our heads were one foot apart.

'What's your sun sign?' he said, staring at the sky above.

'My birthday was just a few days back,' I said.

'Gemini then. There, see, those are the Gemini twins,' he said.

'What's yours?'

'Taurus. See, over there,' he said. He pointed to a group of stars that outlined a bull.

'Wow,' I said.

We became quiet and enjoyed the silence and isolation. I felt calm because of the surroundings. Maybe the champagne also had something to do with it. I could hear him breathing. I stretched my legs. A wave touched my foot. I moved in reflex. As I did that, my ankle brushed against Neel's. He turned his head and looked at me.

'I am sorry,' I said.

'It's fine,' he said, rather whispered. We looked at each other and smiled. I don't know why, call it girl intuition or whatever, I felt like something was going to happen. I could have moved away. But I didn't. Maybe because I wanted it to happen.

He leaned forward. He placed his lips on mine. They felt as warm and gentle as the water on my ankles. I closed my eyes. My hands moved halfway to stop him but lost the resolve to do so as the kiss felt amazing. He kissed me long and deep as dozens of waves broke and touched the soles of my feet. He lifted his arm to draw me closer. Neel Gupta, partner, two decades older and my boss's boss, held me tight and kissed me. This was not supposed to feel good. But never had a kiss felt this good. I didn't protest. Maybe I should have. But when something feels so right it is hard to do so. I placed my palm on his face. The face I had seen every day for so many months, but never touched. I felt connected to him. I felt like the entire island existed only for this one reason, our kiss.

A relatively stronger wave came and hit us higher, leaving us wet waist down.

He continued to kiss me, the intensity increasing with every passing second. His fingers lingered down the back of my neck. Goosebumps broke out all over my body. If he could kiss like this… His other hand went to my thigh and my heart started to thump louder.

Should I stop him? I wondered. I placed my hand on his wrist but offered no resistance. Another strong wave came up and wet my entire dress. His fingers stroked my thighs.

Am I really doing this? my rational mind asked me one last time in a meek voice while I moaned. Nobody cared about the rational mind tonight. My hand slid under his linen shirt, already wet due to the water. I touched his hard chest, and circled my index finger around his left nipple. He bit my lower lip in excitement.

We sat up. He removed his shirt, keeping his shorts on. He pulled up my dress and had me wriggle out of it. We lay down again, the cold sand under our backs. He kissed my navel, touching his tongue to it. My knees lifted a little. I grabbed his head with my hands.

'Neel,' I whispered. He didn't hear me. His mouth and fingers continued to explore me. He traced my bra with a lazy finger. He took his time, to match the slow pace of the island. After a while, he lifted me a little. His hand went behind me and unhooked my bra in one snap. My breasts felt the cold breeze. He paused to look at them, whatever he could see in the moonlight.

He touched a nipple with his fingertip. Took a breast in his hand. I could feel myself melting all over. When my hand brushed over his shorts I knew he was as turned on as I was, if not more. His mouth was on my breasts.

I lifted my hips and he pulled down my underwear. Then we were both naked on the sandy beach. He leaned over me again and kissed my inner thighs. His tongue reached down there and kissed me intimately. I almost jumped up in excitement.

Like all his kisses, he kept this light and slow, till I began to tremble. His tongue began to gather pace. The pleasure became unbearable. I arched my back. Debu had gone down on me before. However, this was a completely new level of sensation and pleasure. If Debu was French fries, this was a gourmet six-course meal. If Debu was beer, this was champagne. If Debu was a boat, this was a luxury cruise. *Stop comparing, and what's with the weird analogies?* I mentally scolded myself, and refocused on the moment. Neel continued to work magic with his tongue. I arched my back further and dug my fingers in his hair.

'Everything good?' he whispered.

I didn't respond. I couldn't. I simply nodded. It wasn't just good. It was divine, sublime, insane Philippines-exclusive-island-level good.

I could feel the build-up of an orgasm within me, as could he. I squeezed his face between my thighs. I came, hard. He lifted himself up and brought his face close to mine. He used his arm to gently part my legs and entered me. He moved with gentle and firm strokes. I felt the build-up again and I came a second time, more intensely than the first. My body shook, I closed my eyes, and I blacked out for at least thirty seconds. This one orgasm had the intensity of ten orgasms.

He paused after I came and pulled out of me. He brought his face close to mine and gently pecked me on the cheek.

'You okay?' he said, his voice tender.

'That...' I said as I gasped for breath. 'That…was something else. How on earth did you do that?'

He simply grinned in response. In embarrassment, I covered my face with my hands. He gently removed my hands and looked into my eyes.

He entered me again. He felt bigger than before. I clenched his shoulders as we continued to make love. Water hit us from time to time. We kissed till I felt his shoulder spasm under my hand and he groaned.

He looked into my eyes and smiled. He played with my eyelashes. He put his arm around me as we lay down side by side, facing each other.

'That was…' he whispered and paused to take a breath before he spoke again, 'something else.'

'I know,' I whispered back.

The stars twinkled above us. My day had started early with a morning flight in Hong Kong. Our frantic lovemaking made me feel tired. Fatigue took over. I closed my eyes.

27

The sun has a way of making everything visible, even your blunders. When dawn broke I opened my eyes. I blinked, trying to orient myself. The seawater glistened in front of me but my mouth felt parched. I felt a headache coming on. Water, I needed water. Neel lay next to me, fast asleep.

'No way,' I mumbled. 'No way, Radhika. No way.'

I smacked my forehead. I found my clothes next to me. I wore them as quietly and quickly as possible. I stood up, wondering if I should wake Neel up. I decided not to. I picked up the glasses and the empty champagne bottle, the catalyst to last night's disaster, and walked back. The sun rose higher. I walked fast. I didn't want to face Neel right now. In fact, I didn't want to face him ever.

Back in my room I lay on the bed, staring at the ceiling.

'Fuck,' I said out loud. 'What the fuck have you done, Radhika?'

I lay there motionless. A million thoughts ran through my mind. *What did I just do? I slept with a partner at Goldman Sachs. I slept with a man twenty years older than me.* I realized Neel was just ten years younger than my father.

Radhika, how could you do it? Mini-me jumped out of her cave. All of a sudden, mini-me had full authority.

There is something wrong, something totally fucked up about you. You are just a bloody useless little idiot.

My happy mood from yesterday had evaporated. Life had just begun to sort itself out. I had closed a great deal. I had been promoted. I had even somewhat gotten over Debu. All this had given me a new shot of self-esteem. Now it meant nothing. I curled up in my bed in tears. Mini-me continued to talk, or rather yell at me.

He's fucking married. He has two kids. There is a wife. They are all waiting in Hong Kong, where both of you live.

Yes, it was true. And I had known it all before. What was I thinking? Or rather, why was I not thinking?

Life is not a private island in the Philippines, mini-me shouted at me.

I know, I know. I had nothing to counter my inner voice with.

This is why Debu left you. Something is wrong with you, seriously, you stupid, slutty bitch.

I sobbed. I don't know why, but I cried and cried. I had crossed the line. Hell, I had not just crossed, but jumped and leaped miles over the line.

You had one thing going for you, your career. Now you have fucked that up too, mini-me said.

I berated myself for a long time. I realized I had to get up. I had to shower, pack and leave on a seaplane in an hour. I didn't know how to face him. I didn't want to. *Could we go back on separate flights? Could I just go drown in the sea outside?*

I wondered where Neel was. *What if he didn't wake up? Should I call him?*

I heard a knock on my door. I froze. I opened the door to find one of the hotel staff.

'Madam, your shoes. You left them in the restaurant last night.'

'Oh, sure, thanks,' I said.

'I returned sir's shoes to his room.'

'Great. Was he there?'

'Yes, he was. He asked me to tell you to meet in the seaplane reception area in thirty minutes.'

'Sure,' I said, relieved. I didn't have to talk to him just yet. I showered and changed into a charcoal-grey suit. It was too formal and a misfit for my location but apt for my mental state. As if he would see me in this work suit again and things would be back to normal.

Funnily enough, he did seem pretty normal.

'Hey, good morning,' he said and smiled. He wore sunglasses, just like me. We had found a way to avoid eye contact.

'Hi,' I said.

'All set? Time to say goodbye to the Pengalusian,' he said. His voice seemed casual. He seemed calm, unlike the neurotic mess I was.

We sat in the plane. The pilot gave a thumbs-up as we took off. I ignored the beautiful scenery below us, as my mind was flooded with doubts. Instead of regret, another set of thoughts gripped me.

How is he is so calm and casual? Did it mean nothing to him?

I looked outside the window, away from him. My mind was on nothing but him.

Is this a regular thing for him? He doesn't think this was special? Have there been other girls? Oh, am I also just a conquest now? I hate him.

The seaplane landed. We stepped out and took a car to the Palawan airport. He looked at me. I looked away. We reached the airport and took our connecting flights back to Hong Kong. On the way, we spoke little, limiting ourselves to stupid conversations like 'Where's the gate?' at the transit airport in Manila or 'Can you pass the pepper?' during our meal in the Cathay Pacific aircraft.

I don't know why grown-ups behave in such a stupid manner. Pepper seemed more important than anything else. I opened my laptop and pretended to work. He did the same. My mind raced up and down with thoughts. *I have been such a fool. He will go home, tick another box in his conquest list and laugh about it. He will be like, that Indian VP chick? Check. Been there, done that desi babe. Damn it, Radhika. Stupid. Stupid. Stupid.*

We landed in Hong Kong. We went to the airport car pick-up point. We waited for our respective cars, which Bianca had booked for us. Our two black cars arrived. I proceeded to step into mine.

'Radhika,' Neel said.

'Yeah,' I said and turned to him.

'I know you probably have a million thoughts in your head. So do I.'

'What thoughts?' I said. 'Excuse me?'

Let's pretend nothing happened. That would be a mature way to deal with it, right?

'About last night?' he said, puzzled.

I shrugged my shoulders.

'Haven't really had a chance to think about it,' I said. *Yeah, more like, haven't thought of anything but that.*

'Well, I have been thinking about it all day.'

Good, mister, at least it freaking matters. Go on, I said in my head as I continued to look at him.

'And while I am still working through my thoughts, I just wanted you to know that last night was special for me. I can tell you, haven't felt that way before.'

'Oh,' I said, my mouth open. I did not expect that. 'Oh okay, well,' I said and went into clueless and silent bimbette mode. I looked at him with a blank face.

'Yeah, it was tender and wonderful and touching and so many things,' Neel said, moving his hands around as he spoke.

'That's interesting,' I said.

Okay, what kind of an idiotic response is that? Interesting? Like really, Radhika?

'Interesting?' he said, surprised at my stupid response.

'I better go. See you later,' I said. The driver opened my car door.

'Sure,' he said and waved at me. He looked pained at what would have seemed to him my indifference. The car drove off the airport terminal. I noticed him continue looking at my car until he went out of sight.

My car zipped across the highway as Hong Kong's flickering skyscraper lights became visible again.

Pretend it never happened, maybe that will mean it never did, I said to myself as the car reached my home.

28

Two weeks later

'Okay, enough. We do need to discuss what happened,' Neel said.

'Why?' I said. Neel had called me to his office. We sat facing each other at his desk.

'Because it's not good to not talk about it. You've been avoiding me ever since we came back from the Philippines.'

I studied my fingernails. 'What is there to talk about? It was wrong.'

'Well,' he said and paused before he spoke again. 'Define wrong.'

'It was wrong, Neel. And you know it,' I said, looking up.

'Okay, maybe it was a little wrong. But it felt right.'

'Really?'

'Didn't it? Didn't it feel just right?'

'It doesn't matter, Neel.' I started counting on my fingers. 'I work for you. You are married. You are a dad.'

'I am aware of that.'

'So then what is this all about? Let it be a one-off. A one-off blunder. And let's move on.'

He stood up restlessly and walked to the window. Staring into the harbour he spoke again. 'I can't call it a blunder. How does one call the most special experience of one's life a blunder?'

He has a way with words. Be careful, I told myself.

'Call it what you want. Point is, it was not real. We can put it down to the setting, the drinks, the air... It won't happen again. It won't,' I said, my voice as agitated as his was quiet.

Neel came back to his seat and sat across from me.

He held his chin with his right hand.

'Okay, okay, calm down,' Neel said. 'I get it.'

'We should focus on work,' I said briskly.

'Fine. We cool then, otherwise?'

'Yeah,' I said.

'So if there's another deal I want to staff you on, I can?'

'Of course. You are the boss.'

'Even if it is with me?'

'Do you have to staff me in particular?'

'Greenwood wants to buy some more distressed hotels in Korea. They want us to look at some options. They liked your work. So…' He left the sentence hanging.

'Whatever you say,' I said.

'I won't staff you if you don't want to. Should I say you are not available?'

'So I lose my clients now?' I said.

'Of course not. You are on. The target company is in Seoul. Let's go there soon.'

◆

'I am looking for a sofa. A two-seater, please,' I said.

'Would you like a simple sofa or a sofa bed?' the salesperson said.

I had come to IKEA, the Swedish furniture store, on the weekend. The huge, 20,000-square-feet IKEA store is located in Causeway Bay.

'Sofa bed,' I said. At some point, if I had guests from India, I would need to provide a place to sleep. The IKEA salesperson led me to the sofa bed area.

There were a dozen models, from Japanese futons to clever snap-shut mechanisms.

'Do you have a colour preference?' the salesperson said.

'Not really. How about the steel grey right there?' I pointed at one.

'Oh, that's a bestseller. Comfortable and minimalist,' she said.

I sat on the sofa to see how it felt.

'Good,' I said. 'I like it.'

'Hi.' Someone waved at me from a distance.

I looked up. 'Neel?' I said.

He stood at the other corner of the sofa section.

'Hi,' he said again as I walked up to him. 'Good to see you here. We came for some easy chairs. Here, meet Kusum. Kusum, meet Radhika, from my office.'

An Indian woman, around forty years old, stood next to him. A three-year-old boy held one of her fingers. A seven-year-old girl sitting on one of the IKEA sofas played with an iPhone. A twenty-six-year-old girl, or me, wished for an earthquake that would swallow her deep into the bottom of the earth.

'Radhika, so nice to meet you,' Kusum said in an American accent.

She extended her hand.

'Oh, okay,' I said as we shook hands. 'I mean, hi, Kusum.'

'This is Aryan. Aryan, say hi to Radhika didi,' Neel said. Aryan extended his tiny hand as well. I shook it. My heart began to beat fast.

'And that is Siya. Siya, say hi to didi,' Neel said. Siya waved my way without looking up from her screen.

'Not done, Siya,' Kusum said in a firm voice. 'Is that how you wish people?'

Siya recognized authority. She kept the phone aside and came to me with dainty steps.

'Hello, didi. How are you?' she said, in a rehearsed formal routine.

'I am fine. Thank you,' I said.

'That's better. Siya, I don't like bad behaviour,' Kusum said.

I guess more than anyone, I was the badly behaved one. I avoided eye contact with Kusum. I did manage a side-glance. She was slim, elegant and had a straight, upright posture. She was wearing a long black dress with a diamond necklace and matching earrings, the ones you see advertised outside the Cartier store in Hong Kong. I noticed a fat solitaire on her ring finger. Three carats, I guessed.

'Sorry, Radhika, just training her. She's addicted to the phone,' Kusum said and smiled.

'It's okay,' I said, wondering what excuse would allow me the quickest exit.

'Neel's mentioned you,' Kusum continued. 'You recently moved to Hong Kong, right?'

'Yeah, six months,' I said, wondering what else he had mentioned.

'We have been meaning to call the team over to our house. It's my fault, never worked out a date,' Kusum said.

'Not a problem,' I said. I spoke as little as possible to exhaust conversation so I could leave.

'Shopping for home, is it?' Neel said. Well, did he have to talk? I felt guilty just being next to him in front of Kusum. I wished I could hide beneath one of the IKEA sofas.

'Yes. I needed a sofa bed,' I said.

'Where do you put up?' Kusum said.

Is she going to come kill me? Will she knock me out with that diamond solitaire?

'Old Peak Road,' I said.

'We are in Repulse Bay. Do come sometime. Do you miss Indian home food? Have her over, Neel,' Kusum said.

Oh, please, please don't be nice to me, I wanted to say.

'Yeah, why not? You should come,' Neel said, his face as blank as mine.

'Maybe sometime. Anyway, I don't want to impose on your family outing,' I said, hoping to escape.

'What outing? We just came for some errands. Are you by yourself?' Kusum said.

Yes, I am. Single, alone and loveless. No wonder I borrowed your husband.

'Yes,' I said vaguely. 'Sunday, so just thought will fix up the house.'

'I love your dress, by the way,' Kusum said.

God, she is actually a nice person. She had praised my simple white lace dress, even though she probably wore a designer Prada or Gucci outfit herself. She was not a bitch. And that just made me feel worse.

'It's just Zara,' I said.

'Well, you have the figure for it,' she said. She seemed fit too. I looked at her face. She was pretty, fair and had high cheekbones. I would kill to look like her at forty. I noticed she had a small bust. My boobs were better. *Okay, why on earth am I comparing my body to hers? Is that all we women are? I am a vice president in Goldman Sachs. Why doesn't that make me feel as smug as knowing I have bigger boobs than Neel's wife? And why am I comparing myself to her at all?*

'Th...thanks,' I stammered, remembering she had given me a compliment.

'You have lunch plans?' she said.

'Er, actually, I normally don't eat lunch,' I said, making up nonsense as I spoke.

'We are just heading to the food court outside IKEA. Feel free to join us,' Kusum said.

I looked at Neel. *Can the great partner at Goldman Sachs use his brain to get me out of this?*

'Yeah, join us. Because it would be great if you can join us,' he rambled on, 'but not if you don't want to.'

I glared at him. *What do you mean, 'not if you don't want to'?*

'Have a salad. It's not good to skip meals,' Kusum said.

'Oh okay,' I said in meek submission.

'I understand you must be on a diet. Trust me, I go through the same,'

Kusum said and smiled at me.

So now what? Were we bonding together? Wife and mistress? Fuck, did I just call myself mistress? I am not a mistress. I am a vice president, for God's sake.

I followed Neel's family out of IKEA and to the food court in a daze. I saw taxis out on the road. I had the urge to jump into one and scoot away or maybe just jump under one of them and die.

◆

'Mom, I want French fries with my noodles,' Siya said.

'No, I will get you some veggies instead,' Kusum said. Siya made a face. Kusum glared at her daughter. Siya got the message and began to eat her lunch. Aryan had home food. Neel ordered a chicken wrap, Kusum a quinoa salad. I went for fried rice, though I ate it like a little bird, one grain at a time.

'Liking Hong Kong?' Kusum said.

'Yeah,' I said. 'Compact, convenient. Work is good.'

'Made some friends?' she said.

'Well, work people, mostly,' I said.

'That's Goldman for you. They make you work so much, you don't have a life outside.'

'That's not true,' Neel said. 'I come home on time.'

'You are a partner. These poor associates and VPs have to do the grunt work.'

Neel shrugged.

'You have to pay your dues,' he said.

'I couldn't handle it. JP Morgan for eight years. I just quit.'

'Oh, you were in banking?' I said. Neel never told me that. Well, he never told me *anything* about her.

'Yeah, equity sales. I had enough. Although busier now with these two little ones. Sometimes I do wish I could escape to office.'

'We don't escape, we work,' Neel said.

'Yeah, whatever. You at least get weekends. Mothers don't. The errands never stop. That reminds me, I had to call...' Kusum opened her Louis Vuitton handbag.

'Siya, where is my phone?'

'Mommy, I stopped using it when you told me to,' Siya said, slurping up a noodle.

'Oh no. I left it in IKEA. On the sofa.' Kusum jumped up. 'I will just go to the store and check.'

'You want me to come?' Neel said.

'How? Kids and food are all here. No, you stay. I will be back in ten minutes.'

'Do you want me to go and check?' I said. I'd do anything to get away from this sweet domestic scene.

'How kind of you to offer.' Kusum smiled. 'Don't worry. I will be back in a minute. Neel will handle the kids.'

She left Neel, Siya, Aryan and me at the food court. I had the most awkward meal of my entire life. I couldn't talk freely to Neel. Siya might understand, after all.

'Eat the vegetables too, Siya,' Neel said.

Siya didn't comply. Neel moved over to her and began to feed her with a spoon. I ate my rice in silence. Aryan ate butterfly-shaped pasta with red sauce from his lunch box. He smeared the red sauce all over his face and hands. With every bite, Aryan looked messier. I could see Neel wanted to attend to his son but had to feed his daughter.

'Do you mind?' he said and gestured to me. I looked around, took a deep breath and slid next to Aryan. I took a tissue and wiped his face.

'Eat slowly, Aryan, okay?' I said.

'You feedy me,' he said.

'What?' I said.

'You feedy me,' he said again.

Neel smiled at me. *Really, Neel, this is funny to you?* Aryan jumped into my lap and handed me his fork. I fed him with one hand and kept a tissue in my other hand to wipe his mouth.

'I didn't expect to run into you,' I said.

'Well, I had no idea you would be here,' Neel said. Siya looked at both of us one after the other, with an innocent expression. We decided not to pursue the topic further.

'You go to daddy office too?' Siya said.

'Yes,' I said. 'How about you? Which class are you in?'

'Grade three,' she said.

'What's your favourite subject?' I said, as Aryan took a bite off the fork.

'Math,' she said.

'Radhika didi is really good at it,' Neel said. He looked at me and smiled, as if he meant not just math.

'Are you really smart?' Siya said.

'I am okay smart,' I said.

'Enough feedy,' Aryan said to me, as he felt neglected.

'No, you have to finish your lunch, Aryan,' I said. I don't know how I ended up feeding Neel's child. It was awkward, sure. Yet, somehow, seeing Neel taking care of his children made him more real, more human. *Is this what it would be like to have a family?* I wondered what Neel thought when he saw me feed Aryan. His favourite distressed debt analyst could wipe tomato sauce off a toddler's face too.

Neel looked at me and smiled. *Do I make a good family person, Neel?*

'Found it,' Kusum said as she held up her iPhone. She noticed me with Aryan.

'Oh my God, I am so sorry. Aryan, you can eat on your own.'

'I like didi feedy me,' he said.

Kusum put out a hand for the fork. I surrendered it. She was staking her claim. She wanted her family back. Aryan went into his mother's arms. My lap, and even I on the inside, felt empty. I realized I wanted this too. I wanted kids. I wanted messy pasta dishes. I wanted iPhone-addicted daughters who had math as their favourite subject.

'Say thank you to didi,' Kusum said.

Aryan didn't say thanks. He bent forward and kissed me on my cheek. He had his father's charm. I melted at the little boy's display of love. I wanted to kiss him back. I didn't. I couldn't. How could I? It's somebody else's family. *Will I have a son like this one day? Will I ever have kids?*

'I better leave,' I said. 'I remembered my part-time help is coming. She doesn't have the keys.'

'Oh, you haven't finished your lunch,' Kusum said.

'I am quite full. Really, thanks so much,' I said.

'Really?' she said. 'We hardly spoke.'

'I am sure we will meet up soon,' I said.

'Of course,' Neel said, adding a comment when there was no need to.

'Bye, Siya. Bye, Aryan,' I said.

'Bye, Feedy Didi,' Aryan said and everyone laughed.

Feedy Didi dashed out of the food court.

29

For most women, it is that time of the month. For my mother, it is that time of the week. The time when she goes hysterical on the phone and wants one thing more than anything else in the world—my marriage.

'Not today, mom, please. Any other day,' I said.

'Why? It's Sunday. It's the only day you are relaxed and can talk properly.'

'I am not relaxed today,' I snapped. I opened my laptop and logged on to Facebook.

'Why? Are you working?'

'No.'

'So? You are at home, right? Did you go to that Ikka shop to get the sofa bed?'

'IKEA. Eee-Kee-Aaa.'

'Whatever. Did you get a sofa bed?'

'No. I went there this afternoon. I liked one. I didn't get a chance to buy it.'

'Why?'

'Leave it, mom. I told you. Not a good day.'

'How will we come if you don't have a sofa bed?'

'I'll get it, I promise.'

'Why are you so irritated?'

'Because I know what you are going to say.'

'What?'

'Register your profile. See some boys. Mom, why are you obsessed with me getting married?'

'If I don't care what will happen? You will continue buying sofas alone. Is it even a woman's job? To buy furniture?'

'Don't start, mom,' I said. I searched for Debu. He had kept his profile private. I don't know why, I wanted to see his profile picture. Maybe he was single again.

'Okay, listen to just one proposal,' she said.

'See, I knew it. That's the only thing you talk about!'

'Chemists.'

'Chemists?'

'I know what you are thinking. But this is a family with six chemist shops in the heart of Delhi. They even have one opposite AIIMS. Do you know how much business that can do?'

'Mom, you want my husband to sit in a chemist shop?'

'He manages the shops. He doesn't just sit there dishing out strips of Crocin.'

'What's his qualification?' I said.

'You have this hang-up about qualification.'

'Mom, how is education a hang-up? I am an MBA.'

'So he has done BPharm. He is thinking of doing an MBA,' she lowered her volume, 'through correspondence.'

'Correspondence?'

'You can even do it online these days.'

'Mom. Bye.'

'They have a kothi in Bengali Market. The boy's own floor has four bedrooms.'

'I don't care. I am not looking for real estate.'

'Talk to him once?'

'Why? Mom, you know I am working abroad. Why would I quit and come for this?'

'What do you want then? NRI? I can look.'

'I don't want anyone. Please leave me alone.'

'What has happened to you today?'

'I have to go. Bye.'

I ended the call. I saw the Facebook page in front of me. Avinash was still Debu's friend. I could ask him. I called Avinash in New York.

'Hey, Radhika. Been ages,' he said.

'Yeah. What's up?' I said.

'Just woke up. Sunday morning here. How's Hong Kong? Work?'

'It's good. Busy. Hey, Avinash, can I ask you for a quick favour?'

'Sure.'

'Promise you won't judge me, or tell anyone.'

'Sure.'

'I want you to check Debu's profile on Facebook.'

'Really?'

'See. You are judging me, right? This idiotic girl who moved continents but can't move on.'

'No, no. Wait. I am not judging. What do you want me to do?'

'I will FaceTime you. You point your phone camera to your computer screen. Load Debu's profile on your computer.'

He laughed. 'That's innovative.'

'It is also desperate.'

'Hey, that's fine. FaceTime me.'

I gave him a video call.

'Here we go. Debashish Sen,' Avinash said. I could see his computer screen on my phone. He zoomed in closer to Debu's profile picture. He stood there, grinning in Central Park with a red-haired white girl three inches taller than him. My heart sank. He had switched at least two women after me. I, meanwhile, had run into the wife and kids of the boss I had slept with.

'His last post was at a colleague's birthday party. Do you want me to enlarge the picture?'

'Yeah, sure,' I said.

Debu sat at a restaurant table, holding up a bottle of Corona beer. He still had his beard and curly hair. The tall white girl sat next to him, a glass of wine in her hand. He looked happy. She looked happy. The wine looked happy. Who did not look happy? Me.

'You want to see more?' Avinash said.

'Thanks, Avinash. That's enough,' I said, my voice flat.

'We miss you. Don't you miss New York?'

'Yeah, I do. Miss you guys,' I said.

I finished the call and sat in my bed. I saw the time; it was midnight. I changed into my nightclothes. As I put my white Zara dress into the laundry bag, I noticed a tiny red pasta sauce stain on the sleeve. I don't know why but I felt horrible. I felt lonely. I imagined Neel at home, kids in his lap while he told them bedtime stories. I imagined Kusum wearing designer sleepwear and cuddling Neel. Why was I imagining all this? How did it matter to me? I knew he had a family all along, right?

My phone buzzed. WhatsApp message from Neel.

'Hope you recovered from bumping into me today. Sorry about that.'

Okay, so he wasn't spooning in bed with his wife in pretty sleepwear. He was typing a message to me.

'Not your fault,' I messaged back.

'Strangely, I liked that you met my kids.'

'Really?'

'Yeah. They are a huge part of my life. Nice to share it with you.'

Somehow, he made it all seem less terrible.

'That's sweet of you to say. They are amazing kids.'

'Thanks. They liked you. Aryan kept saying Feedy Didi.'

I sent a smiley back.

'You don't even talk to me these days,' Neel sent another message.

'What's the point?' I replied.

'We can only know the point of talking if we do the talking, right?'

'It's fine. Nothing to be said. Mistakes happen.'

'Stop calling it a mistake. Please.'

'Fine.'

'Can we talk? Like catch up properly? Instead of avoiding each other.'

'I don't know, Neel. I am not in a good place.'

'What happened?'

'Nothing specific. Just low.'

'Can I be there for you? At least a little bit?'

'We will talk later,' I said.

'We are going to Seoul next week. Can we catch up then?'

'Sure,' I said.

'Thank you. Just don't avoid me.'

'Can't seem to, as it turns out. Even on weekends,' I said.

'You are funny. Anyway, goodnight.'

'Goodnight. By the way, Kusum is really sweet.'

'Thanks,' he said. 'She liked you.'

'Because she doesn't know me,' I said.

'Don't say that.'

I sent a smiley back. He replied with a long message.

'Anyway, Kusum is nice. I am not going to say she is a horrible person, Radhika. But she and I just don't share that connection. Not even a tenth of what you and I have. None, actually.'

I read the message and didn't reply.

'What?' he sent another message.

'What do you want me to say? Go see a counsellor? Work on your marriage? What?' I typed back.

'Nothing. I am telling you facts from my side. All I want is for you to admit to some of your feelings.'

'Why? Why do you want to know my feelings?' I replied.

'Because even though this is totally wrong, the fact is I love you. Goodnight,' Neel replied.

◆

We didn't talk in Seoul. We made love. We made crazy, crazy love. And we did the same when we went on other business trips, ten more times in the next three months. Each time our intimacy felt deeper than before. Despite feeling immoral, there was also the matter of my loneliness—he made me feel less lonely. I wanted Neel in my life. Someone to treat me like I was special and make me feel loved, every bit of me. Maybe I gave him something too. A bit of the youth he wanted to hold on to. The lightness and brightness of me.

As our business trips increased, our guilt trips decreased. He said he and Kusum disagreed on many things, from raising kids to how hard he should work. He said I accepted him the way he was. With every night we spent, flight we shared and meal we had together, I felt closer to him. I still showed some restraint. He told me 'I love you' every time we met. I never did. He never pushed me to reciprocate either.

The Greenwood quest for more distressed hotels in Korea dragged on. They wanted to see more options. We didn't mind. It meant more trips to Seoul, more companies to look at and more Neel to hold through the night.

30

Three months later

'Who is it?' I said. I walked up to answer the doorbell in my nightclothes. I was watching the Filmfare Awards at my home in Hong Kong. The film *Queen*, about a woman who took charge of her life, was sweeping all the awards. The doorbell rang again.

I opened the door.

'Neel?' I said. I checked the time: 11 p.m.

'Sorry, I didn't mean to disturb you,' he said.

Neel and I had some unspoken rules. He never came to my apartment. I had never gone to his house either. We had never got together in Hong Kong. Somehow, intimacy on a business trip far away felt less sinful than in the city we lived in.

'What's the matter?' I said.

'Can I stay here tonight?' Neel said.

'Why?' I said. 'I mean, we don't really do that.'

'Kusum and I had a fight,' he said.

'Anything major?'

'Things escalated. I didn't want them to get worse. I told her I had to go on a business trip and left. I thought I would go to a hotel in Hong Kong but...' he said and looked at me.

But what? You thought, why pay for a room and be alone when you can get accommodation and sex for free? I thought.

'Yeah, of course. You can stay here. Come in,' I said.

'Thanks,' he said.

'Hungry?' I said.

He shook his head. He held me by my shoulders. He kissed me. He smiled. I did not.

'What am I to you, Neel? A stress ball? To come and play with when you are hassled?'

'No. Not at all, Radhika,' he said. He sounded shocked.

'So why are you here? Didn't we have this pact that we don't do anything in Hong Kong?'

'Did we? I mean, what's the difference?'

'There is, to me. Business trips feel less…wrong. There's also a clear boundary. This is…I don't know what.'

'Why?'

'Because I don't know when you will show up here and when you won't. Today you are at my home because you had a tiff with your wife. Tomorrow she will bake cookies for you and you will be home with her. What does that make me? Ms Standby?'

He pushed back his hair with an unsteady hand. 'I just wanted to be out of there. Fresh air…I thought I will come and check if you wanted to be with me. I am sorry if…'

'It's fine tonight. I just prefer it outside Hong Kong. Helps me keep my sanity,' I said.

'Are you okay, Radhika? I've never seen you like this,' Neel said.

'Let's go to bed.'

◆

We lay in bed. I turned off the lights. He put his arm around me. I didn't reciprocate and lay still.

'I know what you are thinking,' he said.

'What?'

'That this is a booty call.'

'Now that you say it, maybe yes. Maybe that's why you are here.'

'I just wanted to be with you. Let's not do anything tonight. Let me just hold you,' he said.

I looked at him. Even in the darkness I could see his eyes.

'Really?' I said.

'Yeah. Why are you so surprised?'

'You are a guy. We are having an affair. You are okay with not having sex?'

'Of course,' Neel said. He kissed my shoulder.

'We can if you want to,' I said.

'No, not tonight. I just want to be with you,' Neel said. 'Goodnight. I love you.'

'Goodnight,' I said, in mild shock.

I stayed awake as he slept in my arms. He was two decades older, yet I felt I had a baby next to me. He looked peaceful as his head lay on top of my hair. Maybe he did care for me. Maybe what we were doing was wrong, but maybe something good could come out of it.

I checked. He seemed to be in deep sleep.

'I love you, Neel Gupta,' I whispered to his sleeping face.

'I heard that,' he said and turned sides.

'You are so bad,' I said and punched his shoulder as he grinned, eyes still closed.

◆

'I will let Josh do the talking. He is your supervisor. Only fair he gives you your number on bonus day,' Neel said.

Josh sat in Neel's office. I took a seat with them.

'Sure,' I said. It was impressive how professional Neel and I were at work.

Josh gave me a summary of my performance review. My peers had rated me four-and-a-half overall.

'That's a good rating,' Neel said. I wondered what he himself had rated me.

'Thanks,' I said.

'And the bottom line,' Josh said. 'Your number, or your bonus for the year, is 350,000 dollars.'

My heart skipped a beat.

'Wow,' I blurted out, even though I didn't intend to react.

Josh smiled.

'That tells me you are happy. Good.'

'Thanks,' I said, still absorbing my gross compensation. My total base salary and bonus came up to half a million dollars.

'Keep up the good work.'

'I am humbled,' I said.

'You deserve it. Your deals made a lot of money for the group,' Neel said.

He smiled at me. I kept a straight face.

I came back to my desk. I called my mother. She gasped at the number, especially when I converted it into rupees. My father went into shock.

'Of course it's all legal, dad. What are you saying? I promise it's legal. Goldman Sachs is a reputed firm,' I said.

'But three crores a year?' he said.

'That's your little girl,' I said.

He laughed.

'You want to move to a new house in Gurgaon? One of those apartments with swimming pools and gyms?'

'No, beta. We are fine here,' dad said.

'If you need anything, just anything, let me know,' I said.

'You visit us soon,' he said.

'I will,' I said. 'Love you.'

Josh finally left Neel's office at 6, after finishing all bonus announcements.

I knocked at Neel's door a little later.

'Hey, come on in,' he said.

'Tired?' I said.

'Busy day, yes,' he said.

I sat down in front of him.

'Happy with your number?' he said.

'Yeah. I just wanted to be sure of one thing,' I said.

'What?'

'How much of this bonus is due to my work?'

'What?' Neel said, surprised.

'How much is due to my work and how much is due to what we have?'

'Are you kidding me, Radhika? This is all your good work. You know the profits on your deals.'

'Yeah, you said I deserve it. I just want to be sure,' I said.

He shook his head.

'I don't believe it,' he said.

'What?'

'You are paid because you are good. Actually, you deserved more. However, there are limits to what first-year VPs can be paid. I could have asked New York to override the limit,' he said as I interrupted him.

'Please don't do things like that.'

'Well, I didn't. And it's hurtful you think I would. I don't need to pay you more to get your love. Okay?'

'Okay,' I said. 'Thanks then.'

'Stop presuming things. I am trapped in a marriage. I don't have answers. I wish things were different,' he said, his voice agitated. He paused and continued in a calmer voice, 'But I love you. That is why I am with you. I am proud of you. You deserve it. You deserve more.'

'I am sorry,' I said.

'It's fine,' he said.

'How was your bonus?' I said.

'I am not supposed to tell you that.' He grinned.

'You are also not supposed to do a lot of other things with me, mister,' I said.

'Three,' he said.

'Three what?'

'Three bucks.'

'Three million dollars?' I said, my eyes round.

'See, this is why I didn't want to tell you. It sounds like a lot, I know.'

'It is a lot. You made three fucking million dollars in bonus?' I said.

Somehow, life has a way of making you feel inadequate about a 350,000-dollar bonus.

'I told you. You deserve more. Dream bigger, girl.' Neel winked at me.

◆

'You made so much money last year. You are a vice president. What else do you want career-wise?'

'Mom, it's not just career. I am not ready.'

I had surprised my parents. I had come home for the Chinese New Year four-day weekend in Hong Kong. Aditi didi had also come over. Dad, Mom, Aditi didi and I visited India Gate. We took a walk along the lawns. My mother walked with me. As always, she talked about her favourite topic.

'You will never be fully ready. It is already hard to get a boy for you. You are too successful, beta.'

'Is there such a thing? Too successful?'

'For girls there is. What to do?'

'Let's not start again, mom. I am only here for four days.'

'What is the use? At least chat with a few good ones? I will find NRIs, okay?'

'No, mom. I don't want to.'

'Do you have someone?' mom said and looked at me. Her direct eye contact made me uncomfortable.

I have someone, yes. Someone only five years younger than you, mom.

'Not really.'

'Not really means?'

'No, I don't.'

'So? Don't you need a man? Every woman does.'

'I don't think so. I do fine on my own.'

'There is an age, beta. You get the best matches then. After that, a girl's appeal declines. You are twenty-six already.'

'So I am like a car model? Depreciating over the years.'

'You are impossible! I am not talking to you.'

My mother sulked for the next half-hour, which meant thirty minutes of peace. We walked along Rajpath all the way to Rashtrapati Bhavan. Her tough and sullen expression matched that of the security guards on duty.

'What do you want, mom?' I said finally.

'You say you are not ready. But give me a time-frame. When will you start looking at boys seriously?'

'I don't know. Three years. Four?'

'You will be thirty. How do you expect me to find a good guy for you?'

'I will also be an even more successful banker.'

'So? That makes it worse.'

I rolled my eyes.

'I would have a lot of money of my own. That will help me and my husband get a good start in life, no?' I said.

'You don't need to make so much. Your man will.'

'Mom. Please.'

'One year. I will wait one year, then you cooperate. We start looking seriously, okay?'

'Just one year?'

I stopped to buy peanuts from a street vendor. She rambled on while I fed her with one hand and held the peanuts in the other.

'You are so fussy. It will take another year even after I start looking for you. Another year to do the wedding, as NRIs have their own time issues. It is still a three-year process. You will be twenty-nine. Already late. Doesn't listen, this girl…'

'One year. Okay? But don't push,' I said.

'I never push. Do I ever push?' she said.

I looked at her. She seemed so earnest while asking her question, I burst out laughing.

'Please find sensible men. Men with some class, okay?' I said.

'What class? I am going to find some slum-dweller for you or what? I'll find total gentleman, you wait and see,' she said. I mentally grinned at the word 'gentleman', which made me think of Neel. He was what my mother would call a gentleman. Minus his affair, of course.

'I love you, mom. You are too cute,' I said.

'What? And what is this class business when you yourself are eating peanuts on the road?'

31

Dragon-I restaurant, Central, Hong Kong

Neel and I had come for dim sum, the traditional Chinese dumplings, at the posh Dragon-I, a modern Chinese restaurant near our office. I struggled with my chopsticks as I picked up a steamed spinach dumpling.

'So yeah, one year. That's all mom gave me,' I said. I finished recounting my India Gate conversation.

Neel lifted a peanut dumpling with his chopsticks easily.

'So you are getting married?' Neel said.

I looked at him and thought a little before I spoke again. 'I am just tired of my mother's relentless pursuit. I have to listen to her at some point.'

'What about *us*, what we have?' Neel took a sip of Chinese tea.

'Neel, what about my life? Do you care?' I said, my voice firm. We locked eyes.

'Of course, I care. But isn't *us* important?' he said in a reasonable voice.

'For there to be an *us*, there has to be a future. *Us* has no future, right?' I said.

'I don't know. We haven't discussed anything,' Neel said, looking taken aback by how serious the lunch conversation had turned.

'And whose fault is that?' I said.

Of course, it is your fault, Neel, is what I wanted to say.

'The topic never came up, I guess,' he said.

I didn't respond. I just stared at him. I kept my chopsticks down.

'What?' he said, figuring out that something was very wrong.

'What topic, Neel?' I said.

'Us,' he said. 'Us and our future.'

'Us is useless,' I said.

'Us is special,' Neel said.

'Well, all this *us* has done is have an affair for the last year. This *us* pretends to be colleagues in the office. Whereas in reality this *us* sleeps with each other during business trips and, now, even at my place.'

'Can you keep your voice down, please?' Neel whispered.

It only pissed me off.

'See. Even here, even at Dragon-I, we are colleagues. I can't say anything that will give us away. I can't hold your hand here, can I? Even though you do like to spoon me at night, isn't it?'

Neel looked around. The closest customers were three tables away.

'You want to talk, we can talk. About anything. I had no idea you had so much bottled up.'

'How could you? You have it easy. Partner at office. Husband and father at home. Young chick when you want her. What do you have to worry about?'

'This.'

'What?'

'That you are not okay about it. When I thought you were.'

'What made you think I am okay?'

'I don't know. When we make love, or when we work together, or when we chat, isn't it out of this world?'

'Life isn't lived "out of this world", Neel. Life is lived in this world.'

To be fair, even I didn't know why I felt so anxious. Perhaps my mother's one-year ticking-clock deadline had triggered a panic attack.

'You know the problem, Neel. I can't even discuss *us* with anyone. Other girls discuss their boyfriends with their friends. I can't, right?'

I had to stop talking. I excused myself to go to the washroom. I returned after washing my face.

Neel looked at me with concern.

'Sorry,' I said. *Why am I saying sorry to him?*

'You don't have to be sorry. It's your feelings. Thank you for sharing them. I am sorry for not sensing them earlier.'

My plate of vegetable dumplings had gone cold. One of the waiters replaced it. Neel and I ate in silence.

'I love you,' Neel said.

I shrugged.

'So?' I said. 'Kind of irrelevant, isn't it?'

'What do you want, Radhika?' Neel said.

I kept silent.

'A future? I am twenty years older,' he said.

'You said age doesn't matter in love. Didn't you?'

'I am married. I have kids. So much baggage.'

'Exactly. So what am I doing with you?'

'Aren't you happy with just what we have?' Neel said. He seemed to be genuinely confused.

'Would you be? If you were in my place?' I asked, looking him squarely in the eye.

'We have our work. We have love. We have excitement. We have friendship. We don't have the predictability and monotony of a married couple.'

'You make marriage sound so bad. You are married. The whole world gets married.'

'Clarify this for me. Do you want to get married? Or are you feeling stressed only because your mother wants you to get married soon?'

'Eventually I do want to, Neel. How could you think I won't? I want marriage, kids, family.'

'Really?'

'What do you mean, really? I do. I want Sunday IKEA trips with my husband and a whole bunch of kids. I want to wipe my kids' messy faces when I feed them. I want to bake cookies for them. Yes, yes I do.'

'Really, Radhika?' Neel said. He looked at me gobsmacked, as if I had revealed my secret desire to join the ISIS.

'Yeah. Why?'

'I thought you were career-minded.'

'Excuse me? What is that supposed to mean?' I said, my voice ice-cold.

'Nothing. Let's talk later. I'll ask for the bill,' Neel said and signalled the waiter.

◆

'No, Neel. Not tonight,' I said.

We were lying tangled up in my bed. He nuzzled the side of my neck. It signalled that he wanted sex. I shrugged my shoulder, dislodging his lips.

'Radhika, come here,' he murmured my name in a persuasive voice.

'No, Neel,' I said. 'I am tired.'

He had come to my apartment four nights in a row this week. I don't know what story he made up at home. Frankly, I didn't care. Every night I let him in. We watched TV for a while and we went to bed.

He rebuttoned the shirt of his nightsuit.

'This is the fourth time you have rejected me,' he said. He was right.

We hadn't had sex all week.

'Stop assuming. I am not rejecting anything. I am tired,' I said.

'Is it your mother?' he said.

I shook my head.

'Is it me?' he said.

I shook my head.

'It's me,' I said.

'What?'

'How could I let myself get into this?' I said.

'We love each other, Radhika. Stop making it sound so bad.'

I switched on the night lamp next to me and turned on my side to face him. I lifted myself up to rest on my elbow.

'Really, Neel?' I said.

'What?' Neel said.

'I allowed myself to get involved with a married man. Not just a one-night stand. A long and full-blown affair. Hell, I allowed myself to fall in love with you. When there is no future.'

'I have no plans to leave you.'

'But do you have any plans to change anything?'

'Why do we have to change? What we have is perfect.'

'What if Kusum finds out?'

'She won't.'

'What if she does?'

'Don't be paranoid. You are being over-anxious these days. Is it that time of the month?'

He tried to put his arms around me.

'Shut up, Neel,' I said, extracting myself from his grip. 'Don't trivialize it.'

'Your weekend trip to Delhi and talking to your mother has really shaken you up.'

'Maybe I needed to be shaken up. To really think about what I want.'

Neel sat up in bed.

'Sorry to say this, but you aren't thinking clearly. If I go by what you said in Dragon-I,' Neel said.

'I said I want to have a family. Have kids. Be a good mother and look after them well. That's not thinking clearly?'

'You are a star at work. What is all this mundane stuff you are talking about? Any woman can do all this.'

'But I can't?'

'I didn't say that.'

'So?'

'I see you as someone exceptional. And special. You could be an MD, a partner.'

'Yeah, I will be. I like my work too.'

'But you said you want marriage, IKEA, bunch of kids. Baking cookies, really?'

'Yes, I want all that too.'

'Radhika, you are getting carried away. You saw Kusum the other day and you are getting competitive over me.'

I too sat up in bed, almost panting in anger.

'It's not always about you, Mr Neel Gupta. I am talking about myself. *My* needs. Do you get it, Mr I-am-so-smart Goldman Sachs partner?'

'It's just that...' He turned silent.

'What?' I said. He did not respond.

'Say what you wanted to say, Neel.'

'It's just I never thought of you as the maternal type. I don't know if you were even meant to be a mother.'

I felt my face turn hot. My whole body began to quiver. Neel figured he had said something really, really wrong.

'Okay, that did not come out right.'

'Get out,' I said, my voice calm.

He didn't move.

'Please leave my apartment, Neel. Get out now.'

'Come here, I will make you feel better,' he said, leaning forward. He tried to kiss me.

Slap! I gave him a tight one across his face. I didn't care who the fuck he was.

'How dare you? How dare you fucking say that?' I said.

'I am sorry.'

'Just leave. Or I will send an email to all of Goldman Sachs tomorrow. About us. Would you like that?'

He slithered out of bed. I kept a stern gaze on him as he dressed, picked up his laptop bag and left.

I curled up in bed, tears rolling down my cheeks. I cried and cried.

I buried my face in the pillows, including the one that smelt of Neel, and just cried.

You are so stupid, Radhika, I said to myself.

What was I thinking anyway? Neel and I would walk off into the sunset? He thinks I wasn't meant to be a mother. How could I ever love this man? Did I not know this day would come?

My stomach hurt. When I went to the bathroom I discovered that Neel was right. It *was* that time of the month. In the middle of all this drama I had to deal with the first day of my period. Did I tell you it sucks to be a girl sometimes?

◆

'What's this?' Neel said, surprised.

He slid the letter on his desk towards me.

Josh Ang,
Distressed Debt Group
Goldman Sachs

Dear Josh,

I would like to submit my resignation from the position of vice president in the Distressed Debt Group.
Thank you so much for the wonderful experience.

Radhika Mehta

'That reached you real quick,' I quipped.

'Of course. I have to sign off on it,' Neel said.

'Can you please do that, sir?'

'Will you stop it, please?' Neel said, his voice low.

'Fine. Whatever. I'll be quiet.' I exhaled and kept quiet.

'This is your career,' Neel said after a few seconds.

'I know what I am giving up. My career is the one thing I truly had as my own,' I said.

'So why?'

'I have no choice. My career is intertwined with you. If I have to leave you, both have to go.'

'So don't leave me.'

'And do what? Become your mistress?'

'What rubbish.'

'What else am I? Mistresses at least get some rights and privileges. I am worse, actually.'

'You are no mistress. You make your own money. Mistresses take money from the man. They are dependent. You do it out of choice.'

'Which in some ways makes it even worse. Can we hurry up, please?'

'You won't let go, is it?' Neel said.

'I have decided, Neel. As you can see, I have nothing to lose. You do. So please.'

'I am sorry about what I said yesterday, okay? That mother thing.'

'It's not just what you said or didn't say. This whole thing is wrong. And now if I have any self-respect left, I need to end it.'

Neel looked at me carefully. I kept my eyes on the view outside the window—the Hong Kong harbour.

'You make me feel so bloody guilty,' he said.

'You should feel bloody guilty,' I said, still without looking at him.

'We did this together. Nobody forced you.'

'I know. I feel guilty. So about time you do too.'

'Give me two hours.'

'What?' I said, turning to him.

'Come back in two hours. Can you?'

I shrugged and left his office. I went back to my cubicle.

My desk phone rang after two hours. I went back to Neel's office.

◆

'Leave me if you have to. Don't quit the firm,' Neel said.

'So are you resigning instead?' I said.

'Can you stop being so harsh? We have happy memories.'

I smirked at him. He continued, 'You can take a transfer to another office. New York. London. Wherever.'

I looked at him.

'I suppose not New York,' he said.

Sure, not New York. I had a relationship wreck in that city too.

'I...' I began to speak as he interrupted me.

'You can get jobs outside. But please don't leave the group. We value you. I will never forgive myself.'

'Is that all you won't forgive yourself for?' I said.

He hung his head low. Then he stood up and went to the window. I thought about his proposal for a minute.

'Fine, I can move to London. But it has to feel like a new job. I don't want you in my life. At all.'

'What do you mean?'

'No common deals. No being in touch. Be gone. Clear?'

'How can we...'

'Neel, I am serious. If this is reported, you get into trouble. Not me. You are the boss.'

'Are you threatening me?'

'I am saying I am serious. I am going to be a huge mess. I don't know if I will be able to pick up the pieces again. I don't want you in my life there. That is why I am leaving.'

'Okay,' Neel said in a heavy voice and came back to his seat.

'Thanks.'

'Someone from the London office will call you this evening,' he said.

'Fine. Can I leave now?'

'Yeah,' he said and paused. 'Radhika?'

'Yes?'

'I am sorry.'

'For?'

'I am sorry I let you down.'

I stood up to leave.

'I let myself down, Neel.'

32

I felt a lump in my throat as I replayed Hong Kong in my head. My hand holding the breakfast plate trembled. Neel looked at me. My relatives continued to fill the dining room. I drank a glass of water to buy time.

'Can we talk in private? Please?' Neel whispered.

'How, Neel? Can't you see? I am at my wedding.'

'I have a room here. Come for a little bit. Please.'

'How did you get a room? They told us they were full.'

'It's not important. Please, fifteen minutes?'

'But how did you get a room?' I said. I wanted to scream at the lobby manager.

'I took the presidential suite. That's all they had. Now can you come there? Room 101?'

Of course, Mr Partner had to be in the presidential suite. My cousins waved, gesturing me to come back.

'I need to have breakfast with my cousins. See you in thirty minutes,' I said.

◆

'You said you will leave me alone,' I said as he opened the door. I entered his lavish 3,000-square-feet presidential suite. I sat on one of the sofas in the suite living room. He didn't respond. He went to the electric kettle at the corner of the room and filled it with water.

'Tea?' he said.

'Neel! I don't have time. You said you wouldn't bother me.'

'I cut off for a year. Did I ever bother you in London?' he said. 'Would you like some green tea?'

'What is it you wanted to tell me?' I said.

'Can you relax?' Neel said. 'How about a "Hey, how have you been?"'

'Neel,' I said. 'I don't have time for pleasantries.'

'I am just making conversation. Am I allowed to do that while I make a cup of tea?'

'Sure,' I said.

'We haven't caught up in a year. How was London? You know I grew up there, right?'

'I do.'

'So how was it?'

I just kept looking at him.

'What?'

'I am not here to talk about London.'

'Give me a minute. I need to bring something from the other room.'

I nodded. He went into the bedroom. I looked out of the window. The sea was silent behind the double-glazed glass. Neel's mention of London brought back many memories of my move there.

London

One Year Ago

33

The Goldman Sachs office in London is located on 133 Fleet Street. The office at Peterborough Court is at the same site as the old *Daily Telegraph* building. Patricia, the group secretary, settled me into my new cubicle. The British accent in the London office reminded me of Neel. When you break up, it becomes a habit to remember everything about the man—with my second heartbreak I had learnt this much. Neel was a habit, a bad habit rather, almost an addiction. Like smoking, when you know it is bad for you but you can't seem to leave it. I also learnt that you don't get better at handling heartbreaks. They suck every single time, even though this time was marginally better since I had initiated the break-up. I battled the urge to email him, telling him I had reached the new place.

Why couldn't he email me? Why couldn't he call? Well, how could he? I had threatened to expose him.

I missed his voice. I missed his eyes. I missed his touch. I missed all that he did to me, with me, in bed. *So what if he is married? He loves me, and love is what I need, right?*

See, this is how your mind plays games with you. If it wants you to do something, it will find a hundred reasons to justify it. What's more, the reasons will even make sense. I picked up the internal phone on my desk to call Neel.

The buzz on my cellphone disrupted my thoughts. In the past few months my mother had discovered WhatsApp. She had sent me a message. 'Checked profile?'

You won't give up, will you? I wanted to type back.

'Doing it, now,' I replied instead.

I opened shaadi.com on my office laptop. The screen displayed happy faces of couples in nuptial bliss, who had found each other on this website. Testimonials spoke of how a couple who met on the site married within three months and were now expecting a child. Was finding love that simple? Why did I find it difficult? Why did I have to complicate everything? Or was there something wrong with me?

I logged on to the account my mother had set up. The page opened to a summary of my profile. She had used a picture of mine from India Gate, the one I took when I visited Delhi last time. A shadow fell on my face in the photo. My eyes were half-closed. She could not have chosen a worse picture.

I read my profile.

Hi, I am a young, slim, quite fair, Punjabi Khatri girl aged 26, 5'4" tall. I am currently working in London, but flexible to move anywhere with my husband. I am family-minded and don't mind staying in a joint family.

I reached for my cellphone— to call my mother and blast her. I resisted the urge and read on.

I can cook North Indian cuisine quite well. I have one elder sister who is already married and well-settled in Delhi. My parents have no other liabilities. My father retired from a respected position in State Bank of India and my mother is a housewife. We are well off and can do a high-status wedding.

My eyebrows shot up. I read the next section.

I am looking for a well-qualified, well-settled suitable match from a good Punjabi family. Someone who will look after my family and me and respect elders. If interested please respond with details about you, including horoscope or date and time of birth. Regards, Radhika Mehta.

'Seriously? Mom, seriously?' I said out loud. I closed the shaadi.com window. I had to call mom and talk, or rather shout at her. I couldn't do that in the office. I packed my laptop in my Tumi bag and stood up.

'I am going to get lunch,' I told Patricia and left the office.

I went out on Fleet Street and found Itsu, a Japanese-inspired healthy fast-food chain. I ordered a vegetables and brown rice potsu pot and sat down to eat. Fork in one hand and phone in the other, I called my dear mother. I charged at her as soon as she answered.

'Mom, what are you doing?'

'What?' she said, surprised.

I loaded my profile on my laptop screen.

'I saw the profile.'

'Liked it?'

How do you even begin to answer that?

'Mom, are you serious? What is this?'

'Why? I wrote what will get you the best response. Sharma aunty next door helped me.'

'It's horrible, mom. Really, who is this person you have written about? It is not me.'

'What are you are saying? It is you 100 per cent. Isn't your height five feet four inches?'

'Mom, first of all, the picture is terrible.'

'It's what I had. Send me a better one. We should have done a portfolio when you had come here.'

'I will send you one from here.'

'Send one in Indian clothes.'

'Why?'

'Are you stupid? Are you going to send me a picture in your office suit? Are you applying for a job?'

'It's who I am.'

'Stop it, Radhika. Is the picture the only problem?'

'There are a million problems. Let me start. What is "quite fair"? Tell them my real complexion. Say I am wheatish or whatever.'

'If you write wheatish people think it is dark. You have to write "quite fair". Raise it up a notch.'

'Oh, really? So what if someone writes "dark" then?'

'If someone says dark, it's like black. You know those Negro-type Africans.'

'Mom, that's not a good term. No one says Negro.'

'Whatever. These are minor things.'

'I'll tell you huge things.'

'Say.'

'One, you say "flexible to move with husband". Who said that? It depends, right? Maybe he has to move. It's a discussion. Two, I "don't mind joint family"? Why do we have to put that? Three, my parents "have no other liabilities". What is that? Oh, and don't miss, "we can do a high-status wedding", that is four. Five, why just Punjabi family? Six, I don't need a guy to "look after" me. Seven, "send horoscope". Mom, really, I don't know what to say,' I said.

I had to pause just to breathe. The customer at the next table offered me a glass of water. I mouthed him a thanks and took a sip.

'You have said a lot,' mom said, in her upset voice. 'No respect left for parents, I see.'

'I am not disrespecting you. This whole thing is just wrong, mom. I don't want to be a part of this.'

'I don't think you understand the strategy.'

'Strategy?'

'Yeah. You don't scare away the good guys.'

'Why would they get scared?'

'If they see a girl who is too independent-minded, too qualified, doing too well, they get scared.'

'What nonsense.'

'It's a fact. I didn't make the rules, beta.'

'Oh and one more thing,' I said. 'You barely mention my job. Currently working in London, really? I am a vice president in Goldman Sachs. I make half a million dollars a year.'

'Exactly. Now you see the strategy?'

'Huh?'

'See how we mention it also but hide the achievements also?'

'Mom, can you hear yourself? You are hiding your child's achievements?'

'I am hiding my daughter's achievements. So we get more boys to choose from. That's all. I am not taking away your achievements.'

'So if I were a son?'

'Obviously, we would put your salary first. But now we have to be careful.'

I smacked my forehead. How do I get through to her? I wondered if I had made the biggest mistake of my life. Maybe Neel was right. I was not meant for all this nonsense. I missed Neel. I wanted to call him so bad.

'Are you there?' my mother said.

'Yeah,' I said. My heart ached as I thought of Neel holding me at night.

'I am coming there,' my mother said.

'Where?'

'London. I am going to spend some time with you. We will do this together.'

◆

'Enough, mom,' I said. She tossed another parantha on my plate.

I didn't want a husband. I needed my mother with me in London. So she could cook me hot gobhi paranthas every Saturday morning for breakfast.

'Why do you stay in Chelsea? Southall has so many Indians. Better, no?' she said.

'Have you seen the park view outside? See how charming this is,' I said.

'But do you get achaar and chutney? In Southall you get it. Sharma aunty told me.'

'You get it here too,' I said. I tore open the second parantha. 'Just stay with me. Forever,' I said.

'See, even you miss having a proper home. Is this even a life? Go to office early. Come back late to an empty house.'

'Mom, I have one of the most wanted jobs in the world.'

'And I have one of the most unwanted jobs, but I love it. Taking care of my family,' my mother said and gave me a glass of lassi. She kissed me on the forehead. I hugged her.

'I love you, mom.'

'I love you too. Now show me the responses. You have made me wait all week.'

I had modified my profile on the matrimonial website. I had removed obnoxious bits like 'husband to take care of me' and 'no liabilities'. And added: 'successful career at one of the world's top investment banks'. I also mentioned I wanted a secure and easygoing man.

'Fine,' I said. I opened my laptop and logged in.

'Fifty responses, very good,' she said excitedly. 'Open them.'

'Opening, mom. Be patient.'

The first query came from a Mohit Ahuja, from a business family in Delhi. They owned three restaurants, Mohit managed one of them.

'No,' I said.

'Why?' my mother said. 'They look well-off.'

'I don't want to be with someone who runs a family restaurant.'

'What nonsense!'

'Mom, see the qualifications. BA from some random university. No. Next.'

We continued scanning the responses for the next few hours.

'This one is ugly. I can't wake up next to a man like that,' I reacted to one.

Mom came up with one of her wise sayings: 'There is no such thing as an ugly man.'

Just to get back at her I rejected some men due to their 'looks'. Others didn't make it because they had jobs in India where they earned a few lakhs a year. Despite all my feminist leanings, I didn't want to be with someone who made so much lesser than me. *Why does a woman feel a man's income is more important than hers? Maybe because it is important to men, and very few men are secure enough to just let this issue be.*

'No, mom. He lives in Bulandshahr. Joint family. Family business. No, no, no,' I said as my mother showed me another candidate.

I was realizing by now that sifting through prospective grooms was harder than valuing distressed assets.

'You are not doing this properly,' my mother said as I rejected a guy because I didn't like his printed Hawaiian shirt.

'But I hate that shirt. How could he wear it?' I laughed.

'He is a doctor. We are shortlisting him. You can choose his clothes after marriage,' mom said.

We finished at 4 in the afternoon, with a shortlist of ten potential grooms to be contacted further.

'I'm tired. You want to step out for a coffee?' I said.

'Sure,' she said.

We walked to a Pret a Manger café near Earl's Court tube station. My mother held my hand.

'We have done something together after a long time,' she said.

'Yeah, bonding over shortlisted grooms,' I said and laughed.

'You wait and see. I will find a prince for you,' she said.

34

'Hi, can you see me?' I said. I sat at my dining table, facing my laptop. I had a Skype call fixed with Raj Bakshi, a doctor based in Boston, USA.

'Yeah. It's a little dark though. Can you switch on another light?' Raj said. He was thirty years old, had a thin moustache and wore a light blue shirt.

Before I could respond, my mother switched on all the lights in the apartment.

'Mom? What are you doing here?' I whispered to her.

'Yeah, much better,' Raj said.

'One sec, Raj,' I said and muted him. I bent the laptop screen to cover the camera.

'What happened? Don't keep him waiting. Talk,' mom said.

'Mom, if we are doing this, we are doing this my way.'

'I am only trying to help…'

'Thanks. But let me talk to them without you hovering around.'

My mother made a face and left the room. I resumed the Skype call.

'Hi,' I said.

'Hello. Must be quite late there?'

'It's midnight, yes. London is five hours ahead.'

'Sorry. I just came back from work,' he said.

'You are a doctor, right?'

'Yeah. And what exactly do you do? Your profile said banking.'

'I am in Goldman Sachs. VP in the Distressed Debt Group.'

'Oh,' he said and became quiet.

'So yeah,' I said, wondering what to say next. I don't know why I take responsibility for awkward silences.

'What kind of doctor are you?' I said.

'I am a GP, general practitioner, in the Boston City Hospital. Doing my residency.'

'I could never be a doctor. All that blood. I feel faint in hospitals,' I said and smiled.

'It's a part of life,' he said, his tone sombre. 'People are dying. Someone needs to save them.'

'Ah. Yes. Of course,' I said. *Okay, isn't Dr Bakshi a little too serious?*

'How's Goldman Sachs?' he said.

'Good. Hectic. But I like it.'

'They pay people very well, I hear.'

'It's based on performance, but yes. It's good money.'

'If you don't mind, how much do you make?' he said.

Isn't this too much too soon? What's the protocol? He can ask me all these things in the first call? Can I ask him too?

'Are we sharing compensation already?' I smiled, to lighten his operation-theatre mood.

'Sure. Why keep it hidden? I make 100,000 a year. Plus benefits,' he said.

What am I supposed to do? Clap?

'Okay,' I said.

'And you?' he said.

I don't know why I didn't feel like telling him. Perhaps I was getting tuned into male pride. I could sense which guy could take it and who could not.

'We can discuss all this later. So what do you want to specialize in? Or do you want to specialize at all?'

'I want to be an ophthalmologist. Eye doctor.'

'I know. Good,' I said.

I had a sinking feeling this wasn't going to work. How do you end calls like this?

'So how much is your salary again?' he said.

Okay, he asked for it. Thrice.

'If you must know, I made half a million dollars last year.'

I heard his chair creak in response.

'Five hundred thousand dollars?' he said.

'Yeah. That's what half a million is,' I said. I kicked myself for that patronizing comment. It wasn't funny. I had a feeling nothing was funny to Dr Stuck-up Bakshi anyway.

'Okay,' he said.

Okay? What the fuck is a singular 'okay'? They should ban this one-word reply in conversations. How am I supposed to take it forward from here?

'So yeah. What else do you do apart from work?' I said.

'Excuse me. But I have to go.'

'Oh really? What happened?' I said. I hate being rejected. Even by boring men doing their residency in Boston.

'Nothing... Okay, I will tell you. This is not going to work. Your salary is too high.'

'How can you get too high a salary?'

'I mean for me. I mean compared to me.'

I realized this was a dead end. Why not end it with a bit of fun?

'Oh, so you mean you are not man enough to handle it?' I said.

He hung up without saying bye. Oops, strike one I guess. Ha ha.

◆

Three weeks later we had struck off all the ten shortlisted names from the list.

'It's not going to work, mom,' I said.

We had come to Dishoom, a quirky modern-Indian café in Covent Garden.

We ordered pao bhaji and masala chai, a rare delicacy in London.

'I told you not to mention your career too much,' she said, upset that I had rejected all ten suitors.

'I can't hide who I am,' I said.

'Why can't you be like your sister?'

'Because I am not Aditi didi. I don't want to be her.'

We came back home. She came up with another idea. She wanted to upgrade our shaadi.com membership to the VIP category, where special agents help you get grooms.

'We have special needs. We need special help,' she said.

I guess I was special. Specially fucked up. No wonder she needed an army of specialists to trap a man for me.

She sat on my bed. I lay next to her and turned the other way.

'Do whatever you want, mom,' I said.

'One of my daughters got settled so easily. I just hope and pray God helps us,' she muttered to herself and raised her folded hands to the sky.

'What's with invoking God? Am I some illness? A misfortune?' I said, without looking at her.

'Will you stop being so touchy? It is a fact Aditi's marriage happened so quickly. She has whiter skin, which helps. But she also had a good attitude. You should have an even better attitude.'

I turned towards her and interrupted her.

'What do you mean, even better attitude? I should be more subservient? What is that word in ads? Homely? It just means submissive, right? You want me to be more homely?'

'Well. Yeah.'

'I am not homely. So maybe I will just stay single.'

'Don't say such horrible things.'

'There's nothing horrible about it,' I said.

'This money and international job have gone to your head. You are not even a girl anymore.'

'What?' I said, one eyebrow up in disgust.

'Forget it.'

'Mom, dad used to walk me to the school bus stop, remember? When I was in primary school.'

She looked at me, said nothing.

'He used to tell me, "Beta, when you grow up, you can do whatever you want. The sky is the limit for you."'

'So?'

'Why do people tell girls all this? You ask them to achieve things, but when they do, you can't handle it. Why does it become "you are not even a girl anymore"?'

'I don't know all that. I never worked. I didn't have choices like yours,' she said.

'Neither did you have the courage,' I said.

She paused for a second before she spoke again. 'I don't know. Okay, fine, I don't have courage. Anyway, I think it is better for women if they don't work.'

'Mom!' I screamed in exasperation.

'What?'

'My job means a lot to me. Can you not demean it?'

'Can you not demean me?' my mother said. She broke into tears. Her sobs turned into a full-blown crying fest, as she mourned the loss of her ten shortlisted prospective sons-in-law.

I looked around. I found a tissue box on the bedside table. I passed it to her. She wiped her tears.

'Do you know how much pain I had to bear when you were born?' she said.

It's called labour, mom. I didn't cause it, it is how kids happen.

'I heard you wanted to abort me,' I said.

She looked up.

'Who told you?'

'It's not important how I found out. I heard the doctor goofed up on the sex determination test. He said it would be a boy.'

My mother looked at me in silence.

'Those were different times,' she whispered. 'We had Aditi. Your dadi wanted a boy.'

'You did too.'

'Yeah.'

'Sorry, mom, I came out. You got a raw deal.'

'Don't be stupid. I love you.'

She hugged me and after a moment I hugged her back.

'Then let me be,' I said, 'please. Groom or no groom, doesn't matter. I want you to support me.'

A tear escaped my eye. I buried my face in mom's chest.

'Don't worry. We will go through some more profiles tomorrow. Your rajkumar will be there somewhere,' said mom.

35

Three weeks later

My mother wore her reading glasses. She flicked through the pictures on the shaadi.com app on my phone.

'See this. Why haven't you accepted this one?' my mother said.

We sat in my living room at noon on a Saturday morning, I in blue pajamas–white T-shirt and she in a salwar-kameez.

'Read it out, mom,' I said, typing on my laptop. 'What does he do?'

'He works in Facebook,' she said, and removed her glasses, surprised. 'How can you work in Facebook? He does Facebook all day?'

'No, mom. Facebook is a company. Go on. How old?'

'Twenty-eight. Height five feet ten inches. I will read his profile?'

'Sure. He wrote it?' I said.

'No, it says written by parent.'

'That's two points down.'

'Stop it. Even I had to write it the first time for you, right?'

'I will never forget that. Anyway, go on.'

My mother read from the phone screen.

Our son is an intelligent, humble and simple boy who is looking for a suitable life partner. He prefers a career woman, someone who is willing to live in the USA. He is a systems engineer at Facebook, where he has worked for the last five years. He is based in Menlo Park, San Francisco. He did his engineering in Computer Science from NIT Nagpur, where he topped his class. He did his masters from MIT in Boston, USA. He is our only child. We are a simple Punjabi family based in Mumbai (originally from West Delhi). We want the right girl above anything else, as she will be our new family member.

My mother finished reading and reached for a glass of water.

'Not bad, well-written. Open-minded and honest. Salary?' I said and pressed save on my laptop.

'It says between 150,000 to 175,000 USD, plus stock options. Is that good?'

'Good. Give me the phone.'

I saw his profile picture. A lean, tall and bespectacled man in a beige overcoat stood against the backdrop of the Golden Gate Bridge in San Francisco. He resembled Sundar Pichai, the CEO of Google. Geeks have their own role models, I guess.

'He is handsome,' my mother said.

'He looks like the student who tells other children to stop talking.'

'Any nonsense you say.'

I read his name. Brijesh Gulati.

'Ugh,' I said. 'Ugh. Rejected. I am not marrying someone called Brijesh Gulati.'

'Why? It's a nice name. Gulatis are Punjabis. Don't you know that restaurant on Pandara Road?'

'Exactly. I am not marrying someone whose name resembles a Punjabi restaurant.'

My mother stared at me.

'What?' I said.

'What name you want? Amitabh Bachchan? Akshay Kumar?'

'It's not that. It is just that he's just so...' I thought of the right word, 'typical.'

'I think you are looking for negatives. And you can't find any. So all this name and "typical" nonsense. Tell me one proper thing wrong?' my mother said.

'Exactly. There's nothing wrong with him. But he doesn't have like, any wow or thrill factor.'

'You are choosing a husband. Not taking an amusement park ride for thrills.'

Ah, but love can be thrilling, mom, I wanted to say. Love can mean passion under the moonlight on remote islands. The thought of that night with Neel made me flinch.

'Okay fine,' I said in a brisk fashion and chose the 'accept' option. I kept my phone aside. Ten minutes later my phone made a 'ting' sound. I picked it up.

'I don't believe this. He already sent a "Hi" with his Skype details. Mom, this is desperate, no?'

'This is a good sign. It means God wants both of you to connect,' my mother said. It is amazing how mothers can justify any action as divine intervention as long as it suits them.

'Set up a call,' my mother said in her most royal tone.

I typed back a message.

'Skype call fixed for tomorrow,' I said to my mother.

◆

'Hi,' I said, as cheerfully as possible. One of the most awkward moments in world history has to be speaking to a shortlisted arranged marriage candidate for the first time. I sat in my living room near my window, on Skype with Brijesh.

'Good morning,' Brijesh said. 'Or sorry. Good afternoon.'

'So I am Radhika. You already saw my profile.'

'Yes, I found it quite interesting.'

'Really? Which part?' I said, to enable more conversation.

'I like that you have a good career. Investment banking is hectic, though, isn't it?'

'It is. But I am used to it now.'

'I am sure. And what are your interests?' he said.

'I love to travel. I like music. I like exploring whichever city I live in. How about you?'

'I mostly work. But I like watching cricket and Bollywood movies.'

Really? An Indian software guy who likes watching cricket and Hindi movies? Can it be more stereotypical?

It seemed Brijesh had read my mind.

'Yeah, so typical, right? Cricket and Bollywood. I am kind of boring.'

For the first time a guy had admitted a weakness to me on a Skype call. He *was* kind of boring. But unlike super-bores who didn't even know they were bores, at least he knew he was one.

I smiled.

'If I go to sleep on this call then I am afraid you may be right,' I said.

He laughed.

'You have a good sense of humour,' he said.

'Thanks,' I said.

'Actually, I watch some English movies too. Have to develop a taste. You can suggest some good ones to me.'

'Sure,' I said.

He can praise a woman's sense of humour and even take advice from her—not bad.

He continued to talk. 'I can't pretend to be fake-sophisticated. I grew up in Naraina Vihar in West Delhi and then Borivali in Mumbai. So I didn't have much exposure. But now I want to learn more about the world.'

'Wait a minute. Did you say you grew up in Naraina Vihar?'

'Yeah. Why? It's a small colony in West Delhi.'

'I am from Naraina too,' I said, surprised. 'H block. That's where my parents live.'

'What? I was in G block. G-478. My parents still have a house there. They live in Mumbai now, of course.'

My bedroom door opened. Mom came in.

'Naraina?' she whispered, her face unable to contain her excitement. She had probably had an ear to the door and heard our entire conversation. I shooed her away. I spoke to Brijesh again. 'This is uncanny. Did you shop from Modern Stores?'

'Yes. That fat uncle who never had change?' he said and both of us laughed.

'Anyway, so yes. I wanted someone who has Indian roots but is better exposed to the world than I am. You have been in New York, Hong Kong and now London. I felt you could be an asset to me.'

I wanted to reject him. I wanted one solid reason to do so. I couldn't find it.

He talked about meeting up towards the end of the call.

'I go for work to New York sometimes. It's midway between London and San Francisco. If our calls go well, would it be possible for you to come?'

'Let's see,' I said. 'Skype is good for now. Speak soon.'

My mother entered the living room the second I disconnected the call.

'You can't snoop on me, mom. This is not fair.'

She came up to me and gave me a hug.

'Sorry, my beta,' she said and kissed my forehead. 'But what a great boy. And Naraina? See how Sai Baba's blessed us?'

36

One month later
St Regis Hotel's café, New York

'Radhika, right?'
I heard his voice as I entered. I turned to look at him. He wore beige chinos and a black turtleneck, perhaps his homage to Steve Jobs.

'Brijesh?' I said. We shook hands.

'Yeah. Good to see you in person,' he said, guiding me to a table.

The old-world luxury café had high ceilings and colonial-era furniture. A saxophone player and a pianist played in one corner.

We ordered tea for two.

A waiter brought us tea on a tiered silver tray of goodies—scones, jam, clotted cream, cakes, mini cucumber sandwiches and chocolates.

'Afternoon tea was a great idea. Everything looks lovely,' Brijesh said. He took a few sandwiches and placed them on his plate.

'Glad you like it,' I said.

I wore office attire, a grey suit, partly because I had gone to the 85 Broad Street office earlier to meet Jonathan and Craig. Mostly, I wore it because my mother had told me not to. She had instructed me to wear a magenta salwar-kameez and dangling gold earrings. I told her I wouldn't go to New York looking like I am a part of a Baisakhi celebrations' troupe. In fact, I wanted to be as drab and real as possible. Brijesh could see me as I was and reject me if he wanted to.

'When is your flight back?' Brijesh said.

'9.30,' I said. 'I have to leave for the airport at 7.30.'

We had four-and-a-half hours to decide if we wanted to be together for the rest of our lives.

'So who talks first?' he said.

'Usually I do,' I said and smiled.

'Oh. I would actually prefer that. Tell me about yourself.'

I told him the story of my life from my childhood until now. I covered everything, apart from Debu and Neel.

'So I have been in London for six months. Parents now would like it if I could settle down. Gosh, doesn't that sound so lame?' I said, ending my story.

'What? The term "settle down"?' he said.

'Yeah. Only in India do we use that phrase. Settle down, like in sedimentation everything settles down. Don't move anymore. No risk, no excitement.'

He laughed.

'Our parents valued security over everything else. In their time jobs were few, so you better grab one and settle down. Else you would be on the road,' Brijesh said.

'So true,' I said.

'Even I have settled down in a job,' Brijesh said.

'Really? You are with Facebook. Isn't it one of the most fun companies to work for?'

'See, that's the thing. Everyone thinks I am in this amazing company. How could I even think of leaving it?'

'Do you like your job?'

'Work is challenging. Money is good.'

'So then?'

'Sometimes I wonder…there is so much happening in the tech world. Can't I start something of my own?'

'Of course you can.'

He looked happy at my encouragement. He told me some more about his life. He grew up in Naraina for the first couple of years, after which his parents moved to Mumbai. His father worked in Indian Oil. Brijesh wanted to get into IIT, but couldn't make it despite two tries. He said it was because he was distracted. He joined NIT, topped the class and went to MIT for higher studies.

'And then a typical IT job. That's me,' Brijesh said.

I smiled. We finished our tea. The waiter arrived with the bill.

It was 5.30; we had two more hours.

'Let's take a walk in Central Park,' I suggested.

We entered Central Park on 59th Street, with the Apple store on my right. The green trees and grass around made us forget we were in one of the busiest cities of the world. I thought of Debu. His office was less than a mile away.

'You seem lost. Work?' he said.

'No, it's just…New York brings back memories.'

We walked in the direction of the Central Park Zoo.

'Good memories or bad memories?' Brijesh said.

'Mixed,' I said. 'Mostly good, though.'

We reached the zoo and bought two tickets. We saw the highlight, a pair of baby grizzly bears, born just six weeks ago.

'They are so cute,' I said, as the two cubs, no bigger than rabbits, slept on their mother's back.

'You like kids?' Brijesh said. My heart beat fast. The kids-and-mother question had made me lose men in the past. *Did he mean, do I like kids in general? Or did he mean, would I like kids with him?* My mind went into overdrive, imagining little infants with nerdy glasses, working on Facebook servers.

'Huh, kids?' I came back to reality. 'Yeah, I do like children. Never thought I would but at some point I do want to have messy, naughty kids.'

'Me too,' he said.

We came out of the zoo and walked further north.

We reached the famous Bethesda fountain, located at the edge of The Lake. We sat on the steps and watched ducks with their ducklings swim in little groups. The sun had dimmed, and the water reflected the evening sky.

We sat in silence for five minutes before I spoke again.

'Brijesh, we spoke about several things. We didn't talk about our past relationships,' I said. 'Boyfriends and girlfriends, that sort of stuff.'

'Oh,' he said.

'Yes. Should we or not? We don't know each other so well yet,' I said.

'But isn't that the point? Anyway, better to discuss such things.'

'Yeah. So, you've had relationships?' I said.

He turned his gaze away from the ducks and looked into my eyes.

'Only one,' he said.

'Oh, the special one.'

'I don't know. It was a long time ago. I told you I was distracted during my IIT preparation, right?'

'Yeah.'

'She was in my coaching classes.'

'Okay,' I said. 'A girlfriend?'

'I liked her for roughly two years. She liked me too. Unfortunately we expressed our feelings too late. We only dated for two months.'

'Meaning?'

'Her father took up a job in Saudi Arabia. She moved there with her family.'

'I am sorry,' I said.

'It's okay,' he said and smiled. 'It was a long time ago.'

'How about you?' he said. 'You have had relationships?'

'Nothing in India. I did have a relationship in New York and, well, I don't know what to call it, but something in Hong Kong. So yeah. Two. Or one and a half.'

'Oh,' he said, somewhat surprised.

'Yeah. I did. God, I feel lighter telling you that. I don't know why but I do.'

He smiled.

'It's over, though. Both of them ended. A long time ago,' I said.

'Did it hurt when they ended?' he said.

'Yes, it did,' I said and smiled, 'but I am okay now.'

He did not probe further.

'Would you like to know anything more?' I said.

'Not really. Only if and when you want to tell me,' he said.

We looked at the ducks again.

He spoke after a few minutes. 'So what do you think? About us?'

Did he want a decision from me? After one afternoon tea and one walk in the park? Is that how arranged marriages work? What should I do?

I thought before I spoke.

'Brijesh, I did like meeting you. But this is such a big decision, right?'

'Of course. Take your time. Go back. Think. Reflect.'

'I will. Should we walk out of the park so I can call an Uber to the airport?' I said.

◆

'You won't get such a good match again and again. He is US-based. You can easily get a transfer to his city. He makes good money. He has shares. You say he is sweet. Really, beta, I can't find you anything better than this.'

My mother, back in India now, had called me during my lunch break in office.

'But mom...'

'The Gulatis have called twice.'

'I need time to think.'

'No prince on a horse will come. Certainly not through shaadi.com.'

'I didn't say I want a prince.'

'So come down to earth. What do you know about men anyway?'

Yeah, what do I know, I thought. *If I did, I would have made them stick around, right?*

I remained silent.

I liked him. I could say yes. Maybe not an 'oh my God wow' type yes, but at least 'there's no reason to say no' kind of yes. Still, I wanted to be cautious.

'It's okay, mom. Whatever. Okay, if you guys like him then yeah, it's a yes.'

'Really?'

'Yeah.' I sighed.

'It's a yes! Aditi's papa, are you there? Mubarak,' I heard her scream.

It drowned out everything—my voice, reason and doubts. I, Radhika Mehta, was going to get married,

Congratulations, Radhika, I whispered to myself after I hung up the phone.

37

'Hey, you are here,' Neel's voice brought me back to my present reality. Waves continued to splash on the beach outside. He placed his hand on my shoulder.

'Come, let's sit and talk.'

I brushed his hand aside and turned to him.

'Neel, I need to go. I really should,' I said. My cousins would soon start looking for me for sangeet practice.

'Give me five minutes. I need to tell you something,' he said. He had a large brown envelope in his hand. We sat down on the chocolate-brown sofa.

'Let me talk, okay?' he said.

'Sure,' I said, my gaze away from him.

'And look at me, please,' he said.

I turned to him. The same sparkly eyes, beautiful face and chiselled features. I could see why I had loved him.

'I want to say three things,' he said.

'I'm listening,' I said.

'But before that, may I just say one extra thing? You look nice in this white salwar-kameez.'

'This? Well, thanks. It's for the sangeet practice.'

'I have never seen you in Indian clothes.'

'Really?' I said. Of course he hadn't. He had only seen me in work clothes or, well, no clothes.

'Indian clothes suit you. You look like a little fairy.'

I don't know why he talks like this. Worse, I don't know why it still feels so good when he talks like this.

'You came here for this? To comment on my salwar-kameez?'

'No, no. That is just a side observation.'

'Talk about what you came for.'

'One, Radhika, I am really, really sorry. For how things ended between us. I am just an idiot. A total idiot.'

'Well, we parted ways, I moved to London. End of story,' I said and let out a deep breath.

'Yeah, I never considered that the story could end differently. There were other options.'

'It's history. Leave it, Neel.'

'Well, I can't leave it. Since you left, I have missed you every single day. I can't even bear to pass your cubicle. Every bit of Hong Kong, every business trip reminds me of you. I am filled with pain every time the taxi passes Old Peak Road.'

'There are other routes to your house, I am sure,' I said.

He looked at me. I stared back.

'I am sorry, Radhika. I loved you. So much. You were the best thing to ever happen to me. Or ever will. Smart, young, beautiful, compatible and successful. I had you. You loved me. And what did I do with it? Nothing.'

I didn't respond.

'I made the biggest mistake of my life. I really did,' he said.

Now, where else had I heard that line recently?

He placed the brown envelope on the table. He clasped his hands and lifted them in front of me.

'I know you don't believe me. But only I know the hell I went through after you left. That is why I am here.'

'I believe you, Neel. I missed you too. However, we couldn't do anything about it, right? So yeah, what's the point of you being here?'

'For the second thing I am going to tell you.'

He picked up the brown envelope. He pulled out a set of A4-sized sheets. The first page had a stamp paper.

'I am leaving Kusum. These are the documents,' he said.

I felt dizzy. The suite spun around me. He gave me the papers in my hand. He and Kusum had filed for a mutual consent divorce at the Hong Kong Family Court. My hand began to tremble.

I kept the divorce documents on the table.

'Why?' I said.

'*You* are asking me why?' he said. '*You*, of all people?'

'You had a perfect family.'

'If I did, why did we have what we had?'

I kept silent. His eyes became wet.

'What about the kids?'

'We plan to co-parent. Share custody.'

'What did Kusum say?'

'Not happy, of course. However, she gets it. She knew something was amiss in our marriage. We had grown too far apart.'

'What will she do?' I said. I don't know why I had such concern for his ex-wife.

'She will figure it out. Financially, she is more than okay. I gave her half of whatever I had. No questions asked. In return, she agreed to co-parenting and mutual consent.'

I couldn't believe I was discussing a divorce at my wedding venue.

Neel continued, 'I am sorry, I will skip the details. The point is,' he said and exhaled, 'my marriage is over.'

'I am sorry, Neel,' I said.

'It's okay,' he said and massaged his temples. 'It had to happen. Should have happened long ago.'

I checked my phone. I had missed calls from two of my cousins.

'I hope you are okay. I need to go now. You had something else to say? The third thing?' I said.

'Yes. There's a small plane waiting at the Dabolim airport.'

'Your chartered flight?'

'Yeah, Radhika,' he said and leaned forward to hold my hand. 'Our flight.'

'What?' I said. I didn't withdraw my hand. I just gave a quick glance to confirm the door was shut.

'I know this will be a huge mess for you. Your entire family is here. There are huge expenses. But hear me out.'

'What?'

'I will cut a cheque right now, at the hotel lobby. I will pay for everything your family or the groom's side spent for this wedding. So financially, it's a non-issue. You just come with me, and we fly away on the plane. To Hong Kong. To wherever, actually.'

'Neel, are you kidding me?'

'No. I mean it. I have wasted too much time. I have over-analysed, treated our love like it was a financial deal. It doesn't work like that. You have to do these things from here.'

He touched his chest to indicate his heart.

'You want me to elope with you?' I said, still absorbing his proposal-cum-plan.

'You can talk to your family. I can meet them as well. When we reach Hong Kong we can get married.'

'What if I don't want to be in Hong Kong?'

Neel became quiet for a few seconds.

'It would be nice if we can be there for a while,' he finally said. 'My kids are there. But if it bothers you we can move to another city. I will commute. See them from time to time.'

I looked at him searchingly. I knew him well enough to tell he wasn't lying. Neel Gupta, partner at Goldman Sachs, never uttered a word if he didn't mean it. I kept my gaze on him for a minute.

'Say something,' he said.

'What am I supposed to say? I have to dance to chittiyan kalaiyan now.'

'What's that?'

'A Bollywood song. For my sangeet.'

'Wait, that's Punjabi, right? What does it mean?'

'Fair-complexioned wrists, white wrists, actually,' I said.

'Of course, it's India. Has to be white. So you dancing and all? With all those hip moves?' he said. I nodded.

Both of us laughed. For a moment it felt like old times, when he and I would chat over breakfast at the Goldman café.

'Look, I don't want to deny us a celebration. We can do a court marriage now in Hong Kong. Later, when the dust settles, we can have our own big fat Indian wedding. One in India and one in London, for my folks.'

I realized he hadn't let go of my hand. He slid off the sofa and knelt down. He lifted my hand and kissed it.

'My beautiful Indian princess, rather I should say smart, analytically sound and extremely beautiful Indian princess, will you marry me?'

My heart beat fast. Neel, unattainable crush of most Goldman girls who had met him, the man whom I loved, was in front of me on his knees.

'Please, princess, say yes,' he said.

My phone rang. I wanted a disruption to avoid answering Neel. I picked up the call without looking at the caller id.

'One sec, Neel,' I said.

'Baby, where are you?' Debu's voice on the other side made me jump.

'Hey, I got to call you back,' I said.

'Okay listen, I called home and...'

'Talk to you later,' I said and hung up.

'All fine?' Neel said, still on his knees.

I nodded.

He lifted my hand up again.

'Radhika Mehta, I love you and will always do. Will you marry me?'

I pulled my hand back. I smacked my forehead.

'Fuck, Neel. Really, fuck,' I said.

'What, Radhika?'

'You had to do all this now? Where were you in Hong Kong, when I lay silently crying in bed next to you?'

'You were crying? I couldn't hear.'

'Silently crying. And you said I am not the marriage type. What was that? I am not meant to be a mother?'

'I freaked out. I didn't want what we had to end. I couldn't figure out how to keep you.'

I stood up.

'How did you figure out now?' I said, or rather screamed, and pointed to the papers. 'Did you even suggest any such options then? I was the young VP in office you slept with. That's all I could be, right?'

'I understand you are upset. I didn't treat you right.'

'I came to resign. It didn't matter to you. The best you could do was to arrange a transfer. Wow.'

'Why didn't you shout at me then?'

'Huh?' I said, twisting my dupatta's edge.

'You could have told me that what I was doing was wrong.'

'You had a family. What am I supposed to say to you? "Let's be together. Leave your wife and little kids"?'

'I wish you had,' he said in a bleak voice.

I paced up and down his suite a few times. He sat there, still on his knees.

'Sit on the sofa, Neel. There is no need to be so dramatic.'

He complied and sat back on the sofa.

'Fine. Not dramatic, but be pragmatic,' he said.

'This is so stupid, Neel. Really, I expected better from you.'

'So I acted late. Is that what your anger is about? Go ahead, yell at me.'

'That's not the point.'

'I missed you every day. I didn't contact you. But I did what I had to do with my life. Then I heard about your wedding and it was now or never. So I came here. To take you away. With me. Forever.'

He walked up to me. He held my shoulders with both hands.

'Neel, just stop,' I said.

'Fine, hit me. Slap me. You did it once. Do it again. As many times as you want. But come with me.'

I felt his breath on my face. He had Ralph Lauren's Romance on, the same perfume he used to wear when he came to bed with me.

'Leave me, Neel,' I said, even though I didn't make any effort to extract myself from his grip.

He held my shoulders tighter.

'I said leave me,' I said, my voice breaking. I started to cry.

Radhika, what is with you and your tear taps?

'Shh,' he said, 'enough now. It's okay. I am here now. It's all going to be fine.'

He placed his hand on the back of my head. He pushed my head forward until my forehead rested on his chest. He didn't try and kiss me. He just patted my head a couple of times. He brought his mouth close to my ear and whispered, 'I will be here, in this room. The pilot is waiting for my instructions. You calm down. Go back and think. It's a lot for you to take in. I will wait until you give the go-ahead. Then we will do what we have to.'

I nodded.

I lifted my head.

'I need to go. I really do,' I said.

◆

I raced down the hotel corridor, my mind racing a million times faster than my steps. At the function room entrance, I found Debu.

'Debu!' I said, looking around to ensure nobody saw us. 'What are you doing here?'

'Baby, I tried calling you so many times. You don't pick up.'

I couldn't talk to him here. Anyone from my or Brijesh's family could walk in anytime. I saw a staff door near the function room. I pushed it open. Debu and I entered the kitchen area of the hotel.

'You can't land up here like this,' I said.

'I had no choice. I thought you would be at the sangeet practice. I didn't see you there.'

A chef next to us fried a kilo of onions on full heat.

'You went in?' I said, aghast.

'I pretended to be lost. Another guest in the hotel.'

'Never do that again, okay?'

'Sorry. We only have one more day, Radhika. I called to tell you I spoke to my parents.'

'About what?'

'About us. About everything we had. And the situation we are in now. I had a two-hour call.'

'Debu, I am not exaggerating this. But my head is a big mess and might explode right now.'

My phone rang—my mother was calling.

'I have to take this,' I said. My mother shouted at me as soon as I picked up the call.

'Are you mad? Where have you disappeared? Your cousins are looking for you all over the hotel.'

'I am here only,' I said.

'Where?'

'In the toilet.'

'Why are you taking so long? Is your stomach okay? Eat carefully, don't get loose motions on your wedding day. You need medicine?'

'Mom, I am fine. Two minutes. Okay, bye.'

I hung up and looked at Debu.

'You heard that?' I said. 'See how everyone is looking for me?'

'I am sorry. Anyway, my parents protested a lot, but I convinced them. They want to come here.'

'Please, Debu.'

'I just need your decision. I am your first love, Radhika. First and only. You don't even know this guy you are getting married to.'

I have more choices now, I wanted to tell him.

'What do you want me to say?' I said instead.

I tried to walk past him. He blocked me with his arm.

'Stop this wedding. Tell your parents. I will come with you. It's now or never.'

'Can I,' I said and paused, 'can I think about this, Debu? Really? I have practice now.'

'Yeah,' he said and lowered his hand.

'Thanks,' I said.

'I will love you until the last day of my life,' he said from behind me.

38

'Focus, Radhika madam. Your feet are not matching the beat,' Mickey, the choreographer, said to me. Though he was ticking me off for the fifteenth time he had remarkable patience in his voice. In his place, I would have slapped my student.

'Neither do I have chittiyan kalaiyan in real life, nor can I do the steps for chittiyan kalaiyan,' I said.

He played the original song with Jacqueline Fernandes on the LED screen behind the stage. My six cousins who had to dance with me had mastered each move down pat. I couldn't keep up beyond five steps.

I couldn't hear the lyrics or Mickey's instructions. I only heard the following in my ears:

Debu. Neel. Brijesh.

Debu. Neel. Brijesh.

I heard 'I love yous' in Debu's and Neel's voices. I heard Brijesh saying he wants to go apartment-hunting in San Francisco. I heard Neel talking about the waiting plane. I imagined Debu's Bengali parents packing their bags along with their monkey caps and buying rasgulla tins for their Goa trip.

Mickey paused and replayed the song for the sixteenth time.

'One-two-three, Radhika madam, start,' he said.

Chittiyan kalaiyan ve, o meri chittiyaan kalaiyan ve.
Chittiyan kalaiyan ve, o meri white kalaiyan ve.

I tried to dance. The image of Neel making love to me on the Philippines island flashed in my head. It switched to Debu and me sitting in our Tribeca apartment and watching TV together. I came back to reality, and tried to remember the steps.

'Madam, again you are missing the beat. What is happening? Cut, cut. Restart.'

Three more attempts for Radhika the wobbly-toed bride. Well, turns out I sucked at these attempts too.

Finally, Mickey stopped the music.

'Only Radhika ma'am now. Cousins, please leave stage,' he said. He meant business. He played the song again. I came to the middle of the stage. In the first stanza, I had to lift my wrists to my face and move my eyes. Instead, I stood still. My legs felt weak. I dropped to my knees. I sank on to the stage floor and burst into tears. I cried loud enough to make the choreographer come running to me. He feared he would lose his job.

'Sorry, madam. I am sorry. We don't have to do this dance.'

It wasn't the dance. It was the thoughts that danced in my head. What on earth was I supposed to do?

'Madam, I change song? Romantic song? *Aashiqui 2?* "Tum hi ho"? Just walk around looking sad. Easy. Try?'

I shook my head. My cousins ran up to the stage and surrounded me.

'What happened, didi?' Sweety said.

'Nothing,' I said. 'I am so useless. I can't get these stupid steps.'

'Didi, I can be the centre girl,' Sweety said.

'How can you be the centre girl? Are you the bride or what? Idiot,' Pinky, another second cousin of mine, said.

My mother came up to us.

'What is happening?' she said to me.

I stood up. I gave her a tight hug. I cried again. She patted my back.

'Calm down, my bitiya. Every girl has to leave her parents' home one day.'

Sure, that's what she thought this was. I am crying at the thought of leaving home. Never mind I have not lived at home for years anyway.

'Give her a break. She will do it in a few hours,' my mother said.

'But, madam, sangeet is this evening,' Mickey said in a concerned voice.

'She will do it later,' my mother said in her trademark stern, no-more-negotiation voice.

I came back to my room with my mother.

'Rest, I am sitting here,' my mother said.

I lay down in bed. My mother opened a newspaper and sat next to me.

'Mom,' I said.

'Close your eyes. Try to sleep.'

'Mom, I want to talk to you about something important,' I said.

'What?' she said. 'Oh, did Aditi call the beauty parlour? Their staff should have come. Anyway, what?'

I looked at her face. *Where do I even begin with her?*

'Nothing, mom, it's personal and I don't know if I should…'

'It doesn't hurt so much,' she said.

'What?' I said, surprised.

'Sex. I know you must be tense. It doesn't hurt so much.'

'Really, mom?' I said, my sarcasm not evident to her.

'Yeah. See, I am not like those backward mothers who can't talk frank with daughter. I talk frank. That's what you wanted to say, right?'

'Yeah, pretty much,' I said.

'Good. Rest. And do chittiyan kalaiyan only. No sad tragic songs at my daughter's sangeet.'

◆

Suraj and his team of decorators outdid themselves on sangeet night. Bollywood posters from movies of every decade adorned the walls. Streamers made from fresh white lilies and deep red roses filled the entire room. The stage had the look of a Bollywood item number set, complete with matkis and disco balls. It all felt over the top, like every Punjabi wedding should, and it worked. Guests roamed around the function room appreciating the decorations. I wore an onion-coloured flowing lehenga along with an elaborate diamond set. I looked at myself in the mirror.

'Stunning you look, didi,' Sweety said. I couldn't recognize myself after the one-hour make-up session. For a second, I wished Debu and Neel could see me like this. Yeah, that's how I felt on the eve of my wedding, wishing my exes who waited within bluetooth range could see me dolled up.

After a nap in my room I had gone back for the sangeet practice. Sometimes the only way to calm your mind is to keep it distracted and busy.

I had rehearsed in the afternoon with the doggedness of an Everest climber. I didn't have another financial model to build. I decided to take on chittiyan kalaiyan instead. 'You look beautiful, madam. All the best for the stage,' Mickey said to me in the evening.

Brijesh came up to me.

'You look…' Brijesh said, 'very nice.'

'Thanks,' I said. I kept a straight face. I had to talk to him. Before I could begin, he spoke again. 'Actually, more than nice. Beautiful. Stunning. Basically, great.'

'You look sharp too,' I said. He wore a cream-coloured shervani suit with a self-design. He had switched to contact lenses for the night, getting rid of his Sundar Pichai spectacles.

Together, we met elders on each side. We touched everyone's feet enough times to count as two sets of abdominal crunches.

'Good evening, ladies and gentlemen,' Pankaj mama took the stage. He held a whisky glass in one hand and a mike in the other.

'Welcome to the most beautiful wedding sangeet of the most beautiful daughter of my most beautiful sister,' he said. Obviously, the most beautiful whisky had already reached his head.

Mickey's troupe performed two professional dance numbers first. We sat through them and clapped at the end of each. The highlight of the evening, the aunts' dance performance, came next.

'Now we have the mamis and buas on either side performing to London thumakda,' Pankaj mama announced to thundering applause. He did a little jig on stage himself in anticipation.

Eight aunts took the stage. The LED screen showed a London backdrop with the picture of the Big Ben. Each aunt had enough gold on her to make the down payment for an apartment in London. The stage creaked as everyone took initial positions.

The song began. Richter-scale-nine-level pandemonium rocked the stage. The aunties matched the original steps for fifteen seconds. After that every Punjabi aunt's head, limb and torso seemed to have a mind of its own. Two aunts banged into each other. Another one had her bangles tangled up in someone else's hair. But they continued to dance. The crowd roared.

Tu ghanti Big Ben di
Pura London thumakda

If the British had seen this tribute to London, they would never have colonized us.

Choreographer Mickey's mouth fell open. He covered his face with his hands, wondering if he had chosen the wrong profession. Never had his students massacred his lessons to this level.

Brijesh stood next to me. He looked at me and grinned. I hid a smile; after all, they were my aunts.

I checked my phone. It had two messages each from Neel and Debu.

I didn't open them. Instead, I placed my phone in Aditi didi's handbag.

'Your turn is coming soon,' Aditi didi said.

'Didi, I don't feel like it,' I said.

'What? Your cousins are already backstage. They have waited for this moment since they came to Goa,' she said.

'All the best,' Brijesh said as the time came for me to go backstage.

'Can you get me a drink, Brijesh?' I said.

'Huh? Yeah, sure. What do you want?'

'Anything.'

'Whisky?'

'Sure,' I said.

He returned from the bar with a large peg of Black Label. I chugged it in one shot.

'Take it easy. Don't be tense. It's just a dance,' Brijesh said.

'It's not the dance. We have to talk,' I said.

Pinky came and tugged at my lehenga. I had to go.

'We'll talk later,' I said.

'What? Sure. Hey, rock it!' Brijesh said.

On my way backstage, my mother stopped me.

'What were you doing?' she said.

'What?' I said.

'I saw you. You asked Brijesh for whisky and drank it like a cheap bar girl. In front of him?'

'So?' I said, confidence soaring after the whisky shot. 'I wanted to loosen up before the dance.'

'Do you have any brains? Your in-laws are watching you. What will they think? Their bahu drinks like a jungli bewdi.'

'Mom. My would-be husband gave me the drink. If he doesn't have a problem, what's their problem?'

My mother gave me a dirty look. Pinky pulled my hand.

'My suggestion, mom, is go get a drink for yourself. You need it,' I said to my mother as I left the function room.

◆

I survived the stage. I did not let my choreographer down. I remembered all my steps. I nailed chittiyaan kalaiyaan, even though I found it more challenging than foreclosing the assets of a distressed Chinese factory.

The audience cheered. Mickey kept repeating 'one-two-three-four and turn round and round and one-two-three-four' from behind the stage.

The song ended. My cousins and I finished our performance with a huge group hug. The audience broke into applause.

Why does one have to get married to have so much fun? Why can't extended families just get together once in a while and dance for no reason?

The crowd gave us a standing ovation. Brijesh clapped the hardest, perhaps not expecting his investment banker bride-to-be to break a leg on stage as well.

'You were fabulous. You are a good, good dancer,' he said.

'Oh no, I suck. Those four minutes took four hours of merciless practice.'

'I couldn't do that even with four months of training,' he said.

A waiter with drinks passed us. I stopped him and gave Brijesh a glass of whisky.

'Drink up,' I said.

'Are you sure? We still have to meet so many people.'

'You will need it. We need to talk,' I said.

'What?'

Before I could answer, lights dimmed in the function room. A DJ took over. The stage now became a free-for-all dance floor. In Punjabi weddings this means first the kids take over the floor. Then their elder teen cousins come and kick them off the stage. Next, all the uncles get drunk and shove the teenagers off. Finally, the uncles get so drunk that they even drag their wives, or the aunties, on to the stage.

Brijesh and I also danced to a few songs. Brijesh was right. He couldn't dance. Imagine Bill Gates or Mark Zuckerberg trying to do bhangra. You get the idea.

After three songs, I whispered in Brijesh's ear, 'Brijesh, let's step out and talk.'

39

My ears felt a sense of relief as the DJ's music faded out as we left the function room. We came out to the Marriott garden, dark and silent at night. The December air had a mild chill to it and I rubbed my hands together.

'Where are we going?' Brijesh said.

'Out of sight,' I said. I found a palm tree with a bench underneath it. We sat down, adjacent to each other, facing the sea.

'Isn't it nice to just breathe?' I said.

'It is, but they will look for us,' Brijesh said. 'A search party would be sent soon.'

'It's all a bit crazy. This whole jingbang of two clans. Getting too much now,' I said.

'Don't worry, in two days all the guests will be gone. Just you and me then.'

'Yeah,' I said. I wondered how and where to start. He continued to talk.

'And soon we will be on a plane to Bali,' he said.

'Yeah Brijesh, about that…' I said.

He ignored me and continued to talk, all excited. 'And once we get back from Bali to SF, I have lined up apartment viewings that weekend. Hope that's okay?'

'Brijesh, I can't do this,' I said.

'What? Too hectic? Okay, we can see apartments later. It's just that my current apartment is too small and…'

'I am not talking about the apartment hunt.'

'Then?'

'This. Whatever is going on. I am sorry. I can't do this.'

'What? Relatives? They are getting on my nerves too. How many more feet do we have to touch?'

I held his shoulder. I turned him towards me.

'Brijesh, I cannot get married,' I said.

'What?' he said in genuine confusion. 'Sorry, beg your pardon?'

'You heard me.'

He looked at me and laughed.

'What?' I said.

'You are so funny. Sweet also.'

He pulled my cheek.

'Sweet?' I said. *What is so sweet about me leaving him high and dry at the altar?*

'You are nervous. And so like a little child, you are saying I can't do this. It's sweet only.'

'It's not...' I said as he interrupted me.

'I am scared too. I live alone. Now I will have this other person living with me for the rest of my life. It petrifies me.'

'It does. Yes. And this is just too soon.'

'Too soon? We have planned this for months.'

'We planned the event for months. However, we decided so soon.'

'You said yes. I said yes. We had to reach a decision, right?'

'Brijesh. Can you please trust me? I can't do this.'

He smiled again. He placed an arm around my shoulder.

'From now on, your fears are mine, and mine are yours. So be scared or whatever, I am with you.'

I got off the bench. I turned around to face him.

'Brijesh, I don't think you are getting me. It is not nervousness. There's stuff I need to deal with and my head is a huge squishy mess.'

'I am sorry to hear that. But...' he paused.

'But what?'

'But 200 people are dancing inside to celebrate us coming together. A mood swing cannot dictate our decision now.'

'It's not a mood swing, Brijesh.'

'What is it then? Something you want to tell me?'

'It's my past. I still have to come to terms with it.'

He paused to look at me, wondering what I meant.

'We all do. It happens over time.'

'It's about my future too. About what I want.'

Brijesh's phone rang. He smiled.

'There, the search party is out,' he said and picked up the phone. 'Yeah, dad. I am here, stepped out for some air. Yeah, Radhika is with me. Just chatting, dad. Okay, we are coming.'

He ended the call and turned at me.

'The elders are leaving. They want to bless the couple before they go to bed,' he said and smiled.

'Sorry Brijesh, I…'

'We have to go now. Listen, Radhika, I am no expert on women. Maybe this is how all women think the night before their wedding.'

'Not all.'

'Maybe in arranged marriages they do. We still don't know each other. Can I suggest something?'

'What?'

'Go to your room. Rest. Please sleep. All these guests and huge celebrations are bothering you.'

'Well, I only chose to have a grand wedding like this.'

'Exactly. So maybe your doubts are just irrational last-minute fears. Sleep over it. You will feel better. Let's go now,' he said.

'But…' I said.

'Dad's calling again,' Brijesh said as he picked up his phone.

♦

I took my phone back from Aditi didi's bag when I reached my room.

I checked the time. 2 a.m. I hadn't unlocked my phone to read my messages yet. Message notifications flooded my phone home screen. They read like this:

Debu: Hey baby, what's up?

Debu: Is there anything I can do to help? Can I talk to anyone on your side?

Debu: 5 more messages

Neel: In my room. Here if you need me.

Neel: When can we talk?

Neel: You around? Can we meet? Like for a minute?

Neel: 3 more messages

Brijesh: Hope you are fine? Get some rest, okay?

Brijesh: It's all going to be okay. Stay calm.

How am I supposed to stay calm? A dozen messages from three different men, every hour. And I have a wedding tomorrow. Mine. I have no clue with whom. *How am I supposed to stay calm?*

Aditi didi slept next to me. She woke up for water and noticed the lit phone screen in my hand.

'Sleep, you idiot. You will have dark circles in all your wedding pictures.'

Yeah, that should be my biggest concern. Would the make-up lady apply enough concealer to hide my dark circles? *Why can't I be like other girls? Why am I not thinking about how my lehenga looked on me tonight? Why am I not worried about my nails? Why am I thinking about my dark life rather than my dark circles?*

Ting. Another message.

'Put it on silent,' Aditi didi groaned in a sleepy voice, 'and come to bed.'

I looked at my phone screen.

Suraj: Hope you liked decorations, madam. Your dance was too good.

I shut the phone. I closed my eyes. But I couldn't sleep.

What do I do? Who is it going to be? Debu, Neel or Brijesh? Oh, Radhika the great distressed analyst, how do you analyse your way out of this distressed situation?

◆

Some people are good at taking decisions. I am not one of them. Some people fall asleep quickly at night. I am not one of them either. It is 3 in the morning. I have tossed and turned in bed for two hours. I am to get married in fifteen hours. We have over 200 guests in the hotel, here to attend my grand destination wedding. Everyone is excited. It is the first destination wedding in the Mehta family.

I am the bride. I should get my beauty sleep. I can't. The last thing I care about right now is beauty. The only thing I care about is how to get out of this mess. Because, like it often happens to me in life, here I am yet again in a situation where I don't know what the fuck is going on.

I lay still in bed for another half an hour. I thought about what I could do. I noticed Aditi didi in deep sleep. I stared at the flickering red light of the smoke alarm on the ceiling. At 3.30 a.m., I stepped out of bed. I opened the room curtains. The sea appeared pitch black. The light from a few distant ships flickered in the background. Moonlight filled my eyes.

It's your life, Radhika, take control of it, a voice inside me said. The voice was calm, unlike the hysterical mini-me who usually yelled.

'Who is this?' I said to myself.

It's me. Your inner voice.

'The critic inside me? The one who thinks I am a total bitch?'

No, the one who thinks you deserve to be happy.

'Really? I have a person like that inside?' I said in my head and chuckled.

We all do.

'Well, so what do I do? Who do I choose?'

Stay still, Radhika. Stay still. The answers will come.

I did exactly that. I sat still for half an hour, almost in meditation. I kept my eyes fixed on the dark sea outside. Slowly, a weight lifted off me. I knew what I had to do.

I took out my phone. I sent an identical message to Debu, Neel and Brijesh:

'You there?'

Debu replied first, in a few seconds.

'Yes, baby, trying to sleep but can't.'

'Meet me for breakfast. 5 a.m. Hotel coffee shop,' I answered.

'Oh really? That's great! That's just in an hour. See you!'

He also sent me a few excited and happy smileys.

'Thanks,' I replied, 'see you.'

Neel responded after ten minutes.

'Yes, am here,' he said.

I copy-pasted a line from Debu's chat to Neel.

'Meet me for breakfast. 5 a.m. Hotel coffee shop,' I sent to him.

'Okay sure,' Neel said.

Brijesh replied at 4.30.

'Hey, good morning. You are up early. Did you get some rest?' he said.

'I am okay.'

'Good. What's up?'

I copy-pasted the line from Debu's chat with one modification on the time.

'Meet me for breakfast. 5.30 a.m. Hotel coffee shop.'

'Really? So early?'

'Can you? Please.'

'Of course. See you.'

I kept my phone aside. I let out a big breath. Aditi didi woke up.

'What are you doing on the sofa?'

'Fixing my life,' I said.

'What?'

'Nothing. Just going for a shower,' I said and went into the bathroom.

40

I reached the coffee shop at 5 a.m. Neel and Debu had already arrived. They sat at separate tables, unaware of their common link through me. Debu wore a light-blue kurta and pajama that along with his beard and spectacles made him look like a communist intellectual. Neel wore a crisp dark blue shirt with a buttoned-down collar and a well-ironed pair of beige shorts. I wore a simple light-blue chikan salwar-kameez. It felt ten times more comfortable and lighter than the wedding fineries I had worn all week.

Four IndiGo Airlines crew members occupied another table, sipping coffee before their early morning flight. Apart from them the coffee shop had no other customers. The coffee shop was open on the side, facing the sea. Daylight had just broken. The sky had streaks of pink in it. The morning breeze felt cool in my hair, still wet after the shower.

Neel and Debu stood up at their respective tables as I entered the coffee shop. They walked towards me from two different directions.

'Hey,' Debu said.

'Hi there, you look fresh,' Neel said.

Neel and Debu looked at each other, surprised and confused.

'Good morning. Debu, this is Neel. Neel, this is Debu,' I said.

'Good...morning,' Debu said, as he tried to figure out the situation.

'Hi,' Neel said to Debu.

'Let's get some breakfast,' I said.

I sat down at one of the sea-facing tables. Both of them froze where they stood.

'Come, both of you,' I said and smiled.

They sat down hesitantly. The waiter arrived to take the order.

'I will have a cappuccino and brown-bread toast. With peanut butter and honey. How about you guys?' I said.

Debu and Neel looked at each other.

'Black coffee. Porridge, please,' Neel said.

'Er...orange juice,' Debu said.

The waiter left. I continued to smile, enjoying their confused state.

'Is he a friend?' Neel said, asking about Debu.

'Yeah, you could say that,' I said.

'You want to introduce me properly?' Debu said, clearing his throat.

'Of course I will.'

'Yeah, because sorry, Debu, I don't know you and so it is all a bit confusing and surprising...' Neel was saying when I cut him off.

'Both of you are my exes. My past lovers,' I said.

If there were prizes for priceless expressions, Neel and Debu could both share a Nobel.

'Sorry, I don't understand,' Neel said. 'I am an ex but who is he?'

'Debu. My boyfriend in New York, remember?'

'Oh, *that* guy,' Neel said.

'Neel is your ex too? Sorry, when was this?' Debu said.

'Hong Kong.'

'Oh,' Debu said, and became silent. He studied Neel openly.

'Yeah, he's older, Debu. Much older,' I said. 'Neel's married too.'

Debu realized I had caught him staring at Neel and took his gaze away from him.

'I was. Not now,' Neel corrected me. 'So Debu's come to attend your wedding? That's nice.'

'He's not come to attend it. He's come to marry me. He wants to sit in the groom's place. Right here, in Goa.'

'What?' Neel said. 'I thought things ended badly for you guys. Debu's the same guy who made you leave New York, right?'

'Yeah,' I said. 'Change of heart now. Just like you.'

I guess it takes a while for people to realize my worth.

I turned to Debu.

'And, Debu, Neel is here to stop the wedding too. His style is a bit different. It involves chartered planes.'

Debu's eyes popped open.

'You see, he is rich. Something you always had a problem with.'

'I...I...I...' Debu stuttered as he struggled to string a sentence. 'I have no problem with someone who is rich. Who said I did?'

Neel interjected, 'Radhika, I didn't mean to display my wealth. It just seemed like the best option.'

'Neel, it doesn't matter. But understand the situation, guys. Both of you are here to stop my wedding, which is in a few hours. Not only that, you want me to marry you instead. As you can imagine, you have put me in quite a predicament.'

The waiter arrived with our food. As he served us, Neel and Debu shifted in their seats, avoided eye contact with each other. I leisurely spread peanut butter on my toast. I saw the unease on their faces. Debu spoke after the waiter left.

'Sorry, Radhika. I didn't realize you have another ex-boyfriend here. Was this gentleman even a boyfriend, actually? He is so much older and married.'

'Not married anymore. And my name is Neel, Neel Gupta,' Neel said, loosening the collar of his shirt.

'Yeah, whatever. But, Radhika, I thought you and I are meeting here alone. In any case, you need to come with me.'

'Why? You forgot how you treated her? She had to leave the country for you,' Neel said.

'Even for you, Neel,' I said.

Neel looked at me with a stumped expression.

'Radhika, I said sorry. I never disrespected you. I may have had some confusion. But now I don't. I am only human.'

Debu interrupted Neel.

'Mr Neel, find someone your own age.'

'It's the connection that matters, not the age. And sorry to say, I seem fitter than you,' Neel said.

I couldn't believe the discussion. I had to make an effort not to grin. For a few seconds I relished these two men fighting over me. I imagined them in a fistfight; though I knew Neel would clobber the intellectual Bengali babu in the end, I could have watched them duel all day. But I did not have the time.

'Boys, boys, stop arguing. And listen to what I have to say for once,' I said.

'I know you love me, baby,' Debu said. 'I am your first love.'

'Which is often a mistake. We connect, Radhika, beyond love. We are similar. You know that,' Neel said.

'Why do you guys love the sound of your voice so much? Can I speak, uninterrupted?' I said.

Both of them nodded. Neel clasped his hands and placed his elbows on the table. Debu took a sip of his orange juice.

'Thanks,' I said. 'Sorry, I am doing this to you together. Just more efficient. Also, maybe you can learn something from each other.'

'It's fine,' Neel said, eager not to censure me.

'Debashish Sen, you remember our walk in New York? You said women could do anything. You quoted feminist texts. Essentially, you said women could and should fly.'

'Yeah,' Debu said.

'Nice in theory. In real life the girl throws a party for her guy's promotion but the guy cannot handle the girl's bonus. Yes?'

'That's not...' he said but I stopped him.

'Let me speak. You said fly, but when I flew high, you wanted to clip my wings. Fly, as long as you fly beneath me, is it?'

He looked down. I turned to Neel.

'Neel, you loved me as the flying bird. You wanted me to fly higher and higher.'

'Of course,' Neel said.

'But you know where you went wrong?'

'Where?' Neel said.

'You didn't want me to have a nest.'

Neel didn't have an answer.

'Neel?' I said.

'I believe in equal rights. You know that, right?' Neel said.

'Did you realize that perhaps I did not want to fool around? Perhaps equal rights means giving women the same rights, not the same things? Equal rights to get what *they* want, rather than equal rights to the same things *men* want.'

I noticed Debu scratch his head as he also heard and tried to figure out what I said.

'Meaning?' Neel said.

'What do you want? Career? Home?' Debu said. 'I am really confused.'

'Yeah. What do you want? Choose whatever you like, Radhika,' Neel said.

I took a sip of my lukewarm coffee.

'Ah, choose,' I said and sneered. 'Choice. The benchmark word of feminism, right? I become a great feminist if I give women the choice of home or career.'

'What do you mean? Isn't that how it should be?' Neel said.

'Yeah, why not? Isn't that fair? Giving women the choice?' Debu said.

'No. It is still unfair. Because here's the deal. You know what women really want? We don't want to choose. We want to fly and we *also* want a beautiful nest. We want both. Do male birds tell female birds to choose? "Hey honey, choose. Either fly or sit in the nest."'

'I don't get it. Really,' Debu said. Even Neel looked confused.

'From a man's perspective, men want a career, right? In general?'

'Yeah,' Debu said.

'Men want sex, right? No judgement, but they want sex, right?'

'Yeah,' Neel said.

I collected my thoughts before I spoke again.

'Let's say, in the name of male rights, men are given a choice. Come on guys, choose. You want a career? Go for it, just give up sex. Oh, you want sex? Just worship women all day and give up your career dreams. So choose, we are giving you equal rights. Choose now. Sex or career?'

'Sorry but that is a ridiculous choice to make,' Neel said.

'Exactly, Neel. It is indeed a ridiculous choice. Just as ridiculous as the choice given to women—fly or nest. You want and get both. But a woman must choose?'

I had three sips of coffee before Neel had something to say.

'I get it. Women want everything. To have a lovely home and be a great mother. To also have a chance to shine in their careers,' Neel said.

'Not all, maybe, but for many, yes,' I said.

'How is it practically possible? Career means long office hours. Home means kids, responsibilities,' Debu said.

'Exactly! Have you thought why it's not practical?' I said.

'Why?' Debu said.

'Because men designed this world. They decided office timings, 9 to 6, five days a week. Women weren't in the workforce then. They are now. These office timings work well for men. They don't work for mothers, for instance. What are we going to do about it?'

'We as in us three?' Debu said.

'No, we as in the whole world,' I said. 'When will we say, let's rejig this to ensure it works for women? Forget rejig, when will we even acknowledge the issue?'

I paused to catch my breath, then leaned forward as if to listen to them. Debu finished his orange juice in one quick swallow.

'You have a point. Conceded. I didn't realize your strong need to have a family too. That is why I made a mess last time,' Neel said.

'I imposed my notion of motherhood on you. Ignored your desire to have a good career alongside. But forgive me and come with me. I will support you,' Debu said.

'No,' I said, my voice coming from somewhere deep within me.

'You are making the right choice with me, Radhika,' Neel said.

'No, Neel, not with you either.'

'What?' he said.

I checked the time. It was 5.28.

'I am not coming with you, or with you. There are fundamental things about both of you that won't change. Debu, you say you will be supportive, but the fact that you couldn't handle even a bit of my success means it's an intrinsic part of you. You can't change that. And I plan to be a lot more successful than what you saw. So, sorry, no.'

'But Radhika...' Debu began.

I placed a finger on my lips to shush him right there.

'And Neel, you are amazing, no doubt. The chartered plane, tempting, of course. Now with the divorce and everything I know you love me too. But you know what, you love only half of me. My other half is Kusum, the woman you left. You want a party girl. Someone young, who allows you to cling on to your youth. The same youth you work so hard in the gym for. Well, I won't be this young girl forever. I don't know what Neel Gupta will do with me then. He likes Radhika, his young vice president, but will he like Radhika, the diaper-changing wife and mom?'

'Of course, I...'

'Shh. I am not going to compromise and settle for less. I have made up my mind. Thank you for listening. Now, no more lectures. I will simply tell you the action plan.'

'What?' Debu said.

'Both of you, I need you to leave, right now. This hotel, Goa and my life. You will not bother me, my family or my guests. No messages, no calls. You are my past, but guess what, I am done with my past. So please,' I said. I pointed to the exit.

'But,' Debu said.

'I am saying fuck off in the nicest way possible. Please do appreciate that. And do fuck off,' I said.

Debu and Neel looked at each other. They looked at me once more and stood up to leave. In silence they walked out of the restaurant.

Together. Out of my life.

Brijesh entered the coffee shop just as they left. He came up to me. He wore grey workout clothes. He noticed the used crockery and cutlery on the table.

'Good morning, wife-to-be,' he said. 'These people? They came to see you?'

'Good morning, Brijesh, come. We need to talk,' I said. He saw my serious expression and sat opposite me looking a little baffled.

'Yeah sure,' he said. 'By the way, white suits you.'

'Thanks.'

Brijesh ordered a plain dosa and coffee.

'Feeling better from last night?' Brijesh said after the waiter left.

'Sort of.'

'We always feel more anxious at night,' Brijesh said. 'Don't worry. Remember, whatever happens in life, eventually it is all going to be okay.'

'You really believe that?' I said.

'Yes.'

'Good. So Brijesh, I thought about it all night. This just doesn't seem right. I can't get married to you today.'

'What?' he said. 'Are you serious? Some nervousness is understandable but...'

'I am going to inform my parents now. After that I will talk to your parents.'

'What?'

'Unless you can talk to them first. I prefer that. Put the blame on me.'

'Radhika!'

I ignored him and continued, 'I will settle all bills. Nothing needs to be paid from your family's side. I am so sorry for this and...'

Brijesh interrupted me.

'Who the hell do you think you are?' Brijesh said in an out-of-character high pitch.

I looked at him, surprised.

'I am sorry. I can understand you are upset,' I said after a pause.

'You understand? That's it? My entire extended family is here. They have celebrated with us for a week. The morning of the wedding what do I tell them? The bride says no? She has cold feet?'

'It's all my fault. I accept that.'

'Everyone is here, Radhika. Everyone.'

'I know.'

The waiter arrived with Brijesh's dosa and coffee. Brijesh left them untouched.

'Can I ask why?' Brijesh said, his voice under control again.

Tear rolled down my cheeks in response.

'Why, Radhika?'

'Those guys who you saw leave. They are my past. My exes.'

He looked back at the restaurant exit.

'It's okay. They are gone,' I said.

'You invited them?'

I shook my head. In brief, I told him what had happened to me all of last week in Goa. He listened with full interest, and had a shocked expression at the end of it.

'That is some story,' he said as what I had told him sank in.

'Yeah, that's my week.'

'What did you decide finally?'

'I told them to leave. Get out. Out of Goa and my life, forever.'

'Good. Then what's the issue? Your past is gone.'

'But I am not in the present either. I am nowhere, really. I need to find myself.'

'Find yourself?' he said, a bit of sarcasm in his voice. 'You have told me you had two relationships. As long as they are in the past, I don't care.'

'No, Brijesh. This wedding stands cancelled. I am sorry,' I said and stood up.

He looked at me. He could see from my expression that I offered no scope for negotiation. He remained silent. I turned around and left the coffee shop.

41

My room in Goa resembled a funeral scene. Despite the five-star luxury and the gold around my aunts' necks, people had a sombre expression. I had communicated my decision. My mother had displayed her hysteria. Dad sat stone-faced, unable, as usual, to react to any conflict situation. My aunts had gathered around my mother, offering fake sympathy and condolences. I could sense their glee. I was providing family gossip for months.

Kamla bua had still not given up.

'Brijesh said anything to you? Be honest,' Kamla bua said.

'I told you several times, he has nothing to do with it. He is quite sweet.'

'So what is the problem, you mad girl?' my mother screeched at the top of her voice.

She came and stood in front of me.

Slap! Before she could deliver another slap Kamla bua held her down. I didn't react.

'No, Aparna, no. Keep control. Sai Baba will make it all okay,' Kamla bua said to my mother.

'What will be okay? We are ruined. Look at her, still glaring at me.'

'There's no need to hit me, mom,' I said, my face red as I fought back tears.

'So what should I do to cure you of your madness? Look at Aditi. In third year of college she was engaged. Married after a simple graduation.'

'I am not Aditi.'

'This is what happens when you educate girls too much,' Kamla bua said in a low, consoling voice.

'It's her father's fault,' my mother snapped. 'He never said no to anything. Ahmedabad, New York, Hong Kong, wherever she wanted to go, he would let her.'

'Can you keep dad out of this, mom?' I said, my voice muffled. I turned to everyone and folded my hands.

'All of you, I have a request. You are all my extended family. Yes, I take full blame for the debacle that happened. You can judge me all you want. But can you please not judge my parents for this?'

My aunts and uncles looked at each other.

I continued, 'Treat it like a Goan holiday. That's it. My treat. I need your support. My bigger issue is Brijesh and his family. They will be hurt much more. I need grown-ups from my side to be with me when I tell them.'

Nobody gave me a response.

'Fine, I will talk to them on my own. Please enjoy your last day in Goa. Those wanting to fly out earlier, talk to Suraj to change flights,' I said.

The tableau continued. I turned to leave.

'Wait, I will come,' Aditi didi said. 'I don't understand what you are doing. But I will come. Can't let my sister do this by herself.'

She stood next to me and held my hand. I smiled at her and held back tears.

'I will also come with you,' Pankaj mama said. 'Come, Richa, we can't let her go alone.'

Richa mami debated between the roles of obedient wife and offended aunt, and chose the former.

'No need,' my mother said. 'She does everything alone anyway.'

'Dad, you should come,' Aditi didi said. My father stood up.

'Come, Aparna,' my father said in his soft voice. My mother looked at everyone. With much reluctance, she stood up.

'Yes, let's go. Let's get fully shamed,' she said.

◆

I rang the bell. Brijesh opened the door. He didn't say a word and stepped aside to let me and my relatives enter. The room felt ice-cold, and not because of the air conditioning.

Mr and Mrs Gulati, Brijesh's parents and my almost in-laws-to-be, stood with glum faces. Brijesh's relatives, his father's brothers along with their respective wives, sat gingerly on the bed. Brijesh's mother's sisters— Rohini masi and Gunjan masi—sat on the sofa. Everyone looked like they had had knives stabbed in their backs. Brijesh had already told them.

I struggled to figure out where to start. This is where age helps. For my mother seemed to know exactly what would be a mature reaction. She burst out crying and went straight to Brijesh's mother to bear-hug her.

'Somebody's cast an evil eye, Sulochana,' my mother said. Her lone hysterics made everyone in the room feel even more awkward. Brijesh's mother didn't hug my mother back.

'We are ruined. I had no idea my girl would do this to us. What do you do when your own child is defective?' my mother said, howling at top volume.

'Sit down, Aparna ji,' Brijesh's father said.

I realized I had to take control. I went to the centre of the room and addressed everyone.

'Hello everyone, I will just take a minute. To all in this room, I am sorry. I am really, really, sorry. I am sorry because I was not prepared for this marriage but I said yes. I am sorry because I brought shame to your relatives. I am sorry because I ruined your happy moment. However, I did this because I felt going ahead would not be fair on Brijesh and his family.'

'This is fair?' Brijesh's mother said. Her voice had a sharp sting to it.

'No. But going ahead would be even more unfair. Between two unfair things, this felt less unfair.'

I fought back tears as I listened to Brijesh's mother.

'In this room it is just us close relatives. You realize what we have to go through with all our acquaintances who are also here?' she said.

'I do. I am sorry,' I said, tears flowing. I folded my hands. 'I really am sorry, aunty.'

Brijesh looked at his mother and then me. He stood silent with arms crossed on his chest.

'You look so good together,' my father said. 'Can't we do something?' I shook my head.

'Our relatives are here. The arrangements are all done. We can still end this drama, Radhika,' Brijesh's mother said. 'Nobody will know. The marriage can still happen.'

'No, aunty, I am sorry,' I said.

'What kind of a girl is this?' Brijesh's mother said.

'I told you. I have a defective piece. My other daughter is golden. Such a nice, good bahu she is,' my mother said.

'Enough, Aparna aunty,' Brijesh said. Everyone in the room looked at him, surprised. 'She may regret her decision to marry me. It doesn't make her defective.'

Through my tears I looked at Brijesh. Despite what I had done to

him, Mr IT guy could still actually stand up for me. It only made me
feel worse.

'And mom, she has made up her mind. We may not like it, but she
has,' Brijesh said.

'But, beta, all arrangements are in place and everyone is here and...'
Brijesh's mother said.

'Mom, we can't get married just because it is convenient,' Brijesh said.

I gestured a thanks to Brijesh. He nodded. He handed me a box of
tissues to wipe my tears. His kindness, even at this moment, killed me.

'All of you are still our guests,' my father said with folded hands. 'And
from my daughter's side, I say sorry.'

I could not see my father grovel. I wanted to leave so I could cry
freely.

'Suraj will help you if you need anything. All your bills will be settled.
Thank you,' I said and ran out of Brijesh's room.

◆

The Gulatis and Mehtas checked out of the Goa hotel at noon the next
day. Both sets of families avoided eye contact. Things had indeed changed
from the sangeet night two days ago when people could not take enough
group selfies.

The Mumbai flight for the Gulatis left earlier than ours. They took
their places inside the bus.

'Brijesh, one second,' I said, as he wore his backpack to leave the
hotel lobby.

'Yeah?' he said, his voice curt.

'Can we talk for two minutes?'

'Really? Why?' he said.

I kept quiet. He took a deep breath.

'All right,' he said. 'But not here, in full view of everyone. Meet me
on the beach in five.'

◆

'Thanks for supporting me in front of the elders yesterday,' I said.

We walked on the Marriott beach one final time.

'I don't like raised voices, or insulting people, especially in public,'
Brijesh said.

'You had every right to insult me too. You can now. We are not even in public.'

He looked at me for a second. He shook his head and gave a sad smile.

'I guess I never understood women anyway. I thought I did, a little bit. Clearly, I still have a long way to go,' he said.

'You understand people and you understand kindness. You are a good guy, Brijesh. I am the one who is messed up. I need clarity.'

'Hope you find it. What do you plan to do, anyway?'

'For now, I will go back to work. Maybe apply for some visas. Then take a long vacation. Maybe one of those round-the-world tickets. The ones that let you fly in one direction. Just keep going.'

'Well, the world is round. So you can't keep going. You will eventually have to come back home. Come back to reality.'

'That's true, unfortunately,' I said.

'Bye then,' Brijesh said.

'Bye, Brijesh.'

'You aren't coming back to the hotel?' he said as he turned to leave.

'I will. I just want to watch these waves for a few more minutes,' I said and looked into the horizon.

42

**Three months later
El Albergue Hotel,
Ollantaytambo, Peru**

I sat in the café and sipped my coffee. The tiny blue trains to Machu Pichu came and went at regular intervals. I downloaded my trip photos from my phone into my laptop as a backup. My laptop flashed the date, 23 March, with a reminder saying 'Message B'. It had been three months since the Goa fiasco. Despite the reminder I found it difficult to gather the courage to message him. I flipped through every picture from my trip to distract myself.

In the past month, I had started eastwards from London. I visited Berlin, Cairo, Beijing and Sydney before taking a flight to Lima in Peru, South America. From Lima I landed up in Ollantaytambo, or simply Ollantay, the base point to visit the famous ruins of Machu Pichu. I stayed at the historic and charming El Albergue hotel, located right at the mini train station that one uses to visit Machu Pichu.

One hour and two cappuccinos later, I took out my phone.

Radhika, just do it. What's the worst that will happen?

I sent a WhatsApp message to Brijesh.

'Hi.'

I waited for another half an hour, until the blue ticks appeared. He had read my message. He didn't respond. My heart sank. This was all a bad idea anyway.

'Hi. Wassup?' he typed back a few minutes later.

'Today would have been three months. Of our almost wedding anniversary,' I replied.

He sent a smiley.

'Sorry again,' I replied.

'Hey, all part of life. How are you doing?'

'Good. Travelling. Took that trip I told you about.'

'Round the world?'

'Yes.'

'Reached full circle yet?'

'Almost. I still have two more flights to go.'

'Cool. Where are you now?'

'Peru. Came to see Machu Pichu.'

'Nice.'

'Where are you right now?' I said.

'At work. No such luck like you!'

'Brijesh, I wanted to ask you something.'

'Sure.'

'My next stop is San Francisco. I am there in three days.'

'Oh, cool.'

'Yeah. Was wondering if you want to meet for a coffee?'

He didn't respond for a few minutes. I had a sinking feeling about this. I sent him another message anyway.

'I totally understand if you can't or if you don't want to.'

'Sorry, my boss had called me. Yeah sure, would love to have coffee.'

'Really? Great.'

'Yeah, can we do it in Menlo Park? Easier for me.'

'Of course. Whatever is closest to your office. How's Wednesday?'

'Sure, Philz Coffee at Menlo Park. 4 p.m.'

◆

Philz Coffee
Menlo Park

I reached five minutes early. Philz Coffee is located just outside the sprawling Facebook campus. I took a seat by the window, looking at the offices of a company that connected a billion and a half people around the world. I wore a blue-and-white checked dress, which seemed to reflect the Californian sunshine.

'Hi,' Brijesh said as he came up to my table. I stood up. We hugged cursorily.

'Thanks for meeting me,' I said, a little self-conscious.

'No issues. Welcome to my city,' he said. He wore a black hoodie and blue jeans. His shoulders seemed broader, as if he had bulked up. He wore a Facebook corporate ID badge around his neck.

'Strange to see you like this, at work,' I said.

'Yeah, without any relatives. I see you and feel an aunt is going to pop in any minute,' he said.

'Totally. I am like, where are the buas and the masis?' I said.

'Yeah, I feel this urge to touch someone's feet,' he said.

Both of us laughed.

He went up to the counter and came back with two cappuccinos. I spoke after he sat down.

'I can never apologize enough, but again, sorry,' I said, 'The one Indian girl whom you finally came down to marry created such a drama.'

He waved his hand.

'You don't need to anymore. I am mostly over it. Life goes on. I reflected in the past two months too. On why you did what you did, and said no to the wedding that morning.'

'What did you infer?'

'That frankly you, or for that matter, any girl, doesn't need a man to define her. You need a man to support, inspire…understand you. Help you be the best person you can be, banker, mother, both, whatever. And until you find a man you trust enough to do that, why settle?'

I looked at Brijesh, admiring his wisdom.

'You think so?' I said.

'I do. And you are not just one Indian girl. You are one special Indian girl.'

I smiled and gestured a thanks to him. He nodded.

'I still blame myself. A lot. For making you look bad in front of your relatives.'

'Don't. I don't even think about my relatives when I think about Goa, actually.'

'That's good. No regrets?' I said.

'Not really. Okay, just one regret.'

'What?'

'You remember that night at the police station?'

'Oh yes. When we went to Anjuna? That inspector. Our parents rescuing us. Terrible.'

'Yeah. And all that we did, the grass, driving without a licence—I would have never done all that without you.'

'Well, I am bad company. That was a mad, crazy night.'

'Yeah, so the thing is, I had begun to look forward to a mad, crazy life with you. That didn't happen so, oh well…That's the regret.' He shrugged and smiled.

Our eyes met. I didn't have a suitable response for him. I decided to change the topic instead.

'Your shoulders. You look fitter,' I said.

'I joined a gym. Try to go every day.'

'It's showing.'

'Thanks. You look relaxed too. Your face seems…clearer. More peaceful.'

'So is my mind. A month of travel helps calm you down.'

'Yeah, I'm sure. You look nice,' he said.

I smiled. We sipped our coffee.

'How is work?' I said.

'Good. But my business idea is taking shape. A service provider for developing Internet of Things or IoT apps. IoT is the next big thing. A company that helps make IoT apps has scope.'

'Of course it does.'

'Just that I need this formal business plan to raise money from VCs. It is a pain. They want financial models and projections and what not.'

'I could help if you want,' I said.

'Really?'

'It's what I do on a daily basis,' I said and smiled.

'Oh yeah, of course.'

'I will need to understand the business. And turn it into a spreadsheet full of numbers. I do it all the time.'

'I will share the details with you. How long are you here for?'

'I have five more days of vacation left. I could make a quick model in the next couple of days.'

'You would? That would be amazing. Can we work on it over the weekend?'

'No problem,' I said.

We sipped our coffee in silence for a minute before he spoke again. 'Also, if you are here this weekend, there's an Arijit Singh concert.'

'Oh cool. I like him,' I said. He had simply informed me about the concert. I couldn't assume he had asked me to go for it with him.

'Yeah, so,' he said and took another sip of his coffee. A sliver of foam stuck above his lips.

I pointed to his lip.

'What?' he said.

I opened the camera on my phone and turned it into selfie mode. I showed him his face and smiled.

'Oh no,' he said, embarrassed. He wiped his foam moustache with a tissue.

I gathered the courage to ask him a question.

'Brijesh, would you like to come to the Arijit Singh concert with me?' I said, my heart beating fast. I had to be prepared for any response, including a bitter, biting rejection.

'Of course, that is what I meant. You will be helping me with the business, so we could go together to the concert later, right?' he said.

'I would love that. To go to the concert with you,' I said.

'Yeah, I would love to spend more time with you too.'

Our eyes met again, this time for longer. He took another sip of his coffee. It created an even bigger foam moustache. He also had some foam stuck to the tip of his nose. I showed him his face in my phone's camera again. He smiled. I smiled. We looked at each other for a few seconds. Then we laughed. And then we laughed some more.